WAVES OF DESIRE

The water splashed in a fine mist and Rue blindly clutched at Hawke, grabbing his shoulders. She breathlessly clung to his hard, warm body, staring down at the blue water swirling around them. It took her a moment to realize that strong, possessive arms had wrapped themselves around her waist. When Hawke pulled her tightly against his body, his breathing fast and harsh, she grew alarmed. She gazed into his eyes and saw the light of desire illuminating them.

"Let me go!" she panted, pushing against his shoulders. "I don't want—"

Hawke's mouth swooped down to take hers, silencing her protest. *I don't want this,* she cried inwardly as she twisted and turned her head, trying to free herself from the deepening kiss, the tongue that darted around in her mouth, coaxing and teasing.

Suddenly, without warning Rue's body quivered in response. She sagged against Hawke, every nerve awake in her body. He gave a sigh of satisfaction and his hand slid to her breasts as he moved against her, purposely making her aware of his arousal. She moaned softly, lost in a passion she'd never known existed.

Other Leisure Books by Norah Hess:

DEVIL IN SPURS

NORAH HESS

HAWKE'S PRIDE

LEISURE BOOKS   NEW YORK CITY

To
Patty,
Jim and Patrice

A LEISURE BOOK®

January 1991

Published by

Dorchester Publishing Co., Inc.
276 Fifth Avenue
New York, NY 10001

Printed in the United States of America.

CHAPTER ONE

"There goes Buck DeLawney's girl. Skimmin' over the ground like a wild Indian."

"You mean Rue?"

"Yeah. Wonder why he ever gave her such an odd name?"

"Cause he rued the day he ever married her loose mama, most likely."

"Wouldn't be surprised. I never could figure out how he come to get tangled up with Becky. By the time she was fourteen she'd laid with half the men around here. It just about broke his parents' hearts when he married that one."

"He cut and run, though, when she had herself a woods colt."

"Ain't nobody blamed him though, his wife

5

whorin' round like she did. It's a shame
though, he didn't take his own youngun' with
him."

"That would have been a mite hard on
Buck, draggin' a three-year-old round with
him. You got to remember he was awful
young, just turned twenty. A man don't always
think straight at that age, especially if he's
blind mad."

"'Spect you're right. How long has he been
gone now, do you reckon?"

"About sixteen years, I figure. Rue is nineteen now, and she was three when Buck up
and left. Ain't never been seen nor heard of
since."

"That poor child ain't had it easy all these
years. Becky whorin' and all, bringin' two
more bastards into the world for Rue to take
care of. Her too drunk all the time to tend to
them herself."

"And don't forget the girl havin' to put up
with her shiftless stepdaddy."

"Yeah, Sly Burford, the lazy no-account.
Somebody ought to have shot that man the
first time he showed himself around here.
That man ain't got no shame nor morals at
all."

The old couple watched Rue DeLawney's
slender figure disappear into the tree-studded
foothills, then set their rocking chairs to
creaking. They leaned their heads back, their
faces lifted to the noon sun beaming down on

the small porch, their young neighbor and her problems slipping from their minds.

Rue's long legs flashed smoothly up the steep incline, her bare feet making no sound on the thick carpet of fallen pine needles as she hurried along. She paid no attention to the stately spruce and pine that seemingly towered to the very sky. They were a familiar sight; she had passed beneath them too many times to be impressed by their green splendor. She had traveled this path, daily, ever since she could remember.

She paused once, long enough to pat gently the chicken-pox scabs on her face with a rag she carried for that purpose. It was Indian summer and the sun was still scorching hot, causing perspiration to bead on her forehead, then inch downward onto her sores.

Her thin face grimaced, they itched so and she was hard-pressed not to scratch them. But Grandma DeLawney's warning was ever with her. "If you scratch them, honey, you'll be dreadfully scarred," she had cautioned. "And for life. There's nothing that will take them away." She had then lovingly brushed the red-gold curls off Rue's wide forehead and said, "I don't want anything to happen to that pretty face of yours. You won't catch yourself a husband if your face is all pockmarked."

Rue's shapely lips curled scornfully, remembering her grandmother's last caution.

She hadn't told the sweet old lady that she would never marry, never put herself at the mercy of some man. That it had been her experience, with the exception of her grandfather, that men were brutes and self-serving. She could live very happily without a husband.

Putting the distasteful thought of men from her mind, Rue daubed at her face again, thinking of her three half brothers. Sixteen-year-old Jimmy had taken to heart her advice not to scratch his sores, but the four- and two-year-olds dug at their faces continually. She hated to think what their skin was going to look like later on for surely they would be scarred for life.

For life, she thought sadly. *But how long a life for them?* She couldn't imagine they would be long ones. From the day their drunken mother brought them into the world, having no idea who their fathers were, the children had been sickly, undernourished because her stepfather was too lazy to provide for them.

Rue sighed raggedly. If Granddad DeLawney hadn't had any luck hunting yesterday, she didn't know what she would give the children for supper. This morning she had given them some cornmeal mush with a few scraps of salt pork in it. She and Jimmy had shared an apple he had filched from a neighbor's tree so that at least the edge of his hunger would be eased a bit.

Rue sighed again. Would they all starve to death, come winter? For the time being there was the small vegetable garden patch she and Jimmy had planted. It hadn't done well though. Rain had been scarce that summer and most of the plants they had worked hard at sowing, the seeds coming from Grandma DeLawney, had shriveled up and died. Although what had survived had helped toward their meager diet, they had not produced enough to put some away for the cold months ahead. And Granddad was getting too old to hunt their meat all the time.

"Damn Sly Burford's soul to hell," she gritted out. "It was a sorry day he came into our lives."

Rue could only vaguely remember her father, a big laughing man who had gone away when she was just a tot and Jimmy only an infant. As she grew older, she pestered her mother for the reason her father had left them. Becky had always ignored the question until finally one day, hate flashing in her eyes, she had snarled, "Because he's a no-good bastard, that's why. Now don't ask me about him again."

But shortly before her seventh birthday Grandma DeLawney told her the real reason Buck DeLawney had left his wife and child and hadn't been heard of since.

She had known of course that her home life was different from that of the children she occasionally attended school with. Day or night, often both, some man or other would climb the trail to the DeLawney shack and knock on the door. Her mother would smile at him and take him into the only bedroom. After a spell of springs creaking and the headboard banging against the wall, the man would leave, avoiding eye contact with Rue and Jimmy. Consequently, when her schoolmates would chant at her, "Your mother is a dirty old whore," she knew what they meant. At first, she had shed many tears at the cruel taunts, but over the years, she had grown a skin so tough, insults could no longer penetrate her heart. Not even the sly remarks and salacious invitations she'd had to endure as her ripening body and pretty face drew the attention of the gawkish teenagers she'd run into.

Her trips to the village had been curtailed, however. One day on her way home from the grocer's she had almost been raped by two youths who lay in wait for her in an old abandoned cabin. As she kicked, screamed, and scratched, ironically, a man on his way to visit her mother had heard her. He had dragged the boys off her, cuffed them a bit, then sent them running off. He had helped her up then, saying kindly, "Best you don't walk alone anymore, Rue."

To this day, Rue shivered every time she remembered that day, the boys' rough hands on her body, their fingers digging into her flesh as they tried to drag off her bloomers. She had had nightmares about the assault for a long time. She remembered longing to tell Becky about it, but she had never been close to her mother and had kept it all locked up inside her.

Becky had never been close to any of her children for that matter, Rue recalled. And for a very simple reason. She was a hard and uncaring woman who didn't look for, nor want, a tender relationship with her off-spring. She hadn't wanted them in the first place.

In the eleven years that Becky had whored for a living, she had managed not to get in the family way. Then four years ago that all changed. The old herb woman who had kept Becky supplied with a concoction guaranteed to kill any man's seed took sick and died, taking the secret of her mixed herbs with her. Almost at the same time, Sly Burford appeared at their shack.

Rue, fifteen then, had taken a dislike for the man on sight. She was repelled by his gross stomach hanging over his belt and the way his fat, squinted eyes roamed over her budding curves. Wise beyond her years, her hard blue eyes had warned him away. He had turned his attention on Becky then and had flattered her so that she had taken him into the bedroom without charging him. Rue and Jimmy had looked at each other with raised brows. Never had that happened before.

And surprising them even more, the fat man had stayed with Becky all night. None of the other customers had stayed more than an hour, most of the time only minutes. She and Jimmy had waited for Burford to leave the next morning, but he was still there at suppertime.

Sly Burford was still with them a week later, with Becky turning away the men who made their weekly trip to the old canting shack. Meanwhile, the fat man chopped the wood, carried the water from the spring a half mile away, mended the leaky roof, and made himself useful in a dozen different ways. He spent a lot of time with Jimmy, taking him hunting and fishing. And Jimmy, never having had the attention of a man before, thought that Burford was wonderful, the best thing that had ever happened in their mother's life. But despite his overtures to Rue of being careful to look only at her face, and speaking to her kindly as a father would do, Rue was still wary of him. She had not forgotten how his eyes had undressed her the first time she saw him. He looked to her like a lazy man, putting forth an effort that would benefit him some way.

When at the beginning of the following week, Sly married her mother, Rue, along with their neighbors, asked themselves why he would marry an aging, worn-out whore.

Not that Burford was all that good a catch himself, being fat and smelly.

The answer was made clear to the two DeLawney women in a short time.

Becky learned first, and Rue a few hours later.

Becky, her new husband, and her children had returned from the preacher's house only a short time when Jimmy, standing in the open doorway, called over his shoulder, "Ma, there's a couple men comin' up the hill."

"Let them come, for all the good it will do them," Becky said with relish, her chin proudly in the air. "I'm a married woman now." She slid her arm through Sly's. "Ain't gonna be but one man in my life from now on."

"Well now, Becky." Sly removed her hand and stepped away from her. "Don't be too hasty. The money your business brings in will come in handy, cold weather comin' on and all."

When Becky told him absolutely not, that she was tired of lying with any man who had the price, Sly looking sad and distressed, took her arm and sat her down at the table. Then, his hand on her shoulder, he began to speak as Rue and Jimmy watched. Disillusionment clouded the boy's eyes, but Rue's shot sparks of hate and disgust.

"I should have told you, Becky"—the fat lips whined the words—"but I got a bad back. I can't hold down a job more than a week or so before it goes out." He paused to give a long sigh. "Then I'm laid up for months."

Becky's own disillusionment quickly changed to one of rage as she realized she had been duped. She jumped to her feet, shaking with fury. She tore into her new husband, calling him every vile name she could think of, ending with, "You're a rotten, deceitful swine!"

The subservience that had for over a week lay like a cloak around the fat man was wiped away as though it had never existed. His eyes narrowing menacingly, Sly clamped biting fingers onto Becky's shoulders.

"You fat old whore," he sneered, "surely you don't think that I married you out of undyin' love." His eyes skimmed Becky's body, ranging from the sagging breasts to the body that was going to fat. "I figure you'll be a good meal ticket for a few more years."

He turned her around to face the bedroom, then giving her a hard shove, growled, "If you don't want to feel the weight of my hand, you'd better carry on as usual."

Becky stumbled, caught her balance, then turned back as though to defy the man she had foolishly married. But while Rue silently urged her to fly at the man, to scratch his eyes out, adding that she and Jimmy would help her, Becky shrugged and entered the bedroom. When a moment later there came a knock on the doorframe, Sly invited the men in, his hand held out for their money.

Rue, her shoulders slumped, watched the pair file into the small room, seeing a bottle of whiskey shoved into the back pocket of the man bringing up the rear. It was but a short time later that Becky was laughing and urging the men on.

"See." Burford leered at the brother and sister who stared at the floor. "She enjoys it. She was just bein' stubborn."

Neither brother nor sister made a response to the crude remark. Rue ran outside. She had to get away from that loathsome man, the grunts and groans, the sound of the shuddering bedsprings that carried through the small shack. Although the noise wasn't new to her —she had heard it ever since she could remember—Sly Burford had made it seem obscene somehow.

Tears pricking her eyes, Rue ran to the shed at the back of the house. They would be flowing down her cheeks soon, and she would die before she let that awful man see any weakness in her. She entered the dim interior of the small building and started to close the door behind her. The flimsy barrier moved a few inches then stuck. Rue looked up and dread leapt in her pulse. Sly's big bulk blocked the entrance, his pig-like eyes revealing his lustful intent.

Her heart beating painfully in her chest, Rue strove to hold the door fast, her mind racing as she tried not to give in to panic. When she suddenly snatched open the door and launched herself at Buford, he staggered back in astonishment. He let loose a bellow of rage when the nails of both her hands raked across his face, scoring deeply into his flesh.

"Bitch!" he snarled, and grabbing her fragile wrists he stuck a foot behind her knees, tumbling her to the ground.

Rue lay flat on her back, the breath knocked out of her body, and Sly still holding her hands. She opened her mouth to cry out, to alert the two men with her mother. One of them had come to her rescue before and would come again she had no doubt.

But Burford had read the thought in her blue eyes. His cold words drove the idea from her mind. "You get them men out here, and I'll see to it that something happens to Jimmy the next time he goes huntin'. A careless youngun' could easily trip over somethin' and shoot himself."

He tightened his grip on her wrists until she was sure the bones would snap. "Do you have that clear in your mind, Miss high-and-mighty?" His fat, squinted eyes bored into hers. "Are you gonna behave yourself and be nice to ole Sly? Give him what your mama is givin' them two men in the house?"

Rue stared up helplessly at her tormentor. Tears slid down the corners of both eyes as she nodded.

"That's more like it," Sly grunted, and released her hands. "You just lay there nice-like while I get ready."

She watched in horror as her stepfather stood up and unbuttoned his trousers. When they fell down around his ankles, he closed his thick fingers around his swollen manhood, and moved them up and down its long length.

"I can't decide which way to take you first." He leered down at her. "I guess it don't really matter," he said after a moment, still stroking himself. "I'll have you a lot of different ways over the years."

Please, God, don't let him do this to me, Rue was silently praying when a movement behind Sly caught her eyes. A fast, careful glance quickened her heartbeat. Jimmy was slipping up behind them, a good-sized club raised over his head. When Sly dropped to his knees and roughly jerked her legs apart, there came a crack of wood as the cudgel broke over his balding head.

A burst of bird song overhead interrupted Rue's reliving the past. *I should be getting on to Granddad and Grandma's house,* she thought, but her mind was stuck on the way her life had been for nineteen years. Then hardly aware of it, she sat down on a rock and picked up where her dark musings had broken off.

Her stepfather had not been knocked unconscious, but he was stunned enough to allow her and Jimmy to run to the house. Her heart was a loud drumbeat as she sat down at the table, rubbing her bruised wrists, her hatred of men strengthening. She looked up at Jimmy when he placed a glass of water in front of her. Would he, too, grow up to be like Sly and like those two men in the bedroom, cheating on their wives?

Her trembling hand lifted the glass of water to her lips, and Jimmy sat down beside her. "Look, Rue," he said earnestly, gazing into her tear-streaked face, "he's going to be pestering you all the time. You've got to learn how to protect yourself. I might not be around the next time, so here is what you do to the bastard if he corners you again."

Jimmy had spent several minutes explaining the method she could use that was guaranteed to work every time.

Rue smiled grimly, remembering that she'd had occasion to put Jimmy's instructions into action later that same evening.

The two men had left and Becky, stumbling drunk, came from her room, loudly, in a quarrelsome voice, demanding her supper. When Sly and Jimmy joined her at the table, Rue placed a platter of pan-fried steak and mashed potatoes before them, then walked outside. To eat with Sly Burford was beyond thinking about.

She moved out into the gathering dusk and sat down on a patch of grass beneath a tall cottonwood. What if Jimmy's advice didn't work? she worried, leaning her head back and gazing up at the evening star. And what about Jimmy himself? He had received his share of threatening looks when Sly followed them into the house a short time later. Would it be safe for him to leave the area of the house now? she wondered, remembering the fat man's threat to the young lad.

The soft crunching of footsteps turned Rue's head toward the sound. "They've gone to bed, Rue." Jimmy's teeth flashed in the darkness that had fallen. "Come in and eat your supper now."

He reached a hand down to her, and grasping it, Rue pulled herself to her feet. "What are we going to do, Rue?" Jimmy asked as they walked toward the house.

"I don't know, Jimmy," Rue said quietly with a tired shrug of her shoulders. "I'll have to think on it."

They entered the house and Jimmy sought his straw pallet laid out in the corner of the room. It was quiet in the bedroom as Rue ate her cold supper, then washed the dishes, and put them away.

Should she tell Granddad and Grandma DeLawney about the incident with Sly? she wondered as she prepared for bed. No, she decided a moment later as she slid beneath the rough blanket. The pair were too old to be worried with that. Granddad would be outraged and would tear into Sly, threatening him with bodily harm and the much younger man wouldn't hesitate to use his fists on the dear old man.

Rue stared into the darkness, her tired body slowly relaxing. A gentle smile curved her lips as she listened to Jimmy's even breathing. Only sixteen years old and already so wise, so dedicated to watching over his big sister. She stretched and yawned and her lids began to droop.

Rue was half-asleep when a stealthy noise brought her wide awake. She opened her eyes a slit, sure of whom she'd see. In the moonlight streaming through the window, Sly's naked body loomed over her. A coil of fear tightened around her heart. The sneaking bastard had been lying in there, waiting for her and Jimmy to go to bed.

Jimmy's instructions came to mind, and she wondered if she could follow them. *First you must keep calm,* she warned herself, *and pretend that you are sleeping if you want to catch him off guard.*

Never had Rue's heart beat so loudly, nor had her nerves ever screamed in such protest as she willed herself to lie perfectly quiet while waiting for Sly to reveal that vulnerable spot between his hairy thighs. A moment later it was all she could do not to flinch and cry out when he slowly lifted one fat leg over her hips, then carefully positioned himself over her.

"Now!" a voice whispered to her as Sly

hung over her and fumbled at the hem of her nightgown. Gritting her teeth determinedly, Rue quickly brought up a knee, held it a split second then lashed out with her foot as hard as she could. She heard a crunching sound as her aim found the fat crotch, quickly followed by a screeching yowl. Sly fell to the floor, where he curled up in agony, screaming and swearing. Jimmy sat up with a startled jerk, and while he grimly smiled his satisfaction, Rue watched the man crawl into the bedroom.

Burford was unable to leave the bed for three days. In the meantime Rue and Jimmy were barred from the house as Becky entertained her customers in Rue's bed. Ever since that night, however, Sly never touched her again. But he still watched her, revenge and hate replacing the lust that had stared out of his gimlet eyes.

And strangely, that made Rue more uneasy than his pawing hands. The man was a danger to her, he meant her harm. Finally, in desperation, she had gone to her mother, telling her all that had happened, explaining her fear of Sly's retaliation, that she believed that given the chance the man might even kill her.

She had received a slap in the face for her trouble, not to mention the tongue-lashing that had followed. "Do you think you're too good to spread your lily-white legs for a man?" Becky had railed at her. "You're fifteen years old and should have been doin' it a couple years ago, help bring some money into this house. I had my first man when I was thirteen."

Rue had stared at Becky, complete bewilderment on her face, not wanting to believe what she had heard. Surely, no mother, no matter how uncaring she might be, would want her daughter to sell her body.

But as Becky raved on Rue had to admit that her mother meant exactly what she said. Rue also learned that day why she hadn't already been forced into a life of prostitution as her mother drunkeningly complained, "The village men have no qualms about usin' Buck DeLawney's wife, but, damn them all, his daughter is somethin' else. Every last one of them have refused to lay a hand on you."

Sick to her soul, Rue had left the house and tramped the woods for hours, bitter hot tears washing down her cheeks as she cursed the father who had gone off and left her to be brought up in such an environment.

It had been late in the fall when Rue noticed her mother was gaining weight. When Rue mentioned this fact to Becky, she had laughed mirthlessly and grouched, "My new weight will disappear in the spring."

Rue had paid no attention to the slurred conjecture. As usual by midday Becky was well into her daily bottle of whiskey, and very little sense came out of her mouth after sucking at the raw spirits. However, near the end of winter the drunken sentence came back to Rue and she realized that her mother's words hadn't been senseless ramblings after all. Becky was going to have a baby.

On a blustery March morning Becky was delivered of an undersized baby boy who was too weak to cry. The doctor wrapped the mewling infant in the white square Rue had cut from an old blanket, and handing the wizened body to Rue, said disgustedly, "I'll send a nanny goat up here to provide milk for the poor little mite. All he'd get from his mother's breast would be straight whiskey."

Three more years followed in which another baby came along. This one, also a boy, had fallen to Rue's care as well.

Then one morning, two weeks ago, Sly came from the bedroom and callously announced, "Old Becky died sometime last night."

Jimmy had gone for the doctor, and after the white-haired man had examined the wasted body, he had snapped his black bag shut and said to no one in particular, "Probably all the whiskey she consumed through the years ate up her liver."

Not one person from the village had attended Becky Burford's funeral, nor had her husband, Sly. And no tears were shed as her two eldest children watched their mother's body lowered into the ground. The woman had loved no one, and no one had loved her, except maybe Buck DeLawney when he first married her.

Becky's passing, however, had made an impact on her children's daily lives. There was no more money coming into the house, and with Sly making no effort to find work, it soon became a desperate situation. Everyone's bellies rumbled from hunger. The sickly little ones hung on to Rue's skirts, and she felt guilty that she couldn't love them. All she could feel was pity.

She had expected, hoped, that her mother's husband would leave now. There was no reason he should stay. Was there? The man still watched her, the hate in his eyes seeming to grow daily. A suspicion had been growing in Rue that he was waiting, waiting to take revenge on her before leaving.

A couple of months ago, by accident, she had overheard her stepfather ranting to Becky that he would get that wildcat. The wildcat was not an animal, she learned as Sly raged on, but herself.

"When she kicked me that night four years ago, she ruined me, took away my manhood. I can't get it up anymore." Rue heard his fist hit the wall. "And so help me I'll find her alone someday and that'll be the last anyone sees of Rue DeLawney."

Rue picked up a handful of pine needles and idly let them slip through her fingers.

"Somehow I've got to get away from here," she whispered. "Far away where that devil can't find me." It had gotten to the point where she was afraid to go to bed, fearful that her stepfather would kill her while she slept. And sweet little Jimmy, he never went far from her side.

A soft inquiry broke into Rue's dark musing. "Why are you sittin' there, granddaughter? Have you changed your mind about visitin' us?"

Rue jumped up, her even white teeth revealed in a glad smile. "I was just resting a minute, Granddad, thinking about all the injustice in this world."

"There be a lot of that, child." The old man nodded. "I ponder it myself sometimes. It don't seem fair that some folk get more than their share of bad times."

Shaking off her troubled thoughts, Rue changed the gloomy subject. It was bad enough that Granddad knew they were practically starving, he didn't have to know that she feared for her life. It was probably all in her imagination anyway. Sly was surely smart enough to know he couldn't get away with murder.

Looking at the glass jar in the gnarled hand, then lifting her eyes to John DeLawney's wrinkled visage, she asked, "Are you sap gathering, Granddad?"

Blue eyes like her own, only faded a bit with

age, twinkled back at her. "That I am, child. Your grandma has been fussin' that she's about out of salve. Give me a hand a bit, then we'll go on to the house. Maddy promised to bake me a berry pie for lunch."

"How long have you been out?" Rue fell in step beside the old man.

"Sun wasn't up yet when I rolled out of the blankets." He looked down at the rifle in his hand. "Brought along my Henry. Thought maybe I might see a squirrel before it warmed up. Most animals hide when it gets hot."

"Oh, Granddad!" Rue half cried. "Are you telling me that you didn't have any luck hunting yesterday?"

"Now don't go gettin' upset, Rue, honey." John put an arm around her narrow shoulders and squeezed them affectionately. "I bagged me a fine young doe, fat as butter. I got it butchered and stowed away in the cellar, next to that cold spring water that flows through it. The meat should keep a couple of weeks."

"Thank God." Rue sighed her relief. "I've been wracking my brains about what to give Jimmy and the little ones for supper in case you hadn't shot anything."

"Dad blame it, Rue, it gets my hackles up that you have to worry whether or not them younguns' get to eat. What you aimin' to do, let them drag on you the rest of your life?"

"Oh, Granddad." Rue sighed. "I don't know

what to do. I don't worry about Jimmy. He's a good lad and doesn't have a lazy bone in his body. I'm sure somebody would take him in. But the little ones, sickly and all, who'd want them."

"Well, the way I see it"—John passed over Rue's concern for the two little boys— "although Burford has good cause to doubt that either child is his, he owes it to them to see that they eat. He kept their mother in the business that brought them about. Lined his pockets too, I'll bet.

"And I'll tell you something else, I'm gettin' dad-blamed tired of trampin' this mountain lookin' for game while that one sits on his fat rump doin' nothin.'"

"I know, Granddad," Rue said, her eyes full of apology. "But he doesn't care whether they eat or not. It doesn't bother him at all to listen to their hungry cries."

"What does that hog do for his own grub? I can't see that he's lost any weight." John ran his eyes over his granddaughter's thin body. "The way you have."

"He rides down to the village every day. He probably eats there, using the money Mom made to pay for it."

"Damn his rotten soul!" John kicked angrily at a rock. "I think it's time I called a meetin' of all the men around here and discuss this situation. We don't need men of his sort among us."

And wouldn't it be a blessing to see the last of Sly Burford, I could sleep nights then, Rue thought as the subject was dropped, and she walked along with her grandfather, their attention on finding trees where the bark had cracked and its substance oozed out.

From this gum Maddy DeLawney made a potent salve that helped various cuts and bruises to heal. It was the same ointment that covered the eruptions on Rue's face.

After about a half hour, John held the jar up and squinted at it. "I think we got enough," he said to Rue, who leaned against a tree, patting her sweaty face with the scrap of rag. "Let's get on up to the house and sample some of Maddy's pie."

"My, you do look a sight, child," Maddy DeLawney greeted her granddaughter as the girl proceeded John into the neat, orderly cabin. "Let me see how those scabs are coming along."

She led Rue to a window and carefully scanned her face in the sunlight pouring through shiny glass panes. She nodded her head finally. "They're coming along just fine. I see you took my advice and haven't been scratching them. A few weeks from now you'll have your creamy complexion back again.

"You had the worst case of pox I ever saw." Maddy shook her head. "There was a couple times John and I thought we might lose you, your fever was so high.''

Rue kissed the soft, wrinkled face. "It was a lucky thing for me that I was visiting you the day my face broke out. If you hadn't put me to bed and doctored me through the worst of it, I'm sure I wouldn't have pulled through.''

She looked tenderly at the old woman. "It was kind of you to send some of your salve down to the others.''

Maddy shrugged her shoulders. "Poor little scraps, I knew Becky wouldn't do anything for them. Anyway, John said they had a light case of the disease. It took hold of you hard because you'd worn yourself out taking care of them.''

She brushed the hair away from Rue's face. "You should keep your hair cleaner, honey. It's so greasy you might get your sores infected, with it hanging against your cheeks that way.''

Rue looked uncomfortable, embarrassed by the tangled condition of her hair. "I know, Grandma.'' She pushed the oily strands behind her ears. "I tried washing it yesterday, but without soap the water just ran off it.''

Maddy patted Rue's arm in sympathy. "I made some of my rose soap this morning. It's not quite set yet, but it'll be ready when you come visiting tomorrow.''

"Oh, Grandma, what would I do without you and Granddad.'' Rue threw her arms around the slight body and hugged it. "I would really have a miserable existence if you two weren't here to bring a little normalcy to my life."

Pain flickered in Maddy's eyes as she returned the hug. "I don't know what John and I would do without you, honey. You bring us so much pleasure. You're a piece of our Buck."

She motioned Rue to sit down at the well-scrubbed table, and John took a seat across from her. His mouth watering as his wife cut into the juicy pie, he said, "I still can't believe that Buck never sent us a letter in all this time."

"I worry about that too." Maddy sighed, pushing a plate of the pastry in front of her husband and granddaughter. Then sitting down with her own helping, she continued, "Buck was always a thoughtful son, and he was crazy fond of you, Rue." She stared out the window as Rue and John hungrily attacked the pie. "He's been on my mind a lot these past weeks. I keep getting the feeling that he's coming home."

John patted his wife's work-worn hand lying beside her plate, but didn't speak the doubt in his mind. If they hadn't heard from their son in sixteen years it was doubtful they'd ever hear or see him again.

And Rue made no remark either. It mattered less to her whether her father ever returned or whether he was six feet under the ground. Hadn't he gone off and left her to a hellish life? In her opinion he wasn't worth wasting a thought on.

The sun dipped toward the west and Rue reluctantly said that it was time she was getting back down the mountain. "I told Jimmy to come meet me around four if he could get away."

"Jimmy's a good lad, no matter who his father is." John stood up, and walking to the trapdoor in the center of the room lifted it up. "It's some relief knowin' he is with you," he added as his head disappeared down the cellar steps.

You'd be more relieved, Granddad, Rue thought, *if you knew the times he's protected me from that fat hog we live with.*

By the time Rue had finished her coffee and Maddy had wrapped a piece of pie for Jimmy, John returned with a large chunk of venison. Rue's mouth watered as she watched her grandmother wrap it in a white cloth. There'd been no meat in the house for three days.

"It will make a good strengthening stew, honey." Maddy handed the meat to Rue. "But don't you let that fat Sly have a bite of it, even if you have to beat him off with a club."

Rue assured her grandparents that she would do just that if necessary, then kissing each of them on the cheek, and promising that she would see them tomorrow, Rue started down the mountain.

Jimmy was waiting for her, leaning against

a tree a short distance from the DeLawney cabin. "Have you been here long, Jimmy?" Rue asked. "It's not safe to leave the children alone too long. You know that Sly won't watch them."

"The younguns' are asleep," Jimmy answered, eyeing the smaller package in his sister's hand. "And Sly took off about a half hour ago. I thought I ought to get up here just in case."

Rue didn't have to ask in case of what. She knew. In case Sly was going to wait and waylay her along the mountain path. "You did right, Jimmy," Rue assured her brother, as she looked fearfully around. There were a lot of places the fat man could hide while he waited for her.

She looked at the club in Jimmy's hand, then picked up one of her own from the forest floor. Noticing her brother's absorption with what he hoped was a treat for him, she grinned and held the package out to him. "A piece of berry pie," she said.

Jimmy almost snatched it from her hand, and as they moved on and Rue scanned the forest for signs of Sly, the boy consumed the pie in three bites.

Rue heard the children crying before the shack came in sight. Sighing, she hastened her pace. She must get the stew on as soon as possible.

CHAPTER TWO

The September day was hot and listless under the Nebraska sun as Hawke Masters stood beside an open grave. He flinched each time a clod of earth hit the lid of the stark pine coffin.

Earlier there had been an excavation beside the one he stared into, but that one was filled and mounded now. Sara Masters, his sister-in-law, had been laid to rest before her husband. Now it was his brother, Ben's, turn.

The tall, broad-shouldered man looked down on the curly head of his five-year-old niece, who tightly clutched his hand. Poor little Susie, she hardly knew what was going on. His eyes moved to ten-year-old Tommy, who held his sister's other hand. The lad knew what was happening and was manfully trying to hold back his tears.

Hawke's gaze moved to his father's weather-worn face. Tears rolled freely down those brown, wrinkled cheeks as the man stood bareheaded, his old straw hat gripped in his hands. Jeb Masters had lived long enough to know there was no shame in shedding tears when a man was being torn apart inside.

Although Hawke Masters was wracked with the same tearing emotion, none of his pain was visible on his stony face. If one looked closely, however, one would see his muscular throat working as he swallowed back his grief.

No two brothers had ever been closer, three years separating the pair, Hawke being the eldest. As youngsters they had shared dreams and secrets, then as adults they had drank and raised hell together, even occasionally sharing the same woman. Then when war broke out they had joined the Army and fought side by side.

But previous to the war Ben had met and married gentle, brown-eyed Sara. From that day he'd never looked at another woman with lust in his heart. While Ben sired two children and worked his father's farm, Hawke had continued on in much the same manner as before. His dissolute lifestyle caused his father to worry, to wonder where the wild streak in his firstborn had come from, and would he ever tame down.

The war had been over about a year when Ben started dreaming of going West. The old family farm was worn out, he claimed, and each year he worked harder and grew less in the depleted soil. He wanted something better to leave his son someday.

He'd had little trouble convincing his foot-loose brother to come along, only his father had been reluctant to make the move. At Jeb Masters' advanced years he didn't like change. Also he was loath to leave their mother's grave in the small local cemetery.

How Pa had loved his wife, Hawke thought, shutting out the scraping sound of the shovel as he remembered the two of them together. Pa had aged terribly since Ma's death a few years back. The pain of losing her still lingered in his eyes.

Why was it, Hawke wondered, and not for the first time, that the other two Masters men had found undying love, while he at thirty-two had never had his heart touched by a woman? At least one appealing enough to spend the rest of his life with. Once Pa had said that Hawke never gave a woman a chance, simply because he didn't want the responsibility of a wife and family. Also that the type of woman he seemed drawn to wasn't good wife material anyway. Pa had ended by predicting that if Hawke managed to make it to an old age he'd be sorry he hadn't married.

"You'll be mighty lonesome, son. I'm

thinkin' it must be terrible to die alone, with no one to grieve your passin'."

Hawke looked at his father again. The twisted pain on the thin face made Hawke wonder if it wouldn't be better to die alone, to leave no one to endure what this fine old man had when he lost his beloved wife, and the agony he was enduring now.

His lips twisted stubbornly. His way was best. He had no desire for marriage, so why should he tie himself down to a woman just because it was accepted as the normal thing to do? Besides, didn't he have Lillie? She fired his blood, gave him a satisfaction that few women ever had. And being his neighbor's wife put her out of bounds for matrimony for which he was thankful. Lillie wasn't good wife material either. She was good in bed, he'd give her that, but a man couldn't stay in the blankets all the time. But actually, Lillie was a little on the stupid side. She was fox sly about a lot of things, but he couldn't remember them ever having a normal conversation of any importance.

Hawke kept his thoughts on Lillie, anything that would remove him from the painful present. He drifted back to the first time he'd seen Lillie, and the two years that had led up to their meeting.

He had left Pa and Ben on the Nebraska border where they had settled down to farm once again, and had headed across to Colorado. Staring at a mule's rump day after day was still not for him. So, for over a year he did odd jobs as he wandered. He drove a stagecoach for a while, then dealt poker in a fancy saloon, punched cows for a few months, in other words, just plain drifted.

However, as he journeyed across the beautiful country he'd seen thousands and thousands of wild cattle grazing, belonging to the man strong enough to corral them. There was born in him the desire to have his own ranch. He did not want marriage and a family, but he was tired of his lifestyle and wanted to settle down to something. Pa had insisted he take a share of the money received from the sale of the old farm in Ohio, and Hawke had decided he would invest it in something tangible, a worth he could see, could touch.

He had then spent a week intensely scouring the terrain, looking for the right spot to start his, what he laughingly called, empire. One day he had found some abandoned buildings nestled at the edge of the Rocky Mountain foothills. Inquiring at the government agency in the small town of Raffin, he learned that the deserted ranch consisted of five thousand acres. That it was mostly all prime land, two-thirds grassland and containing a narrow river that never dried up.

He had hurried to file a claim, then almost winded his stallion in a race to take over *his* property. His first action was to paint in big letters on a weathered board, "Hawke's Pride," then to place the sign about a mile from the ranch house. The next day he had gone over the roof of his new home, replacing rotten shingles, insuring that he wouldn't be leaked on the next time it rained. His next chore had been finding men to help him run his ranch.

It had taken a couple weeks. He wasn't going to hire just any man; he wanted trustworthy men, ones not afraid of work, ones who knew what they were doing. Finally he had hired six cowpunchers and started rounding up the wild longhorns.

He had worked harder than any slave the following year, but his physical effort had paid off. He now had a herd of over two thousand, not counting the thousand head he had driven to Abilene this past spring.

It was in Abilene he met Lillie.

It was dusk when he stepped out of the saloon where he and his men had stopped for a drink of whiskey to cut the dust of two weeks from their throats. He had paused a moment outside the swinging doors, wondering which bordello to visit. It was then he spotted a female figure strolling down the wooden sidewalk, her voluptuous figure very inviting as it swung along.

Hawke had thought her a whore when he went in pursuit of her. Her mode of dress, the way she walked, all said that clearly to him.

And when he overtook her and looked into a painted face of coarse attractiveness, he was surer than ever. But as he walked alongside her, hinted at what he was looking for, the woman turned insulted eyes on him.

Flashing a wedding band on her left hand, she snapped, "I'm a married woman, Mister."

Nevertheless, there had been an invitation in the eyes that had swept over him, and in less than ten minutes he had talked the woman into accompanying him to his hotel room. Hawke smiled thinly. Lillie had entertained him in such a way that there was no doubt that, though she no longer worked her trade, she had at one point in her life.

Before Lillie left him a couple hours later, he learned that her husband was twice her age and was no longer very active in bed, and that his ranch lay only thirty miles from Hawke's Pride. Since that first encounter, he and Lillie met once a week in an old line shack halfway between the two ranches. There they spent a couple hours on a pallet of hay, wearing each other out.

A hand on Hawke's shoulder brought him back to the present and a shamed blush to his face. He shouldn't have been thinking about Lillie and the line shack, he swore silently in self-disgust as his father said, "Come on, son, it's over. Go thank our neighbors for attending, then let's get these younguns' back to the house. They're worn out. Besides, Tommy has to get off alone so that he can cry."

Hawke shook hands with the scattering of people who had gathered for the burial, thanking them, then picked up his young niece. Jeb led the way from the cemetery, an arm around his grandson's shoulder as they walked down the hill to the neat set of buildings nestled in a stand of cottonwoods.

They entered the house that was strangely empty, the absence of Ben and Sara leaving a lonesome void. A shuddering sigh escaped from Jeb's mouth before he said, "Let's change into our work clothes, Tommy. It will be dark before long."

Hawke shook his head as the elderly man and his grandson headed for their bedrooms. Life must go on. There were hungry animals to be fed and watered, cows to be milked and chickens to be tended. Tasks that couldn't wait, even for death.

When his father and nephew headed for the barn a short time later, Hawke built a fire in the kitchen range. Then with his niece's big eyes watching him, he started preparing supper.

As Hawke sliced ham into a skillet and peeled potatoes to fry, he remembered all the good times he and Ben had enjoyed together, and deeply regretted that he hadn't been able to see his brother before typhoid fever took him and his wife. But Pa's letter hadn't arrived in time for him to ride across Colorado and say all the things that were in his heart.

An hour later Hawke breathed a sigh of relief when his two male relatives entered the kitchen, a pail of milk in Tommy's hand. Little Susie had begun to cry for her mama, and he was at a loss how to console her.

He watched his father pick up the little girl and, sitting down in a rocking chair, cuddle her close and set the chair in motion. Smoothing the brown, curly hair with a work-calloused hand, he explained gently to the child that her mama and daddy had gone away for a while, but that she would see them again at a later time. That in the meantime she had Grandpa, her brother, and Uncle Hawke to love her.

All three men smiled their relief when red-swollen lids slipped over wet eyes and Susie drowsed. Jeb continued to rock the small body until Hawke announced that supper was ready.

An hour later the meal, mostly picked at, was over. While Hawke cleaned the kitchen, Jeb helped the children to get in bed. Darkness had set in by the time the two men sat outside, having a last smoke before retiring too.

"So, Pa," Hawke broke the silence that had fallen over them, "what happens now?"

"I don't know, son." Jeb rubbed a hand wearily over his face. "I'm gettin' too far on in years to raise a couple younguns', especially a little girl. I probably won't live long enough to see them become adults."

Hawke knew a gut-wrenching pain at the thought of his father also dying someday. He was ready to exclaim, "Don't talk that way, Pa, you've got a lot of years ahead of you," when Jeb spoke first, stunning Hawke with his words.

"I been thinkin' it would be a good idea for you to live here with us. Take over the farm, be a daddy to your brother's children."

While Hawke gaped at his father, there flashed before him his ranch, his big herds of cattle, the long green valleys, the tall rugged mountains. He loved that wild country, could not visualize ever leaving it for good.

He looked at his father and said gently, "Look, Pa, you know how I feel about farmin'. I still hate all aspects of it. Besides, I have a very prosperous ranch in the makin'. My dream is to become a land baron someday."

"I can understand that." Jeb looked up at the stars that were beginning to appear. "And I want you to know that I'm proud and happy that you've finally found an interest in life. I wouldn't for the world jeopardize your chance to realize a dream. Dreams are important in this cockeyed world. Sometimes they are all that keeps a man goin'."

Hawke continued to smoke his hand-rolled cigarette in the silence that developed, his green eyes narrowed in thought. Then, as though coming to a decision, he flipped the cigarette into the dusty yard, its lit end making a glowing arc in the darkness.

"Pa," he said, "I have a better idea. Why don't you and the kids come live with me?"

Jeb was stunned now. He could only look blankly at his son. Hawke hurried to take advantage of his father's temporary loss of speech. Fired by the idea of having his remaining family with him, he rushed to say, "The house needs some repairs, but it's big, plenty of room for us all." Hawke sat very still, hardly breathing as he tried to read the expression on the face turned in profile to him.

Maybe I should have waited until morning to spring my idea on him, Hawke thought when Jeb made no answer. *A sleepless night of worrying would make my suggestion more conducive, to going west with the children.*

Yes, I should have, Hawke decided when a moment later Jeb shook his head and declared softly, "I couldn't go off and leave more of my family in the ground, Hawke. There'd be no one to visit Ben's and Sara's graves. At least there are relatives back in Ohio to look after your mama's resting place, say a prayer, bring flowers."

Hawke was uncertain what to say next. He understood what the gray-haired man meant, knew that besides his grief there would be guilt at leaving the two lonely graves. But, damn it, Pa couldn't stay here alone with

Susie and Tommy. Like he himself had said, he was getting too old to raise them by himself.

"Look, Pa," he said earnestly, "I know the thought of moving on again is a hard decision to make, but bear this in mind. The way you've always carried Mama in your heart no matter where you were, the same will be true of Ben and Sara."

He laid a hand on Jeb's shoulder and squeezed gently. "Your grief will be easier to bear in new surroundings. And it's beautiful country, Pa. Rough and wild. The kids will love it."

Hawke saw the wavering in Jeb's eyes and pressed on. "Tommy especially will fall in love with the land. He can have his own horse, ride the range with me. By the time he's grown, he'll be a fine cowman. Ready to inherit the ranch when I retire."

Jeb looked at his son affectionately, although frowning a little. "That's right fine of you, Hawke, thinkin' to make Tommy your heir. But, surely, you plan on marryin' someday, have sons of your own."

Hawke shrugged dismissively. "Stuck with one woman is not for me, Pa. I'm too old, too set in my ways to let a woman take me over. I'll be content raisin' Ben's children."

Jeb laughed softly. "Thirty-two is far from bein' old. Someday you just might run into a woman who would make you like it just fine if she took you over."

"Ha!" Hawke snorted. "There's not a woman alive who could make me give up my independence."

"We'll see." Jeb grinned. "I hope I'm around to see it if it happens. You men who hold out so stubbornly fall like a rock dropped in a well when love hits you. You'll go stumblin' around like you've been smokin' locoweed."

"It's a bet, Pa." Hawke grinned. "Come back to the ranch with me, and if that happens, you can crow your heart out."

Jeb made no response to the half-jokingly made bribe. Instead, he gazed out into the moonlit night, occasionally drawing on his cigarette. Hawke knew he was mulling over everything they'd said, weighing each argument put to him. Again Hawke held his breath, waiting for his father's decision.

Finally Jeb broke his silence. "What about Susie? Who would take care of her while we're out chasin' them cows of yours? A five-year-old can't be left alone."

"That'll be easy," Hawke answered eagerly. "I'll hire a housekeeper," then added silently to himself, *damned if I know where I'll find one though*.

Jeb fell silent again, and from the concentrated look on his face, Hawke was aware that he was still turning over in his mind the pros and cons of disrupting the children's lives.

Finally Hawke couldn't bear the suspense

any longer. "Well, Pa," he prodded, "what about it? Are you comin' back to the ranch with me?"

A sigh of relief whistled through Hawke's teeth when Jeb answered, "I reckon it's the sensible thing to do, Hawke. I'm not goin' to be around forever. Sooner or later the younguns' would end up with you anyway."

The gray-haired man grew silent again for a moment, then, his voice husky, he added, "I like the idea of spendin' my last years with my firstborn. Never did get to see much of you since you was sixteen. Seems like you was everywhere but at home."

Unhappily conscious of the neglect of his parents over the years, Hawke couldn't speak over the lump that rose in his throat. He could only grip the knobby hand that lay on a bony knee.

Sensing his son's choked emotions, Jeb said matter-of-factly, "It'll be two to three weeks before we can come, though. There's the farm to sell, the furniture. The livestock to get rid of, some of the crops still to be harvested."

Hawke's blood raced joyfully. He'd have a family with him again, family that he hadn't realized how much he had missed. There would be company when the long winter set in, keeping a man mostly housebound. He wouldn't be so damn lonesome like all the previous years.

"Better bring the furniture, Pa." He

laughed. "I've only got a few sticks, and they should have been thrown away years ago. Truth be told"—he smiled crookedly—"the house is pretty much a boar's nest I'm afraid."

A frown wrinkled Jeb's forehead. "Are you sure you can get a woman to work in the kind of place you just described?"

"Don't worry about it, Pa, I'll get someone." The confidence in Hawke's voice wasn't shared by his thoughts. Damned if he knew where he'd find a woman willing to take over his household, plus a couple of youngsters.

I'll think of something, he told himself, then yawned loudly. "I'm beat, Pa. I think I'll go to bed. I made the trip here in three days where ordinarily it takes at least five. Anyway, I'm headin' back tomorrow and I want to get an early start."

Both men stood up. "I don't know where you can sleep, Hawke." A worried frown creased Jeb's forehead. "You can't use Ben and Sara's bed, you might catch the fever. I'll be burnin' the mattress and linens tomorrow."

"That's all right, Pa." Hawke shrugged indifferently. "A pile of hay in the barn will be fine. Most of the time I sleep on the ground anyway." He held out a hand to his father. "Actually it's better I sleep in the barn. I won't wake up the kids when I leave. So I'll say good-bye now."

Jeb took his son's slim hand and held it. "I'll

fill you a bag of grub and put it just inside the barn door."

Hawke nodded, squeezing his father's hand before saying, "I'll see you in two or three weeks then."

"God willin', we'll be there," Jeb answered, and released his hand.

"Pa." Hawke paused, his hand going to his hip pocket. "I brought along some money in case you'd need it. Five hundred dollars. I want you to take it."

Jeb shook his head. "Thank you, son, but I don't need it. Me and your brother have made out real good with the farm."

The sun was barely above the tree line when Hawke left the farm in Nebraska and cut across the state line into Colorado. As he kept Captain, his stallion, at an easy lope, his lean face wore a worried frown. It had struck him fully that raising his brother's children was a grave responsibility and the thought hung heavy on him. Until now his only obligation had been to himself.

Was he capable of putting himself second, he asked himself, cater to the needs of others for a change? Yes, he decided. For Ben's children he could, and would, do it.

Now, the next question. Where would he find a woman who would be willing to live with the loneliness of his ranch? Pa and the children wouldn't be much company for her, and the nearest white woman was Lillie Meyers. A wry grimace twisted his lips. That one wouldn't bother herself with a female.

The hours passed, the miles stretched out behind the tireless stride of the big black stallion. The animal occasionally snorted his desire for water, and his master's stomach rumbled from hunger. Hawke frowned into the westward sun. It would set soon, and he hadn't come across any signs of water. The water in his canteen was warm and brackish and needed to be replenished for tomorrow's travel.

There was about an hour of daylight left when Captain lunged up a rocky hill and Hawke spotted what he thought was abandoned buildings. "Maybe there's a well there, Captain." He patted the mount's sleek neck as he sent him down the hill.

A moment later he was reining in beside a dangerously slanting shack. He slid stiffly to the ground, eyeing the building, wondering if it was safe to spend the night in. He started then, as from inside came the fussy wailing of a child. Impossible as it seemed, people evidently lived here.

"Lazy nesters." His lips curled contemptuously as he looped the stallion's reins over a bush. "Clutterin' up cow country with their piddly farms and their barbwire fences that cut and rip the cattle to pieces."

The crying inside stopped when Hawke's

knock on the flimsy door pushed it open. He stood in the opening, blinking, adjusting his eyes to the inside where the only light came from a very small window. A movement to his right caught his eye. The thin figure of a young woman stood beside a rusty stove, a long-handled spoon in her hand. As his gaze rested on her sore-infested face, he thought to himself he had never seen a female less comely. He looked into her stormy blue eyes and realized he had never been so fiercely glared at either.

He shifted his eyes to the tangled mass of hair, and wondered what color it was beneath the dirt and grime, when the girl spoke over the resumed crying of the small youngster hanging onto her skirt.

"Becky is dead," she said coldly, impatiently freeing her dress from the small clutching fingers. "So you can just turn around and ride back down the hill."

Hawke glared back at the unattractive girl, anger at her sharpness tightening his lips. "Look, miss," he growled. "I don't know any Becky. I'm just ridin' through. All I want is to water my horse."

"There's a river about half a mile down the hill," the ungracious young female said shortly, then turned back to stirring whatever was simmering in the pot.

An unreasonable desire to bait the unpleasant girl, to crack her aloofness, to remove the unwarranted contempt from her eyes, rose inside Hawke. When another, younger tot toddled its way into the room, also crying, he leaned back against the doorframe and sneered, "You've been a busy little miss, haven't you. How many more do you have runnin' around?"

He received a baleful look and a short, "That's none of your business, Mister."

Hawke studied the thin faces of the children and thought, *They look like her with the same disgusting sores on their faces.* "Where's your man?" He shot at her.

The girl gave him a look of intense dislike, then said begrudgingly, "I don't have a man."

That doesn't surprise me, Hawke snorted. Besides her ugly face, what man would tolerate her sharp tongue? "Are you tellin' me that you live alone here with these younguns'?"

"No, I'm not telling you that!" A lid was slammed on the steaming pot and the two crying children were firmly removed from the girl's hem. "My brother and stepfather live here too."

Oh-ho, Hawke thought. *It's that kind of household is it?* His lips curled in disgust. He'd heard of cases like that. The mother dead, or gone away, then the stepfather taking over the daughter.

He studied the marred face, the lank, oily hair hanging alongside her cheeks, the rail-thin body. The man couldn't have much pride in himself to take something like that to bed. Nor was he much of a provider either, Hawke thought, his lips tight. He ran his eyes down the slim body clad in homespun, patched many times, but surprisingly clean. *She looks half-starved,* he told himself, shifting his eyes to the shelves attached to the wall a few feet from the stove. He frowned at the small bag and five potatoes lying there.

His eyes swung back to the girl, noting how proudly she held her small head, the straight line of her back. His eyes narrowed indignantly. What made the ugly bitch think she was special? He reluctantly admitted that she had a nice way with the tots, who were again whining and hanging on to her. The resigned look on her face said that the little ones were hungry, and that they had a right to cry.

The little ones suddenly stopped their whimpering and scurried from the room. While Hawke's startled look followed them, he heard a heavy tread on the porch. He straightened his slouched position as an obese man and a young teenager stopped just outside the door.

Yes, he thought, *this one would take the girl to bed; he'd lie with a dog.* He glanced at the boy, his eyes widening at the hate in the dark eyes. *For me, or the fat man,* he wondered, then looked back at the man when he spoke.

"Howdy, stranger." Fleshy lips parted over large yellow teeth. "I expect you're lookin' for

Becky, huh?" A sham sadness flickered in the ferret-like eyes. "It grieves me to tell you that she's been dead a couple weeks now." He held out a dirt-grimed hand to Hawke. "The name is Sly. Sly Burford."

Hawke reluctantly took the outstretched hand, noting there were no calluses on the palm as he introduced himself.

"Take a seat," Burford invited, stepping past Hawke and lowering his big bulk in the only chair the room boasted of. "Smells like Rue's stew is about ready to be et. It would pleasure me if you'd eat supper with us."

Hawke remained in the door. He didn't like the man, didn't like the sharp-tongued girl. And although the stew smelled mighty appetizing, the cook didn't and he'd just as soon pass on the invitation.

"I'd like to water my horse first," he said, knowing that he would ride on once the stallion had quenched his thirst. "The girl tells me there's a river nearby."

"No need to make that trip." Sly rose and picked up a pail of water from the table. "He can have this."

Hawke glanced at the girl and knew from the stiffening of her body that she had been the one who had lugged the water from that long distance.

"No, that's all right," Hawke waved a dissenting hand. "A half mile is a long way to fetch your drinkin' water."

"Don't worry about it," his fat host insisted. "Rue won't mind bringin' up more, will you, girl?" The question was asked with a sly maliciousness.

He's a mean bastard, Hawke thought angrily, and wondered if the girl would suffer if he refused the water. With a mental sigh, he stepped into the room. "Maybe just a couple of dipperfuls to hold him for a while."

A fast glance at the girl showed her relaxing a bit, but the shaking of her hands told Hawke that she was raging inside. When she made no move to produce a basin, Sly, sending her a look of promised revenge, jerked one off the wall, and picking up the pail again, emptied half its contents into the chipped pan.

Hawke started to object then closed his mouth. There was bad blood between these two and he wanted no part of it. As he took the vessel and walked outside, he expected to hear a violent argument erupt behind him. But no sound came from inside the small quarters, except for the ceaseless whining of the hungry toddlers.

He hunkered down beside the stallion and as its nose whiffled the water, the mouthwatering aroma of the simmering stew drifted from the door. Would he be able to say he wasn't very hungry and only take a small portion of the venison? The girl and the little ones, not to mention the boy, were god-awful hungry, he knew. It would be criminal of him, a grown man, to take food away from those who needed it so badly.

Hawke stared down at the ground, with half a mind to climb on Captain's back and ride away, not even bothering to say good-bye to the obnoxious man and sharp-tongued girl. He gave a startled jerk when a voice spoke behind him, a voice that was still changing, shifting from the high treble of a youth, to the deep resonance of a man.

It was a man's tone that rasped, "Me and my sister don't want you here. So get on your mount and ride out."

As Hawke looked up at the boy with open-mouthed surprise, the young man flourished a wicked-looking butcher knife. "If you stay and take Sly up on his offer to sleep with my sister, I'll put this between your shoulder blades."

Still too stunned to speak, to declare that he couldn't be paid enough to bed the unattractive girl, Hawke gaped as the brother walked away and disappeared into the house.

So that's how the bastard makes his livin', Hawke thought, scowling as he remembered Burford's smooth palms. He rose and gathered up Captain's hanging reins. "We're gettin' out of here, boy," he muttered, lifting a foot to the stirrup.

Ready to swing a leg across the saddle, he swore softly under his breath as Burford called to him from the door.

"Supper's on the table, Masters. Come and get it before it's et up."

Hawke opened his mouth to say that he had decided to ride on, then the boy appeared beside his stepfather, his dark eyes threatening, ordering him to be on his way. *Why you little pissant!* he swore to himself, half in anger, half in amusement. *I'll just stay and let you sweat a bit, then really rile you when you discover I only hold contempt for that slovenly sister of yours.*

Everyone but Sly was at the table when Hawke entered the shack and hung his hat on a peg driven into wall beside the door. The girl ignored him as she filled plates for the two little ones, who watched her avidly. He looked at the single unoccupied place at the table and frowned. The ugly one didn't welcome him, and damned if he'd eat what wasn't gladly given.

When Hawke was about to turn away, Sly pushed him forward, saying heartily, "Sit down, Masters. Looks like Rue can't count. I'll get myself a plate."

Although his stomach was growling with hunger, it was with reluctance Hawke slid onto the end of the bench. He ignored the black look she sent him, as his attention was on Rue's slender hands. If they looked anything like her face, he wouldn't be able to choke down a bite.

Relief rolled through him. The tapering

fingers were free of any soil or grime, including her nails. *Strange,* he thought, *considering the rest of her.* He shifted his gaze to Sly when the fat man came lumbering over to the table, a tin plate in one hand, a stool in the other.

"The girl ain't much good at most things, but she sure can cook." He slid a sly intimate look at Rue as he slapped the tin on the table and carefully lowered his large bulk onto the three-legged seat.

Hawke glanced at the girl, expecting to see fire shooting out of her eyes at Sly's thinly veiled insinuation. But they showed no emotion, as she spooned food into the youngest child's mouth.

Then, when Sly reached for the wooden ladle, smacking his fat lips in anticipation, the girl erupted like a wildcat. Her hand swept down beside the bench and came up with a club, two inches around and two feet long. The blow she delivered to Burford's wrist brought a scream of pain from the fat man.

"You lazy bastard!" she panted, ready to let go again. "My grandfather tramped the mountains half a day to shoot this venison. I'll crack your head open if you touch it."

For a long tense minute the pair glared at each other, Burford nursing his wrist, his hate for the girl a living thing. Hawke had no doubt who would look away first as he wondered at the strange behavior between the pair, thinking how fierce their coupling must be.

As Hawke had expected, Burford broke eye contact first. Staring down at his wrist, he whined, "You didn't have to break my arm, you bitch. I won't be able to do a lick of work for weeks now."

Brother and sister snorted disgustedly, implying, "As if you ever do."

His face purple with rage, Sly stood up and kicked the stool across the floor. Then, his pig eyes glaring murderously at Rue, he gritted between his teeth, "You'll pay dearly for this, missy. See if you don't."

Hawke saw a flicker of fear in the blue eyes as Sly stomped outside. *The rag-tail girl is courageous,* he thought, digging into the plate of stew she silently handed him, *but she knows she's licked, that sooner or later she'll pay dearly for her stand against that brute.*

As Hawke slowly chewed and swallowed, giving his stomach time to fill, he let his gaze slip over the room and its furniture. He was reminded of his own few pieces back at the ranch—a chair that needed mending, the long table and two benches on which they sat, a sagging bed in one corner, and the rusty old stove. Surprisingly, however, the room was spotlessly clean.

He shifted his eyes to Rue, and as he wondered at the complexity of the girl, he found her blue eyes studying him. When he lifted an inquiring eyebrow at her, she looked away, and after jumping to her feet, gathered the dirty dishes. When he saw no evidence of coffee to finish off the tasty stew, Hawke started to swing his feet from under the table. He would thank the girl and be on his way.

"Sit a spell longer, Masters." Burford had come in from outside, a bottle of whiskey in his good hand. He plopped the bottle on the table and ordered his stepson to fetch cups. Then turning to Rue he added, "Put them younguns' to bed. I'm sick and tired of their infernal whinin'."

As the children were hustled out of the room by Rue, Sly splashed the clear liquid into the tin cups the boy had sullenly put before them. "It ain't the best in the world," he said, pushing a cup toward Hawke, "but it'll warm your innards."

Hunching over the table, the flickering lamp touched the fat man's face with grotesque shadows as he downed his drink in one swallow. Lowering the empty vessel, he looked across the table to Hawke. "Masters," he began, "as you can see, me and the girl don't get along at all, and I'm through takin' her sass. It's been on my mind for a long time to get rid of her, bind her over to some family." He paused a moment, fixing his eyes on Hawke's. "What if I bound her over to you, say for about three years? Could you use a bound girl?"

Hawke heard the swift intake of an angry breath, mingling with his surprised one. It could have come from the girl, who had returned to the room, or from her brother, who came swiftly to his feet. Hawke shook his head as if to clear it, telling himself that Burford wasn't serious, that it was a cruel joke meant to torment the girl for the whack on his wrist. The man only wanted to torment her.

Well, you fat bastard, he thought, *I'll put an end to that real quick.* He emptied his cup of whiskey, then drawled, "No thanks, Burford. I don't want no diseased female in my household."

He was aware of the blue flame of outrage in the glare the girl gave him as Sly asked testily, "What do you mean, diseased? She ain't got no disease?"

"What about them sores on her face?"

Sly hunched around to look at Rue. "I hadn't noticed before," he said after a moment, "but she's probably broke out from somethin' she's et. Them crazy old grandparents of hers are always diggin' up somethin' from the woods and feedin' it to her. It'll clear up in a few days.

"I'll let her go cheap," Sly pressed when Hawke made no response. "She's always givin' me trouble, and I want her out of this house."

"I'm not interested, Burford." Hawke shook his head, still thinking that the man only wanted to torment his stepdaughter. "Anyway, what would I do with her?" He pretended to go along with what he thought was a sham.

"Well." Sly smirked, "Besides beddin' her, she could cook and clean for you. Like I said, she can sure cook up a good meal."

Hawke knew suddenly from the urgency in the man's voice, that he was serious. He did want to get rid of the girl. Well, he wanted no part of what Burford offered.

"Sorry, Burford, I repeat I'm not interested in . . ." He let the rest of his denial die on his lips. "Cook and clean" had clung to his brain. Here, right under his nose, was the solution to his problem. Someone to take care of his niece and nephew. In three years Susie would be old enough to more or less take care of herself and then the girl could go.

But what about the girl's younguns'? he remembered with a frown. Would she be taking them along? He wouldn't care to have them around, whining like they did. Still, he couldn't bring himself to separate a mother from her children.

He looked up from studying his clasped hands. "What about the youngsters? Are they part of the deal?"

"Not unless you want them," Sly answered.

"I don't want them, but I'd hate to take the girl away from them."

"Hell, Rue won't care. She ain't all that crazy about her half brothers."

Hawke gave a surprised start. He'd have

sworn the children were hers. Then strangely, he was relieved that this strange girl wasn't a mother. He folded his arms on the table and prepared himself for a long haggle. The fat man would try for a good piece of cash for his stepdaughter.

"She's a weedy-lookin' thing," he began coolly, flicking a running glance over the girl who stood as still as a statue with a look of incredulity on her face. "And I'm still not convinced she's not diseased."

"I told you she ain't diseased!" Burford slammed a fist on the table.

Hawke kept a look of doubt in his eyes. *Let the no-good sweat for a while, rethink the price he'd planned to ask for the girl.*

When Burford almost shouted, "Well, damnit, what's your answer?" Hawke still took his time to reply.

Finally, when sweat broke out on Burford's bulging forehead, Hawke said, as though in doubt, "I guess she'll do . . . if the price is right."

"Like I said before, I aim to be reasonable." Sly sat forward, an avaricious gleam in his eyes. "But you got to keep in mind she's only nineteen and has a lot of good years ahead of her to work for you." He sat back and stated coolly, "I want five hundred cold cash."

"You're loco, man!" Hawke stiffened. "I could get five hundred head of cattle for that much money. I'll give you three hundred."

Sly helped himself to more whiskey, then wiping a hand across his lips, said with finality, "I'll come down another hundred, but not another cent. Four hundred greenbacks and she's yours."

Hawke was about to agree when a slim bundle of fury dashed to the table. Blue eyes looking stormier than ever, and blinking back tears of rage, Rue cried, "You will not sell me, Sly Burford! I'm not some animal to be bargained over!"

"That's right!" The teenage boy rushed to his sister's side. "If anybody is gonna leave here, it'll be you. You've done nothin' but leech off our mother for the past four years."

With an amazing swiftness for a fat man, Burford was on his feet, his beefy hand lashing out, catching the boy across the face, sending him reeling halfway across the room.

Then before anyone could move, he had Rue by her thin arm, twisting it cruelly behind her back. As she cried out, he jerked her hand up between her shoulder blades, hissing, "I've had enough of you, you mountain witch. Goin' around with your sneerin' mouth, the hate in your eyes." Shoving her arm a little higher, making her face whiten with the pain of it, he continued, "You'll either go with Masters, or I'll sell you to some Mexican. He'll soon take the starch out of you. They don't take no guff from their wimmen."

Hawke knew, as well as Rue did, the amoral

man would do exactly what he threatened, that someday he would find her alone, and no one would ever see her again. When Rue's head sagged in defeat, Hawke suffered the same emotion. He felt obligated now to take the poor wretch with him, without arguing over the money either. The life that was planned for her if he didn't take her would be a short one: toiling under the sun all day, and working under her harsh master every night would soon take its toll. In five years she'd be worn out from hard work and childbearing.

When numbness crept through her body, and reached even to her spirit, Rue said no more. When the gripping fingers released her, she walked silently to the bedroom door and disappeared through it. Shivering, she lay down with the youngsters and pulled the thin blanket up over her shoulders.

CHAPTER THREE

Rue lay on her side, facing the window. Dry-eyed, she watched the shadows in the pines, only vaguely aware of the pattering of mysterious feet, the whispering and sighing of the breeze in the forest behind the shack.

A shamed sickness crept over her. Bound girl, sold like an animal. Dear God, what was she going to do? At last, tears gathered and ran freely down her cheeks, spilling onto the pillow. That cold-eyed stranger who had haggled over the price for her would expect her to ride off with him in the morning, taking her to only God knew where.

At least he won't take you out of the country, her inner voice whispered. *Wouldn't it be better to go off with him than to end up with a man who would probably take you to Mexico, a place alien to you, where you don't even know the language.*

Rue nodded as if in answer to the hidden voice. If she was doomed to go with one or the other, Hawke Masters would be the better choice she guessed. At least with him she might be able to escape someday.

But it's unfair and inhuman that I have to be sold to any man, Rue thought fiercely, *and there must be some other way I can get out of Sly Burford's reach, to prevent his plans for me.*

She tossed and turned, seeking a solution to her overwhelming problem. Her mind a turmoil, alternating between hope and dejection, her thoughts moving from one possibility to another, and discarding them all, she became sure of one thing. She had to see her grandparents, tell them good-bye. She hated to think what Sly might tell them if she just disappeared.

But what could she tell the old couple that wouldn't upset them, cause Granddad to come after her stepfather? She decided finally that the only explanation that might work was to convince them that she was leaving with the stranger because of love.

But did she dare make that trip up the mountain at this hour? She had never visited her grandparents after dark. The forest was full of wolves at night, hungry, ready to attack man or beast.

As if in answer to her question, a wolf howled mournfully across the mountain, and far off in the darkness came the faint answer of his mate.

After several minutes of indecision, Rue knew she had to make the trip. She had to see those two dear people, probably for the last time in her life.

She pushed the fear of the wolves from her mind and waited for the shack to become silent.

The rise and fall of male voices ceased after about fifteen minutes. Then the sound of the outside door closing told Rue that the stranger had left. A disquieting thought gripped her. Maybe he and Sly hadn't reached an agreement, after all. Maybe he had left for good. Would Sly sell her to a foreigner tomorrow?

Rue slipped out of bed and hurried to peer out the window, toward the barn. Shortly she saw a tall male figure pass through the sagging door. She held her breath. Would he ride out on his big stallion?

Several tense minutes passed before she could relax. The gaping black hole of the doorway remained empty. If the stranger was going to leave, he'd have gone by now.

She returned to the bed, and sitting on its edge, careful not to awaken the sleeping youngsters, waited for Sly's snores to fill the cabin. They came finally, loud snorting, rasping sounds. She stood up and slipped quietly to the window again, wishing that she dare go into the other room and awaken Jimmy to go with her. But that would be taking a big chance she knew as she slowly eased up the sash. If Sly should learn what she was up to, she'd never get out of the house.

For a moment or two Rue straddled the windowsill, her courage deserting her. There were at least two wolves out there somewhere, but the question was where? They had sounded far away when she first heard them, but the animals could travel fast. For all she knew, they could be at the back of the house now.

As she sat, wracked with dread and uncertainty, one foot on the floor, the other dangling in the air, her inner voice spoke again, *Get going, girl. You're not going to solve anything straddling a window.*

The night was cool and still with a few stars in the sky when Rue's bare feet landed on the dew-wet grass. The trail to her grandparents' home lay dim and shadowed as she fearfully moved down it.

Rue sped along, her heart near to bursting as she ducked her head to avoid low-hanging branches, sure she could hear the drumming feet of wolves close behind her. She dashed across a narrow glade, also sure that an Indian lurked behind each tall boulder looming up in the gray night.

After what seemed an eternity to her, Rue finally emerged from the shadows of the forest, and her grandparents' small house stood before her. A light glimmered in a window, and with a small thankful cry she dashed across the yard, hopped on the porch, and burst through the door.

Maddy sat before the fire in her nightgown, while John filled his pipe for a last smoke before retiring. Both white heads jerked around when the door flew open, banging against the wall. Faded eyes stared at their frantic-looking granddaughter.

Maddy was the first on her feet. Hurrying across the floor, she took the shivering girl's arm. "Rue, honey, what's wrong? You're as white as a sheet."

The concern and caring in the old woman's touch and voice was Rue's undoing. Forgotten were the words of assurance she'd planned to tell them. Only the frightening outrage that was being perpetrated on her remained in her mind. "He sold me, Grandma," she wailed. "Sly has bound me over to a stranger for three years."

John jumped from his seat, his mouth open, unable to speak. It was his wife who finally managed to say, "You must be mistaken, child. We're not living in the South where human beings used to be sold."

"Oh, yes, he'd do it," John declared angrily, finding his voice. He sat back down when

Maddy led Rue to the fire and pushed her into a chair. "That one would sell his own mother if he could get away with it. He needs money now, what with Becky's income gone."

Maddy sat down in the chair next to Rue. "Catch your breath, honey," she said soothingly, "then tell us everything that happened. Who is the man, and where does he come from?"

It didn't take long for Rue to tell her story, for it hadn't taken Sly long to sell her to the stranger. While Maddy called down every evil she could think of on Burford's head, John lit his pipe and drew on it in deep concentration, seemingly unaware of his wife's angry tirade.

The old mantle clock began to bong out the time, and Rue unconsciously counted the nine strikes as John stood up and knocked his pipe out in the fireplace. Her eyes followed him as he walked to the door and took down the lantern that hung there. He sprung the chimney, then scraped a match against the wall, and held its flame to the lantern's wick. He snapped the glass globe back in place, then picked up the rifle that was always propped beside the door.

"Come on, honey." He smiled at Rue. "I'll walk you back now."

While Rue looked at her grandfather in bewilderment, her grandmother demanded sharply, "What do you mean, you'll walk her back? I don't understand you, old man. Are you going to let that evil man sell our Rue without a fight?''

"Calm yourself, Maddy," John answered as Rue stood up. "I'm not about to let the bastard sell her. You wait up for me. We've got a lot of talkin' and plannin' to do before we sleep tonight."

"Well, I should hope so." The somewhat mollified wife followed them to the door. "That man should be tarred and feathered."

John and Rue were halfway back to the shack when John began to speak. "I expect that man—Hawke Masters you called him?—will want to get an early start tomorrow mornin' so you look for me to get to the house around dawn. In the meantime, you act as though you're goin' along with everything."

"What are you going to do, Granddad?" Rue whispered as they came to the fringe of trees that grew up to the edge of the weed-filled yard.

"I ain't got it all clear in my mind yet, Rue, but you can rest easy in your mind that you ain't gonna be sold to nobody."

Rue stretched up to kiss the sunken, be-whiskered cheek, then hurried across the short distance to her bedroom window, and climbed inside. Altogether she'd been gone just a little over an hour.

The hours passed slowly as Rue sat on the edge of the bed, waiting for the eastern sky to turn pink. It was the longest night she'd ever known as she stared into the darkness, wondering what tomorrow would bring. What was Granddad's plan to save her from becoming some man's chattel?

Finally the stars grew paler and Rue knew that dawn was not far off. Was Granddad already on his way to save her? Maybe he was outside right now, watching the house.

Daylight came swiftly. One moment there were only dark shadows in the room, the next it seemed they were assuming form and definition. Rue heard the bed in the other room squeak, then Sly's lumbering tread crossing the floor as he walked outside to relieve himself.

Rue glanced over her shoulder at the sleeping children, then sighing raggedly, she stood up carefully, stiff from sitting so long. As she smoothed her dress and combed her fingers through her untidy hair, she paused, her nerves taut. Sly had returned inside with the stranger.

She gave a nervous jerk when her stepfather called loudly, "Rue, get out here. Masters wants to be on his way."

A wild, trapped look jumped into Rue's eyes. Where was Granddad? Was she to be taken away before he arrived?

I must kill some time, she thought frantically. *Give him a chance to get here.* She opened the door a crack and said calmly, "I'll be out in a minute."

She had lingered in her room perhaps three minutes when Sly roared that she had better come out or he would come in after her. She closed her eyes as a tremor of dread went through her. All was lost. Granddad wasn't going to get there in time.

She stiffened her spine, and with her stormy blue eyes flashing scornfully, she opened the door and stepped into the main room.

Rue was met by a battery of eyes. A malicious satisfaction held Sly's features, while a grimace of distaste curled the stranger's lips. But it was Jimmy's white face her own gaze clung to. In his eyes lay hopeless despair. He knew he was helpless to defend the only person he had ever loved.

Rue took a step toward him, then Sly growled, "Don't just stand there, the man is in a hurry. Get your ass outside and climb on the mule."

Rue sent Burford a startled look. "Our mule?" Her voice was sharp. "How do you plan making a garden next spring? Hitch Jimmy to the plow?"

His face red, Sly took a step toward Rue, his large hand raised. Rue flinched, but the blow wasn't delivered. The irate man's wrist was caught and held.

"You forget yourself, fat man," Hawke said, with steel in his voice. "She's my property now and I'll hand out any punishment I think she deserves."

The harsh warning had barely been uttered, and Rue was about to declare that she was no man's property, when the outside door suddenly slammed open.

Everyone swung around to see John DeLawney standing in the doorway, a Henry rifle lying in the crook of his arm. Rue gaped at her grandfather, for never had she seen him look so formidable. The genial twinkle that usually looked out at the world was gone, replaced by cold fire.

Fixing that coldness on a shrinking Burford, John said in a voice that could freeze a man, "You cowardly blusterer! You ain't sellin' my granddaughter like she was some kind of animal!"

His face a pasty gray, Sly edged along the table until it stood between him and the man with the rifle. "You gonna stop me, old man?" he asked with a bravado that came out in a shaky squeak.

"You can bet your rotten soul I can stop you," John grated, and Rue's uneasiness increased at the sound of the trigger being cocked. Would Granddad really shoot her stepfather?

While she stood rooted to the floor, Hawke's body went rigid and Sly shivered. Death for both men was in the old man's eyes, the set of his lips. But the promise of death came mostly from the rifle barrel pointed at them.

Then, without taking his eyes off the pair, John called out, "Come on in, Reverend," and stepped aside so that a tall, gaunt man with a grizzled beard could enter.

Rue blinked rapidly. Why in the world had Granddad brought Preacher Hawkins with him? Surely he didn't think that Sly Burford could be swayed by prayer.

When it was made clear why the preacher had accompanied John, Rue could only stare at her grandfather increduously as Hawke's explosive, "What!" echoed her own bewilderment.

"You heard me, stranger," John said, then repeated his words. "If you want my granddaughter, you're gonna have to marry her."

The color drained from Rue's face. Had Granddad taken leave of his senses? There was no way in the world that arrogant man would marry the likes of her. He had nothing but contempt for her.

In the heavy silence that followed John's decree, Hawke took a step forward, the veins in his neck corded. He stopped abruptly however when he found the rifle aimed at his belt buckle. He didn't have to be told that another step would put a bullet in his belly.

As Hawke kept his eyes on the old man's trigger finger, he was conscious of the inspection from under the bushy white tufts of eyebrows, and instinctively squared his shoulders. The old man reminded him of his father, upright and honorable. He wouldn't hesitate to blow a hole through him, or Sly, to save his granddaughter from being dishonored.

He held back a sneer, thinking, *As if she hasn't already been dishonored many times by Burford.*

But while Rue held her breath, her features strained, fearful of the outcome, Hawke asked himself if it would be all that terrible, married to the unattractive girl. Since he was positive there wasn't a woman alive he'd ever fall in love with, or want to marry of his own free will, why not wed this one?

The idea appealed to him more and more. There were good, sound reasons for this marriage to take place. As his wife, the girl couldn't up and leave if the loneliness of the ranch became too much for her. And, wouldn't he be taking her away from a worse situation, bound over to some other man who in all likelihood would use her for his physical needs, and work her like a slave?

Hawke chose to ignore that maybe his decision had a lot to do with the guilty feelings the grandfather had roused in him. He spoke and broke the charged silence. "All right, old man, I'll marry her if that's what you want."

John's tightly held lips loosened in surprise. He hadn't expected such an easy capitulation from the stony-faced stranger. From the moment he'd burst through the door and saw the broad shoulders and the strong chiseled features of the man, John's hopes of carrying out his plan had lessened a bit. He had thought he'd be facing a man like the cowardly Burford, not one who looked capable of fighting his way out of any situation he might find himself in.

John continued to study the man a moment longer, then asked abruptly, "And you'll be good to her?" His eyes dared Hawke to lie.

Hawke held the fierce blue-eyed gaze, wondering what this old mountain man wanted him to say, that he would cherish his granddaughter? Well, the old devil could shoot and be damned. He'd never say that. Finally he said, "I'll not beat her, if that's what you mean."

John's eyes challenged Hawke's for a tense moment, then he nodded his head. "I guess that's what I mean." He turned and beckoned a stunned Rue forward. "Come and stand beside him, honey." And then to the preacher, "Let's get on with it, Reverend."

Never before had Rue heard the clock tick so loudly as she took her place beside the man who, very much against his will, was to become her husband. She felt intuitively that, as he had promised Granddad, he would never physically abuse her, but, as far as mental pain, she was sure she would get plenty of that. Even now she could feel the resentment that gripped him.

Rue was jarred back to the awareness of the

present when the preacher asked, "And you, Rue DeLawney, do you take this man to be your wedded husband?"

Her eyes sought her grandfather's, asking if he was sure she should say the words that would bind her to this cold, uncaring man, maybe for the rest of her life.

When John gave a slight nod, she looked up at the man who had already said his "I dos" and found him regarding her with unconcealed impatience. With a jerk of her head, she crisply said the words that made her his wife.

The words, fatal in Rue's mind, had hardly been spoken when Hawke swung around, demanding, "I'll take my money back, Burford."

Only Jimmy stood behind them. Burford had slipped away. "That mangy polecat," Hawke ground out, and bolted for the door.

"He can kiss his money good-bye," John said with some satisfaction. "As far as I'm concerned, he deserves to lose it. Willin' to buy another human bein'." He looked at his granddaughter, took in the trembling lips, the dread of the unknown in her eyes. He crossed swiftly to her side and folded her in his arms. "Try not to worry, child. I'm a pretty good judge of character. Although Masters appears to be a rough one, you'll be better off with him than stayin' on here. There's no future for you on this mountain."

Rue silently agreed, then turned to Jimmy when he tugged at her arm. Her heart went out to the sixteen-year-old, who was blinking rapidly, holding back the tears that glistened in his eyes. They reached for each other simultaneously.

"I'm going to miss you dreadfully, Jimmy." Rue held the thin body fiercely. "If ever I can, I'll send for you."

"I'd sure like that, Rue." Jimmy stepped away from her, knuckling his eyes. "Do you know where you're goin'?"

Rue shook her head and John said forcibly, "I'll find out before you leave. I'm not about to let you just walk out of our lives and never hear from you again. Maddy will want to write to you."

The outside door slammed and everyone turned to look at a furious Hawke. His green eyes snapping, he growled to no one in particular, "I can't find the sneakin' bastard."

"He's hidin' up in the mountain somewhere, waitin' for you to leave," John said.

"I should have kept my eyes on the skunk." Hawke took his rifle from the table where he had placed it earlier. He glanced at Rue. "Come on, let's get the hell out of here."

It's all happening too fast, Rue thought in near panic, running her eyes around the familiar room, looking for the last time at the sagging bed in the corner, the lower legs propped up by two rocks of uneven height, the inch-wide cracks in the floor boards, letting in the cold at winter, bugs in the summer, sometimes a snake. She ran a hand over the splintered surface of the table, remembering her endless and useless efforts at trying to keep it free of stains. Surely wherever this new husband of hers was taking her couldn't be worse than what she was leaving.

She stiffened her spine and started for the door, then paused when from the bedroom came the sound of soft whimpering which would soon reach a wailing level if empty little bellies weren't filled with something.

"Go on, Rue." Jimmy nudged her back. "I'll find something for them to eat. Sly's got money now, he'll bring us somethin' when he's sure the stranger has left."

Rue knew better as did Jimmy. Sly Burford wouldn't care if they all starved to death. Before she could utter her thoughts, John had her firmly by the elbow and was leading her outside where Hawke waited, a black scowl on his face.

The old mule stood hipshot a short distance from the big black stallion, switching at flies with his bushy tail. "Keep faith, Rue girl," John whispered as he helped her onto the broad back, a folded blanket her only saddle. "Everything will work out fine for you. As well as the others," he added.

Her eyes smarting from withheld tears, Rue nodded, and as she tugged at her skirt, finally getting it down to her knees, Hawke looked up from tightening the stallion's belly cinch.

"Where are your clothes?" He frowned, seeing no bundle tied behind her.

Rue blushed and pretended she hadn't heard him. She owned only one other dress and it was in worse condition than the one she had on. The fact that Grandma was making her a new one wasn't of much significance at the moment.

Hawke opened his mouth to repeat his question and John was suddenly beside him, giving him a warning jab in the ribs with a sharp elbow. "I ain't put her clothes on the mule yet," he said. "Before I do, I want a word with you."

Rue couldn't hear what was being said between the two men, but it was of short duration before her grandfather was back by her side, handing her a cloth-bound bundle.

"Your grandma finished your dress last night," he said softly. "She put a few other things in it too."

Hawke, watching the pair impatiently, dropped his eyes to Rue's narrow bare feet. They were dusty, but clean. *No shoes either,* he thought in disgust as he flipped open his saddlebag and took out a pair of small moccasins he'd forgotten to give to Tommy. He walked across to Rue and held the pacs up to her.

"Here, put these on." His gaze was drawn to

her shapely calf and dainty ankle. If they weren't so marred with sores, he'd say they were the prettiest he'd ever seen. He was always disappointed when he saw Lillie's legs. They were quite heavy with thick ankles.

But ole Lillie had other attributes that pleased him just fine, he smiled inwardly. And he meant to enjoy them before this trip was over. He swung into the saddle and put Captain in motion even while Rue was still pulling on her new foot gear.

"God be with you, child," John said softly when she straightened and picked up the reins.

Rue's throat was so choked she couldn't speak as she looked into her grandfather's face with a sense of finality. She would never see his or Grandma's dear faces again. What would she do without their love, their caring kindness? She'd be on her own now, with no one to give her a kind thought or word. She lifted the gnarled hand that rested on her bare knee and brought it to her lips. She kissed it lovingly, then dropping it, nudged the mule, signaling him to move out.

Just before Rue entered the fringe of trees that would hide the cabin from her, she looked back, her throat constricting. She could not see her grandfather or the preacher, but Jimmy stood on the broken porch, staring after her, his narrow shoulders drooping. He was crying she knew, crying for many reasons, losing a sister he loved dearly, his hungry little half brothers, the desolate future stretching out before him.

"I'll help you, Jimmy," she whispered. "Someday I'll help you get away from here."

She jabbed the mule with a heel and caught up with Hawke just as one of the children let out a piercing howl for her.

Without looking at Rue, Hawke grunted, "I hope the fat man hasn't planted his seed in you."

Rue choked back the blistering words that hovered on her lips. She guessed it was only natural he would think that way, considering how Sly had hinted at sharing her bed with him. Nevertheless his words had wounded her deeply, and reasonable or not, pride made her strike back.

Speaking with pretended carelessness, she retorted, "You'll just have to wait and see, won't you?"

Hawke gave her a grim look. "Don't think that I'll give my name to your bastard."

Rue flinched at the harsh words, but her hurt wasn't heard in her voice when she snapped back, "I wouldn't do that to an innocent babe. It's bad enough that I have to carry the Masters's name."

Hawke's broad back stiffened. *Damn, there's that sharp tongue of hers. I swear I'll cut it out of her mouth someday.*

* * *

It had been skin-shrinking cool when Rue and Hawke started out in the early morning, but now, three hours later, the bright sun bore down on Rue's bare head relentlessly. She used the piece of white rag in her hand often to pat at the perspiration that gathered on her forehead and upper lip, the saline burning like fire when it seeped into her pox sores.

Thankfully, most of the scabs were quite dry now, and would soon begin to fall off. Rue looked forward to the day when she could once again wash her face in a normal way and leave off the dark, oily salve.

She forgot about her discomfort and fastened her gaze on the man, her husband, riding up ahead of her. There had been no communication between them; in fact, he seemed unaware of her presence. *And that's the way I like it,* she told herself as the stallion and mule clipped along at a steady gait. The wrong that had been done her was too dark a passion in her heart to carry on a conversation with the man, providing he was inclined to talk.

The sameness of the trail Hawke kept to was broken occasionally by small clearings dotted with stumps, and a log house in each cleared space. And though Rue scanned the little places with interest, the flowers blooming around the doors, evidence that the wife took pride in her home, her companion looked on the rudely constructed buildings with different eyes.

Each time one came into view, he would mutter disparagingly, "Damn lazy nesters."

Rue knew that she was lumped in there with his sentiments.

As the sun swung ever westward, it became apparent to Rue that there would be no stopping for a noon meal. Her stomach was growling loudly and night was almost upon them when Hawke finally halted the stallion in a stand of pines and swung to the ground. With a long sigh of relief, Rue slid carefully off the old mule's back. She wore only the patched homespun, and her inner thighs were rubbed raw from the scratchy horse blanket she had straddled all day. What she wouldn't give to sit in a tub of water for a while.

Wishful thinking, she said to herself as she removed the blanket from the mule, slipped the bit from its mouth, then hobbled him in a patch of grass. She stayed beside the old animal a minute, rubbing his back. He was part of her past, a part that made her wonder how Jimmy and the children were faring. Had young Jimmy been able to scrounge up some food for them? Were their little stomachs as empty as hers was at the moment?

She forced her half brothers from her mind and turned her attention to the man who had taken her away from them. He, too, had attended to his mount and was now gathering up small pieces of dry tree limbs scattered about. He was skilled at making camp, she noted as he quickly started a fire in the wide area he had cleared of brush and dry grass. *He understands the dangers of starting a forest fire,* she thought, watching him remove a grub sack from beside his saddle and spill its contents onto a piece of canvas he'd spread on the ground.

When he hunkered down and rummaged through the paraphernalia, Rue wondered if she should offer to help. But looking at his stony countenance she decided to wait until she was asked—or ordered.

Rue continued to stand beside the mule as Hawke set aside a blackened frying pan, a slab of bacon, and two small cloth bags. Then sweeping up a battered coffeepot he rose and strode away. For the first time she became aware of the murmuring sound of running water.

"Thank God," she whispered. "I'll be able to bathe my chapped thighs and put some salve on them."

She untied the bundle her grandfather had handed her that morning and tears smarted her eyes when they fell on the familiar piece of blue, small-flowered calico her grandmother had turned into a dress. She smiled through her tears then. Lying on top of the dress were two bars of rose soap, plus a glass jar of Grandma's healing salve.

The articles were rolled up in two pieces of soft white cloth. A small one for washing, the larger one to be used as a towel. Smoothing her hands over the pieces, Rue's tears fell so fast her throat hurt. She hadn't been able to say good-bye to the sweet old woman whose counsel had kept her going when all around her was dark and bleak, with no sign of ever changing.

Rue scrubbed away her tears with the back of her hand. Grandma, like the boys, must be put from her mind if she was to make any kind of future for herself. She would need all her strength of mind to rise above what life with this rough man she had married might hand out.

Putting all her attention to what she was doing, Rue lay everything except her dress aside. She folded it neatly and placed it on a rock. She would not wear it until they arrived wherever they were headed. It would only be ruined in the heat and from perspiration. When Hawke returned with a water-filled pot and put it on the fire, she picked up a bar of soap, and the two pieces of cloth and followed the direction her companion had taken.

A thick layer of fog lay over the narrow river when Rue knelt beside it. Shadowy with an unnatural silence, she remembered the river back home was the same way, and wondered why rivers took on that eeriness after dark as she dipped her hands into the water and cupped it to her face.

She caught her breath at its iciness, and worked hurriedly at swishing the washcloth into the water, then lathered it with the precious, scented soap.

In all, it took Rue about ten minutes to wash her face and tender thighs, then smooth on the salve. When she returned to the campfire, feeling almost human again, her mouth watered at the aroma of fried bacon and brewed coffee. Hawke was already bent over a plate of meat and beans and she stood uncertain, wondering if she was to share what he had prepared, or if she was to make her own supper.

Hawke solved her dilemma by motioning to a tin plate and cup. "You'd better eat before it gets cold," he said gruffly.

Rue muttered, "Thank you," and after filling her plate and pouring a cup of coffee, sat down on the ground, across the fire from him. She picked up the tin fork and shoved it into the mound of beans. It was hard not to wolf the food down. She hadn't eaten all day, and precious little all week.

But she sensed that sardonic green eyes were watching her with amusement, so she forced herself to take small bites and to chew them slowly.

Encouraged by the few words Hawke had spoken to her, Rue asked as she sipped at the strong coffee, "Are there Indians where you live?"

"Some, but nothin' to worry about," he finally said, after waiting so long Rue didn't think he was going to bother answering her. "Most Indians, you treat them right, they'll treat you right, even though they have good reason to hate all white faces."

"Yes," Rue agreed, eager to continue the conversation. "We have treated them shamefully," she began, then in the middle of her sentence Hawke rose and stalked off into the darkness.

Rue's surprised eyes followed him. "So much for conversing with that one," she muttered.

As she sat before the dying fire, a thought that had niggled at the back of her mind all day, came full force to the front as retiring time approached. Would her new husband demand his conjugal rights tonight? She cringed at the possibility. With the exception of her grandfather and Jimmy, she hated all men and had sworn to herself that never would one touch her in an intimate way. Ever since she could remember she had sometimes seen, and always heard, the disgusting things that had gone on between her mother and the men who had come to the shack.

Rue remembered her grandmother talking to her once about what went on between a man and woman, tried to explain that lust was what Becky shared with the men who paid to use her. "But, honey, when love is involved, it's a natural and beautiful act that completes a couple's love for each other." She had patted Rue's hand. "You'll meet the right man someday, then you'll understand what I'm talking about."

Rue hadn't told the old woman that she was mistaken, that no man under the sun would ever make her granddaughter care that much for him.

But whether she cared or not, she asked herself bitterly, what could she do if Hawke Masters demanded that she be his wife in all ways? There would be no contest between their strengths. He could force her to do anything he wanted. She shuddered, remembering things she didn't want to.

Rue gave a startled jerk when Hawke was suddenly back, dumping the remains of the coffee on the fire and unrolling his bedroll. She watched him stand up, remove his holster, then jerk his shirttail free of his twill trousers. When he shrugged out of the flannel garment, her eyes shone in admiration. This man she was married to was certainly put together right. *Silk and steel*, she thought, gazing at the wedgelike frame, the broad chest amply covered with crisp black hair, the flat stomach. She hadn't realized a man's body could be beautiful.

As Rue compared Hawke's muscular build

to that of Sly Burford's, all fat and flab, she idly lifted her eyes to the man she was admiring and blushed furiously. He was watching her watching him.

His lips curled contemptuously. "Don't have any hope that I intend to bed you."

Rue's eyes widened a trifle, then she looked away with complete indifference. *Stupid man,* she thought, *you should know how much that pleases me.*

But Hawke did know. He had seen how her body had relaxed in relief at his stinging words, and suddenly it was he who felt rejected. Anger flared inside him. This ugly scrap in patched homespun was relieved that she didn't have to share his blankets! He who could have most any woman he wanted.

He spent another moment looking at the smoldering dislike on his wife's face, then without further words to her, wrapped himself in his blankets.

Rue sat, her body unwinding from the nervous tension that had gripped her ever since they had made camp. She had been so sure that the hard, arrogant man would take advantage of his marital rights once they retired. She grinned ruefully in the darkness. Although she was relieved at the surprising outcome, her husband's rebuff had nicked her ego. Even though she would have fought him off had he come near her blanket, still she didn't like thinking that she was repulsive to the hateful man. The young men back home hadn't seemed to think she was unsightly. Their eyes always followed her when she went to the village.

She hadn't been to the village, though, since two of those young, admiring men had tried to rape her, she remembered disquietly.

Rue leaned back on her elbows, listening to the hooting of an owl, the fussing of the birds roosting in the trees, the flowing murmur of the river a few yards away. *It's so peaceful here*, she thought, then suddenly sat up and peered out into the darkness. The night had gone very quiet, except for the sound of the moving water.

What had stilled the birds and the owl? she asked herself. A wolf, an Indian? She strained her eyes and ears to catch an alien sound, to see whatever was lurking out there.

The hair on the back of Rue's neck rose when in the silence there came the definite sound of a twig breaking, as if something heavy had stepped on it. She sat frozen in place, wanting to awaken Hawke, but dreading the verbal abuse she'd receive if she roused him for nothing. It would be like him to think that she was trying to lure him into her blankets.

During the time she tried to decide what to do, the owl took up its hooting again and the birds resumed their fluttering. Rue relaxed, yawned, and stretched. It had probably been a deer who had come to browse in the tall grass. She unfolded the blanket that had been her saddle all day and rolled up in it.

It was impossible to sleep. Rue grimaced, a chill breeze making her twist and turn, vainly searching for comfort. Finally she gave up, and turning on her back, looked up at the stars, wondering what the future held for her. The next thing she knew the sun was shining in her face, and she was being prodded on the hip, none too gently.

She opened her eyes, blinked, then seeing Hawke standing over her, she scowled up at him with stormy blue eyes.

"Don't ever kick me again," she hissed.

Hawke matched her glare for glare. "First, I didn't kick you," he grated. "I only poked you with my foot. And second, you wildcat, I didn't dare get close enough to lay a hand on you for fear I'd draw back a stub."

When Rue continued to glare her dislike at him, he ordered coldly, "Roll out and eat your breakfast. I want to get on the trail. If you're not ready in ten minutes, I'll ride off without you."

Does he mean it? Hope flared in Rue's eyes as she thought how easy it would be to turn the old mule around and take the direction they'd come from. *But to where?* the question quickly followed her excited impulse. She couldn't go back to the shack. Sly would hustle her off to the village saloon before she could catch her breath. Before another day dawned, she'd belong to some other man.

She sighed resignedly. For the time being, her future was cast with Hawke Masters. She would have to bide her time, be patient, lay her plans.

The decision made, Rue ran a careful palm along the insides of her thighs and sighed with relief. Grandma's salve had worked wonders. The flesh there was only a little tender. She threw back the blanket, stood up, and then hurriedly folded it. Keeping in mind that her uncaring companion wouldn't hesitate to ride off without her, she stepped quickly to the fire.

She stared down at wet, gray ashes. Anger tightened her lips. The revengeful devil! He was going to make her go without breakfast. As she prepared to walk to the river to wash up, however, she spotted a plate of beans and bacon, plus a cup of steaming coffee beside his grub sack. "He could have awakened me sooner," she griped aloud, hurrying on to the river at a half run.

A fast scoop of water on her face, a hurried application of salve on her face, and Rue was back to the dead fire. Using the crisp bacon as a spoon, she shoveled the beans into her mouth. The coffee was scalding hot, bringing tears to her eyes as it burned its way down her throat. She threw Hawke a murderous look. Damn him for not giving her time to eat like a human being!

Rue had just flipped the folded blanket over the mule's back and was tying her small bundle to it when, without a look or word to her, Hawke climbed onto the stallion, clicked his teeth, and moved out.

"Damn the miserable beast," Rue whispered, scrambling the best way she could onto her mule's back and jabbing him gently with the heel of her foot.

CHAPTER FOUR

Each morning found Rue and Hawke mounted and pushing farther westward. One day followed another, the night camps essentially alike, and outside of what was necessary, there was no communication between the pair.

Each talked silently to himself, however. Staring between the mule's pointed ears, Rue told herself that she didn't care if the man up ahead ever spoke to her, that she liked his silence just fine. She didn't want them to become acquainted, maybe develop a liking for each other. The next step from there would surely lead to bed, and she wanted no part of that.

And Hawke stared stonily ahead, his body

loosely swaying with the motion of the stallion, as he mostly cursed himself for a fool. Had he really tried he could have disarmed that old man. He could have then hired some young Indian girl to keep house for him and his family. And even if the children didn't take to an Indian and her different ways, they'd have still been cared for. And who could say the children would take to that scrawny, ill-tempered girl plodding along behind him? She was an unpleasant witch if ever he saw one.

The frown on his forehead deepened. He had a strong premonition that somehow his unwanted wife was going to upset the course he had planned for his life. He hadn't figured out how yet, but the feeling persisted.

On the second day on the trail Rue and Hawke had to take cover once. They had almost ridden into a party of Indians. Only the pricking of the stallion's ears had warned Hawke in time. Luckily there had been a deep gully nearby, and crouching in its bottom, hands on the flaring nostrils of their mounts, they waited, barely breathing. The thud of hooves and creaking hackamoors seemed to go on forever as the group passed within feet of them.

"Would they have taken us prisoner?" Rue asked when the last bronzed body rode out of sight and she and Hawke were leading their mounts out of the earth's deep depression.

"I don't know," Hawke answered in a tone that said he'd rather she kept her questions to herself. "They might have been friendly, then again they might have been a bunch of renegades."

Rue wanted to ask what renegades were, but had the sure conviction that Hawke wouldn't bother to answer her.

Twice since hitting the trail, Hawke had pulled in the stallion and peered into the forest. The last time Rue ventured, "What is it?"

"I've got the feelin' we're bein' followed. Felt it yesterday too."

"I had that feeling the first night we camped out," Rue said, bringing the mule up closer to Hawke as she looked worriedly over her shoulder. "An Indian, do you think?"

"Maybe," Hawke answered, then ordered, "keep the mule away from Captain if you don't want a chunk taken out of his rump."

Rue sawed on the reins, pulling her mount away from the stallion. The ornery beast was just like his master. "Are you going after whoever it is?"

Hawke shook his head. "If it's an Indian, there's no use tryin' to follow him if he knows you're after him," he answered brusquely, and lifted the reins, urging the stallion on.

There had been no sign of habitation all day, then near sunset Rue and Hawke rounded a bend on the rocky trail and spotted a spiral of smoke through the trees. Hawke reined in and motioned Rue to do the same.

"A campfire, do you think?" Rue whispered.

"Maybe," Hawke answered, wondering to himself if it was, and if so who sat beside it? White man? Red man? Whomever, what would be their attitude? All kinds of men roamed the West today, outlaws, rustlers, the scumy remains of the war, still set on fighting it.

Hawke's lips twisted wryly. Sitting here wondering about it wasn't going to answer the questions. He lifted the reins, sending the stallion forward, directing Rue softly, "Follow quietly behind me. We'll ride on a little farther, see if we can spot anyone."

A couple of hundred yards had been covered when they came upon a narrow path branching off from the main trail. Hawke reined in again, then at the sound of an axe biting into wood, he urged the stallion on, commenting sourly, "Probably another nester."

Rue parted her lips to ask angrily just what it was he had against nesters, but instead she let out a small cry and pulled her knees up as a large, mean-eyed dog dashed out from under a growth of bushes and came toward them.

Hawke paid no attention to the animal as he kept the stallion moving down the path. Rue followed more slowly, but the mule still bumped into the stallion's rear end when it was stopped short by the dog jumping in front of him. The placid old mule stood quietly, but the horse snorted his unease and danced around nervously. Hawke calmed him with a few softly spoken words, then in a harsher voice ordered the dog away. But the large, half-wolf canine paid him no heed. He continued to stand on braced feet, the hair on his neck bristling, warning growls issuing from his throat.

Rue glanced at Hawke and noted that his right hand rested on his thigh, only inches away from the heavy Colt in its holster. A pucker of anxiety drew her brows together. Surely he wasn't going to shoot the animal.

It became evident that someone else wondered the same thing as a dry, cracked voice warned, "You pull that gun, Mister, and you're a dead man."

The words were followed by the click of a trigger. Hawke peered through the trees and boulders, trying to locate the body of the voice. "I have no intention of killin' your beast, Mister. I was merely goin' to shoot into the air, scare him away."

A short silence followed, then, "What are you doin' round here? I ain't got nothin' worth stealin'."

"I'm not lookin' to steal anything," Hawke answered impatiently. "We've been sleepin' on the trail for the past three nights. I thought maybe we'd be offered a spot under a roof for a change."

This time a longer silence followed during which the dog maintained his threatening stance. Hawke was about to turn the stallion and ride off when some brush crackled and an old man stepped from behind a large boulder. He walked toward them, toe in, like an Indian, his fringed buckskins rustling softly. A rifle lying in the crook of his arm, he peered up at Hawke, his clear, bright eyes going over every feature.

Hawke held his gaze evenly, doing his own study of a face corrugated with wrinkles and a balding head shiny with perspiration.

Finally the thin lips moved. "Round here you trust no one you don't know real good."

"I can understand that." Hawke nodded. "Isolated like you are."

Narrow shoulders shrugged indifferently. "It's a bit away from civilization, but I'm a trapper and that's the way I like it. I don't care much for people."

The old-timer turned his gaze on Rue, his piercing eyes softening as his gaze moved over her face. When she smiled at him shyly, his eyes widened a bit, and he studied her more intently. When Rue blushed uncomfortably and looked away, he turned his attention back to Hawke. "Is she your woman?"

The saddle creaked as Hawke stirred impatiently, reluctant to admit the uncomely girl was his wife. When the old man cocked an eyebrow at him, he muttered, "I guess you could say that."

The wrinkles on the trapper's forehead deepened in a frown as he noted the embarrassed red of Rue's face. He swung narrowed eyes on Hawke. "That's a hell of an answer, Mister. Is she your wife, or just a bed partner?"

Hawke glared back at his inquisitor, then looking away, said gruffly, "She's my wife."

"You're a lucky man to get one who is both young and pretty." The thin lips smiled at Rue. "Usually a feller don't get it both ways."

Only Rue heard Hawke's soft derisive snort. She flinched, but said nothing.

"The name's Adams," Rue and Hawke were informed. After Hawke gave his and Rue's name, Adams called off the dog. "My place is just a little piece ahead," he said. "You can water your mounts at the spring back of the cabin, then stable them in the shed you'll find there. They'll be safe from the wolves that come around at night."

The old trapper led the way around a lightning-blasted pine tree and his one-room cabin stood before them. Its rustic appearance blended so perfectly with the surrounding timber, only a trained eye would have noticed the time-weathered building among the scattering of boulders, some taller than the cabin.

"You folks come on in when you're ready," Adams said, heading for the heavy door constructed of slender split logs. "I've got a venison stew simmerin' over the fire."

In their usual silent fashion, Rue and Hawke watered their mounts, then led them to the shed attached to the cabin. It didn't take Rue long to strip down the old mule. While he chomped at the forkful of hay Hawke had tossed him, she wiped down his dusty, sweated hide with a scrap of burlap she found in a corner.

She worked swiftly, hoping to finish the grooming before Hawke was done with currying the stallion. She felt that if she didn't get away from him for a while she'd have a screaming fit. Three days and nights of his blatantly contemptuous regard was wearing her nerves thin.

But as Rue walked through the shed door, Hawke was at her heels. *Damn him! He does it on purpose*, she swore softly to herself, wishing she had the nerve to slam the heavy door in his face.

But since she wasn't all that brave, she followed the path that ran alongside the small building and stepped on the narrow porch and pushed open the door.

Rue stood a moment, blinking her eyes.

There was one window in the room, but when the door was closed, most of the light came from a large, burning fireplace. She felt the old man's expectant eyes on her and sensed that he waited for words of praise from her. She hurried to say, "You have a fine place, Mr. Adams. It's sound and snug. I'll bet the winter winds don't get through to you."

A pleased grin widened Adams's lips. "I built it ten years ago. The first winter I was here my home was nothin' but a hole in the ground with boards laid over it. I cooked all my meals outside. A couple times I thought I'd freeze to death."

He smiled as though remembering. "The first thing I done when spring came was to start buildin' this place. Soon as I got a roof over it, I hiked over to a spot along the river where a small tribe of Indians had made winter camp. I traded six of my finest beaver pelts for the prettiest little squaw you'd ever want to see."

A soft, faraway look came in Adams's eyes. "She was as pretty inside as she was outside. She'd been with me two months when I looked up a preacher and made her my true wife."

Rue let out a breath she hadn't realized she'd been holding as Adams stopped talking. She had been held captive by the love that threaded the old man's words, his joy, his contentment, of his young wife. She had found another good man. Was she to run into others? she wondered. Would she have to rearrange her opinion of the male species, admit that there were some good ones among the bad?

But not yet, she thought. Mr. Adams and her granddad were only two good men stacked against the many bad ones she'd known. She would have liked to ask what had happened to the young wife, but a shuttered look had come into Adams's eyes, warning that he would say no more about his mate.

Rue wondered if Hawke had been affected by Adams's love for his wife, but a quick look at his stony face revealed nothing. *What does that one know about love*? she snorted to herself, and turned her attention back to their host as he removed the black pot that had hung over a bed of glowing coals and carried it to the table.

When generous amounts of stew had been ladled into the plates, Adams said, "Come, sit down." Then he sliced into a loaf of sourdough bread. When Rue and Hawke slid onto opposite benches, he said, "I expect you folks are hungry."

"I sure am." Rue's white teeth gleamed in a wide smile, failing to note that Adams had paused, knife suspended as he looked at her closely.

"Well, dig in," he said finally, and resumed slicing up the rest of the bread.

The stew was surprisingly good, flavorfully seasoned with wild herbs. And the bread was as light as any Rue's grandmother had ever baked. Rue swallowed her first bite and commented on its taste and texture.

"My woman taught me how to make it." The trapper smiled his thanks, a brief sadness flickering in his eyes.

Rue wondered if she might question him about his wife now, since he had brought her up again.

But Hawke spoke while she was deliberating, and about a different subject. "I expect it won't be too long before you'll be settin' out your traps." Hawke glanced at the dozens of traps hanging from the walls.

"Yeah, fall is about upon us." Adams stood up to bring the coffeepot from the hearth where it had been keeping hot. "The first hard freeze and I'll be settin' out my line."

He filled the tin cups with the steaming brown liquid, then after returning the pot to the fire, he took a pipe and bag of tobacco off the mantle. Seating himself again at the table, he began to tamp the home-cured long green into the well-seasoned, smoke-stained bowl as Hawke fashioned himself a cigarette.

Rue was unaware that she was being studied as she sipped her coffee, savoring its flavor. She gave a slight start when Adams asked, "You're just gettin' over the chicken pox, ain't you, girl?"

"Why, yes, I am." She looked surprised, unaware that Hawke's face held the same expression. "How can you tell?"

"I lost my woman to the pox. Her face had the same sores." And while Hawke stole a look at Rue's face, Adams continued, "I see you've been careful not to scratch them. That's good, you won't have any scars."

He turned to Hawke. "In a week or so she'll be as pretty as ever."

Hawke made no response, but the half-veiled sardonic look in his eyes said that the old man was blind. This time, instead of the usual anger Hawke always aroused in her, Rue knew a deep hurt. Must he always show how unattractive he thought she was. She choked back the lump that rose in her throat and stared down into her coffee.

Adams leaned his elbows on the table and puffed contentedly on his pipe. "As you've probably noticed, Masters"—his lips twisted humorously around the pipe stem—"most wimmen can talk all day without sayin' a thing worth hearin'. What about your wife, is she a talker?"

Hawke stood up from the table, and, as he took a seat in front of the fire, shrugged his shoulders indifferently. "Not much. Not to me at any rate."

"Well, that's kinda a shame." Adams followed Hawke to the fire and sat down beside him. "I bet anything that what she'd have to say would be right interestin'.''

Hawke's only answer was a dry grunt.

It was taken for granted that Rue would wash the dishes. As she went quietly about it, she listened to the two men talk, and learned a lot about her husband. Most importantly that he owned a cattle ranch situated at the foot of the Rockies. Until now she'd had no idea where she was going.

I will like that, she thought, scouring out the cast-iron pot with wood ashes. *I love horses . . . also my faithful old mule*, she added guiltily to herself. Although he had been the means by which she and Jimmy had managed to raise a small garden, he had also been the nearest thing to a pet they'd ever owned.

When it seemed she might slip into melancholia, Rue forced her thoughts to return to the ranch Hawke spoke so eloquently about. She had often wondered how it would feel to sit in a saddle, ride a high-stepping mount, not to demean her plodding old mule, of course. Her hus—Masters rode a black beauty, proud and arrogant, just like his master, with the same, don't-mess-with-me message in his mean-looking eyes.

At last, having scoured every pot and pan the old man owned, which wasn't many, Rue looked longingly at the vacant rocking chair before the fire. It had been a long day and the old mule's jolting, clipped walk was tiring to the body. She hesitated to join the two men only because she'd had more than enough of Hawke Masters's company, his scowling face, his disregard of her as though she wasn't even with him. She was near her breaking point, and she wouldn't be responsible for what she might do if he made some sneering remark to her.

Old Adams made the decision for her. "Don't scrub them utensils too good, missy," he called. "They ain't used to it." He set the chair next to him rocking. "Come and join us. It's been a long time since I've listened to female talk."

"I thought you didn't like female company." Hawke watched the cigarette smoke drift toward the fireplace, his lips curved in amusement.

"Yeah, well, like I also said, I bet this one could be real interestin' if a man got her started. My wife was like that. I never got tired of her company. We'd sit in front of the fire of an evening, goin' over the events of the day, plannin' what we'd do tomorrow." He sighed heavily. "Our one big disappointment was that we never had any younguns'."

"Did it bother you all that much?" Hawke asked. "This idea that man must reproduce himself?"

"Not a whole lot. It would have been nice to have a son, though," Adams said after a thoughtful pause. "It's the wimmen who hanker the strongest for babies. It was a sorrowful thing for Star Shine that she couldn't give me a son.

"What about you and your woman?" He looked at Hawke. "You got a family started yet? You'll need big strong sons to help you on that ranch when you get too old to run things."

Hawke stretched his long legs out in front of him, crossing his ankles. "A rancher owner can always hire a good man to run things if he gets too old to do the job himself," he hedged lazily. "Besides, I have a nephew who'll inherit my ranch someday."

Well, Rue thought dryly, *that pretty much tells me how he feels about my welfare*. Since Masters was thirteen years older than herself, the chances were good that she might be a widow for a long time in the years to come. How was she to support herself? Of course, there was the real possibility that he didn't intend that she be with him for any great length of time. Maybe he planned that when he had no more use for her he'd send her on her way.

Had Hawke or Rue looked at old Adams they'd have seen by the look on his face that the same thoughts as Rue's were running through his mind also. He didn't mention them though when he spoke. "How do you feel about havin' a family, girl?" He looked at Rue. "Don't you want children, a bond between you and your husband?"

Rue shook her head so vehemently she was

stared at in surprise. Her mind raced with legitimate reasons she could give for not wanting children. She couldn't say that she despised the man who was her husband, that she felt that way about most men. But she didn't want to say that her husband felt the same way about her, and that since they would never be sleeping together naturally there would be no children.

Finally, conscious of Hawke's jeering eyes on her, she said, "Perhaps . . . someday, a long time from now, I shall want children. At the moment, however, I am child-weary. Until I got married, I was responsible for raising my half brothers. Frankly, I'd like a rest from whining, crying children." She glanced at Hawke and wondered at the amused smirk on his face. It was as though he knew something that she did not.

Rue grew silent, and after a close study of her face, Adams changed the subject to trapping. As he talked on and on, diverging into reminiscences, Rue stared broodingly into the leaping flames. She did want children, strong, healthy ones, but considering the manner in which they were obtained, she would never be a mother. No man was ever going to get that close to her.

The drone of the old man's voice lulled Rue into a state of drowsiness. When unconsciously her lips parted in a long yawn, he broke off his long-winded story and grinned at her. "I reckon I've about talked you folks' ears off. 'Spect it's time we turned in. You two can take the bed next to the window."

Rue glanced at the two bunk beds attached to the wall, constructed of spruce poles strung with strips of rawhide. Each bore a straw tick, covered with gray, woolen blankets. Two people could fit comfortably enough, providing they were in love. Then they would be unaware of the narrowness as they lay clasped in each other's arms.

But that was not the case here, Rue reminded herself with firmed lips. She would sleep on the floor first. She turned her head and found Hawke's green eyes mocking her.

He spoke before she could. "The bed looks a little narrow, Adams. I'll just spread my blankets here in front of the fire."

"You will?" The old man peered at Hawke curiously. "Close quarters never bothered me and my woman. The closer we could get together, the better we liked it. It's mighty cozy-like in the winter."

"Yeah, well." Hawke stretched his arms over his head, then added at the end of a loud yawn, "It's hardly winter, is it?"

Adams shot Rue a searching glance and she lowered her eyes against the sympathy she saw in his. What was he thinking? she wondered. That probably she wasn't even married to the hateful man sitting beside him, that he only had her along to use occasionally.

"Well, you folks turn in whenever you've a mind to." Adams knocked out his pipe in the fireplace. "I'm gonna hit the blankets now."

"I think I will too." Rue stood up, not about to be left alone with her husband. She moved across the floor to the bed indicated by Adams, kicked off her moccasins, and slid under the itchy blanket.

She lay on her back, staring up at the rafters, listening to the rustling of the bed behind her as the old man made himself comfortable. In a short time he was snoring, keeping her awake. She turned on her side, and with her hands folded under her cheek, she was able to study Hawke Masters freely for the first time.

Although he was handsome enough, she thought, with his firm jaw, wide forehead, and black hair curling loosely to his collar, there was a suggestion of ruthlessness in the chiseled lips and green eyes.

He's a hard man, she told herself, *one who always hits harder than his opponent*. She continued to study him as, his face dark and moody, he stared into the fire. Was he thinking about her? she wondered. Cursing the fact that he was saddled with a wife he didn't want?

Rue pretended to be asleep when Hawke flipped his spent cigarette into the fireplace, then stood up. After a moment there came the soft scrape of the small shovel as he banked the fire for the night, then the whisper of his boots being tugged off. A few minutes later his deep, even breathing told her he was asleep.

Old Adams's snores continued to echo through the room, seemingly louder in the total darkness. Rue was sure she would never fall asleep against the background of that racket.

When Rue's shoulder was firmly shaken, it took a moment for her confused brain to realize that she had fallen asleep, after all. She blinked her eyes rapidly as Hawke, in his usual impatient way, ordered, "Get up. I want to get goin'. We're runnin' a day late as it is."

Resentment flared in Rue's eyes. She knew without him saying it, he was blaming her mule. The old fellow had been unable to keep the galloping gait set by the big stallion. "Hateful devil," she muttered under her breath as Hawke stamped away.

She noted as she slid out of bed and fumbled her feet into the pacs that he had already rolled up his blankets and placed them beside the door. A mischievous desire to test his patience came over her and she took her time smoothing the covers over the bed, tucking them in neatly, and fluffing up the pillow. She was aware that Hawke's narrowed eyes watched her, knew that he was cognizant of what she was up to.

Finally, she could no longer draw out the bed-making. To do so would be admitting that she was being pettish. Ignoring Hawke's dark look, she turned from the bed and smiled a greeting to Adams.

The old man smiled back and motioned to a basin of water on a small table. "I warmed you some water to wash your face in. Ain't got no soap, though. Ran out a few weeks back."

"I've got some," Rue said, and moving across the room to where she had placed her small bundle, again taking her time, she unfolded it and removed the rose soap, washcloth and jar of salve. Keeping her head averted from Hawke's scowling features, she unhurriedly washed her face in the soft spring water, sighing aloud at the pleasant feel of the warm suds caressing her skin.

Rue was additionally pleased that when she rinsed the cloth in the basin, several black scabs floated in the water. Good, she thought, they were finally beginning to fall off. She smeared the dark salve over her clean face, rolled the jar in the washcloth, then taking a seat at the table, laid it beside her plate.

As the bread had been light and tasty last night, so were the flapjacks this morning. When Adams urged a second helping on her, she didn't refuse. It would be dark before she ate again. Hawke hadn't broken his habit of foregoing a noon meal.

"You got much further to go, Masters?" Adams asked after a long swallow of coffee.

"Naw. If that lazy mule can step along a

little faster, I'll be at my ranch by dark."

Adams narrowed thoughtful eyes on the man who had spoken so carelessly. "You say that *you'll* be back at your ranch. Does that mean that your wife ain't goin' with you?"

Hawke looked up startled, then looking slightly discomfited, amended, "I meant to say we."

Adams's eyes pierced him another moment, then turning to look at Rue, said softly, "I never did get your name, girl."

"It's Rue." Her lips twisted wryly. The old man's eyes widened a trifle and she added, "I doubt if there are any more females hung with such a handle. My father named me." She paused with a short laugh. "For a reason I won't mention."

"You said last night that you have half brothers. Is your dad dead?"

Rue shrugged her thin shoulders. "I don't know, nor do I care. He went off and left me when I was three years old. No one has heard of him since."

"There might be a reason," Adams began, but Hawke had risen from the table, ordering Rue to get a move on.

"You've dillydallyed long enough."

The old man followed them outside to where Hawke had the mounts saddled and waiting. He accepted Hawke's thanks and returned the handshake. He turned then and helped Rue to scramble onto the mule's bony back. "Thanks for everything, Mr. Adams." She smiled down at him warmly.

He gazed up at her and said earnestly, "If you ever need help, child, you know where to come."

"Thank you," she said softly. "I may have to take you up on your offer someday." She leaned down and gripped his shoulder, then jabbed the mule lightly with her heel. Hawke was almost out of sight.

Adams stared after her, shaking his head sadly. The girl wasn't going to have it easy with that insensitive cuss she was married to. He just might look her up one of these days, remind her that she had a friend.

The mule didn't catch up to the stallion all morning. Rue didn't urge him to do so. She liked it fine, lazing along behind Hawke, a distance far enough away that she couldn't see his face, or hear any cutting remark he might make.

The sun rose higher, grew hotter, burning through Rue's clothes. Perspiration wet the back of her dress and made her skirt cling to her legs. She grew thirsty but refused to catch up to her companion to ask for a drink from his canteen.

It was early afternoon when the mounts moved out of the woods and into a grassy swale. In a grove of cottonwoods, just beginning to lose their leaves, lay a scattering of buildings.

Is this my new home? Rue wondered, her spirits lifting as she took in the well-cared-for house and barn and several sheds. As Hawke prodded the stallion into a gallop, she urged the old mule to keep up.

CHAPTER FIVE

The tall, dark woman sitting on the long porch gave Hawke and Rue a startled look as they clattered into the yard in front of the clapboard house. Rue's eyes fastened on the voluptuous, attractive female and knew immediately that this was not Hawke's ranch. This woman in the blue poplin, low-cut dress, with tiny puffed sleeves, was the mistress here.

How appalling I must look! Rue thought, cringing inside, conscious of her patched, sweat-stained dress, her dirty stringy hair, and scabbed face. However, when she found the woman's curious eyes on her, she looked back proudly. Her grandparents had taught her to bow to no one.

Frowning, the woman shifted her gaze to Hawke. He slanted her a lazy smile as he leaned forward, his arms crossed on the pommel of the saddle.

"Where's Sam, Lillie?" he asked softly, a knowing look in his eyes as the woman ran a tongue around her lips before answering breathlessly.

"He's ridin' boundary today. He won't be home for two or three hours."

Lillie Meyers walked across the porch, her ample breasts juggling so that Rue held her breath, expecting them to escape the scanty confines of the bodice. When she stood at the edge of the porch, she looked archly at Hawke and asked, "Are you gonna sit that horse all day, or are you comin' in for a visit?"

Hawke gave her a salacious grin. "I thought I might come in for a while . . . Have a cup of coffee, or somethin'."

When he dismounted and stepped on the porch, Lillie slid her arm through his and shifting her eyes to Rue sneered through thin, painted lips, "Who, or what, is that on that sorry-lookin' mule?"

Hawke tossed Rue a careless glance. "Her? Why that's my wife."

Lillie jerked her arm out of his. "Your wife? I don't believe you." Her slitted eyes traveled contemptuously over Rue, missing nothing. "You wouldn't marry a rag-tail like that."

Hawke chuckled and pulled Lillie's arm back through his. "Come on inside and I'll tell you all about it."

Rue stared after them as they disappeared through the door. She couldn't remember ever being so angry, so completely insulted. She had been discussed as though she were an inanimate object, without sense or feeling. She felt sick with the hatred she felt for her husband and his paramour. When the sound of his jingling spurs and the woman's high-tapping heels disappeared into the back regions of the house, Rue slid to the ground.

She stretched her sore muscles, then rubbed her rear, thinking she just might walk the rest of the way to wherever they were going. The old mule brayed and nudged her shoulder. "You're thirsty too, huh, old fellow." She looked around the yard. "Come on," she said, turning the animal toward a long trough beneath a cottonwood tree. The stallion snorted and stamped his great hoofs, and only for a second she ignored him. She tied the mule at one end of the trough, then went back for Captain.

"You can't help how your master is," she said as she led the animal to the other end of the trough and tied him to a limb.

Rue licked her dry lips as the mule and horse drank their fill, but couldn't bring herself to drink after them. The water was full of darting tadpoles.

While the mule lipped at a tuft of grass, and the stallion snorted and champed his bit, Rue walked back to the porch and sat down on the top step. Her eyes smoldered with resentment as the sun poured down on her bare head. She hadn't even been offered a cup of water, never mind coffee.

From inside came the faint voices of Hawke and the woman he called Lillie. Rue's lips straightened in a tight line every time low laughter punctuated their conversation. No doubt they were talking about the "rag-tail wife" baking in the sun while they carried on in the coolness of the house.

He's a fool, she thought. *Careless and danger-loving, messing around with another man's wife.*

A half hour passed in which Rue's thirst grew, tightening her throat, roughening her tongue. Rebellion rose inside her. Invited or not, she was going to march inside that house and get herself a drink of water.

She started to rise, then slowly sank back down. A white stallion had broke from a fringe of trees at a full gallop. The rider pulled him to a rearing halt in front of the porch, his sliding hoofs throwing dirt and gravel over Rue. She choked and coughed, then peered through the settling dust at the man astride the big horse.

The coldest eyes she'd ever looked into, stared out of a thin, scarred face. *He's well in his sixties*, she thought. Then apprehension coursed through her as, dusty-booted and long-spurred, the man left the saddle and clanked noisely onto the porch.

His eyes swept over Rue with no hint of friendliness. Even before he asked, "Who are you?" she knew Lillie's husband hovered over her.

And what would he say about his wife being in the house alone with the handsome rancher? Rue wondered. A *young, handsome* rancher, she tacked on.

Returning the intent stare, Rue said cooly, "My name is Rue Masters. Hawke Masters is my husband."

She wanted to giggle as the steel-gray eyes widened and a flicker of surprise stirred the stoic features. Her answer had been the last thing he had expected to hear, she was sure. No telling who or what he thought she was.

Regaining his composure, Sam Meyers asked with a hint of contempt, "Why are you sittin' out here alone? Where is Masters?"

For a fleeting wild moment Rue was tempted to answer, "He's lying with your wife, in your bed." She aborted the thought almost at its conception. This man wouldn't hesitate to put a bullet in Hawke, and would enjoy doing it. And as much as she despised the man she was married to, she wouldn't want to be the cause of his death.

She swallowed hard, and in a wave of confusion blurted out, "He's inside having a cup of coffee."

Sam stared down at her, his gaze measuring. "Why aren't you havin' coffee too?"

Rue gave a small wave of her hand and remarked indifferently, "I don't like the stuff."

There was an undercurrent of mockery in Meyers's voice when he muttered, as though to himself, "Especially if you weren't invited inside to have some."

"Oh, but that's not true," Rue began, then stopped as Lillie walked out of the house, followed by Hawke.

A frisson of fear ran down Rue's spine as, ignoring Lillie's cheerful, "Sam, dear, you've finished early, how nice," the older man looked at Hawke with smoldering dislike.

Rue looked at her husband, trying to read what was in his eyes, but strangely, he seemed to be avoiding looking at her. She turned her head back to Meyers when she saw him take a step toward Hawke.

"A man's a fool who stumbles over the same stone twice, Masters," the rancher said harshly.

Rue held her breath, waiting for Hawke's reply, for there was no mistaking the warning in the cold voice. Hawke straightened out of his lounging stance against the porch post, and with a cool smile wreathing his lips, said, "I agree with you, Meyers. I'll let you know the first time I stumble."

"Don't bother yourself." Meyers's fists clenched at his sides. "I've a feelin' you've already stumbled more than once." He looked at Rue. "You've got your own wife now. I don't want to see you hangin' around mine."

"Sam! What are you thinkin'?" Lillie tucked her hand around her husband's arm and rubbed her large breasts against it. "Hawke is our neighbor. He only stopped by for a friendly visit, and to introduce his new wife."

A sneer lifted Meyers's thin lips. "Is that right? Tell me, Lillie, what is his wife's name?"

Uneasiness swept over Lillie's hard, attractive face, and she looked at Hawke, plainly asking for help. When she started to stammer, fumble for words, Hawke said offhandedly, "Come on, Rue, it's time we get goin' if we're gonna make the ranch before dark."

The thought of waiting a minute longer for a drink of water brought all of Rue's pent-up fury bursting loose. "Hawke Masters, I'm not leaving this porch until I get a drink of water," she declared tightly.

The three stared at Rue, blinking at the fire shooting from her eyes. Hawke stirred uneasily as red crept over his face. He should have seen to it that she got some water. His guilt intensified when Meyers mocked, "You sure look after your new wife's comfort, don't you, Masters?"

Before Hawke could answer, for what could

he say, the rancher turned to his highly agitated wife still clinging to his arm. "It would appear, Lillie, that your graciousness doesn't extend to our neighbor's wife. Go fetch her a glass of water, a cold one, from the spring."

Rue had a suspicion that Lillie Meyers had never moved so fast in her life. But during the few minutes it took her to return, the air was highly tense and Rue wondered if she shouldn't have kept her mouth shut and managed somehow to tolerate her thirst until she reached her new home.

However, when Lillie held out a glass of water to her, Rue practically snatched it from her hand, spilling some on her way to her mouth. Never had anything felt so good as that cold liquid running down her throat. As she thrust the empty glass back to Lillie, and smiled her thanks to Sam, both Meyerses took a closer look at the small, delicate face. A satisfied smile lifted the man's lips, while the woman's pouting ones curved downward. Her narrowed lids said that it was possible that later on she might have competition from Hawke's very young wife.

Hawke was mounted and waiting impatiently as Rue scrambled onto the old mule's back as best she could while trying to keep her skirt pulled down around her knees. A sidelong look showed her Lillie's smirking face. *It pleases the bitch that my husband treats his stallion better than his wife*, she thought darkly, and kicked the mule so hard it jolted him into a half trot.

She rode alongside Hawke in silence for a minute, then unable to hold her tongue any longer, asked flatly, "Are you carrying on with your neighbor's wife?"

Hawke looked at her as though she were an annoying fly buzzing around his head. But as she returned his gaze steadily, he looked away, muttering inaudibly.

"I'm sorry, but I didn't hear what you said," Rue prodded, determined that he answer her.

"I said"—a muscle twitched in Hawke's cheek—"what's it to you if I am? Did you have the crazy idea that I was goin' to be true to my little wife?"

Cut to the quick by his sneering words, Rue burst out furiously, "I never thought that for a minute. Men of your caliber are always tomcatting, married or not. But it's plain Sam Meyers is crazy about his whoring wife and I don't see why you can't leave her alone."

Hawke felt a sting of guilt. Old Sam did love Lillie, probably in the same way Pa had loved Ma, and Ben had loved Sara. It struck him for the first time how his father and brother would have felt had their wives gone to bed with another man.

Nevertheless it irked him that the thin, mountain girl riding beside him had made him see the wrong he was doing his neighbor. He sent her a look from beneath hooded eyes and sneered, "I expect you're an expert on whores. Like always recognizes like."

It was all Rue could do not to fling herself at the hateful man and scratch his face to ribbons. But knowing that he would never let her get started, she used her tongue as a weapon. "You low-life womanizer," she ground out. "I hope Sam Meyers kills you someday, then I'll be rid of you."

Hawke laughed easily. "That won't happen, little girl, so get it in your head; you're stuck with me until I no longer need you. I lost a lot of money on you, and, by God, you're gonna earn it back for me."

Rue made no response and silence prevailed between them until Hawke surprised her by saying, "I didn't take Lillie to bed today, if that's what you're thinkin'."

"I'm not thinking anything," Rue retorted. "It's nothing to me how many women you lay with. I just think it's a shame that you go after another man's wife."

Hawke sent her a searching glance. Could his unattractive wife be jealous? But there was only chilly unconcern in Rue's eyes, and for some reason her obvious lack of interest rankled him. As did her arrogant aloofness. He swore under his breath. He'd take some of that out of her before he was through. He'd see to it that she worked her rear end off around the ranch. By the time she cooked and cleaned and looked after Susie and Tommie, she'd be so tired she wouldn't have the strength to raise that stubborn chin so high.

He lightly nudged Captain into an easy lope. Let the smart-ass bitch ride alone.

Hawke's thoughts went backward to the Meyers. Why, he wondered, hadn't he taken the willing Lillie to bed? He'd had every intention to, had thought about it all the time on the trail. But when Lillie would have led him to her bedroom something had held him back. He was at a loss for the reason, but suddenly he'd had no desire for the woman he'd lusted after for two years.

When a small voice suggested, *Maybe you didn't want to cheat on your wife*, he scoffed at the idea. That one would never keep him from going to bed with another woman. It probably had to do with the strain he'd been under, losing his brother and all.

Captain lunged up a small rise and the rich, green valley lay before Hawke. Long shadows of approaching twilight covered half its length. He pulled in the stallion and waited for Rue to catch up.

"There it is," he said, pride in his voice, "my ranch."

Rue looked down on the darkening length of land that lay on both sides of a river, scattered with growths of pine and spruce. *It's a wild land this man has brought me to*, she thought. *There's nothing but trees, sky, and mountains. And no doubt wolves howling in the night.*

But, oh so beautiful, she added as Hawke lifted the reins and rode toward the buildings nestled in the foothills of the mountain less than a mile away.

A lone rider, keeping in the cover of a wide pine, watched Hawke and Rue until they faded into the distance. Eyes full of hate looked out of the man's fat, heavily whiskered face. His hand stroked the butt of the rifle shoved in its sheath.

"No," he rasped, "shooting is too good for the bitch. She must suffer."

Sly Burford stroked his maimed manhood, his eyes glittering as he thought of ways he'd get his revenge on Mrs. Rue Masters. He lifted the reins of his stolen mount and turned it in the direction of Sam Meyers's ranch. A fancy big spread like that one would always need extra help. He'd hire on there and bide his time.

Rue smiled thinly as she and Hawke arrived at the large native stone and pine log house. This husband of hers did have finer feelings after all, she mused as she watched the softening of his features as he gazed at his home.

She gazed at what made satisfaction glow in his green eyes. The roof of the wide porch running the length of the house sagged in the middle. The porch had several floorboards missing, and the warped shutters hung askew at the windows. The yard was rubble and weed-filled, with a narrow path cutting through it to the house.

Rue stared at the place for a long time. Although it was shabby and run-down, it fired her imagination. Strangely it didn't have that aura of poverty, of hopelessness, like the one she had grown up in. There was a stability about it, a promise of better times. She determined that for whatever time she might be here she would make a home in this untamed West.

Hawke interrupted her silent vow. "Go on in the house and start supper." He slid to the ground and reached for the mule's reins. "You'll find everything you need in the cupboards."

Rue slid to the ground, grabbed her small bundle, and watched him lead her old pet away. She felt a sense of loss as its bony rump swung awkwardly away. He was the last link to her old life. Would her future one be any better? she wondered as she carefully stepped on the rotting porch and pushed open the heavy door.

She stepped into a large room and stood a moment, adjusting her eyes to the gloom. Only the weak rays of the setting sun through a dirty window gave any light. Her vision cleared and the first thing to catch her eyes was the huge fireplace situated in the center of the right-hand outside wall. It was constructed of fieldstone and open at both ends. It had a raised hearth, high enough so that large backlogs could be slid in from either side. Heat from it would flow in three directions. She had no doubt that this room would be cozy and warm come winter when the fierce winds blew.

She turned slowly, taking in the rest of the room. There were only two pieces of furniture, two rockers badly in need of repair. She doubted either one could take Hawke's weight without falling apart.

With a deep sigh, she walked across the dirt-littered floor and stepped through a door that led her into a kitchen. Her lips pursed as her eyes went at once to the rusty range in a corner. It didn't look in much better condition than the one she had sweated over making the skimpy meals for her half brothers.

Her gaze was drawn next to the rough, dirt-grimed table. Every inch was covered with dirty dishes, pots, and pans. She advanced into the room, picking up a bench and aligning it with the table. She bumped her knee on its mate as she skirted the table and went through another door leading into a long hall.

Four doors led off it. Three rooms were empty, the fourth holding a sagging bed and a rickety table beside it. A kerosine lamp, with a smoked chimney, sat on its surface, a box of matches beside it.

The bed was unmade, its covers tossed in a rumpled pile. At least a month's supply of soiled, male clothing had been tossed in a corner. Rue frowned. What did he do, buy new ones every time he needed a change of clothing?

"There's a main of work ahead of me," she muttered, returning to the kitchen. But that was all she'd ever known, so she dismissed it from her mind as she tackled the old stove, building a fire inside it from the plentiful supply of wood stacked a safe distance away from the black monster.

She set the rusty damper, then turned to the table with a sigh. She glanced at the water pail among the mess. Was it possible it held any water?

It was empty. "Damn," Rue muttered. How far would she have to walk to the water supply? And where was it? she wondered, picking up the pail and going through a side door that took her outside.

Another path lay in front of her, leading off through waist-high weeds. Speculating that it led to a source of water, it being so well-trodden, she followed it around to the back of the house and on to a high formation of rocks and boulders rising in a thick stand of cottonwood.

She heard it before she saw it. A rushing torrent of water. It gushed from under a large boulder, lashed against the rocks in its path, filled a scooped-out hole lined with smooth stones, then disappeared into a dense thicket.

Rue dropped to her knees beside the small pool and dipped her fingers in its icy coolness. There would be no more half-mile walks to fetch water from a river. She had a constant flow of healthy, gravel-strained water only a few yards away from the house.

She filled the pail then hurried back to the kitchen where she poured half its contents into a big black kettle on the range. While it heated, she attacked the table. While she scraped dried food off plates and out of bowls, she muttered, "I doubt if there's one clean piece of crockery, or anything else for that matter, in this entire house."

The kettle steamed and Rue poured the hot water over a bar of yellow, lye soap she'd unearthed in a bottom cupboard. She swished the piece of rag that had been wrapped around the soap in the water until she had a good amount of suds. Then picking up the stack of plates, she plunked them into the pan, adding the bowls, cups, and eating utensils.

While they soaked, she inspected the plentiful supplies stacked neatly in an upper cupboard. With a sharp pang, she remembered how bare the shelves were back at the

DeLawney shack and wondered if her half brothers had eaten that day.

The sun had slipped behind the mountain when Hawke entered the kitchen and sniffed hungrily at the mouth-watering aroma of frying meat. His eyes widened as they lit on the scrubbed table, the two shiny plates with knife, fork, and spoon placed beside them, two bowls filled with steaming fried potatoes and string beans, and a platter of lightly browned slices of ham.

By the bright light of the lamp in the center of the table, its chimney sparkling clean, its wick trimmed, he watched Rue take a pan of biscuits from the oven. *At least she's not lazy*, he thought, removing his hat and hanging it on a nail beside the door. Wordlessly, he sat at the table.

At Rue's raised eyebrows, he growled, "I washed up at the horse trough," and began heaping food onto his plate. Rue filled the two cups with coffee, then placing the pot within his reach, took a seat across from him.

The meal was eaten in silence, only the scraping sound of forks and knives heavy in the air. Hawke glanced at the silent girl across from him a couple of times, thinking that he should compliment her on the delicious supper. He couldn't remember ever tasting anything better. But she wore that same aloofness on her dirty face and he held his tongue. He would only receive a sharp retort for his trouble.

When he had cleaned his plate and poured a second cup of coffee, Rue stood up and cleared the table, placing the dirty dishes into a pan of fresh, sudsy water. Hawke scowled at her back as she walked to the kitchen door and leaned in the opening, her stance saying plainly that she was waiting for him to finish his coffee and leave.

Her obvious dislike of him was strangely disturbing to Hawke. Why did she have such low regard for him? he asked himself. She should be damned grateful that he had taken her away from that shack . . . even married her . . . Sly Burford's castoff. And he still didn't know whether or not she was carrying the fat man's seed.

What if she is? Hawke pondered. What could he do about it? Besides needing her to care for Susie and Tommy later on, he was legally married to her. By law he couldn't just tell her to leave.

He stood up, deciding he'd worry about that problem if and when it came up. Taking down his hat from where it hung just a few inches above Rue's head, he said brusquely, "You can use the bed. I'll be bunking in with the cowpunchers."

Rue heard the front door close behind him and muttered, "Your way of letting your men know that your dowdy wife doesn't appeal to you. Well, that's fine with me." She attacked the pan of dirty dishes with a fury that made her pause after a moment, wondering at her anger.

Why was she so angry? she asked herself. Weren't things working out the way she wanted them to? Hadn't she told herself over and over that she wanted as little as possible to do with that man?

"But it hurts," she whispered, tears stinging her eyelids, "To know that the man you're married to has nothing but contempt for you, that you might have to spend the rest of your life unwanted and unloved.

Rue wiped an arm across her tearing eyes and told herself to stop thinking foolishly. Very few men ever loved deeply and for any length of time. Didn't she have plenty proof of that? Look how Sly had used her mother, making her continue to sell her body. And what about those men who came to the shack every night? More than half of them had wives.

"No," she said firmly. "I can live without a man's so-called love."

In a short time the kitchen was cleaned, and two large pans of water were heating on the stove. Before she went to bed tonight, she was going to have a warm, soaking bath, and scrub away the dirt and grime of the trail.

Rue picked her bundle off the floor where

she had laid it in a corner upon arriving. Opening it up, she unfolded the new dress, shook out some of the wrinkles, then spread it out on one of the benches. Next, she placed one of the rose-scented bars of soap, washcloth, and towel on the table, then busied herself with dropping the long bars across both outside doors. Going to where a large wooden tub hung from the wall, she struggled it to the floor and dragged it to a spot well away from the window. One of the hands might be lurking around outside, hoping to get a glimpse of the wife their boss didn't want to sleep with.

Rue soaked in the hot water until it grew cold. When she stood up, a good amount of dark scabs floated on top of the water. As she dried herself off, most of the remaining ones came off in her towel.

"At last." She laughed softly, and hurried to pour warm water into a basin to wash her face. When she finished lathering and rinsing, she peered into a broken off piece of mirror propped on the windowsill. Her white teeth gleamed in a wide, pleased smile. Every last scab was gone. There were only spots of pinkish dots which would fade by morning.

Rue held her greasy hair away from her face and for the first time in her life studied her features. She saw a creamy, honey-tanned complexion, a straight, of moderate length nose, full, red lips above a stubborn, little chin. The high cheekbones beneath stormy blue eyes she had inherited from her father and grandfather.

She blinked her heavily lashed eyes against tears as she remembered her grandfather. How worried he and grandma must be about her. Maybe someday she could get a letter off to them.

Rue let her hair fall back to her shoulders, undecided whether to wash it now or tomorrow. She came to the decision that she better wait as she ran her fingers through the long, heavy tresses. She needed the sun to dry it fully, or to sit before a fire for an hour or so.

"And I'm too tired to stay up that long," she muttered, yawning. And still naked, she blew out the lamp, and in the soft glow of moonlight coming through the window, she walked to Hawke's bedroom and crawled into his bed.

Somehow, Hawke's scent wasn't repulsive to her as she immediately dropped off into a dreamless sleep.

Rue yawned and stretched, and waited for the little ones to start their hungry whining. Then she caught Hawke's scent and her eyes flew open. She wouldn't be hearing those whimpering cries anymore. She was married and hundreds of miles away from them. She pushed away the pictures of their thin, little faces and leaned up on both elbows to peer at the window at the foot of the bed. A rosy glow in the east managed to penetrate the dirty windowpanes. The sun would be up soon. She sat up and swung her feet to the floor.

"I'd better hustle if I'm to have his lordship's breakfast on the table by the time he comes stomping in," she muttered, walking across the floor, flinching as her bare feet trod on a fine film of gritty sand and small clods of dirt. She imagined the lumps of dirt came from Hawke's spurs and boot heels. She promised herself that today the entire house would get a thorough sweeping.

In the kitchen Rue picked up her new dress and pulled it over her head. Its new crispness was rough on her tender skin, abrasive against her firm, jutting breasts. She buttoned up the bodice and ran her hands down her rib cage where the material clung snugly before easing to shape over her breasts. There was a belt to nip in her narrow waist where the gathered skirt fell gracefully to her ankles. She smiled. Grandma had fitted her perfectly.

The dress rustled softly as Rue hurried about, building a fire in the rusty range, brewing the coffee, then slicing salt pork into a frying pan before mixing a bowl of flapjack batter. Between her trips from table to stove, she glanced often out the window, anxious to have everything ready the moment she saw Hawke leave the bunkhouse. She didn't want to give him any cause to wag his caustic, abusive tongue at her.

I'd better unbar the door, she suddenly remembered. And while she was occupied with the front door, she missed seeing Hawke leave the bunkhouse and walk toward the house. She was slapping a plate and silverware on the table when he stepped quietly into the kitchen, then paused in the doorway.

Caught in profile, her slender body gracefully poised over the table, Hawke couldn't take his eyes off her. Used to Lillie's voluptuous body, heavy breasts that had lost their firmness, hips that were wider than his own, the gently rounded body of his wife was like a breath of springtime. His eyes lingered on the incredibly small waist, then traveled up to the proudly jutting breasts that could fill his hands to perfection. He suddenly had the urge to feel their heaviness in his palms.

His eyes then lifted to the oily, stringy hair, and the spell was broken as he remembered where he had found her, plus the fact that she might, right now, be carrying Burford's bastard. He gruffly cleared his throat to announce his presence, and wordlessly took a seat at the table.

Rue was momentarily startled by Hawke's unexpected arrival, but quickly composed herself. In her usual aloof way with him, she placed golden fried salt pork in front of him, followed by a stack of steaming flapjacks. As she poured his coffee, again placing the pot within his reach, Hawke noted for the first time that she had set no plate for herself.

Anger stirred inside him. She had shared his supper, so why not breakfast? He lifted his head to demand an explanation and caught the flash of her skirt and the wooden pail disappear out the door. Swearing under his breath, he savagely jabbed his fork into the stack of flapjacks. High-nosed bitch, who in the hell did she think she was? Ignoring a man as if he wasn't even there. He seemed to have forgotten that he had treated her the same way all across the state of Colorado.

Hawke shoveled the food into his mouth so fast he was gone by the time Rue returned from the spring, a full pail of water swinging from her hand.

A sigh of relief drifted through her lips when she found the kitchen empty. She hoisted the pail to waist level and poured its contents into two large pans. While it heated, she made another trip to the spring, listing in her mind the things she would do today.

The first thing was to get her old dress washed and dried. She had much to do and it all involved dirty, sweaty work. She didn't want to mar her new dress with perspiration stains. And after she cleaned the house, she continued her mental list, she would wash her hair.

Twenty minutes later the much-patched homespun was washed and spread on a bush to dry. Rue then washed the dishes Hawke had used, and the pans and skillets in which she had prepared the meal. Without pausing, she went to the bedroom to make up the bed.

As she smoothed the sheet and plumped up the pillows, she caught Hawke's scent and was surprised again that she wasn't repelled by it. It carried a fresh, clean scent of outdoors and his own particular odor. Nevertheless tomorrow the bed linens would get a good scrubbing, as well as the pile of clothes tossed in the corner.

Returning to the kitchen, Rue set a bowl of sourdough to rise, then went outside to check on her dress. The thin material had dried rapidly. There was only a dampness along the sleeves when she plucked it from the bush. *That doesn't matter*, she told herself, drapping the faded article over her arm. It would be completely wet with perspiration before the hour was out.

Changed into the soft, loose dress that had once been her mother's, Rue grabbed the broom and started in. She paused once in her sweeping to make a sandwich from the cold meat left over from breakfast. She finished eating it with a cup of coffee, then resumed her fight against the dirt and grime.

It was around two o'clock, according to the placement of the sun, when Rue finished doing all that she could to the old house to make it clean. Every room, every corner, had been swept, windows freed of several years of grime, the kitchen floor scrubbed.

She stretched sore muscles. "Time to wash my hair," she said. Then as she filled a pan with water from the kettle on the stove and dropped the bar of soap into it, she chided herself for talking to an empty room. Her husband would think her loony, besides all the other disparaging things he thought about her, should he overhear her.

This habit of talking to herself was one of long standing. From early childhood speaking aloud her grievances had been her only source of ridding the anger, the bitterness, and despair, from her mind. As far as she was concerned, nothing had changed.

It took several washings and rinsings before Rue's heavy hair cleanly squeaked between her fingers. Toweling it briskly, she walked out onto the back porch to let the sun finish drying the long tresses.

As a hot breeze blew the old dress against her slimness, drying the perspiration on her body, Rue leaned against the railing, gazing out at the dusty yard. Her eyes lit on a straggly rose that looked parched.

"I'll give you a drink as soon as my hair dries," she said, and smiled.

She had found a piece of broken comb in Hawke's room, and she now pulled it through the wet, tangled hair, fanning it out, letting the sun and breeze move through it. Soon its red-gold sheen glinted in deep, warm waves past her shoulders.

And Hawke Masters, riding around the corner of the house, thought he had never seen a more beautiful sight than that golden flow of hair. It was all he could do not to dismount, jump on the porch, and run his fingers through it.

And draw back a stub, he reminded himself.

CHAPTER SIX

Rue had been married for two weeks the morning she stood at the kitchen window, watching the ranch hands ride out.

They were rugged, unshaven cowboys, and Mexicans with peaked sombreros and tight trousers. Most, she noted, possessed a lean, wiry hardness of muscle and frame, a hawk-like look in their eyes. They would be fierce enemies, she thought, unyielding to one who was foolish enough to double-deal them, or play them false. Although, on the other hand, the same men would stick by a friend, risk their own lives if necessary.

The hoofbeats deadened, then died away, leaving clouds of dust to drift from the trail.

Rue turned from the window. It would be quiet around the bunkhouse today. Last night she had overheard Hawke tell the ranch foreman that they would start branding tomorrow morning, and that all hands would be needed.

Rue decided that it would be a good day to go for that ride she had been promising herself. She busied herself with putting the kitchen to rights, then hurried to make her bed. Fifteen minutes later she left the house, her dress gathered up above the damp grass, her hair tossing in the airy breeze.

"I hope there's someone around to show me how to saddle a horse," she said, and frowned. She had never sat a saddle, and hadn't the slightest idea how to put one on a mount.

When she entered the shedlike barn and walked down its dim aisle, she found that every stall was empty. A frown of annoyance creased her forehead. All the horses had been turned into the corral. She might as well forget about riding, for she would never be able to catch one.

Fighting back her disappointment, Rue left the stables and walked the several yards to the wooden corral. Five beautiful horses came galloping up to her as she leaned on the top rail.

"Oh, you are such beauties," she exclaimed as they pushed their sleek heads at her, plainly wanting to be petted. "You must be Hawke's prized mounts he brags about so."

She scratched the ears of each in turn. "I wouldn't dare ride one of you even if I knew how to get a saddle on you. He'd skin me alive if he even saw me talking to you."

A long welcoming bray took Rue's attention from the horses. A glad cry escaped her as she spotted her old mule galloping toward her. She had worried about what had happened to the old fellow, but hadn't asked Hawke, afraid of his answer. What if he'd told her that he'd had the old crow bait shot? The way he had complained about the mule's slowness on their trip it wouldn't have surprised her if he'd had him killed.

But her old friend was very much alive as his rough gray head poked over the corral, nudging at her shoulder. She stepped up on the bottom pole so that she could throw her arms around his short, thick neck. "I've missed you, old fellow, worried about you." She dragged an arm across the wetness of her eyes. "But look at you, getting fat and lazy. I'll have to hitch you to a plow again and get you trimmed down." Her voice was soft and teasing.

As she stood with her arms around the mule's neck, her forehead pressed against his, wondering how Jimmy and the little ones were faring, a loud clearing of a throat brought her head up and swiftly down from the pole to the ground.

"Did you want somethin', Miss . . . Mrs. Masters?" A tall man with easy, sinuous grace was coming toward her. Rue recognized him as Hawke's handsome, lean foreman, Josh Malone, a man in his late thirties. She had caught him watching her as she went to the spring for water, or hung up her wash.

She had taken no offense, though. For some reason all the ranch hands ogled her. She had reasoned that they were curious about the woman Hawke Masters refused to sleep with. It would never enter her mind that she was breathtakingly lovely, that any man would stare at her, or that even her husband did when she was unaware.

"I wanted to go riding," she explained to Josh when he stood in front of her. "Unfortunately I have no idea how to go about catching a horse and saddling him."

Gray eyes smiled down at her, then shifted to the horses that still leaned against the corral, vying for Rue's attention. "That bay mare is gentle," Malone said. "What if I saddle her up for you?" He moved to stand beside Rue, propping an elbow on top of the pole fence, uncomfortably close to her head. "You won't get lost with her either. She knows her way home if you give her the reins."

"Oh, I don't think I should ride one of Hawke's private stock." Rue looked doubtful. "I'm not all that good a rider."

Malone frowned at her curiously. "Why

152

shouldn't you ride one of his pets? It's true that none of us hired hands would be so brave as to saddle one of these beauties for himself, but you're his wife." He peered intently into Rue's eyes. "You are his wife, aren't you?"

Rue didn't mean to let her bitterness show, but it crept out in her voice when she answered, "Oh, yes, I'm his wife all right."

Malone's teasing smile faded and his eyes became serious. "But in name only, huh?" he questioned softly.

Rue's face flushed and she lowered her eyes against what she was sure she'd see in the man's face—pity, and, maybe even scorn. He wouldn't have much respect for a woman whose husband didn't want to share her bed.

Her eyes snapped open when gentle fingers stroked her cheek. As her startled gaze met Malone's, he said, as if to himself, "Masters is blind to turn his back on . . ."

Rue moved back before he could finish his sentence, and the palm that had cupped her cheek was removed, and the conversation brought back to the original one.

"Should I saddle the mare then?" the ranch foreman asked, a slight huskiness in his voice. When Rue looked undecided, he said, almost impatiently, "For heaven's sake, woman, he's not gonna beat his own wife for ridin' one of his horses, is he?"

"No, of course not." Rue squared her shoulders. "Go ahead and get the mare ready." She smiled at Malone and added, "Please."

"Good girl." Her smile was returned, and fifteen minutes later she was being swung astride the little mount, fighting her skirt down over her knees.

"Don't ride too far, and always keep the house in sight," Malone cautioned, handing her the reins. "And for Lord's sake, take that worried look off your face. Masters may never know you rode the mare."

That's true, Rue thought, and relaxed at that possibility. She lifted a hand in farewell and turned the mare's head in the direction of the mountain, unaware that thoughtful gray eyes stared after her.

Rue reveled in the mount's smooth, rocking lope. How different it was from her old mule's spine-jolting trot, she mused, deciding that she would ride down the valley instead of up the mountain. She would tackle the rougher region when she was a more accomplished rider.

After about an hour, the little mare responded at once at the tightening of the reins, and stood quietly in the shade of a cottonwood as Rue stared back in the direction from where she'd ridden. She could still see the house, so she turned around to look ahead. She could see the distant river, cutting a threadlike gash through the valley, and could see on either side of it a sea of cattle. An incessant bawling rent the air, and Rue held her breath as a dozen riders rode among the cattle, separating calves from mothers. She watched the youngsters being driven off to one side where a fire burned, heating branding irons she was sure. She wondered how badly the red-hot irons hurt the young animals as one was thrown on its side and Hawke's brand pressed into its haunch.

When the calf was released and ran bellowing to its mother, Rue swung her gaze around the valley. Was there a more beautiful spot in the world? she wondered. In less than the two weeks she'd been here, she had found a near contentment. She couldn't call it happiness, knowing that she wasn't truly wanted, that her presence was actually an aggravation.

A small frown worried her forehead. She still hadn't figured out why Hawke had married her. She didn't do a great deal for him. Only cooked his meals and washed his clothes. Cookie, who made the ranch hands meals could have fed him too, had in all likelihood done it before.

Lillie Meyers's lush curves appeared in Rue's mind and her eyes widened. Of course. Why hadn't she thought of that before? Hawke had married her as a smoke screen to alter Sam Meyers's suspicions that his wife was sleeping with his handsome neighbor.

Rue's bottom lip drooped. Her husband was crazy if he thought someone like herself could throw the cattleman off the trail. The man was sharp and wouldn't be fooled for a minute, especially after finding her sitting alone on the porch while his wife entertained Hawke in the house.

She shook her head. She was afraid her husband was courting a bullet in his heart.

The thought became more forceful a few minutes later when turning north, she saw a rider galloping toward the herd. Her lips tightened. She'd know those broad shoulders anywhere. Where had he been? At the Meyers ranch to visit Lillie?

When she saw Hawke veer Captain in her direction, she turned the mare's head toward the river into a loping run. She was going to catch hell from him for riding one of his horses, and she didn't want the hands to hear it.

Rue didn't know it, but Hawke had been watching her for ten minutes before galloping down the valley. She also didn't know that this was his habit to watch her when she was unaware of it. Had someone told her that she fascinated Hawke, she would have asked if that person had been smoking locoweed.

Nevertheless it was true. It had started the day Hawke took the time to take a good look at his wife, to see what it was about her that made his men's eyes follow her every time she was outside.

He had been stunned by her delicate beauty. In the past he had been mesmerized by the glorious color of her hair, but he'd had no idea that she had a face equal in loveliness. And if that wasn't enough, her cool aloofness, her obvious dislike of him, drew Hawke like the West drew the sun. Each day he had to fight harder the desire to grab her, carry her into the bedroom and make love to her until they were both exhausted.

As Rue had thought, Hawke had come from visiting Lillie at the line shack. But not to indulge in a couple of hours of lust. He had gone this morning to break off their relationship. Besides no longer having a desire for her, his young wife had made him ashamed of his affair. That was a new emotion for him and he didn't like it at all.

When Hawke told Lillie that he would no longer be meeting her at the shack, black anger shot out of her eyes. He prepared himself for a screeching onslaught of recrimination from the twisted, painted lips, then blinked at the change that came over the coarse features.

"I understand," she said, her voice and eyes soft. "The new wife, and all. Actually, it's been on my mind that we should stop seeing each other. Sam is becoming suspicious and I don't want to chance losing my comfortable life."

She held out her hand. "From now on we'll only meet as neighbors, all right?"

Hawke had heartily shaken her hand, relieved that she had taken his decision so well. As he rode away, however, he didn't know that Lillie watched him with grim determination. Nor did he know that as she stood there Sly Burford rode up and swung to the ground beside her.

The river was at a low level, Rue noted as she rode alongside it. She'd heard Hawke complain that there hadn't been any rain for a month, and that the grass was drying up. "We'll be drivin' a bunch of bones to market," he'd added sourly.

Rue looked over her shoulder again to see if the house was still in view. She smiled. There it was, drowsing in the sunshine, old and mellow with memories. Mostly good ones, she imagined. She could visualize a young couple setting up housekeeping, in love, raising a family derived from that love.

Unlike my mockery of a marriage, Rue thought, turning her head from the old house. She sighed resignedly and quelled the unhappy thoughts that nagged her.

She had just decided to return to the house when she heard bawling a few yards down the river. It sounded like one of the herd was in trouble and shifting the mare from a leisurely walk into a long, running lope, she rode toward the distressful sound.

Moments later she was murmuring, "Ah, poor thing," as she reined in and slid from the saddle. At the edge of the river, a yearling was stuck in the mud, almost to his belly. The more he struggled to free himself, the deeper he sank.

Oh dear, how could she help him? Rue stared down at the mud-roiled water. The bank sloped sharply to the stream, its summit about ten feet high. She studied the threshing animal thoughtfully a moment, then scrambled down the slippery bank and slid into the water. She briefly worried about her dress, hoping it wouldn't be stained beyond redemption.

But the dress was soon forgotten as the river brought her dangerously close to the steer's head, its eyes rolling in terror, the lethal long horns swinging from side to side. She carefully dodged them while making her way to the animal's rear end. There, she hoped to push it free of the sucking mud.

Putting a hand on each broad hip, Rue pushed with all her strength. She received a mud-heavy tail across her face for her trouble. The animal hadn't budged an inch. And worse, she could no longer see the beginning of the animal's belly.

She was standing mid-thigh in the brown, swirling water, trying to get up the nerve to approach one of the cowboys for help, when Hawke brought Captain to a sliding halt on the riverbank. He took in the young steer's dilemma, and in seconds he was off his horse and grabbing the looped rope off the pommel. As Rue silently watched, he tied one end to the saddle horn and fashioned a loop on the other end.

"Stand back," he ordered as he twirled a running noose over his head.

Rue started to scramble out of the way just as he let the rope swing out toward the yearling's head. Instead, it struck Rue's shoulder, and fell limply into the water.

"Damn it to hell!" Hawke yelled furiously as he glared at Rue. "I told you to stand back!"

"Don't yell at me, you ornery rattlesnake!" Rue yelled back. "You didn't give me time to get out of the way. It's not easy, moving around with soaked skirts hampering my movements."

"Well, don't just stand there," Hawke shot back as he began to widen the rope for another toss at the steer. "I don't know what in the hell you're doin' down there in the first place."

"I don't either," Rue muttered angrily, sloughing her way toward the bank. She should have known the varmint wouldn't appreciate anything she tried to do.

The loop swung out again, this time encircling the six-foot spread of horns, then settling neatly over the narrow head. With a word to Captain, the horse moved backward until the rope was taut. Hawke pulled off his boots and socks, then wading into the water, he moved behind the frightened bull. Putting his shoulder to the bony rump, he gave a short, sharp whistle.

Rue gaped as the horse responded to the whistled order by moving backward while Hawke pushed the animal from behind. Slowly the animal was inched from the drawing mire. Hawke hurriedly slipped the rope off its head, and freed, it lunged up the bank, heading for the herd, its tail straight up in the air.

Winding the rope from hand to bent elbow, Hawke scowled at Rue and criticized her sharply. "Why didn't you go for help? While you were dillydallying, the animal could have broken a leg."

Damn him! Rue fumed, her throat tight with anger as she climbed the bank behind him. He always had to find fault with her. She opened her mouth to retort that she was going for help when he arrived, but the words didn't leave her mouth. Hawke, in his hurry to scale the gravelly riverbank, was slipping and sliding, struggling not to fall on his face. He twisted his body violently to regain his footing, and would have succeeded had she not been following so closely behind him. She reached out a hand to steady him but only got in his way. He tottered an instant, then fell back into the water, tumbling her along with him.

The water splashed in a fine mist and Rue blindly clutched at Hawke, grabbing his shoulders. She breathlessly clung to his hard, warm body, staring down at the blue water swirling around them. It took her a moment to realize that strong, possessive arms had wrapped themselves around her waist. When Hawke pulled her tightly against his body, his breathing fast and harsh, she grew alarmed. She gazed into his eyes and saw the light of desire illuminating them.

"Let me go!" she panted, pushing against his shoulders. "I don't want—"

Hawke's mouth swooped down to take hers, silencing her. *I don't want this*, she cried inwardly as she twisted and turned her head, trying to free herself from the deepening kiss, the tongue that darted around in her mouth, coaxing and teasing.

Suddenly, without warning Rue's body quivered in response. She sagged against Hawke, every nerve awake in her body. He gave a sigh of satisfaction and his hand slid to her breasts as he moved against her, purposely making her aware of his arousal. She moaned softly, lost in a passion she'd never known existed. She was unaware of the slim fingers that loosened her buttons, freeing her breasts.

"Ah," she whispered when a warm mouth opened over one breast and urgent lips suckled and tugged at the nipple. *I wish it could go on forever*, she thought as Hawke moved his head to take the other breast into his mouth, his lips drawing on it as his fingers stroked the wet, abandoned one.

The spell was abruptly broken when Hawke raised his head and looked into her face. With an almost dazed look in his eyes, he said harshly, almost as if against his will, "God, how I want you."

All too clearly Becky's face appeared before her, along with all the men who had lusted after her mother. They had wanted Becky also, but none had loved her. And neither did Hawke Masters love his wife. He only wanted to use Rue, to bring release to that appendage that jabbed at her.

Well, by God, the daughter wasn't like the mother. Although it was true she had learned she was capable of passion, that her blood could race in desire, she would not play the whore for any man. Not even a husband.

Hawke was unaware of Rue's inner turmoil and she had no trouble freeing herself from his loosened hold on her. He stared at her in bewilderment when with stormy eyes she gritted out, "Want and be damned!"

She struck out for the bank again, her fingers clumsy as she rebuttoned her bodice.

"Where in the hell are you goin'?" Hawke raged behind her. "You little whore, you can't just walk away from a man after drivin' him crazy with wantin' you."

"The hell I can't!" Rue yelled back, stung to her soul by what he'd called her. "It's my body and I can do whatever I want with it. And I don't choose to let you use it."

She swung onto the mare's back, her wet dress clinging to her thighs. She glared down at Hawke still standing in the water and bit out, "I am no whore, Hawke Masters, and don't ever forget that! No man will ever slake his lust on Rue DeLawney's body."

"Like hell," Hawke growled as Rue sent the mount galloping toward the house. "You're a little pepper pot if ever I saw one. You can't go much longer without havin' a man between your legs again."

But as Hawke waded out of the river, climbed onto the stallion, and followed along behind her, he wished with all his being that it wasn't so. He would give all he owned to be the first man with Rue. The first and the last.

As Rue reined in the mare next to the stables, she was angrily aware of the dull ache that still coiled in her loins, and the tenderness of her nipples. As she swung to the ground, her self-disgust was so intense she felt sick from it. What had she been thinking of to allow him such intimacy?

"I hate and despise that man," she muttered, then wondered what to do with the mare. She felt confident that she could unsaddle the little mount, but where would she put everything once she had stripped the animal. She hadn't seen where the attractive ranch foreman had taken everything from, and he didn't seem to be around to help her now.

Rue suddenly felt the presence of someone, or something, behind her. She swung around and uttered a small cry of alarm. An old Indian with snowy-white hair straggling to his shoulders, and a deeply wrinkled face, stood staring stoically at her. His hand rested on the head of a young boy about eight years old.

Don't be afraid, she told herself. How could these two harm her, one so old the other so young? She forced a quivering smile to her lips.

"My name is Rue De . . . Masters." She stepped away from the mare. "Is there something I can do for you?"

Both pair of black eyes were fastened on her hair, the sun making it look like silver-streaked gold. And though the younster continued to stare at her, the old brave brought his gaze to her face. He withdrew an envelope from the breast pocket of his buckskin jacket.

"White man give me this." He held the much-handled envelope to her. "He say find Masters's ranch and give it to the mistress there."

"Oh, thank you!" A smile lit up Rue's face. "It must be from my grandparents."

The stony-faced Indian shrugged his shoulders, then speaking a word to the boy, turned to leave.

"Don't go yet." Rue took a step toward the pair. "Won't you have a cup of coffee first?"

She smiled at the youngster and added, "I baked some cookies this morning. I think you'd like them."

"No . . . thank you. We must be on our way," the old man refused proudly.

Rue saw the disappointment in the boy's eyes and suggested softly, "Couldn't I please give some to your grandson to eat along the way?"

The red man's stern features softened a bit when he read the silent plea in his grandson's eyes. Then he nodded and said, "The small brave has developed a liking for the white man's sweets."

Rue ignored the slight disapproval in the old man's guttural tone and raced to the house where she tied a good amount of sugar cookies in a piece of clean rag. Hurrying back to the stables, she handed them over to the boy. "What's your name?" she asked when he grinned his thanks.

"He is called Little Star," the grandfather answered.

She waited for the old man to give his own name, but when it was not forthcoming, she said, "Well, I am happy to know you, Little Star, and I thank you and your grandfather for bringing me this letter. It is very important to me."

With a curt nod from the old man, they disappeared into the pine woods behind the stables. Rue shook her head, then turned back to care for the mare, anxious to hurry to the house and read her letter.

She stared, bewildered. The mare was gone. "Oh, God!" she gasped, feeling dizzy. Had the old Indian taken the horse and hidden her while she was in the house getting the cookies for his grandchild? She hoped not. She would be greatly disappointed if that were the case, for he had seemed like a nice man even if he hadn't been very friendly.

Hawke will absolutely beat me if I've lost his prize horse, Rue thought, ready to weep. She leaned dispiritedly on the corral, only half noticing the pall of dust and sand in the far corner of the pen. When from the yellow cloud a horse appeared and shook itself, it took her a couple of seconds to recognize the little mare.

"Well, I'll be." She smiled, weak with relief. "The old Indian took care of her while I was gone." Then she hurried to the house, anticipating the news from home.

Hawke, concealed beneath a large, low-spreading pine, had watched Rue and the Indians through narrowed, brooding eyes. He was discovering that there was more to this girl than just a beautiful face. She had been so hard, so cold, back in the shack from which he had rescued her. She had shown some softness for her older brother, it was true, but he hadn't seen any affection for the smaller children. Yet, with the Indian boy she had been kindness itself. And she had felt pity for the dumb stray that had got himself mired in the mud. Surprisingly also, she was a fine cook, he'd never seen better. And she kept the almost-bare house spotlessly clean.

Had he read her wrong? Was she a decent young woman? He remembered then how Sly had talked about her, right in front of her, and directed a scornful grunt at himself. "She's no virgin," he muttered, and wheeling Captain, loped back toward his men.

CHAPTER SEVEN

Rue thought Hawke would never finish eating breakfast and leave the house. She wanted to read her grandmother's letter again. She knew that she was being silly, for she had already read it three times and knew almost every word by heart. But it comforted her to handle something the dear old woman had held, to see the words she had penciled.

She slid Hawke a sideways look, wondering why he was dawdling this morning. Usually he gulped his breakfast down and was gone from the house within fifteen minutes. And last night he hadn't even put in an appearance for supper.

Leaning against the dry sink, sipping her coffee, Rue remembered that she hadn't been surprised when Hawke hadn't eaten the meal she had prepared. He and his foreman had fought because of her in the late afternoon, and Hawke coming out on the short end of the argument had taken his spleen out on her by staying away at mealtime.

The argument had been in progress when she had stepped outside to cool off from the heat of the kitchen range. "Just understand that the girl is not to ride off unless I give the word," Hawke had said angrily.

Then Josh Malone had come back just as heatedly, "Why do you keep callin' her 'girl'? She has a name. If you can't bring yourself to say 'wife', at least refer to her as Rue."

"It's none of your damn business what I call her. And like you said, she's my wife and you can damn well stay away from her."

"Why? You don't give a damn about her. You think more of Meyers's whore."

There was a silence, then Hawke blustered, "I don't know what in the hell you're talkin' about."

"Like hell you don't. All the hands know that you sneak off once a week to meet ole Lil, waller around with her for a couple of hours. You've been seen out there with her." There was another silence, then Josh added in a calmer voice, "If we know about it, Hawke, so do Meyers's men. It's just a matter of time before one of them gets up the nerve to tell the old man about it. He'll come after you with his guns blazin'."

Rue hadn't waited for Hawke's reply, but had hurried back into the house, strangely wanting to cry. She told herself now, as she waited for the silent man to leave the table, that it had been hurt pride that made tears smart her eyes. Any woman's pride would feel trampled on, knowing that her husband preferred a whore to his wife.

Hawke's thoughts were also on the argument he'd had with his foreman as he lingered over his coffee. He'd been too stubborn and proud to tell Josh that he'd made his last trip to the line shack, and that his young wife had all his attention now. And yesterday, when he said all those hurtful things to her, calling her a whore, he was sorry for them as soon as they left his mouth. He owed her an apology.

He sighed silently. He was trying to get up the nerve to do it this morning. That was why he kept sitting here like a bullfrog on a lily pad. And he owed it to her to explain that his father, niece, and nephew would be showing up any day now, that she would have the extra burden of taking care of the children, plus more work all round.

Hawke was suddenly struck with a disturbing thought. What if Rue left when she learned of the underhanded trick he'd played on her? Josh Malone was crazy about her and wouldn't hesitate to take her away. Nor would any of the others refuse her, he thought glumly. It hadn't escaped him how their hungry eyes followed her every time she stepped outside.

Well, then, you'd better spit it out, Masters, he told himself. *You can't sit here all day. Give her the apology she deserves.*

Hawke cleared his voice and looked up to give his prepared speech and looked around, dumbfounded. The room was empty. In her usual fashion, his girl-wife had slipped away.

"Damn!" He pushed his coffee cup away in irritation. He wasn't going to chase after her like some lovesick calf. If Pa and the kids surprised her by arriving today, it would be her fault.

All too aware that his reasoning was that of a spoiled child, Hawke jerked to his feet and stamped through the door, slamming it behind him.

In her room, Rue's lips curled in satisfaction. She hoped he was so angry he would choke on his bile. "It will do you good to get your tail out of joint once in a while, Mr. Masters," she muttered, then smoothed out her grandmother's letter.

September 11, 1868

Dearest granddaughter,
Your granddad met this man who is traveling to Jackson, Colorado, and he agreed to take a letter to you if he can find your husband's ranch. I hope it eventually falls

into your hands.

Many things have happened since you left. First, Sly Burford never came back. I guess he took your husband's money and left the state. Becky's little ones were taken in by different families here in the area. At least now they will have a chance in life, and enought to eat. And this will surprise you, I guess, but Jimmy is living with us. I never realized what a nice youngster he is. He's such a help, and keeps us from missing you a little.

Rue, dear, Granddad and I pray every day that your marriage works out although it had such a rough start. John is sure that your reluctant husband is an honorable man despite his rough ways and will never be mean to you. And that is very important in a marriage, honey. Sometimes more important than love. I have seen those who profess love for their wives, then turn around and beat them unmercifully. To me, that is a poor kind of love.

So, Rue, if you have to settle for respect only from Mister Masters, you will be better off than most women.

I must close now, dear granddaughter, the man is anxious to leave. Granddad and Jimmy send their love. Our thoughts and prayers are always with you.

        Love, Grandma.

Rue let the letter drop into her lap and stared sightlessly out the window. "Ah, Grandma," she whispered, "I don't even get respect from my husband. Yesterday, if I would have allowed him, he'd have used me like a whore."

She folded the letter and slid it back into the envelope. Although she had no idea how she'd ever get a letter to her grandparents, later on she would write to them. Write some lies that would make them rest easier about her.

Shoving the white square under her pillow, Rue walked into the big front room and stood a moment before continuing on to the kitchen. Her glance ranged around the clean-swept floor and wondered if the two chairs in front of the huge fireplace were the only pieces of furniture she'd ever have in the parlor. She imagined they would be. Even if it should enter Hawke Master's mind that she might like a few more items, like curtains at the windows for privacy, he wouldn't bother to purchase them. He probably felt that as long as he provided her with a bed and food to eat that was sufficient for the likes of her. He had seen the conditions in which she lived when he married her and he would never dream that she yearned for more, that her heart cried out for some beauty in her life.

"Naturally he doesn't care if the house is comfortable," she muttered, "He only enters it twice a day to fill his gut." She consoled herself with the thought that at least she didn't have to worry anymore about Sly trying to harm her, as she walked into the kitchen.

That in itself is something to be thankful for, she thought as she began scrubbing her good dress that had been soaking over night. She prayed the muddy stains would come out. There was no telling how long the dress would have to last her, and she would never ask her husband for a new one. She would wear his castoffs first.

Her lips twisted wryly, as she examined the dress for stains. Actually having to wear his clothes might not be too far off. The dress was becoming a bit snug as she continued to gain weight. The darts in the bodice strained over her breasts so, that she was afraid that any day the seams might split apart. She didn't know what she would do then. She had no needle and thread.

Rue carefully wrung the water from the garment and carried it outside where she spread it over a bush to dry. She stood a moment, examining the rose bush that had responded to its daily watering and was covered now with a profusion of blooms. She picked a few fat pink buds, and in the kitchen she found a jelly jar and filled it with water. She sniffed the flowers' sweet, heady fragrance, then placed the stems in the jar.

She had just finished washing the breakfast

dishes and sweeping the floor when the sunlight in the open door was blackened out. She spun around and almost dropped the broom when she saw Hawke standing there. As she watched him, he entered and laid a chunk of freshly butchered beef on the table.

"I thought we'd have a roast for supper," he said gruffly as Rue stared at the piece of raw meat.

She looked up at him, then back at the blood oozing onto her clean table. Good Lord, it must weigh at least five pounds, she thought in bemusement. Way too much for the two of them.

She pushed a strand of hair behind her ear. Not to mention how the kitchen would heat up. She'd have to keep the old range fired up for at least two hours. She looked back up at Hawke and found him regarding her intently. *He looks as though he wants to say something*, she thought, and waited for him to speak. But after shifting his feet, he turned and left.

And while Rue was placing the beef into a big roasting pan, Hawke swung angrily into the saddle. "Why in the hell did I lose my nerve?" he muttered. "Why didn't I just up and tell her that Pa and the kids will be here in an hour or so?"

One of his hands had reported to him that he had talked to Hawke's father earlier, and that Pa was about ten miles away. Hawke rode off, cursing himself for being a coward, as he headed toward the branding site. He was slinking off like a coyote, lacking the courage to be at the ranch when his family arrived.

Rue watched Hawke ride away, gripped by a restless foreboding. In the next hour she made numerous trips to the window, looking for what she did not know.

She had just put the roast in the oven when she heard the creaking of wheels and the clinking of harnesses and traces. She hurried through the house to the front door. She stood immobilized, her lips parted in surprise.

A large prairie schooner was pulled up alongside the porch, a pair of tired mules hitched to it. When she lifted her gaze to the man on the high springboard seat, then shifted it to the two youngsters sitting beside him, many things became clear to her.

There was no mistaking who the smiling older man was. His resemblance to Hawke was startling. And the children, although not green-eyed, shared some of his features.

She was gripped with anger and bitterness. Her deceitful husband had married her to raise his children. And he thought so little of her, was so careless of her feelings, that he hadn't even thought it necessary to tell her. She thought of the big piece of meat in the oven and knew why it was so large. The conniving devil had known there would be extra people at the table tonight.

Rue drew in a breath that was half sigh, half sob. There was nothing she could do about it. God knew she had no say-so in this household. She was no better than a housekeeper. Not even as important. A housekeeper would have been asked if she was willing to care for two children.

Making sure that her face did not show her thoughts, she stepped onto the porch when Hawke's father jumped to the ground. He was a tall, thin man with a weather-wrinkled face and thick gray hair that retained a shading of black in it. She responded to his friendly smile and gripped the work-roughened hand he extended to her. If only his son was so nice, she couldn't help thinking.

The kindly green eyes wrinkled with speculation as he gazed into Rue's still stunned face. "I'll bet that son of mine didn't tell you that we'd be arriving today."

An almost hysterical fit of laughter rose in Rue's throat. Her husband never found it necessary to tell her anything. She managed a careless shrug. "He's always so busy, he probably forgot," she said quietly.

Jeb Masters ran a glance over the vast and lonely land that stretched as far as his eye could see. "Hawke said he'd have a housekeeper by the time we arrived but I had my doubts he'd find a woman who'd be content to live in such loneliness." He turned back to

Rue and smiled. "Let alone one so young and pretty."

Would Hawke try to pass her off as his housekeeper? Rue wondered. She wouldn't put it past him to try. Suddenly she was tired of being treated like something shameful, something to be kept secret if possible, providing gossip for the cowhands. She lifted her chin proudly and said clearly, "I'm not the housekeeper, Mr. Masters. I'm your son's wife."

She looked down at her old raggedy dress, her good one hadn't dried yet, at the scuffed moccasins Hawke had given her, then back at the father she was sure would reject her claim. Her amazement was total as the elder Masters opened his arms with a wide smile.

"I can't believe it!" he exclaimed, his long arms wrapping around her shoulders, giving her a warm hug. "I had about given up on my firstborn ever giving me a daughter-in-law."

Tears scalded Rue's eyes. She was wanted, was appreciated—at least by Hawke's father. She blinked away the tears as Jeb released her and turned to lift his arms to the small girl who had sat next to him. "This is Susie." He set the child on her feet.

The little one was five or so, Rue judged, blond-haired with a crop of freckles across her nose. She stood close to her grandfather's leg, a finger in her mouth, shy and doubtful, as she watched Rue. But when Rue smiled warmly at the little girl and spoke her name gently, she smiled shyly, showing that she was missing a tooth in front.

"And this is Tommy," Jeb said proudly, a hand on the shoulder of the ten-year-old who had jumped from the wagon.

Rue nodded solemnly at the shy youngster, and to make him feel like an adult, she offered her hand to him and said gravely, "I'm happy to meet you, Tommy."

The lad's surprise, followed quickly by a pleased, blushing smile, told Rue that she had made a fast friend. Nor did she miss his grandfather's appreciative look. "There's a platter of cookies on the table in the kitchen," she said. "If you're hungry, go help yourself."

Forgetting his promotion to adulthood, Tommy grabbed his sister's hand and raced through the house. Rue grinned after them as their childish voices broke the usual brooding silence of the old house. She turned back to Jeb Masters. "I take it their mother is dead."

"As well as their father." Jeb nodded sadly, not noticing Rue's surprise. As he told of the death of his younger son and daughter-in-law, Rue angrily asked herself why she should be glad that Hawke wasn't the children's father. She didn't care in the least if he'd been married before.

She blinked, coming back to the present when Jeb asked, "Are you used to children?

Do you like them?"

Rue took a moment to mull over his question. Yes, she was used to children, but not ones like these two who were smiling and healthy. As for liking children, she truly didn't know. She hadn't liked her poor little half brothers. Their constant, hungry whining had made her life a misery.

But as for these two bright children, she was sure she would like them. "The answer is yes to both questions, Mr. Masters." She smiled.

"Hey, now." Jeb laughed. "If you don't feel like callin' me Pa, at least call me Jeb."

Rue returned the friendly grin. "All right . . . Jeb. And you must call me Rue."

"I'll do that . . . Rue." Jeb mocked her hesitation at his name. They both laughed then Jeb said, "I wonder if there's anyone around who could give me a hand with unloadin' the wagon."

"Well, I don't know," Rue said doubtfully. "I think everyone is helping with the branding."

The last part of her sentence was drowned out as a horse thundered into the yard, scattering a cloud of dust and gravel. Hawke was out of the saddle before his mount had completely come to a halt. Pumping his father's hand and thumping him on the back, he exclaimed, "I see you made it, and in good time. Where are the children?" He looked around, avoiding Rue's eyes.

"Here we are, Uncle Hawke," young Tommy yelled, and threw himself off the porch to wrap his arms around the smiling man's lean waist.

Rue felt an unexplained jab to her heart as she watched her husband affectionately knuckle Tommy's head, his face softening with the love he felt for his nephew. She wondered if there had ever been a woman who had brought that same look in his eyes. When he made love to Lillie, did his face show the same tenderness?

Her ruminating was cut short as Susie, calling her uncle's name, burst through the door, tripped on a loose board and fell flat on her stomach. Simultaneously Rue and Hawke rushed to pick up the crying child. Hawke reached her first, and looked a little put out when the little one pulled away from him and stretched her arms out to Rue.

And that was the moment love for the little orphan girl blossomed inside Rue. She held the plump, warm body close to her breast, crooning sympathic words of comfort. This little one would be the daughter she would never have herself. She didn't see the uncertain look in Hawke's green eyes as he hunkered beside her. She did feel the warm strength of his hands as they gripped her arms and lifted her to her feet, Susie still clinging to her like a little monkey.

Rue tried to ignore the excitement Hawke's

touch had caused to shiver through her body when he ventured in a conciliatory tone, "I should have told you that Pa and the kids would be makin' their home with us. It was just that I—"

He broke off his faltering apology, an uneasiness growing inside him. While he had talked to her, she hadn't once looked at him, only stared straight ahead, her face closed and stony. It was clear his wife wasn't interested in his excuses.

He dropped his hands from her arms, and continuing to ignore him, Rue walked into the house, speaking softly to Susie, asking her if she would like to help her make a raisin pie.

As Rue's musical low voice and Susie's high treble faded into the region of the kitchen, Hawke continued to stand on the porch, confusion running through his mind. "Why should I care about her good opinion?" he muttered finally, jumping off the porch and striding over to the wagon to help unload the many articles his father had packed. Still, as he lifted out boxes and crates, his mind was on his wife.

Rue never got around to baking the pie. She had just lifted a bag of flour onto the table when her father-in-law appeared at the kitchen door. "Come show us where you want everything put, Rue," he said cheerfully.

Rue stared at him, her hands still gripping

the bag. This very nice man didn't know the situation in this household. He didn't know that her opinion was considered lower than anyone on the ranch.

While she searched for words that Jeb Masters would understand and accept, Hawke appeared behind his father. "Why don't you leave the pie for tomorrow night's supper?" he said, a smile tugging at his lips, but not quite confirmed.

Rue eyed him suspiciously, trying to read what was in his eyes. There was some reason he was behaving in a half-decent manner to her. He had never before involved her in anything that went on around here.

She knew suddenly that it had to do with his father. He wanted that honorable man to think that theirs was a normal marriage, one made from love. Well, she wouldn't be a part of his deception.

But when she looked at Jeb, ready to tell him the whole wretched story, the happy expectation on his face stopped her.

Sliding Hawke a look that said he wasn't fooling her with his sudden congenial manner, she returned the flour to the cupboard and followed them outside with Susie at her heels.

The first items to come out of the wagon were rolls of hand-loomed carpets. Enough for each room in the house, Rue thought happily, barring the kitchen, of course. When the largest one had been smoothed out on the parlor floor, Jeb looked at it with pride and sadness.

"Hawke, it took your mother three years to fashion this floor covering on her loom. She wove it into six-foot widths, then joined the strips together.

"Its good and sturdy, Rue." He bent over and ran a palm over the woven material. "It'll last you a lifetime, and the colors won't fade either. Hawke's mother dyed the strips of cloth with sassafras root before she strung them though the loom."

Rue dropped to her knees beside Jeb, and running her own palm over the soft red carpet, said softly, "It's beautiful, Jeb, and I'll do all in my power to keep it this way."

"I know you will, daughter." Jeb rose and helped her to her feet.

Hawke and his father had just finished laying out the carpets in each room when the cowhands rode in. "Come on, men," Hawke called, "give me and Pa a hand with the furniture."

With much laughing and joking, and getting into each other's way, beds were carried in and set up in the rooms Rue thought were appropriate for each member of the family. Then dressers, chifforobes, tables, chairs, and a settee were carried in.

Her face aglow with pleasure, Rue rushed around in an excited daze as she directed the furniture's placement. She felt like a child at Christmas or at least the way she imagined children felt on that special day. She had no way of knowing. Christmas at the hilltop shack had been like any other day—bodies shivering with the cold and bellys aching from hunger.

Finally everything was out of the wagon and put in its proper place, leaving only some food staples and a half-dozen barrels sitting on the rickety porch to be stored away at a later date. Jeb explained that the barrels contained bed linens, curtains, clothes, and some little gee-gaws his daughter-in-law had to brighten up the rooms on their farm.

"I didn't leave a damn thing for that damn German who bought the place," he said in vexed tones. "He argued me price on every animal and every piece of farm machinery. I didn't leave him so much as a straw from my old broom."

Also on the porch was a big black cookstove. Every time Rue walked past it, she eyed it with pleasure. Until the rusty old thing in the kitchen cooled off, the new stove couldn't be moved in. She smiled in anticipation. She couldn't wait to test her culinary skills on such a grand piece.

In between directing where the furniture should be placed, Rue had snatched up a squash from the porch, one of many Jeb had brought from his garden, and put it in a pan alongside the beef roast to bake. She had also found the time to peel potatoes and to boil them in a cook pot. And now that the cowhands had left and the house had settled down, she carried a stack of plates to the smoothly finished table that had replaced the old crude and scarred one.

As Rue lifted the roast from the oven, she smiled at the little girl, who hadn't let her out of sight. "Do you want to put the silverware and glasses beside each plate?"

Susie nodded eagerly, and as the beef sat in its own juices, Rue mashed the potatoes, then whipped canned milk into their fluffy whiteness. When everything was ready, she sent the little girl to tell the Masters menfolk that it was suppertime.

Everyone dug in with hearty appetites, Jeb declaring that he had never eaten more tender, tastier beef. As usual, Hawke didn't say anything about the food he shoveled into his mouth, but when Rue sent him a resentful look she was surprised to see pride in his face. Was it possible he was proud of her cooking? she asked herself, then mentally shook her head. He was probably thinking about his horses and cattle; they made him proud.

Darkness had set in by the time the evening meal was finished. As Rue lit the lamps, she noted that Susie was nodding over her plate, her eyes half-closed. She smiled tenderly at the child. It had been a long tiring day for the little one.

Jeb, too, had seen his granddaughter drowsing. "Hawke," he said, "fetch in that barrel of bed linens so Rue can get Susie settled in."

Rue lingered in the kitchen until she thought Hawke had finished his task. She walked toward the hall, then came to an abrupt halt. Hawke lounged in the doorway. She knew that he wouldn't budge, that he meant for her to squeeze past him. Oh, how she'd like to slap the devilish amusement off his handsome face.

But that would please him, she knew. It would give him the excuse to retaliate, in God knew what way. Maybe to kiss her. And by no means must that happen. There was but one way to get by him.

She lifted her chin and plowed past him, knocking him off balance. This time she was amused as his disgruntled swearing followed her. "Randy bastard," she muttered, entering the bedroom next to hers.

Rue hurriedly made up the bed, then went back to the kitchen to wash Susie's face and hands. By the time a nightgown was pulled over the child's head, she was falling asleep. Rue tucked her between the blankets and smoothed a blond tress off Susie's rosy cheek, then straightening up, hurried to put linens on Tommy's bed across the hall from his sister's. He had looked ready for bed also. She would do the other beds when she got around to them, she decided.

It was at least an hour before Rue finished washing the dishes, pots, and pans and got back to making beds. She entered Jeb's room first, next to his grandson's. As she smoothed on sheets and a light blanket, she could hear father and son talking on the porch, could see the glowing ends of their cigarettes as they drew on them. The Masters were a close-knit family, she thought, and suddenly wished that she was a part of it.

"Wipe such thoughts out of your mind, girl," she whispered. "You're no more than a hired hand around here, and that's all you'll ever be."

Rue's body sagged from fatigue when finally there remained only her own bed to prepare. She had the sheets on and was ready to smooth on a blanket when Hawke walked into the room. After one swift glance at him, she carried on as though she wasn't aware of his intense study of her face.

She looks about fifteen, Hawke thought, *with her hair pulled back and tied with a strip of rawhide.* He smiled wryly. It had been no teenager he'd held and kissed that day in the river, he remembered. An unwonted arousal suddenly pushed against the front of his trousers just thinking about it. She had forgotten herself and responded to him, arousing him as no other woman ever had. Would she react to him in the same way again? he wondered.

He walked slowly to the foot of the bed. "Nice large bed," he said offhandedly. "Plenty of room for two."

Rue gave him a startled look and frowned at the serene confidence glowing in his green eyes. Was he hinting that he would share this bed with her tonight? Had he decided to claim his nuptial rights? Her lips firmed in a tight line. She hoped not, for he would be in for a big surprise if he thought that.

She glanced down at the suspicious bulge in his trousers and knew that she was right. *That settles it*, she thought, *and I'm not going to pretend that I don't know what he's talking about.* There would be no beating around the bush, no unmeaningful sweet talk.

She gave the blanket a last smoothing pat and straightened up. "Look," she ground out the word, her blue eyes stormier than usual, "if you think you're going to share this bed with me, you've been out in the sun too long."

Hawke's confident smile didn't falter. He'd expected her to reject his idea at first, but he would talk her into it. If he could just get his arms around her, fasten his mouth on her ripe, red lips, she'd soon melt and eagerly accept him into her bed.

The argument he gave Rue was true, as well as the fact that he wanted her dreadfully. "Look, Rue," he began coaxingly, "Pa will think it strange if we don't sleep together. He's old-fashioned that way.'' He waited a moment to play what he felt was his trump card, the one he was sure she was waiting to see. "I've been thinkin' a lot lately about our marriage, how it got off to a bad start. I've decided to make it a real one.''

Rue stared at Hawke in blank astonishment. *He* had decided to make this marriage work, never mind how she felt about it. Was she supposed to feel honored, bow down and kiss his hands?

Well, you're not fooling me for a minute, you randy tomcat, she thought. Oh, she realized it would probably embarrass him for his father to know that he slept in the bunkhouse with the cowboys, but he was the one who had made that decision from the beginning and, as far as she was concerned, that was the way it would continue.

But the real issue niggled in her mind. Winter was not too far off and he would be unable to visit Lillie once snow covered the valley several feet deep. So the conniving devil was trying to pave the way now, insuring that his needs would be taken care of until spring when he could return to Lillie's arms.

Her small head held proudly and with her hands on her hips, she flung at him, "You're wasting your breath, Hawke Masters. For your information, I will be the one who will decide when our marriage will be a normal one, if ever. For right now I like it just fine the way you set things up when you first brought me here. As far as I'm concerned, I see no reason to change it."

Hawke stared at Rue, thinking of a dozen reasons the present set up should be changed. The anger rolled inside him. He was damned if he would beg her. She had a hell of a nerve, refusing him entry to her bed, a woman who had slept with the likes of Sly Burford.

His eyes raked over Rue scathingly as he grated out his lie. "I didn't have in mind to make love to you. My only intention was to put up a front for Pa's benefit." And before Rue could answer that she didn't believe him for a minute, he wheeled and stalked from the room.

Left weak and trembling from her confrontation with Hawke, Rue left her room and walked out onto the front porch. She sighed and leaned against a supporting post. There was such a heaviness in her heart that she wanted to howl like one of the wolves that roamed the mountain. But crying never solved a problem, Grandma always said, and hadn't she already found that out?

A streak of lightning lit up the sky and for the first time Rue became aware of how humid the air was, its stillness. They were in for a storm. She turned and walked back into the house and on into her bedroom. She was bone-tired as she changed into her old patched dress. She couldn't sleep bare anymore, with her father-in-law and the children sharing the house.

As Rue stretched out between the sheets, delighting in the comfort of her new bed, the storm broke. Loud claps of thunder reverberated through the mountains, and the rain beat against the window, as though determined to get inside. Her lips curled sourly as she drifted off to sleep. Her high-and-mighty husband would at least be happy about the rain. The grass would become lush for his cattle and prize horses.

CHAPTER EIGHT

Hawke left the ranch house, bristling with anger. Never had a woman so vehemently refused his attention before. *She's damned painfully frank*, he swore silently, flinching at her remembered words. "Tears into a man. That sharp tongue of hers slicin' at him like a skinnin' knife," he muttered to himself as he entered the dark bunkhouse and fumbled his way to his bunk.

"And I'm damned tired of sleepin' in this boar's nest," he added under his breath. The rancid odor of dirty socks and sour body sweat seemed to hang over him like a cloud. He was reluctant to take a deep breath for fear he'd choke. He tried to shut out the different snores and snorts that beat at his ears as he tugged off his boots.

Shucking off his denims, Hawke recalled the odor of the fresh clean sheets his stubborn wife had spread over the big comfortable-looking bed and her faint rose scent.

He flung his shirt on the floor and stretched out on the thin mattress. Resting his head on his folded arms, he stared into the darkness. Things could not go on as they were, he thought, blinking as a streak of lightning zigzagged across the sky. His wife's coldness, the unappeased hunger he had for her, was interfering with everything he attempted to do whether it was rounding up cattle or settling arguments between his cowhands. Her constant rejection was driving him crazy. Hell, he didn't even want Lillie anymore.

A twinge of uneasiness stirred inside Hawke at that thought. Now thinking it over, he wasn't so sure Lillie had taken his breakup with her as calmly as she had pretended. He knew she was a vindictive bitch, and he wouldn't be at all surprised if she showed up at the ranch someday. There would be hell to pay if she said the wrong thing in front of Pa. He'd nail his eldest son's hide on the barn door.

As for Rue, he sighed ruefully, she wouldn't give a damn what Lillie might say.

Another streak of lightning lit up the night, followed by a loud roll of thunder and the hard pelting of rain on the roof. Its fierceness distracted Hawke's musings about his wife. At last the infernal heat would break and the grass would become green again. His herd would be fit by the time the cattle drive began, a drive of two hundred miles to the nearest railyard.

Hawke's thoughts had drifted back to Rue when the first drop of water splatted on his forehead. "What the hell!" he muttered as the single drop grew into a steady peppering on his face. "The damn roof is leakin'."

Now what? he wondered as his swearing was joined with that of the others who had been jerked awake by the chill of water hitting their bare flesh. The line of bunk beds were nailed to the wall so they couldn't be moved to dry spots.

As Hawke jumped out of bed and groped for his discarded clothing, the thought hit him that maybe the roof of the house might be leaking also. Although he believed that he had replaced all the rotten shingles, he might have missed some. Someone lit a lamp, and by its dim light he pulled on his trousers, trying not to laugh at the cowpunchers, who gazed sleepy-eyed, waiting to be told what to do.

They'll figure out something, Hawke thought, heading for the door, shirtless and barefoot. He paused a moment, his hand on the doorknob. His foreman, Malone, was missing. A brief smile twitched his lips. Romeo was probably tomcatting in Jackson, snug and dry with his favorite whore.

Hawke dashed through the rain and mud and hopped onto the broken porch where water ran like a sieve through the rotting boards of the roof. "Gotta get that fixed," he muttered as he pushed open the door.

He breathed a sigh of relief. The house was in darkness and all was quiet. Evidently the roof was sound. But he'd better make sure, he decided, and crossed the parlor hurriedly, hoping not to muddy his mother's carpet too badly.

Rue's bedroom door, the first off the hall, stood slightly ajar. Hawke slowly pushed it open, breathing in her scent with deep pleasure. He tiptoed quietly to the bed and stared down at the pillow where her head should be. He caught his breath. In the dimness of the room he made out that, though the covers were rumpled, the bed was empty. She had gone to bed and then got up. Why?

Hawke's eyes narrowed to glittering green slits. Malone's bed was empty also. His hands clenched into fists. The cheating bitch had slipped out to meet his foreman. He twitched his shoulders angrily at the unexpected shaft of pain that jabbed his breast when he thought of them together.

As the lightning flashed and the thunder rolled, he convinced himself that he didn't give a damn if she slept with every hand on the place. But, by God, he added, he wasn't about to let her bring shame to the Masters's name. He would just crawl into the little bitch's bed and wait for her. Give her the surprise of her life when she came creeping in.

Rue fought through the haze of deep sleep. Which of her little half brothers was crying now? What could she give him to eat? She sat up in bed, her mind back at the desolate shack she'd called home.

Dimly then, Rue realized the cries were of fright and not hunger. Also that the child was crying, "Mama" and not "Rue." She bolted up in bed with total recall. It was Susie crying. She had probably been awakened by the storm that raged outside.

As Rue hurried to the room next to hers, lamplight spilled into the hall, and she could hear Jeb trying to soothe the little girl. She stood in the open doorway a moment, watching with sympathy the harried man who was doing his best, but was quite unsuccessful.

"Is she frightened of the storm?" Rue whispered, entering the room and approaching the bed.

Such a look of relief washed over her father-in-law's face that Rue felt sorry for him. She patted his shoulder affectionately as she sat down on the edge of the bed and gently stroked Susie's wet, flushed cheek.

Big blue eyes flew open, and then a small

body threw itself against Rue. When little arms went around her neck in a strangle hold, Rue rocked the sobbing child slowly, crooning a lullaby that an almost-forgotten man had once sung to her.

When the sobs ceased and Susie grew quiet, Rue motioned her head toward the door, silently telling Jeb that he could go back to bed. He gave her an appreciative smile and slipped from the room.

"Susie." Rue lifted the child's chin so that she could look into the tear-stained face. "Would you like for me to sleep with you tonight?"

"Oh, yes, Auntie Rue," the answer came instantaneously. "I'm afraid of storms." She hiccuped. "They make me miss my mommie."

"I know, honey." Rue loosened the clinging arms and helped her get back under the covers. "But Auntie Rue will be here for you from now on," she said softly, blowing out the lamp and sliding in beside the now calm child. She gathered the small body close, settling the blond head on her shoulder. "Let's get back to sleep now, all right?"

Susie scooted closer, and whispered, "All right." Within minutes her body relaxed into sleep and the storm raged on.

Hawke came awake to shafts of sunlight in his face, and a strident voice demanding,

"What in the hell are you doing in my bed?"

Hawke shook his head, as though to clear it, then pinning the furious woman with a scalding look he sneered, "So, finally you're crawlin' home." He sat up in bed, the sheet and blanket falling so low to his waist that a fringe of pubic hair curled against their edges.

Rue swiftly looked away, her face blushing a deep red. Mistaking the reason for her embarrassment he said contemptuously, "So you do have some shame in you."

There was a short silence as Rue jerked her head around and stared at him indignantly. "Don't look at me like a treed cat," Hawke snapped. "If you needed a man so badly, I was willin' and able to take care of your itch. You didn't have to sneak out and meet Malone in the barn."

At first, as Hawke's harsh words lashed out at her, Rue couldn't speak she was so furious. Slowly then, it came to her that his tone had a jealous ring to it. Could that be possible? she asked herself. No, that couldn't be, she decided. Hawke Masters didn't care for her in the least. It was only a case of her belonging to him, and he wasn't a man to share what was his.

The urge to torment him was too strong to ignore. With a defiant tilt of her head, she taunted, "Josh Malone isn't the only man on this ranch. There's others who would gladly meet me in the barn."

There was a tight silence as Hawke glared at Rue, his eyes threatening punishment. Then, a muscle twitching in his jaw, he grated, "But Malone was the only man missing from the bunkhouse last night."

Rue shrugged. "I wouldn't know anything about that." She was deliberately evasive, deriving great satisfaction watching his anger grow.

Hawke started to swing his feet to the floor, then remembered he was naked and that predicament made him even angrier. He could only lie there and shout at her. Susie might walk in any minute. When he finally spoke, his words were low, but savage. "Don't lie to me, woman! You know damn well the two of you made arrangements to meet last night."

Rue cocked her head as though in deep thought. "I don't think I made an assignation with Josh . . . for last night, that is." Then deliberately vague, she added, "I certainly hope not. I don't like to break my word."

"You bitch!" Hawke rasped. "I was right about you all along. You're nothin' but a whore." He swung his feet to the floor, clutching the covers to his middle. "Let me tell you somethin' right now: there will be no whorin' with my men. You will not bring shame to the Masters name."

He grabbed her wrist and squeezed it. "And to make sure of that, from now on I'm sharin' this bed with you every night. I'll ride you so hard, so often, you won't have the energy, nor the desire to go sneakin' off to meet anyone.''

Rue glared back at her husband, hurt to the heart and trembling with blind fury. She sought for some cutting words that would express her contempt for him then had to bite them back when Susie came dancing into the room.

Unaware of the crackling tension between her aunt and uncle, the little girl ran to Rue and threw her arms around her waist. "Thank you, Auntie Rue, for sleeping with me last night." Her small mouth drew into a pout. "Grandpa said I can't sleep with you every night, though. He said that Uncle Hawke would miss you, that he looked real lonesome when he looked in on him this morning.

Susie looked over her shoulder at Hawke. "Were you lonesome, Uncle Hawke? Did you miss Auntie Rue?"

Hawke ran long agitated fingers through his hair, a wave of self-reproach sweeping over him. *God*, he thought, *I wish I could take back those hateful cruel words*.

"I missed her very much, little one," he said softly, then held out a placating hand to Rue.

"Look, Rue," he began awkwardly, "I can't tell you how sorry and ashamed I am for my words and accusations. I was just so sure when I found your bed empty that you—"

"Yes, I know what you were sure of," Rue

interrupted him coldly. She took Susie's hand and led her to the door. "Wait for me in the kitchen, honey." She gave the child a gentle push. "I have something to say to Uncle Hawke in private."

Susie smilingly agreed, and Rue closed the door behind her. "Now, Mr. Hawke Masters." She stamped back to the bed and stared down at him, her fists on her hips. "I know all about your opinion of me, have known all along. But whether or not my morals are good or bad, you will never know. For as far as outward appearances are concerned, I will be the model wife. I have not, nor will I ever *sneak* off to lie with a man—including you."

Rue's voice had risen during her angry retaliation, and she was practically shouting as she flung her last jibe at Hawke. "So if any shame is brought to the Masters name, it will be your doing, messing around with Lillie Meyers."

"Now look, Rue, I've told you how sorry I am." Hawke stood up, forgetting his naked state. "Can't we forget all the hurtful words between us and start all over? As for Lillie, I haven't—"

Rue gasped softly at the sight of Hawke's body. She had never seen a man bare below the waist before. She turned her back to him and snapped, "Will you put on some clothes? What if Susie should come back in here?"

Rue's embarrassement brought a devilish

grin to Hawke's lean face. He sat back down on the edge of the bed and pulled the corner of the sheet across his hips. "I only have my pants," he said plaintively, "and they're still wet from my dash over here in the rain to see if the roof was leaking. I worried about you gettin' wet."

"I'm sure you were worried about me," Rue retorted sharply, then added, "there are clean clothes in the dresser."

Hawke's smile was wicked as he said, "Probably you should bring them to me. As you know, I'm still naked and Susie might—"

"Oh, all right," Rue interrupted him, marching over to the big piece of furniture and jerking open a drawer. She could have left the room, and let him take care of himself. But she still had things on her mind that needed saying.

She snatched up underwear, socks, a shirt, and a pair of denims, and brought them to the bed. "Here," she said, and started to hand them to Hawke.

The clothing fell to the floor as her wrist was caught, given a twist, and she was flipped into Hawke's arms. She felt her old, worn dress splitting at the seams, and when the cool air hit her bare breasts, she began to struggle, to push against the broad shoulders that bore into her.

"Let me up!" she gasped, her curved fingers reaching for his face.

"Oh, no, missy." Hawke grinned down at her as he caught her two wrists in one hand and held them over her head. "You teased and tormented me about Josh; now it's your turn to get a little of it back."

He gazed down at her breasts as he flung a leg across her hips, keeping her pinned under him. His eyes gleaming in appreciation, he murmured softly, "Beautiful."

A mixture of excitement, fear, and anticipation swept over Rue as his head lowered slowly. In fascination she watched his mouth open as it neared a puckered nipple. "Please, don't," she whispered, but his lips were already sucking her, pulling as though he was drawing nectar into his mouth.

She felt a wave of weakness sweep through her at the insistent tugging of his lips, and she gave a deep moan of pleasure. Her body went limp and she was lost in the pleasure of Hawke tasting one breast and then the other.

When he inserted a hand beneath her skirt and laid it against the moist curls between her thighs, she opened eagerly for the finger he started to slide inside her.

When Hawke's mouth and hand suddenly left her, it took Rue a moment to realize someone was knocking on the bedroom door. She hurriedly pushed her skirt down and tried to pull the ripped bodice together as Jeb called in amusement, "I don't want to break up anything in there, but there's a couple of hungry youngsters in the kitchen who refuse to eat anything that Rue hasn't prepared." He laughed dryly. "I hadn't known I was that bad a cook all these past weeks."

"We'll be right there, Pa," Hawke called, his voice hoarse from unreleased passion.

Rue felt Hawke's eyes on her back as he dressed himself, but she was too mortified to look at him. She knew he was thinking that she was easy, that he could have had her if his father hadn't interrupted them.

Anger and shame mingled together and spread through her. He was right. She had been willing to give herself to him. She stared sightlessly through the window. Was she like her mother after all, ready to go to bed with a man only after a few kisses and the stroking of her body?

I must be, she thought dejectedly for she loathed Hawke Masters and yet he was able to set her body afire.

"Are you all right?" Hawke asked gently from behind her, laying a hand on her shoulder.

"Of course I'm all right." She jerked away from him. "Why shouldn't I be? I've been kissed before," she lied.

"Don't be angry," he coaxed. "We won't be interrupted tonight. I'll make it good for you, you'll see. It will be all the better for waiting."

"There will be no tonight!" Rue wheeled on him, her eyes flashing blue fire. "Not tonight, or any other night.''

Hawke grabbed her by the shoulders and jerked her up against his lean body. His partial arousal pressed against her stomach as he glared down at her and growled, ''There will be a tonight. Josh Malone has his eye on you, and I'm not completely convinced that you're not returning his interest. What I said before still goes. I'm gonna see to it that you're fully satisfied every night.''

Just as Rue debated slapping his handsome face, he released her and stamped out of the room, slamming the door behind him. ''We'll see about that, Mister,'' she muttered, looking at the torn dress that was truly a rag now. As she yanked it over her head, she wondered what she'd do for a change of dress now. Resort to men's trousers, she imagined as she did up the buttons over her breasts, the nipples still tingling from the recent tugging on them.

Rue filled the white china basin with water from the matching pitcher and dropped the rose-scented soap and soft flannel into it. She stroked a finger over the red roses painted on the pitcher's side. She had never hoped to have anything so beautiful. Susie had said that it had belonged to her mother.

What had the dead woman been like? Rue mused. Certainly she had been a lady to have had so many pretty things. No one from where Rue came from had owned such nice furniture and pretty personal items.

Rue remembered suddenly that the Masters family was waiting for their breakfast. She hurriedly splashed water on her face, dragged the broken comb through her hair, then hurried to the door.

Her hand on the knob, she paused, nervously biting her lower lip, gathering the courage to face the two Masters men. Her father-in-law had to know that something had been going on between her and his son, and Hawke would look at her with sardonic amusement. She sighed. She couldn't stay in her room for the rest of her life. The sooner she faced them, the sooner it would be over.

Surprisingly, it wasn't too bad. Jeb greeted her in his usual gentle fashion, with a quiet fondness in his eyes. In the clamor of childish voices declaring that they were starving, Rue sneaked a look at Hawke. With him, however, it was a different story. He ran insolent eyes over her body, lingering a moment on her breasts. Then lifting his gaze to her face, he gave her a look that spoke volumes.

Her face beet-red, Rue marched over to the workbench that Jeb had brought, and busily mixed pancake batter. She was flipping over the first batch in the cast-iron skillet when her father-in-law spoke.

"Rue, I've been noticin' that you're built like the kid's mama was. I brought all her clothes along. Me and the younguns' have talked it over, and we'd be proud if you could put them to use."

Before Rue could answer that she would be happy to wear Sara's clothing, Hawke spoke up, angry resentment in his tone. "I can provide for my wife, Pa. She doesn't have to wear hand-me-downs."

Jeb studied his son's flushed face and thought with satisfaction that it seemed that Hawke cared for his wife after all. Jeb had been a little confused when he arrived yesterday. He had not missed the coolness between Rue and Hawke and had decided that it had only been a lover's spat over something of small importance.

"Then it's past time you did, son," Jeb drawled. "I had to look in Rue's chifforobe yesterday for a tin box that contains all my important papers, and all I saw hangin' in it was that dress she has on now."

Hawke's startled eyes jumped to Rue's stiff back, and it was hard for his father not to laugh at the total surprise on his son's face. He mentally shook his head. This eldest son of his had a lot to learn about a decent woman. And Rue was certainly that, Jeb thought. One only had to look at her wide, clear eyes, the innocence on her face. Unbelievably she still had the look of a virgin. His lips tilted a fraction. Fat chance of that, married to his randy son.

Jeb was jarred from his thoughts about the

pair by the bristling argument going on between them.

"How in the hell was I suppose to know you
only had two dresses?" Hawke growled, jabbing a fork into the stack of pancakes. "You've
got a mouth. You could have told me."

"And you've got eyes!" Rue came back,
pouring the second batch of batter into the
skillet. "Only a blind man wouldn't have noticed something like that." She flipped the
browned cakes over. "Anyway, I wouldn't ask
you for a glass of water if my throat was
parched."

"Then don't!" Hawke scraped his chair
away from the table and stood up. "Go ahead
and wear used clothes. It's damned sure I
won't buy any for you." He slammed the
kitchen door so hard behind him, the window
rattled.

As Rue carried the second platter of cakes
to the table the sight of Tommy's wide, uneasy
eyes wiped the anger out of her. She swept
Susie a glance and was deeply ashamed. The
little girl was on the verge of tears. It was clear
these children weren't used to squabbling
parents.

Bringing a bright smile to her lips, she sat
down next to the little girl and joked, "I guess
I told Uncle Hawke, huh? He'll go down to the
barn and pout a while, and then we'll make
up." She stroked the soft blond hair. "Our
little spat didn't upset you, did it, honey? It

didn't mean anything. We were just clearing our voices at each other."

"But Uncle Hawke looked so angry, Auntie Rue," Tommy said, still doubtful. "He looked like he wanted to punch someone."

A forced gay laugh trilled through Rue's lips. "Oh I'm sure he's punched a couple of walls by now, Tommy." She laid a hand on the boy's clenched fist lying beside his plate, and looking across at Jeb's upset face, she said with firm conviction, "I want you all to know that regardless of how angry my husband might get at me, he would never strike me."

She grinned and added, "I might hit him, though."

All three laughed, and the hovering nervous tension evaporated. But Rue knew as she began eating her own breakfast, such outbursts between her and Hawke must never happen in front of the children and Jeb again. It upset the young ones, and Jeb would soon learn that his son's marriage wasn't all it should be. And she didn't want him to know how this strange alliance between her and Hawke had come about.

Breakfast was eaten amid the chatter of the children, Tommy expressing his wish to get to the horses in the corral, and Susie carrying on a conversation with the rag doll that was seldom out of her sight.

The meal was over then, and when Jeb and Tommy went off to the stables, Rue hurried with her chores in the kitchen. She was anxious to go through the barrels of clothing out on the porch. So what if they had been worn before? Wasn't she used to that? The dress she had on now was the only one that she alone had ever worn.

The dishes were finally washed and put away, and Rue fairly ran to view what she might find. While Susie sat on the edge of the porch, still talking to her doll, Rue pried open the barrel that Jeb had said contained the family's clothing.

The top layer belonged to Susie, little dresses, six for play and two more fancier. Sunday best, Rue imagined as she took out small petticoats, ruffled bloomers, and white stockings.

Tommy's came next. They were much the same as his sister's. Everyday shirts and trousers, and a couple of Sunday best. Then there were Jeb's. With the exception of a black suit, everything else was work clothes. She smoothed out the lapel of the suit coat, thinking of the sad event he had worn it to last.

Then there was a mixture of men's shirts and trousers, smaller than Hawke's. His brother's, no doubt. Finally, there lay before her what she had been anxiously looking for.

The first layer was under clothing made of fine material, lace, and ribbon-trimmed. There were also gloves and hose. Rue held these items in her hands a moment, gazing at them in wonder. Her legs had never felt silk on them, nor had her rough, red hands known gloves. Not even in the bitter cold winter.

At last she came to what interested her most. Slowly she lifted six lovely dresses, fashioned from bright calicos, chambray, and muslin. All were trimmed with either ruffles or lace.

Rue gasped her pleasure when she pulled out the seventh dress. Never had she seen anything so lovely. She shook it out, and holding it up, her hungry eyes ran over the garment. The bodice was white lace, cut low, with short, capped sleeves. Attached to it was a full gathered skirt of the sheerest voile which clung to a dark green satin shimmering underskirt.

After a while she sighed deeply and placed the beautiful dress on top of the others. When in the world would she ever wear it? Certainly she could never cook or scrub in it, and that seemed to be her lot in life.

Rue picked up an armful of clothes, then paused on her way to her bedroom at the sound of jingling spurs. She glanced over her shoulder and saw two young cowboys coming from the direction of the bunkhouse. As she watched them, they stopped at the foot of the steps, awkwardly shifting their feet, looking very uncomfortable.

Rue hid her smile, and after greeting them, said matter-of-factly, "I guess you're here to install the other stove." At their quick nod, she said, "The old one has to come out first. I think it has cooled off by now."

One of the shy young men managed to say, "Yes, ma'am," then the pair trooped into the house.

Rue flinched when a minute later she heard the banging of the rusty old stove being dismantled. In her mind's eye she could see ashes and soot flying all over her clean kitchen. "I can't watch," she muttered, and spent the time carrying in all the clothes and putting them away in the proper bedrooms. Susie was her constant companion, chattering away to the rag doll.

To Rue's surprise, while she had been involved with putting away the clothes, the old stove had been carried into the backyard and the new one set in its place. Also, one of the men had done a fair job of sweeping up after themselves.

When she smilingly expressed her thanks, the younger cowboy stammered, "Hawke said . . . said that maybe . . . maybe you'd need us to help hang some curtains."

"Why, yes, I would," Rue exclaimed, surprised that Hawke would be so thoughtful where she was concerned. "Come back in an hour or so. Give me time to find and press them."

"Glad to, ma'am," the spokesman for the two said, then turning quickly, bumped into his companion, knocking him to the ground.

Rue flew to the kitchen to control her laughter, to let the fallen man swear in peace.

The stove drew well, Rue noted as she built a fire, then put the irons on its shiny top. While they heated, she went again to the porch and pried open the barrel that was marked linens. She had just finished pressing dozens of curtain panels when the two young men again presented themselves at the door.

Rue's eyes were alive with pleasure as in the next two hours curtains were hung throughout the house. There were heavy ones for the bedrooms, insuring privacy, and sheer dimities for the kitchen and parlor. Sara also had liked the sunlight, Rue thought.

When the men had left, Rue went from room to room, feasting her eyes on the window coverings, remembering the bare, dirty panes she had stared through at the shack, the broken ones stuffed with rags to keep out the winter winds. She couldn't help thinking how proud Grandma would be if she could see her granddaughter's new home. *It would mean nothing to her though if she knew how miserable and unhappy I am,* Rue thought. *It would grieve her and that is why any letters I write to her must be full of cheer and contentment.*

And what a lie that would be, Rue snorted as she left the big room and crossed into the kitchen. All day, in the back of her mind had lain the dread of bedtime, Hawke's threat of making love to her returning again and again.

"Never," she gritted, as she started preparing a light lunch. "If he so much as lays a hand on me, I'll hit him so hard his head will rock for a week."

When it became evident that the Masters men weren't coming in for the noon meal, Rue called Susie in from the yard and they both bit hungrily into the beef sandwiches she had made. They were topping off the meal with sugar cookies when from outside came the clatter of hooves.

Rue's mouth tightened. Trust Hawke to show up for a meal whenever he pleased. She rose from the table and walked to the window. Her heart lurched and her stomach turned. It wasn't her husband as she had dreaded, but someone just as unwelcomed.

"What is she doing here?" she whispered, her heart picking up an angry, uneasy rhythm as she stared at Lillie Meyers.

With narrowed eyes and clenched fists, she watched the woman swing to the ground, then smooth down the skirt of her blue taffeta dress. *That's hardly an outfit to wear while riding*, Rue thought critically, then remembered her own grimy appearance. Her dress was stained from rummaging through the dusty barrels, and her hair had straggled from the knot she had affixed atop her head before tackling her housework this morning.

Would she have time to change her dress

and comb her hair? she wondered. She shook
her head. No, she wouldn't. She could see
Hawke and his father riding in. Hawke would
be amused if he saw that she had freshened up
for his mistress.

When Hawke swung to the ground, Rue
searched his face, expecting to see pleasure
on it as he walked toward Lillie. To her
surprise, he looked anything but pleased.
Strange, she thought, studying his lean, brown
face. *He's impatient with her, I wonder why.*

Because of his father, the answer came to
Rue. *He doesn't want Jeb to know about his
relationship with his neighbor's wife.* Her eyes
narrowed on her husband. Although he continued to look annoyed, there was a wariness
about Hawke as he approached Lillie. *He's
nervous*, she thought, and grinned. And why
wouldn't he be? He didn't want his father to
know that he cared more for this woman than
he did for his own wife.

Rue couldn't make out the words spoken
among the three, but she knew that Hawke
had introduced Lillie to his father when the
woman smiled brightly and held out her hand
to Jeb. It pleased her tremendously when her
father-in-law unsmilingly gave the ring-
bedecked hand a quick shake, then stepped
back.

"How do you like that, you old whore?" Rue
whispered under her breath. "Jeb knows what
you are."

An angry flush swept over Lillie's face at Jeb's near rudeness. Then, with an indifferent shrug, she slid her arm through Hawke's and hugged it against her full breasts. Rue gritted her teeth when the three climbed the steps to the porch.

Would she be expected to entertain the woman? She doubted that she could. She would rather entertain a rattlesnake.

A quick look at Jeb's frowning disfavor of how Lillie was hanging onto Hawke's arm made Rue feel a little better. At least her father-in-law would be on her side.

It was Jeb who a moment later stood in the kitchen door and remarked in disgruntled tones, "You got company, honey. Some person who claims she's a neighbor."

"Yes." Rue sighed. "I saw her ride up." Jeb looked disconcerted and she knew that he was wondering if she had seen Lillie take Hawke's arm so possessively. She looked at him and smiled. "We'll join you just as soon as I wipe Susie's face."

"Don't take too long," Jeb advised. "That woman doesn't care a whit that Hawke is married."

As Jeb's footsteps faded down the hall toward the parlor, Rue thought how right he was. Wedding vows meant nothing to the Lillie Meyers of this world. Hadn't she grown up with that knowledge? Her mother had taken married men to bed. But, she thought, as she filled a basin with water, there were also women like her grandmother. Women who were true to one man all their lives. She sighed, wishing that she, too, could have a happy marriage like Grandpa and Grandma DeLawney's.

Susie jumped around, excited that they had company, so it took awhile to clean the small mouth of cookie crumbs before sending her into the parlor. Where was Tommy? Rue wondered as she took the time to smooth down her skirt and tuck the loose ends of her hair back into its knot. Eating with the ranch hands, she imagined, then gathered her shrinking courage to go meet the woman she despised with all her heart.

When Rue entered the room, Hawke rose hastily, offering her his seat beside Lillie. "You remember Mrs. Meyers, don't you, Rue?" He smiled, a tenseness to his lips.

Smarting under the older woman's amused eyes, whether at her or Hawke's discomfort, Rue nodded as she sat down and folded her hands in her lap. "How are you, Mrs. Meyers?" she forced herself to ask politely.

"Well, my dear"—Lillie ignored her greeting—"I see that soap and water has improved your face somewhat, but . . ." With a grimace she raked her eyes over Rue's disheveled hair and dirtstained dress. "There's plenty of room for improvement elsewhere."

While Jeb drew in a sharp breath and Rue was too stunned to speak, Lillie patted the space between them. Then, after sending Rue a malignant glance, she smiled coyly at Hawke, and said, "Come sit beside me, Hawke. We haven't talked for a couple weeks."

Jeb shot his son a look that dared him to obey the woman. A visible sweat popped out on Hawke's forehead. He was trapped. Either way he jumped, he'd pay the consequences. He would get a dressing down from Pa, lose more of Rue's respect, and God knew she had little enough as it was, and Lillie, that one was out to cause trouble. If angered, there was no telling what she might say.

He darted a look at Rue's downcast face, then letting out a slow breath, he sat down beside his former lover, wondering what he had ever seen in the bitch. He was going to have a long talk with Rue tonight, make her understand that it was all over between him and the woman who had just placed a hand on his thigh, uncomfortably close to his crotch. And he was damn well going to make this heated bitch understand it too. He couldn't wait to get her alone and cuss her out.

"I must say the appearance of this room has improved since I last saw it." Lillie gazed around as she scooted closer to Hawke. "What about the rest of the house? Are there changes in the other rooms . . . your bedroom?" She looked at Hawke significantly, her meaning clear to everyone. "It was very austere the last time I saw it."

Hawke felt his face growing red as his father looked at him with startled eyes. *Damn the whore!* he thought, not daring to look at Rue, afraid he would see total renunciation on her face.

And though he longed to smash Lillie's mouth, he managed to control his anger as he answered, "I expect all the rooms look different. Pa brought a lot of furniture with him."

"That's nice." Lillie smiled, then sneered, "Will your little wife know how to take care of it? I don't imagine she's too experienced in seeing to fine furniture. Rumor has it that before you married her she lived her entire life in a run-down shack with only a few pieces of homemade furniture in it. Poor child," she tacked on in false sympathy.

Jeb jerked forward in his seat, an angry flush staining his cheeks. When he started to rise, Hawke sent him a look that said, "Wait." Then turning to Lillie, he looked at her suspiciously.

"A rumor, Lillie?" he asked coldly. "Who could have started such a rumor? Who could you have been talking to that would know anything about Rue's former life?"

Lillie frowned at Hawke's tone and shifted uneasily. "Oh, Hawke." She pouted. "I don't know where I heard it. Someone just made it up, I suppose. You know how people like to gossip."

Jeb gave a dry snort and Susie, leaning against his knee, asked, "What does gossip mean, Grandpa?"

"It means, honey, a person who bad mouths another because he fears or envies that person." He looked at Lillie. "Which do you think it is, Mrs. Meyers? Fear or envy, or maybe both?"

"I'm sure I don't know, Mr. Masters." Lillie tossed her head, her thin lips becoming thinner. "I'm sorry I brought it up."

Jeb made no response, but the look he gave the agitated woman spoke his unflattering thoughts clearly.

Rue hadn't uttered a sound at Lillie's attack on her, nor at the exchange between the woman and Hawke, and then Jeb. Her mind was racing with questions. This enemy of hers must have talked to someone who knew all about Rue DeLawney. She couldn't have made it all up and come so close to the truth. But who? She didn't know of anyone back home who would bad mouth her unless . . . Sly Burford. Could he possibly be in the area? Surely not. He'd be too afraid of running into Hawke. He owed her husband a large sum of money.

Rue was abruptly brought back to the present when Lillie suddenly stood up and extended a hand to Hawke. "Come show me the rest of the place," she coaxed. "Give me the grand tour."

Hawke studiously studied the spur on his boot heel, pretending not to see Lillie's hand. "Rue will show you. She knows more about everything."

Lillie's lips tightened and, with what bordered on a threatening order, said shortly, "I want you to do it." She grabbed his hand and pulled him to his feet. With a resigned sigh, and keeping his eyes averted from his father and wife, Hawke followed the woman, who was determined to have him.

In the heavy silence after the pair's departure, Jeb slid a sympathetic look at Rue's bent head then spoke softly to Susie leaning against his leg. "Why don't you go with Uncle Hawke and Mrs. Meyers?"

With a willing nod of her head, the little girl skipped out of the room, calling her uncle's name. Her childish treble rang through the house as she followed Lillie and her uncle, chattering away, explaining in detail which bedroom belonged to whom and that the biggest and prettiest belonged to Uncle Hawke and Auntie Rue.

Rue only vaguely heard the light prattle. She was wracked with an unfamiliar emotion. Jealousy. Like it or not, she was jealous of Lillie Meyers. She wanted to jump to her feet, to dash after the woman and draw her nails across the coarse features, and pull the dyed hair out of her head.

Much sooner than Rue had expected, Hawke was ushering Lillie back into the parlor. Susie still jabbered away, feeling very important, but Lillie's face looked like a storm cloud. She slid Rue a look that said she suspected Rue of sending her niece after Lillie and Hawke.

Plopping herself down on the sofa, making the springs squeak from her considerable weight, she looked at Rue and gibed impatiently, "I must say, *Mistress* Masters, you're not a very good hostess. I've been here half an hour and you haven't offered me any refreshments."

In the thick silence that followed Lillie's sneering delivery, Rue could only return the hostile glare leveled at her. She couldn't believe this woman had the insolence to point out her shortcomings when it came to entertaining a neighbor. It wasn't too long ago when she hadn't even invited Rue to come in out of the heat.

Rue tried to check her rising anger, but lost the battle when Lillie motioned for Hawke to sit down beside her and he meekly did so. In a blinding rage, that these two would insult her so blatantly, she got to her feet.

With her fists on her hips, Rue glared down at the surprised man and woman. "I don't wait on sluts," she ground out. "If you want something to drink, send your sniffing hound after it.'' With a meaningful look at Hawke's stunned face, she stalked from the room, Lillie's enraged voice following her.

"Are you gonna let her talk to me like that, Hawke?'' the enraged woman fairly spluttered.

Jeb, whose wise eyes had missed nothing since Lillie Meyers arrived, looked at his son. He had known within minutes that an intimacy had at one time existed between them, but pray God, no longer. Surely Hawke realized the chance he was taking of losing a wife who was too good to be in the same room with that fleshpot sitting next to him. Jeb waited for Hawke to order the woman from his home.

When Hawke, evading Jeb's eyes, only ran nervous fingers through his hair, Jeb rose, and taking Susie by the hand, left the pair, his condemnation a living presence in the room.

"I don't like that woman, she's an old witch.'' Susie pouted, going straight to Rue and hugging her waist. "She kept telling me to go away, that she wanted to be alone with Uncle Hawke.''

Jeb looked at Rue and saw her need to know Hawke's reaction to Lillie's callous treatment of his niece, but was too proud to ask. Well, by hell, pride didn't stand in his way.

As Rue gently stroked the small head pushed into her side, he asked, "And what did Uncle Hawke have to say?''

Susie's lips curved in a satisfied smile. "He said that I might as well stay, that they didn't have anything to talk about that I couldn't hear."

Jeb smiled his relief. His son wasn't besotted with the woman after all. She was making it hard for him to break off with her, though. He wondered now if Hawke's seemingly ready submission to Mrs. Meyers's arrogant demands was because he was pacifying her for Jeb's benefit.

He glanced at Rue. Had his son been as careful of his wife's finding out about his female neighbor? The pinched look on her face said that he had not. Jeb's lips firmed grimly. His son had a lot to answer for and he hoped that Rue would see to it that he paid dearly, if that was the case.

Rue knew that she should be happy at Susie's answer, and her heart had leapt joyously for a split second. Then she remembered how deceitful Hawke could be, like foisting a ready-made family on her without any warning. And she was quite aware that he didn't want his father to suspect that he was having an affair with a married woman. Consequently, she didn't put much faith in the words he'd said for Jeb's sake.

She came out of her musing when Jeb warned, "You be careful of her, Rue. She'd break up your marriage in a minute if she could."

Rue smiled mirthlessly to herself. *Oh, Jeb,* she wanted to cry out, *there's no marriage to break up. Only a few words spoken by an old preacher under the threat of a rifle. Hawke will have those words set aside as soon as he no longer needs me.*

Jeb waited for her response, and when none came, he took his granddaughter by the hand, and walking toward the door, said, "Let's go scare up your brother. See what he's up to."

Left alone, Rue walked to the window and stared outside, a gnawing emptiness inside her. Some people weren't destined for happiness on this earth, she thought, with slumping shoulders. Certainly in her nineteen years she hadn't had much of it. Actually, she couldn't remember one time being completely happy. The few times had been momentary, fading almost before she could grasp them.

Raised voices in the parlor brought Rue from the window. She walked quietly to the door separating the two rooms and listened intently. Grandma DeLawney had always said not to eavesdrop, but Rue felt she had the right to know what went on between her husband and their neighbor.

Hawke's voice was cold as he said, "It's her home, Lillie. You had no right orderin' her around, treatin' her like hired help."

"Why are you takin' her side?" Lillie demanded, her voice rising. "You don't love her. Your men told my cowhands that you don't even sleep with her."

There was a short, tense silence as Rue waited breathlessly for Hawke's response. She had to strain her ears when he said quietly, but firmly, "I don't love you either. And since she's my wife, my duty is to her."

"Duty, bah!" Lillie snapped. "We'll see how dutiful you are when that big member between your legs gets hungry. You'll come runnin' back to me then. That delicate little miss you're married to will never feed it. She'd faint if you stuck it in her."

Rue could hear the jangle of his spurs as Hawke stood up. "I think it's time you left, Lil," he said coldly. "I think you've said enough. And I don't want to see you around here again unless you come with your husband."

Rue waited to hear no more and hurried across the floor to go outside. She'd be mortified if she was caught listening to that heated argument.

She stood beneath a cottonwood tree, some distance from the house, when Lillie raced away, angrily whipping her mount. Then Rue heard crunching footsteps coming toward her. She knew without looking that it was Hawke.

His laugh was nervous as he stood beside Rue and said, "I hope you didn't pay any attention to how Lillie acted. She likes to stir up trouble just for the fun of it."

Rue wheeled around to face her husband, snorting her disbelief. Her eyes blazing, she said through gritted teeth, "Who do you think you're talking to? Susie?"

"No, by God, I don't think I'm talkin' to my niece," Hawke came back just as fiercely. "I thought I was talkin' to an intelligent woman, one who could see what that woman was up to."

Rue's eyes flashed cool disdain. "You are talking to an intelligent woman, Hawke Masters, and her intelligence tells her that there was no levity in that woman's words or actions. She mistakenly thinks I'm a threat to her. Now, why don't you go after her and give her what she wants and save your family a lot of unnecessary grief and aggravation?" She stopped to catch her breath after the long spate of words, then continued, "You might as well know that none of us want to see her around here again. Neither Jeb nor I will tolerate you bringing your whore into our home, imposing her on innocent children."

"She is not my whore! She's nothin' to me!" Hawke shouted, his face angry. "I told her—"

But Rue wheeled away, running swiftly to the house with tears running down her cheeks.

"Damn the woman!" Hawke swore, the stick he gripped in his hand cracking in two.

* * *

In a white-hot fury, Lillie continued to whip her mount, lashing the poor brute the way she'd like to lash Rue Masters. She had discovered something that Hawke still didn't know. He was in love with his wife. She bared her teeth, and like a wild animal, a growl erupted from her throat.

The enraged woman was but a few miles from home when a wide figure appeared from behind a boulder and grabbed the mount's bridle.

"You're gonna kill that horse, Lillie, ridin' him like that," Sly Burford warned. He studied the angry, petulant features. "What's got you so riled up? Hawke Masters?"

Lillie's small eyes glared down at the fat man, who controlled the lathered, nervous stallion. "Yes, Hawke Masters! Who else can drive me mad?"

Sly peered up at her, then taunted with a titter, "Can't he take care of you anymore?"

"I don't know if he can or not." Lillie slid to the ground and leaned against the heaving horse. "He's all wrapped up in his wife now."

She looked up at the venom in Sly's voice when he muttered, "That little bitch." She had heard his woeful story many times, how his stepdaughter had robbed him of his manhood, that he had followed her here to extract revenge. The beginning of an idea suddenly sparked in her small eyes. If she could convince Sly to take his revenge before Hawke realized his feelings for his wife, he would be hers again.

With furtively calculating eyes, and choosing her words carefully, Lillie asked, "When do you plan on gettin' even with your stepdaughter?"

"Soon." Sly evaded, releasing the horse and moving back. "I've been watchin' her, but she's always got that little girl with her." His fists knotted and his eyes glittered. "But I'll find her alone someday, and then I'll get her good."

Lillie waited a minute, then said bluntly, "I would make it worth your while if that girl disappeared in the next few days."

Sly gaped at the woman as her words took meaning in his brain. Finally, he shook his head doubtfully. "I don't know if I could kill a woman in cold blood, Lillie. I only had in mind to scar up her purty face. Disfigure it so no man would ever look at her without shiverin'."

Lillie made an impatient move with her hands. "I'm not suggestin' you kill her. Just grab her and take her to that renegade Indian village up in the foothills. Old Chief Wise Owl would pay you handsomely for her. Between the two of us, you stand to make a good amount of money."

Greed glittered in Sly's eyes. Lillie was right. That red-gold hair of Rue's would certainly whet the chief's interest. He wondered why he hadn't thought of selling her himself.

Another thought hit the fat man and his avarice grew. He glanced at the woman standing beside him and asked slyly, "What good would it do you to get rid of Rue? You'd still be hooked up with Sam and Hawke might take up with another woman to take care of his relatives."

Lillie started, disquiet settling over her coarse features. She hadn't thought about that. Hawke could very well replace Rue with another woman. He would need someone to keep house and to care for that pesky little niece of his.

She gave the waiting Sly a shrewd look. "Do you have any ideas about that, Sly? Like maybe an accident . . . a ridin' accident?"

Sly smiled thinly. "I might. If the price was right. I'll have to leave these parts after everything is taken care of, and I'll need plenty of money to live on until I can find some kind of job."

"Oh, yes, I'm sure you'll break your back lookin' for work," Lillie sneered. "You're just a workin' fool. I notice how you hustle around the ranch." When a black look came over Sly's face, however, she hurriedly added, "You'll be well paid."

"All right then. Get back on your horse and we'll make some plans while we ride along," Sly growled, ruffled at Lillie's slighting words.

CHAPTER NINE

Rue unwound her long legs and stood up, brushing down her skirt. The sun was dropping low over the Colorado range and it was time she was getting back to the house and start supper. She had been here the better part of an hour, cooling her anger, trying to think logically. She was half sorry she had listened to Hawke and Lillie's conversation. Their angry words and the aftermath had upset her deeply. For she now knew with a certainty that once Susie was old enough to take care of herself, Hawke Masters would send his wife packing.

That he didn't love Lillie either only proved that he was a user. Her full lips formed into a straight line. Luckily she was forewarned, wise now to his treatment of women. More than ever she would keep up her defenses against him. And that would take a lot of doing, she sighed, for the mere touch of his hand sent her heart fluttering.

She stood a moment longer, gazing down at the purple haze thickening in the timbered notches, the gray foothills rolling down from the high country, the sweeping isolated patches of aspen, blazing like gold in the autumn sun. Her eyes lifted to the mountain which sheltered it all from the north.

It is so beautiful here, she thought, her eyes wistful. If only she could live out her life here in all this grandeur. But that would never be, and an empty void settled in her breast.

She gave a start, coming out of her poignant musings when, to her left, long-horned cattle were suddenly rushing headlong down a nearby slope, tearing through the brush, rolling rocks beneath their hooves and bawling hoarsely. While she watched, stupefied, Rue's mare, which she had fondly named Beauty, tensed, jerked her head away from the grass she nibbled, then screamed and galloped away.

"Beauty, come back!" Rue ran screaming after the little mare. But the horse was too gripped with fear, and if she heard the command, she paid no attention.

Rue kicked disgustedly at a stone. She had a long hike ahead of her. She'd be lucky if she got back to the ranch by dark. She looked down at the course she would have to travel. It seemed miles and miles across that wilderness of stone.

With a resigned sigh, she started a zigzag path over the rough, rock-strewn ground.

She had walked but a short distance when the shadows of twilight settled, dark and heavy among the pine and spruce. The brooding, inscrutable silence was interrupted only when a wolf yowled on a distant ridge. Never had the wilderness, the loneliness, struck her so vividly. She walked on, imagining Indians and wolves moving ghost-like through the dimness of the forest.

The moon hung over the mountain, full and resplendent, flooding everything with its silver light when Rue suddenly stood still, frozen in terror. Not a yard away, in her path, stood a wolf, his gray body taut, his eyes red. Wide-eyed, she watched his muscles tighten as he crouched. She braced herself against a tree when she saw him stiffen, ready to spring. She didn't breathe as she waited for the sharp fangs to close around her throat.

Josh Malone, sitting his horse on a distant hill, had seen Rue leave the house and run to the corral where Hawke's special horses were kept. She lowered the bars, and the mare she always rode, Beauty, came trotting up to her when she whistled. The little horse stepped over the remaining two bars and Rue replaced the ones she had moved. His eyes widened when she grasped the flowing mane and swung herself onto the mare's back. He watched her race toward the mountain, her rigidly held body telling him that she was upset. What had her stupid husband done to her now? he wondered.

Should he follow her? Josh asked himself. There were many dangers in the mountains— rattlesnakes, wolves, wildcats, not to mention renegade Indians.

But she no doubt wanted to be alone he decided, so he tailed her, keeping out of sight, and giving her the solitude she wanted. If she needed his help, he would be close by to hear her.

When Josh saw Rue stop the mare, slide to the ground, then climb upon a tall boulder, he pulled his mount behind a spruce and waited. An hour passed, and when the sun disappeared and Rue showed no sign of coming back down the mountain, he became uneasy. Had something happened to her without his knowing it?

Thinking that he'd better take a look, he kneed his mount onto the trail and barely avoided being run over by a riderless horse tearing down the mountain, its nostrils flaring, its eyes terrorized.

Josh recognized Beauty immediately and lunged his own mount up the rocky slope. He rounded a wide boulder and jerked the horse to a plunging halt.

"God," he whispered, jerking his Colt from its holster. He took a hurried aim, and the bullet caught the wolf in the head just as it sprang at Rue. Josh was out of the saddle and catching her in his arms just as she began to fall.

The minutes ticked by as Josh held Rue's shivering body close to his own, stroking her hair, and murmuring softly to her, telling her that she was safe now.

"I was so frightened, Josh." Her words were smothered in his shirt front. "I knew I was about to die."

And you would have if I hadn't been here. The thought made Josh's insides twist. He loved the slender girl he held in his arms, and wanted to beat Hawke Masters into the ground for his callous treatment of her. Didn't the man realize what a treasure he had?

Josh's desire to take Rue away from her husband flamed inside him. He wanted to give her the love and attention she deserved. But now wasn't the time to discuss it with her. She was too upset.

He moved away from her and smiled down at her pale face. "Are you all right now?" he asked when she returned a weak smile.

"I think so," her voice wavered a bit.

His arms still holding her loosely around the waist, Josh said, "We'd better get you home. The family is probably going crazy. Hawke's probably tearing around, cussin' his head off. It's way past suppertime, you know."

Rue giggled, picturing the scowl on Hawke's face when he came in to eat and only found a cold stove.

Her amusement was cut short when a furious voice demanded, "What in the hell is goin' on here?"

The day was drawing to an end as Hawke leaned on the corral, his elbows hooked on the top rail, one booted foot propped on the bottom one. His eyes were narrowed in thought as he gazed unseeing at his prize horses milling around in the peeling paint, post-constructed pen.

What was he going to do about Rue? He absently kneaded the tightness in the back of his neck. She was on his mind all the time, and he ached for her every time she came within sight of him. He gave a derisive snort. Hell, he even found himself listening for the way her laughter would sometimes ring out.

Damn that Lil! The way she had acted so possessive of him today would make it all the harder to get close to Rue now. And if that wasn't bad enough, in trying to keep the damn woman pacified, to keep her from saying something that would make Pa suspicious, he had only made the situation worse. The bitch had arrived bent on causing trouble, and she had succeeded. Pa's face had clearly shown his disapproval when he stamped after Rue.

The big rancher heaved a ragged sigh. The two people he loved most in the world now thought him the vilest creature that ever lived.

Hawke shook his head in stunned surprise. What had his mind just said? That he loved Rue? And as he stood there in the gathering twilight, he realized that he did love his wife. What he had thought was lust, his usual feeling for a woman, was not the case. He felt for Rue what his father had felt for the mother of his children and what his brother had felt for Sara.

One of his horses nudged his arm for attention, but Hawke didn't feel it. He was remembering all the insulting things he'd ever said or done to Rue, the way he had shamed her in front of his hands by not sleeping with her. He cringed as he vividly remembered the day she had been left sitting in the sun while he visited with Lil in the coolness of her house.

God, how in the world was he ever going to make her forget and forgive all his cruelties to her? Hawke massaged his nape again. Yes, he had his work cut out for him, convincing Rue that he was sorry and ashamed for treating her so shabbily. But if it took the rest of his life he would do it. He would court her as no other woman had ever been courted. He would make her believe that he loved her with every fiber of his being.

Possessed with an eagerness to start mending his fences with Rue, Hawke turned from the corral and started toward the house. He smiled when Susie came running to him, her small face pinched, and near tears. "I can't find Auntie Rue, Uncle Hawke," she cried.

Hawke swung his niece into his arms. "Calm down, honey. Isn't she in the kitchen makin' supper?"

"No." Susie half sobbed. "I looked there. I've looked all over. She's gone." This last came out on a wail.

"Have you seen Rue, Hawke?" Jeb had followed his granddaughter, a worried frown on his face. "She's nowhere around. I've searched the house, the stables, everywhere."

Hawke put Susie down and placed a calming hand on his nephew's head when the boy came running up to them, looking ready to cry. The children had become very attached to Rue in the short time they had known her, and he suspected that they were probably afraid that they would lose her as they had their mother.

"Now let's not go off half-cocked," he said, forcing his own face not to show his growing concern. "She's got to be around here somewhere. She wouldn't just up and disappear without sayin' somethin' to someone."

"She damn well might have," Jeb said gruffly. "She had good cause to take off."

Hawke looked away from his father's accusing face. No one knew that better than he. But where would she go? She had no money. She didn't know anyone to ask for help; he hadn't bothered to introduce her to any of the neighbors. That he would rectify as soon as possible.

Shamed, he said, "Look, Pa, I know what you're thinkin', but I haven't visited . . ."—he glanced meaningful at the children—"since I married Rue."

"Well, I'm certainly glad to hear that." Jeb's tone was cutting, implying that he wasn't pleased that his son had dallied with a married woman at any time.

Still avoiding his father's eyes, Hawke said, "I'm gonna saddle up and go look for her. Why don't you take the kids back to the house and fix them a bite to eat?"

"You find her, Uncle Hawke," Susie ordered, her voice trembling as Jeb took her small hand and led her away, Tommy following them.

"I'll find her, little one," Hawke promised, then told himself that he'd better do it soon. Another fifteen minutes and darkness would have arrived.

As he walked along the corral, heading for the stables to saddle Captain, something made him pause to take a close look at his high-bred horses. His heart began to pound. The little mare he had given Rue permission to ride was gone. Rue had left him after all. She had been hurt and angry enough to strike out across the wilderness, chancing all kinds of perils just to get away from him.

Hawke picked up the mare's hoofprints almost immediately. They led toward the mountain. At first he was almost overwhelmed with relief. Rue hadn't left him. Then, on the heels of his relief, he thought of the dangers that lurked up there. Rue knew nothing about them. He had never warned her not to ride there. Hell, he berated himself, he had never taken time with her for anything.

The mountain loomed in front of him as the stallion entered the foothills. Hawke had ridden about half a mile, going over in his mind what he would say to Rue, how he would apologize for what had gone before, to put things straight between them, when he heard the pounding of hoofbeats. His head shot up and he recognized the little mare that shot past him.

"Oh God, what's happened to her?" he groaned, laying the whip on the stallion when a gunshot rang out. Had Arapaho renegades come upon her, then shot her when they had finished with her?

The stallion swung around a large boulder, and with a curse, Hawke jerked Captain to a rearing halt. In the dim shadow of a spruce stood his wife in the arms of his ranch foreman.

Black jealous rage boiled inside him. Forgotten were the words he'd meant to say to her, forgotten was his fear that she had left him. All he remembered was that he had nearly had heart failure when he heard that gun go off. And it had all been for nothing. His wife was quite safe. She had only sneaked off to be with her lover.

In his blind fury, he never questioned why a gun should have been fired, why the mare had bolted. His mind only told him that the woman he loved was playing him false.

Barely in control of his emotions, he barked, "What in the hell is goin' on here?"

Josh swiftly stepped away from Rue, guilt of his love for her clear on his face. Rue, on the other hand, only stared at Hawke, innocently.

But as Hawke continued to glower at her, anger grew inside her. Why was he pretending to be the injured husband? she asked herself. He knew, and she knew, that he couldn't have cared less had he come upon her and Josh making love.

But she would play his game, she decided, and answered coolly, "Very little is going on now. However, if it wasn't for Josh, I would have died a few minutes ago."

Hawke stared down at the pale, lovely face, refusing to see the lingering fear in her blue eyes. "Dream up another lie, you whorin' little bitch," he retorted snidely. "That one is too farfetched."

His eyes raked over a stony-faced Rue, and a scowling Josh. "How long has this been goin' on?" he shot at them. "How many times have you met up here? Twice a week? Every day?"

Rue started to hotly deny Hawke's charges, then thought, why should she? He wouldn't believe her because he wouldn't want to. It would salve his conscience, if he had one, about seeing Lillie Meyers all the time.

With a careless shrug, she tilted her chin, and remarked, "About as often as you sneak off to visit Lillie, I expect."

Hawke almost gasped at the pain her words gave him. If only it was true she saw Josh as often as he saw Lillie, that would mean she hadn't met Josh once.

Josh gave Rue a surprised look, then spoke for the first time. "You've got it all wrong, Hawke. I saw Rue headed up the mountain, and knowing the dangers up here, I followed her." He motioned at the dead wolf a few feet away. "Lucky thing I did. I arrived just as that beast was ready to spring at her throat."

Hawke knew before he looked that he had driven Rue farther away from him. In a calmer moment he would have known that lust hadn't driven her into Josh's arms. Had he controlled his jealous rage, thought a little bit, he wouldn't have jumped to the wrong conclusions. Why was it, he wondered, he couldn't think straight where Rue was concerned?

He gazed down at the dead wolf and shuddered at the thought of those yellow teeth tearing at Rue's lovely throat. His pride, however, wouldn't let him admit he was wrong, wouldn't let him say that he was sorry for what he'd thought and said, and to thank Josh for saving Rue's life.

He only muttered, "I see," then gruffly told Josh to ride to the house and let the family know Rue was all right.

"I'll ride with Josh." Rue started to follow him to his horse.

"You'll ride with me," Hawke growled, and before she could get out of his reach, he grabbed her under the arms and lifted her to sit in front of him. "There's something we have to discuss," he added, wrapping his free arm around her waist.

"I can't think of anything we have to say to each other," Rue gritted, trying to pry his arm loose, the action bringing her in closer contact with Hawke's body. "I think you've said enough already."

Hawke felt a stirring in his loins as Rue's small rear pressed against him. Damn, he wished she'd sit still. If she didn't, she was going to find one hell of an arousal prodding her backside.

There was a huskiness in his voice when he said, "I don't want to talk about what happened back there." His arm tightened about her, jerking her back against his broad chest, putting a few inches between her derrier and his hungry manhood.

"I can't imagine what else we could talk about." Rue watched Josh's mount disappear from sight. "Unless you want to discuss your affair with Lillie. And if that's the case, I don't care how often you see her, so we can leave that subject alone."

Hawke looked up at the sky, a bleakness in his eyes. He'd give half his ranch if his wife did care that he slept with another woman. If only jealously raged inside her as it did in him at the thought of her having a lover.

He thought of all the women he'd made love to, then left them when he tired of their bed, and realized that he was being served a big helping of justice.

"Damn it, Rue!" he grated. "How many times do I have to tell you that there's nothing goin' on between me and that woman?"

Rue made no response, only stared at Captain's ears. But inside her a grain of belief took root. Maybe he had broken all ties with Lillie. The image of the woman's coarse features, the determination in the pig-like eyes and on her thick lips, appeared in Rue's mind. Hawke might think he was finished with her, but Lillie had no intention of letting him go.

Would her husband be strong enough to continue refusing her invitations, or would the time come when he didn't care what his father thought and resumed his affair with

Lillie? Only time would tell, Rue guessed.

"I wanted to discuss our sleepin' arrangements." Hawke disrupted Rue's musings.

"What's wrong with our sleeping arrangements?" she demanded sharply, her heart slightly fluttering. Was he planning to claim a husband's rights? Did he plan on replacing Lillie with her?

Her round chin came up stubbornly. "I like things just fine the way they are."

"Well, I don't," Hawke spoke just as sharply. "Pa is gonna wonder why I'm not sharin' your room. He thinks we have a normal marriage."

"You should have thought about that before you started sleeping in the bunkhouse. Anyway, I don't think Jeb will be surprised that we don't have any kind of marriage after the show Lillie put on today."

"But don't you see, that's all the more reason not to raise his suspicions any higher."

"I don't give a damn what he thinks." Rue began to struggle again, pulling at the whipcord strength of the arm that held her so tightly, her rear again rubbing against that sensitve spot between his spread legs. "I'm not about to share a bed with you," she panted.

"Will you sit still?" Hawke half groaned, feeling himself growing harder and harder. The buttons were going to pop off his fly if she kept twisting in his lap. "I'm not askin' to share your bed, you little wildcat," he managed to say. "I only want to share the room, just a small space where I can spread my bedroll."

To Hawke's relief, Rue ceased her struggling and sat still. And while he willed his erection to go away, she chewed the corner of her lower lip.

Could she trust him to stay on the floor? she wondered. She remembered the time he had kissed her, how hungrily his lips had moved over hers. If he should do it again, could she resist him? She wouldn't want to chance it. Even now, in the circle of his arm, her heart was beating like a hammer. How could she lie next to him in a bed? With one touch of his hand, she would be lost.

Taking her long silence as a continued rejection, Hawke said stiffly, "You don't have to worry about me forcing myself on you, if that's what you're thinking. I'll not come near you unless I'm invited."

"Hah! That's an invitation you'll never hear," Rue retorted, and sighed her relief when the house came in sight.

Jeb and the children waited on the back porch, silhouetted against the lamplight shining through the kitchen window. Hawke reined in Captain and swung to the ground. A wicked gleam of amusement crooked his lips. He lifted the resisting Rue from the saddle and let her body slowly slide down his. When she felt his manhood stir and jump against her stomach, she gritted her teeth, pushing away the heat of desire that scorched through her veins. Her feet touched the ground, and after one little buck of his hips, Hawke released her.

She was grateful for the darkness that hid her flushed face as Jeb and the children rushed to greet her. Susie and Tommy threw their arms around her waist, and with an arm around their shoulders, she answered their questions about the wolf as they walked toward the porch.

"Isn't Josh brave, Auntie Rue?" Susie asked solemnly.

Before Rue could answer, Tommy was adding in awed tones, "Josh said he killed that wolf with one shot. He must be the best shooter around."

Rue heard Hawke's derisive grunt, followed by Jeb's dry chuckle. She grinned. Her father-in-law also knew that his son didn't like hearing Josh Malone being praised.

"You got anything to eat, Pa?" Hawke broke in, stepping onto the porch, putting an end to the lauding of his foreman.

"Me and the kids heated up the stew that was sittin' on the stove. There's plenty left."

"Good. I'm starved." Hawke gave Rue a cool, accusing look. "Chasin' after a contrary female don't feed a man's appetite."

Jeb gave Rue a broad wink, and she turned quickly to hide the amused twist of her lips.

CHAPTER TEN

The morning sunshine flooded through the kitchen window as Rue walked onto the small back porch. She leaned against the railing, gazing at the mist-filled day, and sniffed the sharp pine scent.

She shivered as a cool breeze blew against her. It was nearing the end of November and a hard frost had persisted for the past week. Winter would arrive before long, she mused. But for the first time in her life she didn't dread it. There would be no cold wind whistling through this sturdily built house and the snow wouldn't sift through cracks and broken windows. There would be no white drifts on her bed when she awakened in the morning. And the huge fireplace would keep her warm all day. When she had to go outside, she would wear a heavy jacket and there would be no holes in the soles of her boots.

A sharp gust of wind tugged at Rue's hair and she turned back into the kitchen, her red woolen dress swaying gently as she cleared the table of the breakfast dishes.

It was her favorite dress, she thought, stacking the dirty plates and carrying them to the dry sink. Hawke had bought it and two others for her.

Her hands stilled in the warm, sudsy dishwater as she recalled the day he had walked into their bedroom and tossed a brown paperwrapped package on the bed. Giving her a lazy smile, he had drawled, "A gift from your loving husband."

Rue gave him a scornful look at his description of himself and bent over the package to untie it. When she pushed aside the wrapping, she exclaimed with pleasure as her eyes fell on a neatly folded, blue poplin dress.

"How beautiful," she whispered, holding the garment up, wondering if she'd ever have the nerve to wear it, the neckline was cut so low. Surely it would show half her bosom.

The next dress she lifted up was of black velvet, long-sleeved and just as daringly cut. It was the type of gown a city woman would wear to a ball. What had Hawke been thinking of when he bought it?

The last dress was the red woolen. It was

full-skirted, buttoned to the chin, a white lace collar setting it off. She smoothed her palm over the soft material. This one she wouldn't be embarrassed to wear.

She lifted her eyes to the watching Hawke. "They are very beautiful."

"For a beautiful woman." Hawke brushed his knuckles across her creamy cheek. "Aren't you gonna thank me for them?" he asked, a teasing twinkle in his eyes.

"Oh, I do thank you." Rue smiled back. "I thank you very much. I've never had anything so lovely."

Without warning, his arm snaked around her waist and pulled her against him. "I'd like something better than words," he murmured huskily, and before she could turn her face away, his head swept down and his mouth claimed hers.

Caught unaware, with no time to get her defenses up, Rue's body melted into his. His kiss deepened as her arms went around his neck, his tongue darting into her mouth. She felt his powerful erection press against her stomach and excitement shivered through her. Never had her heart beat with such thudding intensity.

But when Hawke freed a breast from the bodice she hadn't known he had unbuttoned, she stiffened. When he lowered his head and stroked his tongue across her nipple, she returned to reality. This man didn't love her and she refused to be used. Though her breasts ached to have his lips on them, and her body trembled from the desire gripping her, she pressed her palms against his broad chest and broke his embrace.

"Rue, please," Hawke whispered hoarsely as she wordlessly left the room, her fingers doing up the buttons he had freed.

It had been different between them after that, Rue now remembered, bringing her idle hands back to life, scrubbing away at a plate. Hawke was openingly courting her these days. He was full of compliments, the two of them taking long rides together, sitting before the fire, where bit by bit he told her about himself, leaving out, she was sure, all the women he had slept with.

And because of all that attention she was dreadfully afraid her defenses were weakening against him. Of course matters weren't helped any, as she lay every night listening to his even breathing as he slept in his bedroll only feet away.

She had given in to his demand to share the bedroom with him, simply because she didn't want to cause concern for kind Jeb Masters. It had worked out better than she had thought it would—at first. Hawke always came into the bedroom long after she had retired. But since the drugging kiss the day he had given her the dresses, he seemed to come earlier and earlier to their room. A couple of times she had barely climbed into bed when he quietly opened the door.

Rue looked down at the gentle tug on her skirt. "Are you about finished, Auntie Rue?" Susie asked impatiently. "You promised we'd go down to the creek today and have a picnic."

"We will, honey." Rue placed the last dish on the drainer. "Just as soon as I get the beds made."

"Can I wade in the creek like I did the last time we were there?" the little girl asked hopefully.

Rue laughed and ruffled the blond hair. "You silly goose, you'd freeze your feet. Didn't you hear Tommy say that the edges of the water have been frozen this past week?"

"But what can I do then?" Susie plopped down at the table, her small mouth drawn into a pout.

"Well, you can sail the little boat Tommy made for you. That will be lots of fun."

"Yes, it will!" Small hands clapped together as Susie scooted from the chair and followed Rue down the hall to the bedrooms.

Finally everything was in order and Rue went back to the kitchen to make sandwiches for their outing. A few minutes later she had packed two sandwiches, two pieces of cake, and a jar of water in a basket. "Susie," she said, "go fetch a blanket from the linen chest and we'll be off."

The sun had warmed as it rose higher and it

was quite pleasant when Rue and her little charge arrived at the clear, running creek. She helped Susie launch her boat, found her a long stick to control it from the bank, then stretched out on the blanket, the unseasonable warmth bathing her face.

A peaceful hour passed in which Rue managed to keep Hawke out of her thoughts. She mused on her grandparents and Jimmy and wondered how they were, and if she would ever see them again. Maybe she would see Jimmy again. When he became a little older, he could make the trip to visit her. It would be wonderful if Hawke would give him a job. Of course she would never ask him to.

Susie brought her boat in and announced that she was hungry. Rue left off her daydreaming and set out the lunch. As bees buzzed lazily around their heads, the slices of beef between split biscuits were consumed.

While they ate the cake, Rue heard the hollow drumming of hoofbeats. When they stopped suddenly, she shaded her eyes against the sun and peered at a distant knoll. A horse and rider sat outlined against the sky. She frowned. She did not recognize the man as one of their hands, but the large bulk turned toward her looked vaguely familiar. Her heartbeat raced. From here, the man looked like Sly Burford.

Impossible, she told herself. What would her stepfather be doing in cattle country? He was too lazy to work on a ranch.

Nevertheless, she rose to her feet, folded the blanket, and picking up the basket, said, "It's time we get home and start supper, honey."

Thankfully Susie didn't put up a fuss at their short-lived picnic. As they headed toward the house a short distance away, Rue glanced up at knoll. The horse and rider were gone. Still, as she hurried along, Susie's short, little legs running to keep up with her, Rue couldn't shake the fear of impending danger to herself.

The sun was ready to slip out of sight, and long shadows were creeping down the mountain as Rue mashed a large pot of boiled potatoes. She was stirring a skillet of bubbling gravy when she heard the approaching sound of hoofbeats, then a moment later the straining of leather and the heaving of tired horses. The Masters men were home for supper.

She glanced out the window, her gaze unconsciously looking for Hawke. Her eyes roamed over him as he swung from the saddle, taking in the vest that swung open over a soft blue shirt, the checkered kerchief around his neck. As usual, his hard, handsome looks made the breath catch in her throat.

"Stop it!" she hissed under her breath and began to set out the plates.

By the time the horses were unsaddled and put out to pasture and son, grandson and father had washed up at the water trough, supper was on the table, with only the beef roast waiting to be sliced.

"That roast sure does smell good, daughter." Jeb sniffed the air as he hung his hat on a wooden peg on the wall beside the door. "You're a fine little cook." He took his place at the table beside Susie.

"That's why I married her, Pa." Hawke chucked Rue under the chin as he passed her to sit at the head of the table.

Rue's lips moved in a derisory grimace. They both knew why he had married her. A rifle had been trained on him.

"Papa married Mama because he loved her," Susie piped up. "He always said so, didn't he, Grandpa?" She looked at Jeb for confirmation, her eyes large and serious.

"That's right, honey." Jeb patted the blond head. "And Uncle Hawke loves Auntie Rue too. He was only joking when he said that about her cookin'."

"I notice that you and Auntie Rue don't kiss like Mama and Papa used to do." Tommy looked at Hawke.

His eyes shining wickedly at Rue, Hawke answered, "Blame Auntie Rue for that. She doesn't like to kiss me."

"You don't, Auntie Rue?" Tommy looked at her in surprise. "Why not?"

"Don't pay any attention to what your uncle says, Tommy," Rue answered evasively. "He's teasing, just as he was about my cooking." She gave Hawke a look that said he was wasting his time.

Hawke's only response was a raised, mocking eyebrow at Rue. It grew quiet in the kitchen as their hunger was sated, the only sound the scraping of knives and forks. Conversation picked up when Rue placed a cake on the table. As she poured coffee for the adults, the wind moaned through the big spruce in the back yard and the kitchen was filled with cold air.

Tommy ran to slam the door, and as Rue sat back down at the table, Hawke looked at her with slumberous, teasing eyes. "It's gonna be a good night for cuddling if a person has a mind to."

Rue looked away from him, not letting on that she had noted his scarcely veiled hint.

Hawke studied her averted face from beneath his lowered lids for a minute then, rising, he picked up the lantern from its usual place beside the door. "I'm gonna stable my horses tonight," he said, striking a sulphur stick and holding its flame to the wick he'd exposed with a press of his thumb that released the glass globe. "That wind might bring rain, and it will be a cold one."

"He sure is particular about those horses, huh, Grandpa?" Tommy remarked after Hawke left the house by the kitchen door.

"He sure is." Jeb grinned. "They're mighty

special to him. He wants to build up a herd of thoroughbreds.''

Jeb and Tommy continued to talk horses as Rue hurriedly washed the dishes and tidied up the kitchen. Something told her to go straight to bed tonight, not to linger in front of the fireplace talking to Hawke as was her habit. She hadn't liked that devil look in his eyes when he left to tend to his pets.

Thankfully Susie was tired from her busy day and didn't fuss at going to bed an hour early. Jeb and Tommy had moved into the parlor and were sitting in front of the fire when Rue told them good night and went to her room.

As she unbuttoned her dress, she walked over to the window and parted the heavy curtains. A full moon bathed the yard, throwing into relief the waving limbs of the spruce.

It doesn't look like rain to me, she thought, gazing up at the millions of stars twinkling in the sky. But maybe, she allowed, moving to the bed, rain clouds came up quickly in this region.

Rue stripped off her dress, then stepped out of the sheer lawn drawers trimmed with lace and ribbons. She was pulling the matching camisole over her head when she heard a low exclamation from Hawke's bedroll. She swung around and Hawke was beside her, stripped of his clothes.

''No,'' she gasped softly, shaking her head.

"Yes," Hawke persisted gently, his arms coming round her, his palms caressing her back as he slowly eased himself against her trembling body. He caught his breath as they melded, then his mouth was on Rue's with a fierce urgency. Rue felt the powerful beat of his heart against her breast as his kiss deepened and his manhood rose pressing against her stomach.

"Do you know how you fire my blood?" he whispered hoarsely as he released her lips. "How I can't sleep at night from wanting you?"

His hands cupped her proud, jutting breasts, and rubbing his thumbs against the pink tips, he continued, "Do you know how I ache to taste you, to open my mouth over these beauties, draw the nipples into my mouth, and suck them?"

And as Rue stood rooted to the floor, unable even to speak, so weak from the passion his words had aroused inside her, Hawke's hands slid down to her waist and lifted her up. Her hands gripped his shoulders when he held her so that her breasts were even with his mouth. When his lips drew on a nipple, catching it between his teeth and tongue, she flung her head back with a little moan.

Rue's breathing became unsteady and her fingers bit into the bunched muscles of his powerful shoulders as Hawke's dark head moved from breast to breast, his lips dragging on the puckered nipples as though taking nourishment from them. Each one was rosy and swollen when he slid her down his body, pausing to hold her tight against his rigid, throbbing manhood.

He held her there, pulsating between her thighs a moment, then lowered her to stand on the floor. "Touch me," he whispered hoarsely, taking her hand. "Hold it," he urged, folding her fingers around him. "Caress it like I dreamed you would."

It seemed the most natural thing in the world to Rue, to close her fingers around the hard, though velvet, smoothness and gently stroke it up and down. When his manhood moved and jerked in her hand, Hawke arched his neck and closed his eyes as though in pain.

"Oh, God, yes, sweetheart, that's the way. Stroke me, stroke me." His mouth came down on hers and his tongue moved between her lips in a darting action that synchronized with the movement of her hand.

Swaying from the force of desire, and weak from unleashed passion, Rue cried, "I need you, Hawke, right now."

"Not yet, darlin'," Hawke whispered huskily. "I've waited too long for this. I want it to last as long as possible, to be perfect."

He swung her into his arms and lay her across the width of the bed, her legs hanging to the floor. *At last*, Rue thought, then leaned up on her elbows to look questioningly at

Hawke when he knelt on the floor and lifted her legs around his shoulders.

"Hawke!" she exclaimed in a hushed whisper. "What are you doing?"

"I told you I wanted to taste you," he whispered back, a hand on either side of the curly vee between her thighs. "All of you," he added, and lowered his face.

Rue slumped back on the bed, hot liquid seeming to pump through her veins as his mouth covered that most intimate part of her, his tongue delving inside. She thrashed her head back and forth, making little mewling noises as his tongue flicked in and out, his teeth nibbling.

"Hawke, please," she finally begged. "I can't stand any more. Take away my pain."

Hawke answered her plea, rising to his feet, then kneeling between her legs. His eyes were glazed as he gripped her slender hips and raised them off the bed. "The pain will go away now, honey," he murmured, taking his large manhood in his hand. Holding her hips steady, he bent over Rue, guided himself to her pulsating opening, and plunged inside her.

Rue gave a painful cry as he broke the flimsy barrier within her. Mindlessly she struggled to get away from the punishing appendage that seemed to be splitting her apart.

Hawke's body stiffened and grew still. Surprise and wonderment were in his eyes as he stared down at her pain-pinched face. "God, I'm sorry, Rue. I had no idea you had never been with a man before. Why didn't you tell me?"

"I tried to tell you many times," Rue sobbed accusingly, "but you wouldn't listen."

"I'm so sorry, honey." Hawke kissed her smooth forehead. "I have so much to make up to you." He gently wiped away the tears from the corners of her eyes. "Had I known you were a virgin, I would have taken more care. I wouldn't have hurt you so." He smiled down at her. "Do you know you're the first virgin I've ever had? It's goin' to be most enjoyable teachin' you the things I like, finding out what pleases you."

Rue looked up at him doubtfully. "I don't think any part of coupling will please me. It hurts too much."

Hawke's lips curved in gentle amusement. "It only hurts the first time you're entered, honey. After that, it's pure heaven."

"Can we wait until tomorrow night then?" she asked hopefully.

"No." Hawke shook his head. "If we don't finish now, it will hurt tomorrow night too. Don't be afraid." He stroked her cheek. "I'll go real slow and pretty soon all the pain will go away."

Before Rue could say yes or no, he dropped his head to her breasts and drew a nipple into his mouth. As he gently sucked, Rue felt her lower body tingle again and leap in response. Hawke felt her body relax, and keeping his mouth on her breast, he began to move cautiously inside her.

Rue stiffened a moment, then relaxed. The pain was no longer so severe. Slowly Hawke quickened his strokes, going a little deeper each time. When she began to tremble and brought her arms up around his shoulders, he knew she was ready for him. Gathering her close, he pumped his hips in the well of hers in deep rhythmic strokes.

As Hawke irrevocably claimed her body, a warmth built inside Rue, turning rapidly into a consuming fire. Then waves of passion threatened to drown her as they shuddered through her body. She gave an exalted cry as at the same time she felt Hawke's fevered release spill inside her.

Hawke's body went limp on top of Rue. She stroked his sweat-slicked back and shoulders. When his breathing returned to normal, he leaned up on his elbows, taking most of his weight off her delicate body.

"Did the pain go away?" he teased, smoothing the damp hair off her cheeks.

Rue blushed and nodded, wondering when he was going to withdraw from inside her. She accused herself of being wanton when she wished that he wouldn't, that he would make love to her again.

"And did you like it?" He kissed the corner of her mouth. "Do you think you would like to do it every night?"

"Oh, yes." She smiled shyly at him.

"And in the daytime too?"

Rue ran a finger across his smiling lips. "In the daytime too," she whispered.

She felt his manhood growing inside her.

"What about right now?" Hawke whispered huskily.

"Do you mean it?" Rue asked hopefully.

Hawke gave a delighted laugh, and while her body was still moist with spent passion, he moved above her again. His muscled body rose and fell, pressing her deep into the mattress with the thrusting force of his hips. Again they reached the state of delirious relief together.

This time Hawke rolled off Rue, letting her rest. But it was a short time before he pulled her beneath him again, burying himself in her warmth. He couldn't get enough of her, and the way her arms went eagerly around his neck, and her smooth long legs wrapped themselves around his waist, he knew she felt the same way.

It was after midnight when finally exhausted, Rue and Hawke fell asleep in each other's arms.

At dawn, however, shortly before their rising, Hawke awoke, aroused, eager to claim his wife again.

Sometime later, as they lay panting in the aftermath of their vigorous lovemaking, Jeb knocked on the door. "Time to get up, you two," he called cheerily.

"We'll be up in a minute," Hawke called back, lingering passion making his voice husky. When the sound of Jeb's footsteps going down the hall faded away, Hawke slid out of bed and walked across the floor to the door. Quietly he slid the bolt on it.

Rue watched him move back to the bed, his manhood large and hard. When he crawled back into bed, she opened her arms and legs to him. And though they could hear the children running back and forth in the hall, laughing and talking, Hawke took his time stroking Rue to climax at the same time he did.

When it seemed he would claim her a third time, Rue laughed and scooted out of bed. "There's two hungry children out there, you insatiable man. I've got to feed them."

Hawke reluctantly agreed, but while they were dressing, he caught Rue to him, and after giving her a resounding kiss, growled, "I'll be home for lunch. Be ready."

CHAPTER ELEVEN

November passed into December. Frost turned the cottonwood leaves to gold, and they ripened and fell. The mountains seemed the same, yet somehow a subtle change was taking place. In the mornings a thin film of ice was seen along the edges of the river that flowed a mile away, and heavy frosts whitened the ground in the early mornings.

Rue stood on the back porch, listening to the dying clip-clop of Hawke's horse. A softness came over her face as she remembered the sweet lovemaking they had shared a short time ago. Something they shared every morning these days.

She hugged her arms against the cold that nipped at her nose and fingers. She was so happy, completely happy for the first time in her life. Although Hawke had never said that he loved her, she felt sure that he did. His large body told her so every night, as well as every day, beginning with the early dawn and ending after a quick lunch.

He never seemed to tire of her, and, pray God, he never would. He was her whole world.

A cold, damp wind rose and blew around her. Shivering, she turned back into the warmth of the house. Susie still sat at the breakfast table, pushing the remains of a soggy flapjack around her plate, offering some to her rag doll occasionally.

"Don't get syrup on your dollie, Susie," Rue said, on her way to the bedroom to get dressed. Hawke had lingered so long over their lovemaking this morning that she'd only had time to slip on her robe when he finally allowed her to get out of bed.

Shrugging out of the flannel wrap, Rue moved lightly across the floor to the wash basin and pitcher of water. The room was cold, as was the water, and she didn't waste time washing her body. She flinched a bit as the washcloth moved over her tender breasts, then later, again, over the tiny bruises between her thighs. Hawke had been very hungry last night, she smiled, remembering.

She hurried into her underclothing, then stepped into a soft, blue serge skirt. Next she pulled a shirtwaist over her head, a shade deeper than the skirt, and trimmed with black braid. After a few swipes of the brush through her curly hair, she made up the bed. As she smoothed the sheets and blanket, she sniffed Hawke's scent and couldn't wait for lunch time to come.

It was barely daylight when Lillie Meyers and Sly Burford met behind the storage shed some distance from the other ranch buildings.

"Is everything set?" Lillie whispered.

"Yeah, all you have to do is distract Sam so I can get behind him." Sly started to roll a cigarette then thought better of it. The odor of smoke would carry a long way in the cool breeze that had sprung up.

"Do you remember how our conversation is to go once we have the bitch?"

"Hell, how could I forget? You've made me go over it a dozen times."

"I just want to make sure she believes that Hawke is in on her abduction. If I told her, she wouldn't believe me, but if you bring it up, real casual-like, she'll believe it." A thrill of anticipation coursed through Lillie. "I can't wait to see that smug look wiped off her face. It'll kill her to know she's been used by Hawke.

"When will you do it?" Lillie looked nervously over her shoulder. Although she had left

Sam snoring away, he was an early riser and could come stomping out of the house any minute, looking for her.

"I figure *we* will do it as soon as all the hands ride out. It could be over and done with by the time they ride back for lunch."

Lillie nodded then hurriedly slipped through the shadows to the house. And Sly almost rubbed his hands together, thinking of the money that would soon be his. As he carefully made his way back to the bunkhouse, grimacing as his bare feet trod gravel and sharp stones, he damned Lillie for refusing to give him any money until Rue was disposed of.

"Not a cent," she'd said, "until both she and Sam are out of the way. I'm not chancin' you high-tailin' it out of here, leavin' that little bitch still in Hawke's bed."

As if I wouldn't take care of that one, Sly told himself. He had fed on his hate for her for three years. His eyes were still glittering with malice as he slid into his bunk and waited for the others to start stirring, to grunt and groan as they rose to meet another day of hard riding.

It was Sly's job to work in the tack room, to keep all riding gear in good shape. He made sure he followed his daily routine of eating breakfast with the men, then going to the small shed and handing out whatever they asked for.

The sun was about an hour high when the last cowhand rode out. Sly picked up a short, iron bar, hefting it in his hand as he stood beside the cracked, dusty window, his eyes on the ranch house.

Sweat popped out on his palms when the kitchen door opened and Sam Meyers walked out with Lillie behind him. While the rancher kissed his wife, Sly eased through the shed door and ran as fast as his great weight would allow until he stopped behind a wide spruce, only feet away from where Sam's stallion was tied.

He watched the older man walk down the two steps and toward his mount. "Come on, Lil," Sly muttered, "get his attention, say something to him. He's gonna be on that horse and gone pretty soon."

As though Lillie had heard Sly, she called out, "Oh, Sam, what would you like for lunch?"

His foot almost in the stirrup, Sam turned his head and called back, "I don't care, anything will—"

His sentence was cut off as Sly brought the iron cudgel across the back of Sam's head. He sank slowly to the ground without a word.

"Hurry, get him on the stallion before he comes to." Lillie came panting up.

Sly knelt beside the prone figure and felt for a pulse in the limp wrist. After a moment he looked up at Lillie and said callously, "Ole

Sam ain't never gonna come to. You're a widder, Lil."

"You're sure?" Lillie's voice was joyous, yet nervous. When Sly nodded, she urged, "Well, let's get him on the stallion and out of here."

"Not the stallion." Sly shook his head. "Nobody would believe Sam's pet would drag him to death. We'll put him on that wild one that's only half-broken. No one will be suspicious of anything that one might do. They'll think Sam was still tryin' to tame him and got throwed."

"Well, hurry up and saddle him." Lillie's eyes constantly searched the area, afraid someone might ride up.

Sly heaved himself to his feet and hurried to the stable where the unbroken horses were kept. It took him a good ten minutes to get a saddle on the eye-rolling, rearing mount. It took another few minutes to saddle his own mount. Finally, sweating profusely, he led the two animals out of the stable and to where Lillie waited beside her dead husband.

"For heaven's sake, Sly, hurry up!" Her voice squeaked from her dread of them being discovered. "What took you so long?"

"You oughta try saddlin' this wild brute," Sly answered, equally on edge. "He damned near kicked my head off." He walked over to Sam. "Come on, give me a hand gettin' him in the saddle."

With much straining and grunting and the wild horse snorting and sidling at the smell of blood, Lillie's dead husband was finally heaved into the saddle and loosely tied there. Sly then took a short length of rope from a pocket and used it to secure Sam's left foot firmly to the stirrup.

Motioning Lillie to step back, Sly whipped the hat off his head and swatted it smartly across the horse's rump. With a frightened squeal, the horse lunged forward, its pounding hooves at a furious pace as it headed down the valley. Before the animal was out of sight, Sam's body had come free of the rope and was bouncing along the ground, the one tied foot the only connection to the horse.

"Just the way we planned it, Lil," Sly said with satisfaction as he swung onto his mount. "I'll follow that wild bastard until he runs himself out. In the meantime you go on in the house and do whatever you do at this time of day. Don't do anything different."

Lillie nodded, and as she jubilantly walked toward the house, Sly guided his horse into a lope, following the distant galloping wild one, dragging its lifeless burden.

In a short time he reached the animal, its sides heaving and its head hanging. Sly swung to the ground, taking a knife from his pocket. In seconds he'd removed the rope from his ex-boss's body and cut the one that held his foot in the stirrup.

Without another look at the crumpled figure of the man he'd killed, he remounted and headed back toward the ranch, telling himself, that it was a job well done. *And pretty soon you'll get yours, Rue DeLawney,* he promised grimly.

The Masters family had just sat down at the table for lunch, and Rue was ladling chili into a stack of soup bowls when a horse thundered into the back yard. Boot heels rapped across the porch floor, then the door burst open. Everyone stared at a pale-faced young man.

"What's wrong, Bob?" Hawke stood up, recognizing the cowboy from the Meyers ranch.

"Sam's dead!" The panted words fell like a rock in the room.

"From what?" Hawke, stunned, finally managed to ask. "A heart attack?"

"No." Bob shook his head. "His mount threw him and his foot got caught in the stirrup and he was dragged to death."

"That's hard to believe." Hawke dropped back into his chair, motioning the young man to sit down. "Sam was one of the best horsemen around." He shook his head, guilt-ridden that he had once helped put horns on his aging neighbor. "It's a hell of a way for a man like him to go."

The cowhand smiled his thanks to Rue when she placed a cup of coffee in front of him, then said, "It sure is. If he'd have been on his regular mount, it wouldn't have happened.

I still can't figure out what he was doin' on that half-broken wild stallion."

"Was anyone around when it happened?" Hawke asked.

"Not a soul, I guess. One of the boys came across Sam and the mount a couple of miles from the house. The stallion had run himself out, I guess."

The young man cast an uncomfortable look at Rue. "Mrs. Meyers is takin' it real hard." He cleared his throat uneasily. "She sent me over here to ask you to come to the ranch to help her make funeral arrangements."

Three pairs of eyes leapt to the speaker. Hawke's startled look became an impatient one. Even at a time like this Lillie was trying to make trouble between him and Rue. It was on the tip of his tongue to refuse the request, then he remembered that Lillie had never bothered to cultivate a friendship with any of the other ranchers' wives, and now that she needed human comfort she had no one to draw it from.

Maybe for old time's sake he should give her his support, but only as a helpful neighbor in her time of need, he added. He glanced at Rue and found her regarding him with cool eyes. They did not threaten, but rather promised what would happen to him if he went near Lillie Meyers. If he went to the newly made widow, he needn't bother returning to his wife. He chanced a surreptitious look at his father and found Jeb's intent gaze on him. He grinned ruefully to himself. It looked like it wasn't his descision to make.

"Tell Lillie that I'm sorry I can't make it," he said to the waiting cowhand, "but that my wife and I will be attending the funeral."

Almost audible sounds of relief escaped from Jeb and Rue, and a slight smile tugged at young Bob's lips. He, too, was pleased at Hawke's answer. Lillie wasn't a favorite at the Meyers' ranch. Maybe old Sam hadn't known what his wife was, but all his help knew her for the whore she was. Only respect for their boss had kept them from being her willing bed partner.

The wind cut with the keeness of a knife, and Rue was chilled to the bone as she huddled near Hawke, listening to the drone of the preacher's voice, intermingled with Lillie's loud sobs.

She would have felt sorry for Lillie, believed that her grief was real, had it not been for her greeting of Hawke on their arrival at the gravesite. It had been embarrassing, to say the least, the way she had run up to them, throwing herself at Hawke, pressing her full curves against his lean body. The men had looked away uneasily, and the women had looked at Rue pityingly, clucking their tongues in disapproval.

On this cold, overcast day, not one neighbor had come out of sympathy for the widow, Rue suspected, seeing the dislike on male and female faces. It was for Sam Meyers. The stoic man had been a good neighbor despite his stern, caustic demeanor. And though he wasn't one to indulge in pleasant, idle chat, he was highly respected in the area.

Rue unconsciously leaned closer to Hawke, seeking the assurance that he belonged entirely to her. She was afraid of what Lillie would do, unhindered by a husband. Would she sell the ranch and move on, or would she go all out in her determination to have Hawke?

As though he read her mind, knew what her little movement meant, Hawke put an arm around Rue's shoulders and pulled her to his side. Rue smiled up at him, then her gaze encountered Lillie's and she caught her breath sharply.

Pure malice looked out of the small brown eyes, and Rue knew that if the woman had her way, Hawke Masters's wife would tumble dead into the same grave as Lillie's husband's. She shivered and Hawke's arm tightened around her.

"I think the preacher has just about ran out of wind and we can go home soon," he whispered in her ear.

Hawke had guessed correctly. For a few minutes later the man of the cloth said,

"Amen," and shovels of dirt were tossed onto the pine box holding the last remains of Sam Meyers.

Hawke took Rue's arm and led her away, saying, "Let's get you home, honey, and warmed up. I can hear your teeth chattering."

They were almost to their mounts when Lillie came running after them. "Hawke!" she called, near panic in her voice. "You're comin' back to the house, aren't you? The cook has prepared sandwiches and coffee."

Hawke stared down at the black-gloved hand clutching his arm, then frowned into the anxious face lifted to him. "Sorry, Lillie, but we've got to get home. We left the children with the bunkhouse cook, and he's not partial to young ones."

"Well, send Rue on." Lillie had ignored Rue since joining them, and continued to act as though she wasn't standing next to Hawke. "I want to talk to you, get your advice on something."

Hawke moved his arm, dislodging Lillie's grasping fingers. "Not today, Lillie," he said quietly. "I have too much work waiting for me."

The look in Lillie's eyes plainly said that she expected Hawke would soon find a way to elude his wife and rendezvous with his former mistress. "I understand, I'll look for you next week," she purred.

Anxiously, Rue wondered whether her husband would live up to the widow's expectations.

Hawke, untying their mounts' reins that he had looped over a tree branch, missed the gloating look Lillie turned on Rue. Which of them really had Hawke's love, Rue wondered forlornly.

Hawke was about to help Rue mount Beauty when three women approached them. They were hardy, healthy-looking individuals, women who worked hard, mostly out-of-doors from the deep tans on their faces.

"We've been waitin' for you to bring your wife visitin', Hawke," a tall, raw-boned woman somewhere in her mid-forties said, her smile warm, her voice genial. "We about decided that maybe she was ugly and you were hidin' her, seein' as how we met your pa a couple weeks ago."

The woman held out a work-callused hand to Rue. "I'm Molly Jackson, your nearest neighbor." The laughter lines around her eyes deepened. "Hawke sure ain't kept you to himself because you're unsightly. You're pretty as a picture."

Rue's own callused palm met Molly's in a firm handshake as she blushed from the compliment. "I'm afraid my husband never takes time off from work to do anything else." She smiled at the friendly woman. "But maybe I can find my way alone someday."

"Now that's the ticket." Molly nodded her

approval. "And bring the little girl with you. I have a little one about her age. Also, don't wait too long. We're gonna get snow any day now."

A short, plump little woman stepped forward. "Havin' nine younguns', Molly, you've got one for any age a person could mention." Her brown eyes sparkled at Rue, her hand coming forward. "I'm Sadie Larkin, and we're right pleased to have another woman among us. A person sometimes gets the feelin' of bein' overrun with men."

By the time Rue met the other woman, younger than the other two by several years, and expecting her first baby, Rue felt the stirring of belonging, a part of a community. She was no longer a no-account, bred and raised in a dilapidated shack, but a respected rancher's wife, heartily accepted by her peers.

Her face was flushed with pleasure as she said good-bye to her new friends, promising to call on them and warmly inviting them to visit her. As Hawke helped her to mount, his face showed his pride in his lovely wife.

"Did you like them?" he asked as they rode away, Jeb lingering behind, talking to some of the other men.

"Oh, yes. They are very nice," Rue answered, remembering the treatment she'd received from the neighbor women while growing up. None had ever invited her into their homes, hadn't even let on that she was alive, unless they wanted to talk about her and

Betsy's brood.

Rue and Hawke hadn't ridden far when Jeb came galloping up to join them. "That Meyers woman is a bitch if ever I seen one," he said, slowing his mount's pace to theirs. "I wish she'd leave the territory. She's gonna cause a lot of trouble if she's not straightened out." He looked meaningfully at Hawke.

"Don't worry about her, Pa," Hawke said, unconcerned.

Hawke glanced at his wife and wished that she wasn't bothered about Lillie. True, Lillie would make an effort to coax him back into their old relationship, but when she learned she was wasting her time, that he was only interested in his wife, she'd either turn to someone else, or sell the ranch and move on.

Had Hawke known, however, that at this very minute Lillie and Sly were sitting in her parlor, drinking whiskey and laying plans concerning his wife, he would not have been so cavalier in his assumptions. The most important thing on Hawke's mind at the time was would he and Rue find a little time together before she had to start supper and he had to finish up some chores that had been interrupted in order to attend Sam's funeral.

He glanced at Rue, saw the pensive look on her face, and knew that he must find the time to be alone with her. She needed to have her worries about Lillie banished from her mind.

When the three of them reached the ranch

house and pulled up at the stables, Hawke slid from the saddle and swung Rue down beside him. An arm around her waist, he guided her toward the house, calling over his shoulder, "Keep the kids occupied for a little while, will you, Pa?"

Jeb chuckled and Rue blushed.

"Hawke!" she whispered. "You might as well have come right out and said that we wanted to make love."

"Well, we do, don't we?" Hawke moved his hand up to cup her breast, then rub his thumb over the nipple that immediately hardened and pressed against her bodice.

For half an hour, behind their locked bedroom door, Hawke made slow, sweet love to Rue, yet she couldn't help wishing that he'd told her of his feelings instead of just showing her with his body.

Two weeks had passed since Sam Meyers was buried. And in that space of time, his widow had sent three messages to Hawke, reminding him of his promise to stop by the ranch to discuss something that was very important to her. When Hawke ignored each scrawled note, Lillie rode to the ranch, her coarse features set in determined lines.

What went on between the woman and her husband, Rue never learned. They talked at the corral and Rue could only guess what their conversation was as she watched their angry faces from the kitchen window. Once Lillie raised her hand as though to slap Hawke, and he caught her wrists and violently flung it away from him. A short time later, her face twisted with rage, Lillie threw herself on her mount, making it squeal in protest as she dragged her spurred heels across its belly.

Hawke was equally furious, Rue saw, as he stood spread-legged, his hands on his hips, staring after the woman racing away. He spun on his heels then and disappeared into the stables. When he appeared at the supper table later on, his face had assumed its usual calm lines. And though Rue waited, he didn't mention Lillie's visit, nor say what had happened between them.

Rue debated asking him, then decided that it was best not to broach the subject. The important thing was that her husband had rejected the widow.

But the next morning as Rue made beds and picked up discarded clothes, Lillie Meyers was still on her mind. Had the woman finally given up on Hawke? Surely she had after their ugly confrontation yesterday.

Her thoughts left Lillie and Hawke when Susie, coming up behind her, sneezed loudly. She looked down at the child's feet, and chided, "Where are your house slippers, Susie? Didn't you put them on this morning?"

"I couldn't find them." The child sneezed again.

"Well, let's go look for them. They've probably been kicked under the bed." Rue felt the small forehead and found it quite warm. "I hope you're not coming down with a cold."

The fur-lined slippers were where Rue had predicted. She pulled them from beneath the bed and slipped them on the bare, cold feet. Then leading Susie back to the warm kitchen, she said, "Stay here, honey, while I go make a fire in the fireplace. I want you to stay nice and warm all day. Maybe we can knock this mean old cold in the head." She dropped a kiss on the blond head. "We don't want to miss our visit to Molly's tomorrow, do we?"

"Oh, no! I want to meet her little girl. I'll bring my dollie with me."

As the morning progressed, however, it became clear that Susie's cold wasn't getting any better. Rue made her a bed on the couch and rubbed her small chest with a salve she had made just last week, an unguent her grandmother had taught Rue how to make from roots and barks.

It was eleven o'clock when Rue heard the nickering of a horse outside. Her heart leapt. Hawke was home early. She dropped the book she'd been reading to Susie, then almost tripped over the child who had risen from the couch, anxious to see her uncle also.

"Honey, get back in your little warm nest," Rue said gently. "Uncle Hawke will come visit you."

Sulking, Susie turned back and Rue rushed to fling open the kitchen door.

The smile died on her face. Lillie Meyers was holding in a restive horse, a worried look on her face. A furious resentment rose up in Rue. The nerve of this shameless creature, still chasing after another woman's husband. Didn't she know by now that Hawke wanted nothing to do with her?

She gave Lillie a cold look. "Hawke is not here, so I won't invite you in for coffee."

"I know he's not here." Lillie gave her a look that said Rue wasn't very bright. "I know where he is. He's at the line shack. He's been shot and needs help."

Rue felt the blood drain from her face. "Shot? How badly? Where is he shot?"

"Oh, he'll live if the bullet is dug out," Lillie answered shortly. "He caught it in the fleshy part of his thigh." She glanced around nervously. Then looking back at Rue, she asked impatiently, "Are you gonna come take care of him, or let him bleed to death?"

"Of course I'm coming. Just as soon as I get some things together." Rue wheeled around and once again almost stumbled over Susie. She hurried the fretting child back to the parlor, noting how hot she was as Rue tucked her back between the blankets.

I should bathe her with cool water, Rue thought distractedly, but Hawke needed her desperately. "Honey," she said gently, "Auntie Rue has to go help Uncle Hawke. Grandpa and Tommy will be home soon. Will you promise me to stay right here until they come for lunch?"

Susie nodded, her eyes drooping in a fevered sleep. Rue looked at her a moment, torn between the ill child and a husband who might die if she didn't get to him soon. She laid another log on the fire, making sure that Susie would keep warm, then hurried to her room to gather up the items she would need to treat Hawke.

In all, no more than ten minutes had passed by the time she saddled Beauty and joined an impatient Lillie. "Who shot Hawke?" she asked loudly as they pounded out of the yard.

"How should I know?" Lillie called back. "He was lying unconscious on the floor when I walked inside the shack."

Rue felt as though a giant hand had gripped her heart and squeezed it. What was Hawke doing at the line shack? It lay north of the ranch house, and he and the hands had ridden south this morning. She had stood on the porch, waving good-bye to him. Had he doubled back to meet Lillie there? No! She didn't want to believe that.

As the two women kept their mounts at a dead run, Rue noticed vaguely that the sky had become leaden and menacing. It looked as though it would finally snow. "Just so it holds off until I can get Hawke home," she whispered. It was unthinkable to be caught in the line shack by a blizzard without food or heat. Snowstorms sometimes lasted for days.

She nudged Beauty with her heel, urging the animal on to more speed. She was ahead of Lillie by a yard or so when the shack came in sight. She brought the mare to a plunging halt in front of the door. She noted, stepping onto the small stoop, a horse tied at the corner of the shack and wondered where Hawke's stallion was as she pushed open the door and stepped inside.

Rue blinked, blinded for a moment. When shadows took shape, her eyes searched the room for a bunk bed. When she spotted it in a corner, she gave a start. It was empty. Evidently Lillie couldn't get Hawke onto the bed. Her eyes scanned the floor in the dimly lit room, stopping when they encountered a pair of scuffed, run-down boots. A cold chill running down her spine, her gaze lifted to a pair of dirty, twill-covered legs, to a pot belly in a stained, denim jacket, and finally, with dread, to a fat face from which slitted eyes stared with hatred at her.

"Sly Burford! What are you doing here?" she gasped, round-eyed.

Sly's lips parted over tobacco-stained teeth in an unpleasant smile. "Why, I'm waitin' for you, stepdaughter. I've missed you," he jeered as he came toward her.

Ripples of fear slithered through Rue as she

backed away from the obese figure stalking her. Lillie had tricked her into coming here, and Sly meant to kill her.

Well, she wouldn't make it easy for him. She shot a quick glance at the door. She had outrun him before and she could do it again. As for Lillie, if she got in the way, Rue would knock that one flat with one blow of her fist. She had worked hard all her life and she was strong from it.

It was as if she and Sly were doing a slow dance, she thought crazily, she taking a step back, he in the same tempo taking one forward. A dance of death if she didn't get to that door. When a blast of cold air hit her back, she knew she had finally reached the way of escape.

Tightening the muscles in her legs, she spun around, noting too late the satisfied smirk on Sly's fat lips. A booted foot was suddenly stuck in front of her. She tripped, and with an angry cry, she fell. Before she could catch her breath, Sly was on top of her, jerking her hands together and tying them with a piece of rope he yanked from his pocket. She was hauled, screaming, to her feet, then slammed into a chair. Again the breath was knocked out of her. When she was able, she opened her mouth to scream again, but Lillie, standing behind Rue, whipped a handkerchief between her teeth and tied it securely at the back of her head.

"Now, you wildcat, settle down." Sly slapped her hard across the face. As her head rocked, he drew back his hand to slap her again, but Lillie grabbed his arm.

"Don't mark up her face, you fool. The old chief might not want her if she's all battered."

Rue's eyes widened in horror. Dear Lord, what were they planning to do with her? Sell her to the Indians?

A cruel smile curved Lillie's lips as she stood, hands on ample hips, staring down at Rue. "You're thinkin' right, you little bitch. We're sellin' you to that bunch of Arapaho renegades camped up in the foothills." Pure venom shone out of her eyes. "You won't be so beautiful after they've passed you amongst themselves for a while."

Rue shook her head vehemently, guttural noises issuing from her throat as she tried to cry out.

Ignoring her, Lillie gave Sly a barely discernible nod and he launched into the speech he and Lillie had rehearsed over and over. "How much did Hawke say that old chief should pay when we hand her over?"

"Like he told us, *he* doesn't want anything. Whatever you can get for her is yours. All he wants is to be rid of her." Lillie moved to stand over Rue, and looking into her appalled eyes, continued her and Sly's lies.

"It took me and Hawke a long time figurin' out what to do about you. Things have changed now that I'm a widow. Meetin' here a couple of times a week ain't enough anymore. We want to get married, and you can blame that holy father of his for you bein' in this predicament. He would have raised all kinds of hell if Hawke tried to divorce you."

Rue flinched away from the stubby finger Lillie ran down her cheek. "So, you see, my dear, we're forced to get rid of you this way."

Rue felt a cold contraction of her heart. All those nights when Hawke held her close, when she had been sure of his love, it had all been a lie. He had been using her, and she, love-starved, had fallen for his soft words and knowing hands and lips.

A kind of paralysis took possession of her, a devastating numbness of will and flesh. She was incapable of rising to her feet when Sly ordered her to stand. She could only sit and stare at him out of wretched, dull eyes.

With a ground-out oath, Sly yanked her to her feet, and half-carrying her, pulled her from the shack and tossed her onto Beauty's back.

"I'll see you back at the ranch after you've delivered her, Sly," Lillie said. "And, don't forget, her face mustn't be marked, so keep your hands off her."

Sly muttered something under his breath as he put the reins in Rue's bound hands, then mounted the roan Rue had seen upon her arrival at the nightmare she had stepped into. They rode off in the damp, biting cold, Lillie's taunting laugh following them. "Good-bye, Mrs. Masters," she jeered as she carefully moved a stick over her boot prints and her mount's hoofprints, erasing all evidence that she had ever been there.

Sly kept the horses to a jogging trot as he headed down the valley toward the foothills of the mountain. The brisk air and jolting pace, however, drew Rue out of her apathy. She told herself to forget for the moment Hawke's cruelness. A more important issue was at stake now: to keep her wits about her, to try and escape the destiny he had planned for her.

She gave Sly's wide back a look of hatred. She knew he had deliberately set this pace, knowing how difficult it would be for her to keep her seat with the limited use of her hands.

Her knees ached from gripping Beauty's belly when they entered the thick foothills. They climbed upward for about ten minutes, then Sly reined in, and grabbing the mare's bridle, jerked her to a halt also. A cold wind rose at that moment, bringing tears to Rue's eyes, blurring her vision of the Indian village sprawled before them.

She blinked rapidly a few times and saw several buffalo-skin teepees scattered at random. Raggedly dressed children had stopped their play to stare at the strangers, while a group of women stood to one side, also curious.

Before she could scan the area further, she and Sly were surrounded by braves, young and old. She was trying to count how many there were, deciding if she had a chance of escaping them, when Sly heaved himself out of the saddle then stood at the head of her mount.

Rue stared down at his sweating face and realized that Sly was probably almost as scared as she was. The man was a sneaking coward who only felt brave when dealing with women—weak women, that was. He had been afraid of her.

But he had the upper hand now. Her hands were tied and she was in his power. As he jerked her off Beauty's back, the look he gave her said that he knew this, and would now extract his revenge on her.

Rue staggered from weakness as her feet came in contact with the ground, only her natural agility kept her from falling. Above the noise of snarling and sniffing rib-thin dogs, Rue heard guttural murmuring from masculine throats. She shifted her gaze to the red-bronzed faces and shrank from the black eyes that openly assessed her slender figure, blatantly showing their hunger. Her eyes jumped hopefully at the women but then her shoulders sagged. She would get no help from that quarter. They returned her look with hatred.

As the whole tribe continued to watch them wordlessly, Sly cleared his voice nervously, then spoke with false bravado. "Take me to your chief. I want to do some business with him."

"What kind of business?" A tall, young brave stepped forward, his eyes still on Rue.

Sweat popped out on Sly's forehead. It was plain to Rue that he wanted to do business with the head man, that he feared this young Indian might take her away from him.

She watched his thick throat convulse as he swallowed, saw his eyes sliding back and forth like that of a trapped animal. Finally he jerked a hand toward her and managed to get out, "I thought he might be interested in buyin' this woman."

Before the brave could respond, the others were parting, making a path for the elderly Indian coming toward them. His hair was long and white, his face thin and wrinkled, with piercing eyes like those of a hawk. An old scar running from his right eyebrow to his mouth had left his lips permanently twisted. Rue turned her head from the fierce-looking visage, silently praying that the old man wouldn't want her, that instead Sly would kill her.

"I am Chief Wise Owl," the Indian said in an aged, cracked voice as he ran contemptuous eyes over Sly. "Is it not unusual for the white man to sell one of his own race?"

Sly's face paled. He hadn't expected such a question. He had thought that the red man would eagerly snap Rue up, be taken with her beauty, caring less why she was being sold.

"We whites would never sell one of our own," he blustered, "but this woman is a stranger to us. The wives don't want her around because of her beauty."

"I don't know." The chief looked thoughtfully at the ground. "Winter is almost here and it would mean another mouth to feed, more hunting by the braves."

"But she don't eat much," Sly said hurriedly. And as if in a nightmare, Rue listened to Sly discuss her as though she was chattel with no will of her own.

He pointed out that she was young, promised that she would work hard for the chief, that she was mild-mannered, and best of all, she was well versed in how to please a brave in bed and that he had taught her himself.

This last claim by the fat man made Rue want to lose her breakfast. She felt shame that even a red savage would think that she had ever been involved with this repulsive man. From her peripheral vision, she could see that the chief was studying her, his eyes narrowed on her averted face. She gave a small jerk when he ordered harshly, "Look at me, white woman."

When Rue didn't obey the order immediately, Sly advanced on her, his hand raised. She stiffened, marshaling her courage, then met the old Indian's hard gaze unflinchingly, although inside she was a mass of screaming nerves.

The chief closed the short distance between them and she made herself stand still when he lifted a swatch of her red-gold hair and let its softness slide through his knotted, arthritic fingers. "Free her mouth." He looked at Sly.

Sly hurried to obey, giving Rue a warning look to be careful of what she said. When the filthy kerchief was removed, the Indian asked, "What are you called?"

Rue worked her jaws up and down, loosening them, then after licking her dry lips, answered with cool dignity, "My name is Rue Masters."

A gleam of admiration flickered in the black eyes. This white woman had spirit. She would not whine and cry as most of her white sisters would. A man could be proud to call her his woman. He let Rue's hair slide from his hand. "This man who has brought you here looks on you with hatred in his eyes, is this not true?"

Rue nodded. "For a long time he has hated me."

Sly's face clouded and he stirred uneasily. He did not like the turn of this conversation. He grabbed her arm, sinking his nails into her flesh. "Tell him why I hate you, you little bitch. Tell him what you did to me."

"She will tell me later," the chief spoke sharply. "If I decide I want her," he tacked on. He turned his attention back to Rue. "Do you have family, a husband who will come looking for you?"

Rue wished with all her heart that she could answer yes. But it would be a lie, and Sly would be quick to tell the old chief.

She shook her head and answered dispiritedly, "There is no one."

"I find that very strange," Wise Owl spoke as if to himself. "I would think that one so good to look upon would have a man."

While the elderly man talked to her, the young brave who had spoken with Sly came to stand beside the chief. Rue thought she could see a resemblance between the pair, then put it from her mind when the old warrior pinned Sly with a narrow look, and said abruptly, "How much for the golden-haired woman?"

Sly took an eager step forward, avid greed shining out of his fat, squinted eyes. "A hundred dollars, and that's cheap for someone with her looks." When Wise Owl frowned, he added quickly, "When you get tired of her, you can sell her across the border for a good sum of money. The men who own bordellos there are always lookin' for a fair-haired woman."

The older Indian looked at the younger one as if for guidance. Sly waited nervously, shifting his feet while the pair talked to each other in their native tongue. The chief frowned once as if not in total agreement of what the younger man said. Finally, as the brave continued to press his argument with flashing eyes and motions of his hands, the old man reluctantly nodded his head. He spoke a few more words to the young brave, then turned back to Sly.

"My son wants the woman. There will be a wedding ceremony tomorrow."

While Rue bit her tongue not to cry out, Sly's fat lips parted in a smile. If the son was set on having the bitch, there would be no arguing over price. He would take the money and get the hell out of this country—after he had collected from Lillie. He had accomplished what he'd set out to do and, besides, he didn't want to tangle with Hawke Masters should he ever learn what had happened to his wife.

Sly's smile died when the old man spoke again. "As in Indian custom, you may choose six horses from our herd." At Sly's angry start, he pointed out, "Usually only four horses are offered for a woman, but my son is quite taken with the golden-haired woman and does not want to waste time bargaining for her."

His face twisted with rage, Sly cried out. "I don't want your damned horses! I want money! One hundred dollars."

"You are not the woman's family and we need not give you anything if we do not want to," the young brave said coldly, a threat in his eyes that the enraged Sly failed to see as he grabbed Rue's arm and shoved her toward the mare.

"Then I'll just take her back," he growled.

A smile devoid of all mirth stirred the corners of the young brave's lips as he stalked toward Sly and Rue, a knife held low in his hand. "Release the Golden One," he ordered, stopping a foot away.

For just a moment Sly's grip tightened on Rue's arm, then reluctantly he moved away from her. His face drained of color, fear bulging his eyes, he croaked, "You can have her. I'll just be on my way." He started walking toward his mount.

The chief motioned to the braves gathered round and Sly was quickly surrounded. "Take him back in the woods. I would know the whole story of why he brought this woman here. I do not think he tells it all. He is of small brains and I think someone else tells him what to do. This may all be a trick of some kind, a ruse to bring trouble to our village."

Sly was led away, blubbering his innocence, denying that he meant any harm toward the chief and his people. His voice faded away as he was taken deeper into the woods. Rue started to ease her tired body to the ground, then stiffened as a man's scream pealed. She held her breath, wondering what was happening to her old enemy.

Her body jerked when a few minutes later Sly screamed again, and again and again. She stared aghast when suddenly the fat man burst from the forest, running toward the chief. She gaped in horror at the blood running from numerous cuts on his body.

He was within two yards of his destination when he fell face forward on the ground. He twitched a moment, then lay still, the hilt of a knife sticking up between his shoulder blades. Blood trickled from between his lips and ran out on the ground and Rue knew that her old enemy was dead. The young brave stood over him a moment, then walked to his father.

They conversed in low tones with many glances sent Rue's way. They were arguing, she could tell from the stubborn look on the son's face and the dubious one on the father's. Finally the father shrugged, as if to say, "Have it your way," and the young man returned to Sly and retrieved the knife from his lifeless body. She began to tremble when he turned toward her, the blood-stained knife still in his hand. Relief whistled through her teeth when all he did was slice the sharp blade through the ropes that bound her hands together.

In a daze she felt him take her arm and lead her away from the others. Was he going to attack her now, rape her? The question made her tremble all the more.

When they came to the edge of a small growth of pine, she was pushed down beneath a tree. As she stared up at the Indian, preparing to fight him until her last breath, he brought her arms around the tree trunk and tied her hands together. She willed herself not to cringe from him, not to let him know how terror-stricken she was when he squatted in front of her and ran his fingers through her hair.

She almost lost the battle when his lean fingers unbuttoned her jacket, then started on her bodice. She tried to remove herself from it all, to make believe it was happening to someone else. But she gave up the pretense when cold air hit her bared breasts. She saw his hands come up to them and closed her eyes. What cruelty was he going to inflict on her?

But strangely, the young man only stroked the firm white mounds with gentle fingers. Then a moment later, while she held her breath, he rebuttoned her blouse, then stood up, and walked away. A sigh of relief shuddered through her lips, then she shivered violently. This wasn't the end of it. She knew with sickening clarity that later he would return and then . . .

Rue sank back against the tree trunk. How did Indian men treat their wives? She had heard terrible stories of brutal rapes and torturing of their white women victims. Would that be her fate because she was white, or would she be treated less harshly because the brave married her?

She stared unseeing at the sky, cold and hungry, filled with a dread she had never known before. Tomorrow she would marry an Indian whose name she didn't even know. She forced back a hysterical laugh. She had known her first husband's name, but like this impending marriage, she had known nothing about the man. She hadn't known anything about the deceit that lay in Hawke Masters, the mental cruelty he could, and would, impose upon her.

A lone tear escaped her eye and rolled down her cheek. And because Hawke Masters had taken advantage of her, marrying her only to take care of his niece and nephew, tomorrow she would become a member of this renegade tribe which had broken away from a reservation to escape the white man's rule. Could she bear their rigorous lifestyle, or would one winter with them be the death of her?

Her gaze swept over the part of the village she could see from her spot beneath the tree. Children, shy and wide-eyed, watched her from their teepees and the half-starved dogs wandered around, stopping to sniff at Sly's body where someone had dragged it into a patch of weeds. She studied the women moving noiselessly, preparing the evening meal over small fires. There were no smiles on their faces, she noted, but then thought, what did they have to smile about, living a life that kept them mostly on the run, doing all the manual work, never having enough to eat.

Jeb had said once, as they discussed Indians and their habits, that there was a great deal of intermarriage among the Arapaho tribes. That polygamy was practiced, with the men often marrying sisters and their brother's widows. And as for the mother-in-laws, husbands didn't even look or speak to them. She remembered that at the time she had thought that Indian men had no respect for the female species of their world.

Noisey conversation drew Rue's attention to a large campfire in the center of the village. The men sat around it, her future husband among them. He, it seemed, was the center of their attention as they spoke loudly to him, punctuating their remarks with loud laughter and crude gestures as they looked knowingly at her. Her skin crawled and she squeezed her eyes shut. She could imagine what they were saying about her, and what the young brave's answering remarks were.

I've got to get away! she screamed inside. And though her mind raced with possibilities, no solution came to her. She could only wait, be on her guard, and if the slightest chance of escape occurred, she must take advantage of it. Even if it meant a knife in her back. She would prefer death to a living hell.

The hours dragged by and Rue's arms ached from being stretched and her fingers cramped unbearably. She thought of her grandparents, Jimmy, her father-in-law, the children, anything to keep her mind off what awaited her tonight.

Suddenly, like a drape being closed, the sun sank and night arrived, dark and fearful, as a wolf's lonely yowl drifted down from the mountains. The leaping flames of the large campfire threw shadows on the bronzed faces, giving them a cruel, grotesque look. Rue shivered and looked away from the Indians.

A short time later, however, when the men were called to supper, a full moon rose, chasing away most of the darkness. Rue's stomach rumbled from hunger, although it made her nauseous as she watched the men dip their fingers into the bowls of stew. She tried to turn a deaf ear to the obnoxious noises they made, slurping and chewing with open mouths.

Finally the men had sated their appetites and moved back to the fire where one man brought out a bottle of whiskey and passed it around to the others. As the women and children took up bowls and scraped the bottom of the pot for their share of the meal, Rue wondered if anyone would bother to bring her anything to eat. No food had passed her lips since breakfast this morning, and her body screamed for nourishment.

She learned a short time later that she was not to be fed as the women carried the empty bowls and pots to a waterfall to wash them.

Was she to die from starvation? she wondered. When shortly the men staggered around drunkenly, she wondered if that wouldn't be preferable.

Rue's uneasiness of the drunken men grew to fear and dread as they grabbed women, and disappeared into the teepees. She tried to shrink within herself, to disappear, not to draw her future husband's notice.

She drew a deep breath of relief when she saw him lead a young woman toward his teepee. He seemed to have forgotten his captive momentarily.

Rue relaxed a bit, hoping that the tall brave would be occupied for the night. She felt intuitively that none of the other men would bother her, at least not until her intended had had her first. After that, she would probably be fair game for any man who wanted her.

The wind changed suddenly, and the air became sharp, making Rue thankful for her heavy jacket. There would be no blanket for her, she knew, and there was no doubt that it would start snowing before too long. She could almost smell it.

She shivered, thinking of the snow piling up on top of her, smothering the breath from her body. The women wouldn't care, and the men were too drunk to notice.

Rue had just curled her feet beneath her for extra warmth when there came a rustling of leaves, the crackling sound of careful footsteps. She looked over her shoulder and saw the bushes behind her quiver. Something or someone was there, creeping up on her. Was it an animal, or one of the men brave enough to use her before her marriage?

She gave a small cry of surprise when the brush parted and a small, brown face peered out at her. "Little Star!" she whispered. "Is this your village, your people?"

The little boy she had given cookies to crawled over to her side. "Yes," he whispered back, casting a nervous glance at the fire where those who had not yet fallen into a whiskey stupor continued to drink. Then the moonlight glinted on the blade of the knife that slashed through the ropes that held her to the tree.

"Grandfather said to cut you free," Little Star continued to whisper as the ropes fell away. And while Rue rubbed the circulation back into her wrists, he added, "We cannot give you your mount, but here is a strip of pemmican to chew on. It will give you strength."

Rue wanted to kiss and hug the child in her relief, but knew she dare not. The boy would be greatly embarrassed by such an action. She laid a hand on his shoulder and looked solemnly into his eyes. "I will not forget you and your grandfather's kindness," she said, rising to her feet. "I pray that someday I will be able to repay you."

"Where will you go?" the lad asked. "Back to your man?"

"No!" Rue hissed. "Never there! Point me in the opposite direction from his ranch."

"You go east then." Little Star threw another uneasy glance at the men sitting around the fire. "You go now while they drink firewater."

Rue squeezed the narrow shoulder, looked at the men fleetingly, then darted away.

No one's face was turned in her direction as the little boy watched her disappear out of sight. He picked up the piece of rope, then crawled back under the brush, very pleased with himself. Golden One was a good woman, she did not deserve the treatment his red brothers would have given her.

CHAPTER TWELVE

Hawke sat his mount on a lush grassy patch overlooking the river. He looked up at the sky that had turned dark gray with lowering clouds. The grass that reached past the stallion's knees wouldn't be green and tender much longer, he thought. If he was any judge of the weather, they would get snow tonight, covering and freezing everything it touched.

Tonight. He grinned wickedly as he felt a stirring in his loins. He'd gone around all morning in a fevered sweat, thinking of the delights in store for him once he and Rue retired to bed.

His grin widened. He'd get a little appetizer before that though. After he and Rue had a quick lunch, they would lock themselves in their bedroom and make love until Pa pounded on the door, demanding to know if his hoggish son was ready to go back to work. Rue would blush prettily, and he'd just have to take her one more time, no matter who was waiting for him.

His lips twisted sadly. He and Rue's bodies had honed down considerably from their turning to each other so often during the night.

That was another thing he loved about his wife. If she felt the need of his strength inside her, she didn't hesitate to let him know it. He'd awakened to the soft stroking of her fingers, and in seconds he'd be ready to oblige her.

"I just can't get enough of her," he said out loud, marveling at the truth. It had never been like that with any other woman. An hour or so with one would last him for a week or more.

Hawke looked up at the overcast sky and saw that the sun was directly overhead. A slow smile swept across his face. Was Rue watching the clock, counting the minutes until she saw him riding in for lunch?

"Let's go see, Captain." He chuckled and headed the stallion down the back side of the small knoll.

As Hawke rode up to the house, he saw his father and nephew just disappearing inside. He rode on to the stables and, stripping the saddle off the mount, turned Captain into the corral where Jeb and Tommy's mounts were already munching a pile of hay. When the three of them returned to the range later, each would ride a fresh horse.

Jeb met Hawke at the kitchen door, a worried frown on his face. "Susie is mighty sick, Hawke. She's runnin' a high fever."

"What does Rue have to say about it? She's the doctor around here."

"She don't seem to be around."

"She's got to be here somewhere." Hawke pushed past his father. "She wouldn't go off and leave the child alone for too long, even if Susie was well. Maybe she went to the necessary."

"Well, she's not in the house, and I didn't see her around the stables when we rode in. Course I didn't go lookin' in the . . . *here*."

"Let me take a look at Susie, then I'll go scare Rue up."

In the parlor, Hawke looked down at the little flushed face and laid a palm on her forehead. Pa was right, she was burning hot. "I wonder why Rue hasn't been bathing her with cold water to keep the fever down?" he mused out loud.

As if she had heard Rue's name, Susie stirred and whimpered, "Auntie Rue. I want Auntie Rue." There was a glaze of delirium in the blue eyes she turned on Hawke. "Bad witch took her away."

"She's out of her head with fever," Jeb fretted as he left the room for a basin of cold water.

Susie continued to toss restlessly, muttering, "Uncle Hawke is hurt."

"I'll go look for Rue now, Pa," Hawke whispered when Jeb returned with the water, a washcloth floating in it. He was worried himself now by the child's wild rambling.

"Yes, do that, and hurry up," Jeb said anxiously. He noticed Tommy's pale face then, and said in a normal tone, "Not that I'm worried about Susie, you understand. I just think that she'd rest easier if Rue was here."

Hawke went first to the necessary. The door stood open. Almost at a run, he went to the stables next. Inside he walked the length of the stalls until he came to the last one, the one that belonged to Beauty. It was empty. Had Rue taken her and gone for help, looking for him? She would never go to the Meyers ranch for assistance, and she didn't know where her other neighbors lived. He still hadn't gotten around to taking her visiting.

Hawke walked back outside and around the stables and corrals, studying the hoofprints there. He picked up the mare's prints right away. They were easily recognizable, the left front shoe having a wide notch in it. It was clearly defined in the sandy soil, and he followed it away from the churned-up corral area and onto the untrampled stone and grass.

His heart gave a jerk. Now there were two sets of hoofprints. Rue wasn't alone. And whoever was with her was on the heavy side, or at least heavier then Rue because the new set of prints bit deeper into the soil. For some reason, she had ridden away with a man.

It was no Indian, of that he was sure. The red men didn't shoe their horses. Who could she be with? Not Josh. His foreman had been with him all morning; in fact, he could see him and the others riding in right now.

Hawke hurried back to the house and walked into the parlor. When Jeb looked up from sponging Susie's face he said, "Pa, I have a feelin' that Rue may be in trouble. For some reason she has ridden off with someone. She would never leave the little one unless she thought it necessary, or she was forced to."

Jeb stood up, alarmed. "You're goin' after her, of course."

"Just as soon as I can saddle a horse. In the meantime keep bathing Susie and"—his eyes fell on the jar of salve—"maybe rub some more of this on her chest." He handed the small jar to Jeb.

"I will, son, and I pray that you find Rue quickly. It looks like a storm may be brewin'."

In less than ten minutes Hawke saddled a horse and was following Rue's trail. He could tell that the two mounts he tracked had run flat out. The length between the hoofprints indicated it. Wherever Rue was going, she was in a hurry.

Hawke soon noticed that, surprisingly, the tracks led straight toward his line shack. Who could have taken her there, and why? Anxious to find out, he nudged the mount, sending him into a gallop. In twenty minutes the shack came into view.

Nothing stirred around the crude little building when Hawke thundered up to it. He spotted Rue's small bootprints before he sprang from the saddle and rushed into the shack, calling her name.

Only silence greeted him. The small fourteen-by-fourteen-foot room was empty. He swept his eyes over the area, and it seemed the same as the last time he'd seen it. The day he had told Lillie that he would no longer be meeting her there, that their affair was over.

He scanned the room again. There was no sign of a struggle, no overturned chairs or messed-up bunk bed. He went back to the door and stared down at the ground, then ground out an oath.

There was a set of footprints leaving the place, but large ones. Beyond no doubt, they belonged to a man. His heart hammered painfully. His wife had been carried out of the building. By whom and why? His mind raced with questions. Did he have an enemy who would harm his wife to get back at him for some imagined hurt?

Hawke couldn't think of anyone who would take their spleen out on Rue. He knew that there were some men who didn't like him for some reason or other, but they were honorable men, who would never hurt a woman for any reason.

Anxiety coiling in the pit of his stomach, he left the shack and climbed back into the saddle. Rue was indeed in trouble.

When Hawke picked up the tracks with the notch in one shoe, he thought it odd that the mounts now walked. Why the almost leisurely gait, when before they were in such a hurry? Also, he was sure that the new set of tracks were put down by a different even heavier rider. These cut much deeper into the sandy soil. For some reason Rue had been turned over to someone else. He hurried his mount along, afraid to speculate why.

After a half hour tracking, a worried frown marred Hawke's face as his anxiety grew. The two mounts were headed straight for the mountain. Why? Only renegade Indians, wolves, and eagles lived in the wilds.

Suddenly he grew faint. An Indian had Rue. It was the only logical answer. The man was riding a stolen horse, one that still wore shoes.

But how had Rue been lured to the shack? he wondered as he kicked the mount into a fast, hard gallop, his eyes never leaving the trail. *They can't be too far ahead*, he told himself. *The prints are too fresh.* He glanced around at the westering sky. The day was far advanced, and lowering clouds were darkening the sky.

"I hope that Indian village isn't too far up the mountain," he muttered, urging Captain on. He must find Rue before night set in— and before she was ravaged by a bunch of braves.

Hawke had ridden close to an hour when he came to a river. The tracks led into it, and he steered his mount after them. It was a fast stream, but not deep, only a few times coming up to the horse's belly as he waded in a straight line toward the opposite bank.

The blood suddenly pumped faster in Hawke's veins. The mountain was only about a mile away. He could see the top of it looming above the spruce and pine. "Damned if it doesn't look like it's snowin' up there," he swore softly as the horse lunged out of the water and onto the rocky, sandy shore.

Hawke swore again. The tracks he'd expected to see were gone. Rue's captor must have angled the mounts to the left or right, and not moved in a straight line as Hawke had.

Sighing, for time lost, he rode back and forth along the edge of the river, looking for where the two mounts had left the stream. He found a few tracks, but they were days old. "Damn!" He slammed a fist on the saddle. The bastard had followed the river. Maybe for a mile or so. And had he gone up or down stream?

Hawke sat wondering what to do. Precious time could be lost looking along the river, especially if he searched in the wrong direction. And the deepening gloom brought on by the threatening storm would soon make it impossible to see the tracks if he did find them.

Finally he reined the horse toward the mountain. He had a better chance of picking up the trail there. He jabbed Captain with a heel, and keeping him at a run, Hawke came to the foothills in a short time. He reined in sharply at the sound of crackling brush. Had he come upon them already, and was there a gun trained on his heart?

He relaxed when he caught a glimpse of a deer bounding off through the trees. He urged the stallion on, telling himself to get control of his nerves as he rode the edge of the foothills, his eyes fastened on the ground.

After only a few yards he found the familiar hoofprints. They followed a narrow trail, and he steered Captain after them, checking his gun, seeing to it that it was handy to his touch. There was no doubt in his mind that he would have to use it.

After several hundred yards the trail led to a yellowed-walled canyon that opened up into the mountain. As Hawke rode, the air became cold, brittle, and sharp. He pulled up the collar of his jacket, muttering that for sure a blizzard was coming. He was thinking that he must find Rue and get her home before it struck when he saw the glow of a campfire in the almost total darkness.

He reined in. It would be best not to ride in any further. Most likely there were sentries posted about. He would better escape notice on foot.

Hawke slid to the ground and secreted the mount behind a tall boulder. After briefly laying a palm across its nostrils, a signal that Captain mustn't whinny, Hawke began his approach to the fire.

He was as silent as any Indian as he moved from boulder to boulder, coming ever closer to his destination. It was strange, he thought, that he hadn't seen anyone standing guard. Indians weren't stupid. They had to know that stealing a white woman was the worst offense they could commit. Did they honestly think that their village was that well-hidden?

The moon passed from behind a cloud just as Hawke crouched behind a brush thicket, only feet away from the fire. It shone fully on the braves, who slept in a drunken stupor, and the others who sat bleary-eyed, unaware of anything around them. His eyes scanned the area lit by the fire, searching for Rue. When he saw no sign of her, he could only assume that she was in one of the teepees scattered about.

But which one, and who was with her? His chest knotted in pain at the thought of some brave claiming her slender body. With a mingling of fury and helplessness that he had arrived too late spinning in his mind, he dropped down on all fours. He would reconnoiter the shabby village, peer into every teepee until he found his wife. And God help the man he found her with!

Hawke had crawled but a short distance when he froze into place behind a large rock. For suddenly from out of the darkness came a small figure, advancing with short, straight steps, right toward where he crouched. When the lad drew opposite him, Hawke stood up.

In the dim moonlight Hawke recognized the boy, who backed up in alarm. He had seen Rue give the Indian some cookies one day. *Now,* he thought, *how do I go about not frightening the child more than he is already?* He desperately needed the information the youngster could give him.

Making himself relax and erasing the harsh look he knew must be on his face, Hawke spoke quietly, "Little brave, I mean you no harm. I am lookin' for my wife, the one with the golden hair. Her mount's tracks led me to your village. Have you seen her?"

The boy stared at him a long minute and Hawke had the feeling that he was debating whether to answer the paleface. As the seconds ticked by and he was about to give up on the child speaking, Hawke wondered what to do about him. He couldn't let him rouse the camp.

He was thinking that he would have to tie and gag the youngster, when abruptly the little brave spoke. "A fat man brought Rue here, her hands and mouth tied. He tells Chief she is for sale. He wants much money for her."

A fat man, Hawke's eyes narrowed in thought. The only fat man he knew was the storekeeper in Jackson. Certainly it wasn't him. To his knowledge, the man never left his place of business.

"Did your chief pay him the money?" Hawke asked the boy, who watched him warily.

"No. Wise Owl's son say he wants Rue for his woman and offers the fat man six horses for her." The boy rushed on as though to get through the whole story. "The fat man grow angry, say no, that he will take Rue somewhere else and sell her. The brave puts his knife in the man's heart. He is dead." He jerked a small thumb at the large, crumpled heap in the shadows.

His face grim again, Hawke barely glanced at the dead man. Whoever he was, he was glad the bastard was dead. "Which teepee is she in?" His voice was hoarse with emotion.

"Rue is not here." The boy reached into his ragged jacket and pulled out a piece of rope.

"I cut her free."

A wave of weakening relief swept over Hawke. "I owe you, little brave." He clasped the narrow shoulders. "If ever I can help you, it will please me greatly. Now, in which direction did she go, and is she ridin'?"

"I could not get the mare to her," the boy replied. He lifted an arm and pointed upward. "She went up the mountain."

"Up the mountain?" Hawke looked stunned. "Why would she do that?"

The lad shrugged his small shoulders and pointed to his head. "I think she was all mixed up."

Hawke wanted to yell at him, to ask why he hadn't turned Rue in the direction of home. Instead, he sighed heavily. What was done was done. The important thing, she was no longer a prisoner. He debated asking the boy if the brave who wanted her for his woman had spent any time with Rue alone. He decided then that he didn't want to know. The important thing was that he must find her before the storm broke.

Little Star watched Hawke fade into the darkness, a pleased smile on his face. He had done as his friend, Rue, had asked him. He had sent her man off in the wrong direction.

Rue's breath came in labored bursts as she ran along, loose sand and gravel dragging at her feet. The painful stab in her side spread upward to her breasts and she could hear the loud beat of her heart.

Finally she stopped and sat down on a large, flat rock, utterly exhausted. As she rested a moment, chewing on a piece of pemmican, she realized that she had no idea where she was going. She only knew that she was putting distance between her and the husband who no longer needed her, who never wanted to see her again.

When her breathing slowed to almost normal, Rue rose and started on. The rocks in her path were sharp, uneven, and slippery under her boot heels. Nevertheless she moved swiftly, sometimes sitting down and sliding on her rear.

At last she reached the bottom of the foothills and sat down again. She didn't know if she could go on as she listened to the sough of the wind in the trees. She shivered as she felt the ominous quality of the gloom surrounding her. It was as though it waited for her to die, all alone.

She firmed her lips against the thought and dragged herself to her feet. She stood a moment, looking down the long stretch of valley. Only a distant growth of pine offered a place where she might spend the night. She felt in her jacket pocket on the odd chance she might find a sulpher stick. She couldn't believe her good fortune when her fingers found three beneath a wadded handkerchief. At least she would have a fire. All she had to do now was find the strength to reach the stand of trees that was a mile or so away.

Feeling much better and more in control, Rue started out, stumbling a bit, faint from fatigue.

As she staggered on, it grew colder and blacker and no wind disturbed the stillness. Then out of that opaque, obscure grayness came snow. She peered ahead. Surely that clump of trees wasn't far off. She felt like she had been walking for miles.

Rue plodded on, her head bent against the snow pellets stinging her face and soaking her bare head. She was vaguely aware that the storm quickened and that the wind had come back, growing into a howling gale. She could not see a foot in front of her as she forced her feet to move on. She must find shelter and soon. Her strength and fortitude were almost spent.

Her legs became leaden, and she knew that soon they would refuse to move. When she tripped and fell beneath a large pine, she was too weak to gather wood and start a fire. The waiting wilderness closed round her and she slept, the snow covering her in a white blanket.

As Hawke followed a winding path, the only way Rue could have taken, as the forest was too thick to move through, it began rapidly to change underfoot. When the horse stumbled over an outcropped rock and almost fell, Hawke was compelled to go more slowly. If the animal should break a leg and have to be shot, its rider would never get off the mountain alive.

The air grew colder and Hawke worried if Rue wore her heavy jacket. Pray God, he'd find her soon.

His concern increased when huge snowflakes came fluttering down. In a short time the snow was clinging thick and heavy on the fir trees and blanketing the ground with several inches. He rode on, his teeth set and his eyes on the ground. Rue's footprints should start appearing in the snow any time.

The air had turned biting cold when Hawke heard the rattle of a disturbed rock. He pulled the horse in, peering ahead. Was it a wild animal poking around, or a man? If man, was he white or red?

He was ready to ride on when he felt the singe of a bullet pass over his head. Captain spooked at the sound, and while Hawke fought to control his horse, there came a thud in his thigh, followed by a searing pain. His hand shot to his Colt as he peered around, trying to penetrate the double gloom of snow and night. He spotted an Indian then and thumbed the gun back as with a yell and a leap the fierce-faced brave came at him, his scalping knife in his upraised hand.

Hawke's finger squeezed the trigger, the Colt jumped, and his enemy lay in the snow. He twitched twice, then lay still.

The world grew dim for Hawke then and he reeled in the saddle, fighting back the blackness that sought to envelop his mind. He had to get down this mountain and send others to search for Rue.

He managed to turn the horse around, and as the animal began the descent, Hawke fell forward on its neck, groaning his pain in Captain's rough mane and gritting his teeth to hang on.

Old trapper Adams lowered his tired body into his favorite chair and stretched his stockinged feet to the crackling fire dancing up and down in the fireplace.

"Dog," he said, tamping tobacco into a clay pipe, "there ain't nothin' like a cheery fire on a cold night." The big dog's tail whacked the floor as if in agreement.

Adams reached into the fire and brought a flaming twig to the bowl of his pipe. He drew on the stem clamped between his teeth, and when the tobacco burned to his satisfaction, he leaned back and the rocker creaked in motion. He gave a relaxed sigh and watched the smoke curl from his pipe.

Then, as had been his habit for a week or so, in quiet moments, his thoughts turned to the couple who had spent a night with him some time back. Rue had been the girl's name. A strange name, he thought and wondered how was she getting along with that stony-faced husband of hers.

He had puzzled on that strange marriage for a long time after they'd left. There had been no love between them, that was for sure. The only thing they seemed to share was resentment, as if neither one wanted to be hitched to the other. He had especially felt that about the man, Masters. Hell, he slept on the floor rather than share his wife's bed. The girl wasn't having an easy time of it with that hard case, he imagined.

The old man continued to rock slowly, stopping once to add another log to the fire. For some reason he couldn't get that big-eyed girl out of his mind. He couldn't shake the idea that she was in danger, or was about to be.

The wooden clock on the mantle struck ten and Adams yawned, rose, then knocked out his pipe on the hearth. When he had banked the fire and was shucking down to his woolen underwear, he said, "Dog, I'm not goin' to bait my traps after runnin' them tomorrow. The day after, me and you are gonna strike out and see for ourselves how Rue is farin'. I got an uneasiness about her."

The dog thumped his tail again, then stretched out on the hearth, his big head between his paws. Soon Adams's loud snores filled the small cabin.

It was a blustery morning when Adams called the dog and climbed onto the gray mule. There was a feel of snow in the air, he thought as he prodded the animal to move out. "She's gettin' ready for a blizzard, Mule," he said. "So I don't want you dawdlin' along."

The mule stepped briskly along all day, and when Adams made camp at sunset, he was pleased with the distance they had covered. He built a fire in the center of a stand of spruce, then placed an open can of beans close to the heat, and started a pot of coffee brewing. Shortly, as he and Dog shared the skimpy meal, the air became damp and biting.

The lonely howl of a wolf drifted through the night as the old man drank his coffee and smoked his pipe. "You keep your eyes and ears open tonight, Dog." He scratched the soft hair between the brown eyes. "That lobo sounded kinda hungry. I wouldn't want to be his supper."

Later, rolled up in a buffalo robe, his feet to the fire, the stars that looked down on Adams were cold and brilliant, seeming to crackle in the sky. "We're gonna get snowed on tomorrow," he spoke to the dog stretched out beside him. "I hope we make it to Masters's ranch before it gets too deep."

The morning was freezing cold when Adams awoke. He started a fire, and when he picked up the half-full pot of coffee to reheat, he grunted sourly. It was frozen solid.

"It'll take us a few minutes longer to get on the trail, Dog," he said. "And we ain't got all that much time to waste."

While the coffee thawed and warmed, Adams rolled up the buffalo hide and tied it with a thin strip of rawhide. When he walked over to the mule to saddle it, he wasn't surprised to see wolf tracks circling his small campsite. Dog's threatening growls had awakened him a couple times during the night.

When Adams finally resumed his trip, he kept the mule at a trot. The weather grew steadily colder, with heavy clouds building up in the north. He had been riding about an hour when a heavy wind came up and the day turned gray. A worried frown drew his shaggy eyebrows together. He and the animals were in for some rough weather.

It was close to dark when the first flakes of snow began to fall. Soon it became a white curtain, and with the oncoming night, Adam's surroundings were almost obscure. He urged the mule on, his eyes peering ahead, looking for a spot to make camp and wait out the storm. He would never make it to the Masters's ranch this night.

"And pray God I find a sheltered spot soon,"

he muttered. The old mule had just about had it.

Adams continued to squint through the snow, alert to see a boulder, a tree, anything that would cut the force of the wind. Finally, through the screen of snow, he spied the dark shadow of trees. Heaving a sigh of relief, he guided the mule toward them.

He was within half a mile of the sheltering spruce when the dog, a few yards ahead of him, stopped suddenly and raised his head to sniff the air. He darted off then, heading for a large tree that stood apart from the others. When a minute later he set up an anxious barking, Adams called on the mule for more speed. He knew that bark. It was telling him to hurry, that he was needed.

Stiff-kneed and near frozen, Adams slipped off the mule and tramped through the snow to where the dog whined and pawed at a curled up, snow-covered figure. A youngster caught in the storm, he thought, kneeling beside the slight frame.

He gasped in disbelief when he turned the body over onto its back and he stared down at Rue's pale face. "My God, girl!" he exclaimed. He hurriedly felt for a pulse in the cold, limp wrist, and finally felt it, faint and slow.

"We've got to get her blood circulatin', Dog," he whispered in near panic.

With his mittened hands, Adams frantically

scraped the snow from under the spruce, piling it into a wall around Rue. When it was about three feet high, he hurried to the mule and returned with the buffalo hide. He went through the doorlike opening he'd left in the center of the wall, and spread it on the ground.

Adams stood a moment, catching his breath, then brushing the snow off Rue, he lifted her onto the heavy robe. After he folded the edges tightly around her, he ran to search out and gather up pieces of dry limbs beneath the stand of trees. Placing them into a loose pile, he jerked the scarf from around his neck and shoved it under the stacked wood.

Because of his hurrying and his cold, stiff fingers, he broke two sulphur sticks before he got a fire going. When the flames leapt high, he made another trip to the mule, returning with a bottle of whiskey. Kneeling beside Rue, he lifted her head and tilted the bottle to her lips.

"Come on, Rue," he ordered sharply as a father would to his child, "open your lips and swallow this."

Rue, in her semiconscious state, heard the order and obeyed. Her lips parted and the raw whiskey trickled down her throat. She gasped, choked, and coughed. But the alcohol warmed her stomach and sped up the beat of her heart. She opened her eyes and blinked at the old man in confusion.

"Adams," she croaked, "what are you doing here?"

"What are *you* doin' here is a better question?" Adams answered. "What in the blazes are you doin' out in a blizzard alone? You'd have frozen to death in another hour if Dog hadn't found you."

A spasm of pain moved across Rue's face. "I was running from something worse than death," she said hoarsely.

Before Adams could question her strange statement, she cried out in pain. The warmth of the fire and the whiskey had started the blood circulating in her feet and hands. All else was forgotten as Adams removed her boots and socks and began to massage her ice-cold feet.

Slowly the pain stopped as the cold eased out of Rue's body. When the warmth of the fire stole over her, she looked at Adams and her cracked lips parted in a smile. "I didn't think I would ever be warm again."

The old man returned her smile, then asked, "Are you hungry?"

"Starving." She nodded, and the elderly trapper made yet another trip to the mule that stood tail to the wind. He removed the grubsack tied to the back of the saddle, then took the time to lead the animal into the shelter of the trees.

In a short time Rue knew she had never smelled anything so good as the aroma of brewing coffee and frying salt pork wafting toward her. She watched avidly as Adams placed the larger share of the meat on a tin plate, added a piece of hardtack, then handed it to her. She ate ravenously, uncaring that her host watched her with dry amusement.

When the meal was topped off with steaming cups of coffee, Adams lit his pipe, then looked across at Rue. "I'll have your story now."

Rue set her coffee down and stared into the fire, reluctantly remembering what she would like to wipe from her memory. With pain and bitterness threading through her voice, she spoke.

In as few words as possible, leaving out the nights of lovemaking with her husband—she was too ashamed to tell that—she told Adams what had happened since her arrival at Masters' ranch. She ended with Hawke's betrayal, and how she had eventually wound up under the tree where Adams found her.

When Rue finished, Adams shook his head in bewilderment. Never in a million years would he have thought that Hawke Masters was capable of such a dastardly act. He had known right off that the man was hard, but he hadn't read him as being deceitful. He had certainly been outspoken with Rue the night the two spent at the cabin. Why would he back off telling her to her face that he wanted out of the marriage?

Adams grew angry, felt let down. He had always thought that he was a good judge of people. He glanced at Rue's drawn face and at the single tear that slipped down her cheek. "Put it all behind you, girl." He reached over and patted her knee. "All men ain't like that. We'll head for my place in the mornin'. You'll be safe there with me and Dog."

When Rue's eyes thanked him, he added, "It'll be right pleasant, havin' someone to talk to in the evenins'. Dog ain't much on answerin' me." He grinned.

Adams stood up then and stretched his tired muscles. "Finish your coffee, then get back in the bedroll. I'm gonna see how Mule is doin'."

The coffee had grown cold and Rue poured it around the edges of the fire. After making a nature call behind the large tree trunk, she hurried to get into the warm bedroll. She lay a moment, then scooted over to leave room for Adam's skinny body. There were no other blankets, she knew.

As she drifted off to sleep, she heard Adams say, "Dog, you keep an eye on Mule tonight. He's old and stringy, but I'm thinkin' the wolves wouldn't mind that."

Sometime during the night the wind died down and the snow ceased. There was a white silence when Adams awakened Rue at dawn. She found herself refreshed, except for her hands and feet. They were sore from being nearly frozen.

She and Adams shared a can of beans he had warmed and drank the leftover coffee from the night before. The sky in the east was pink when, riding double on the old mule, they started out, the snow up to the mule's knees, and up to Dog's belly.

Jeb Masters stared out the kitchen window, his hands cupped at the sides of his face, cutting down the reflection of the lighted lamp behind him on the table. All he saw was the driving snow and, dimly, the outlines of the outbuildings.

The glass panes reflected his anxiety. Where was Hawke? He had been gone for six hours now, and for the last two the snowstorm had raged. He could only hope and pray that his son had found Rue and that they were holed up in one of their lineshacks, waiting out the storm.

His granddaughter fussed from the parlor and Jeb hurried to her side. He pulled the blanket she had tossed aside back under her chin, then removed the wet cloth from her forehead. It felt hot in his hand as he dipped it into the basin of water on the floor. When he had wrung out the square of soft flannel and bathed the small flushed face with it, he looked over his shoulder at Tommy, who stood ready to help in anyway he could.

"Go fetch another pan of snow, son," he said quietly. "This water is warm."

Tommy grabbed up the basin and half ran to the door, water slopping onto the floor. In his concern for his granddaughter, Jeb didn't notice the wet spots on his cherished carpet. He wouldn't have said anything had he seen it. Tommy was just as worried as he was about the little girl.

He did, however, start to chastise Tommy when a minute later the boy burst into the room, the door slamming back against the wall.

But the words died on his lips when Tommy cried, "Grandpa, Uncle Hawke is outside, slumped over the saddle. I think he's been shot. There's blood all over the saddle!"

Jeb shot to his feet. "Go get Josh," he called over his shoulder as he rushed to the door.

Tommy darted out behind him and was halfway to the bunkhouse when Jeb began to examine Hawke. His eyes were drawn immediately to the dark red stain on the twill material covering the muscular thigh. He noted that the edges of the discoloration was dry and frozen, but when he carefully touched a finger to its center, he found it wet and warm. He shook his head. The wound still bled. How much blood had Hawke already lost? Jeb wondered with a groan.

He was holding his son's limp wrist, checking his pulse, when Tommy and Josh rushed up. "How bad is he?" Josh asked, concern on his face. Although he was jealous of the man, would take his wife away from him if he could, Josh still liked Hawke Masters.

"He's alive, but just barely," Jeb answered, his voice shaky as he dropped Hawke's wrist. "His pulse is very feeble."

"He'll be all right," Josh said soothingly. "Let's get him inside and see how much damage has been done to him. See if he's been shot anywhere else."

Tommy ran ahead and held the door open as Hawke was carefully hauled from the saddle and carried between the two men into the house and then into his bedroom. They stretched him out on the bed and as Jeb removed his boots and then his trousers, he glanced at his hovering white-faced grandson.

"Go sit with your sister, son," he said gently. "Your Uncle Hawke is goin' be all right." As he turned his attention back to his son, Jeb silently prayed that his words were true.

A quick examination showed that Hawke had been shot only once, and that the bullet had gone through the fleshy part of his thigh, barely missing the bone.

Josh stopped pressing around the wound and gave Jeb a reassuring smile. "The freezing weather probably saved his life. It slowed down the flow of blood." He straightened up. "We shouldn't have any problem stopping this seepage. The question is how much blood has he already lost."

"A lot, I think," Jeb answered grimly. "The

saddle and Captain's side is wet with it."

Josh laid a comforting hand on the hunched shoulders. "Why don't you go get me some warm water, a bottle of whiskey, and maybe a sheet for bandages?"

Jeb shook his head in bemusement as he filled a basin with water from the black cast-iron kettle on the back of the stove. Cold water for Susie's fever, warm water for Hawke's wound. He felt so muddled and worried he hoped he could keep them straight.

When he returned to Hawke's room, a basin of water in one hand, a sheet and bottle in the other, he found that Josh had changed Hawke's shirt and somehow managed to get him between the covers. Josh took the water from his slightly shaking hands.

"I'll take care of the wound, Jeb, so stop worryin'. Your son is as strong as a mule and just as stubborn. He's not about to die and leave that pretty little wife of his for some other man to take."

For the first time Jeb thought of Rue and was deeply ashamed. Where was she? Did the Indians have her? Was that how Hawke had been shot, trying to rescue her? Or, was she out there, lost in the blizzard?

He gave a startled jerk when Josh asked the question that had been on the cowboy's mind since entering the house. "Where *is* Rue? Is she sick? Has she caught the little girl's cold?"

Jeb's shoulders slumped even lower. "I

don't know. She's disappeared. Hawke was out lookin' for her when he got shot."

Alarm shot into Josh's eyes and he fired so many questions at Jeb, the older man looked at him curiously. The ranch hand seemed unnaturally worried about Rue.

His tone was a little cool as he answered, "We're just as in the dark as you are. We have no idea how or when she disappeared. All we know is that she's gone. All we can do is wait until Hawke comes to and see if he found any trace of her before he was shot."

CHAPTER THIRTEEN

The pale winter sun had set and darkness was arriving fast when the mule stopped in front of the old cabin. Rue looked at the sturdy little building, a sharp pang jabbing her breast as she remembered the first time she'd seen it. Although it was only months ago, it seemed like a lifetime since she and Hawke had spent a night here.

Her lips thinned in a smile of self-derision. She should have thought back to that night, and all the following days before she lost herself in a fool's paradise.

Her face flamed with shame as she remembered how easily she had let herself be taken in by Hawke, how she had believed his honeyed words, had let him use her. For used her he had. He had spent his lust on an unwanted wife until he could get rid of her and have the woman he loved.

Rue came back to the present when Adams tugged at her leg, and teased, "You gonna spend the night on Mule?"

She gave a small bitter laugh as she slid off the tired mule. "I was just remembering the first time I was here, and of how foolish a young girl can be."

Adams's smile faded and his eyes became serious. "Don't linger on the past, Rue. That's history and hard to change. You must look to the future now, plan yourself a new life."

"I know," Rue said wearily, climbing off the mule and following the old man onto the small porch. "Right now I don't want to think farther than the present."

"You'll feel different in time, after your heart and mind have healed." Adams pushed open the cabin door and stood aside for Rue to enter the dark interior of the single room.

She almost tripped over Dog rushing past her. "That ding-blasted dog ain't got no manners," the old man grumped. "You'd better stand still, Rue, until I light the lamp. It's blacker than a whore's heart in here."

He scratched a sulphur stick on the underneath of the table and in a moment a small flame pushed back the darkness of the room. "Come sit down while I get a fire goin'," he said, kneeling in front of the fireplace.

Rue eased her tired body into the blanket-padded rocker and watched Adams rake away a thick layer of ashes disclosing a few red coals beneath them. He reached a hand into a large woodbox and brought out a handful of wood slivers and laid them on the glowing embers. When they caught and burned steadily, he fed larger pieces of wood to it. After he tusseled a large backlog behind the fire, he straightened up and dusted off his hands.

"There," he said, "we'll be as warm as a whore's heart in no time."

Adams grinned at Rue's startled look. "There's good and bad in all of us, Rue. Even whores." He waited a second then added, "I guess I was just tryin' to make a point."

"Hah!" Rue sniffed, "I hope you're not including Hawke Masters in your dubious observation."

"I expect he treats his father in a good way."

Rue couldn't deny that. Hawke's treatment of his father was above average, as well as the way he cared for his niece and nephew.

When Adams saw that Rue wasn't going to give him a rebuttal, he changed the subject. "I expect you're as hungry as I am. I got a pot of rabbit stew in my little storage shed. I'll bring it in and hang it over the fire. I imagine it's frozen, so it'll take awhile for it to warm up."

When Adams left the cabin, Rue stood up and shrugged out of her jacket and hung it on a peg affixed to the wall. She looked down at her dress and frowned. The hem and several inches above it were mud-stained with two big tears midway up the skirt, caused from her repeated falls in her mad dash for freedom.

She smiled ruefully. She'd have to borrow some clothes from the old man. Luckily they were around the same size, in height at least.

A snatch of cold air followed Adams into the room. "It's gettin' colder and colder out there," he said as he swung a crane out over the fire then hung a black cast-iron pot on it. "It's as cold—"

"As a whore's heart," Rue laughingly finished for him.

"Yeah." Adams grinned, standing with his back to the fire, his palms turned to catch the warmth. After a moment he put his mittens back on, and walking to the door, said over his shoulder, "Keep an eye on the stew, will you, while I go put Mule away?"

Rue nodded and sat back down, rocking the chair with a slight push of her foot. She stared into the flames, trying to keep her mind blank of the last few months, as though she hadn't lived through them. Dog pushed his nose in her hand, and she idly scratched his ears, wondering if her heart and mind would ever heal, as Adams had said they would.

When memories of Hawke persisted in entering her mind, Rue got to her feet and walked to the shelf where Adams kept his plates, cups, and eating utensils. When Adams returned from tending his faithful mule, the stew was beginning to steam, and Rue had set the table and put a pot of coffee on. While Adams took off his heavy jacket, then washed his hands, she dished up their supper. Both were ravenous, and no words were spoken between them as the stew quickly disappeared from their plates.

It was after they'd had their coffee and Rue had cleared the table that the loquacious Adams spoke. His stockinged feet stretched to the fire, his pipe clenched between his teeth, he began. "When I was young, in my twenties, I trapped in Canada one winter. A wild and trackless country with great forests and rivers where great herds of caribou roamed and wolves seemed to lurk behind every tree."

He's like an Indian, Rue thought sleepily as Adams talked on and on, describing landmarks, the freezing weather, the currents and eddies in a river he'd crossed once.

Her head nodded in near sleep when finally the old man wound down and knocked his pipe out on the hearth. He rose and stood looking down at Rue. "I'm wonderin' bout clothes for you," he said as her eyes questioned him. "A pair of my long johns would be warm and comfortable to sleep in." He gave a dry laugh. "As for that, it wouldn't hurt to wear them under your other clothes."

"As for them other clothes." He looked at

her torn and bedraggled dress. "I guess you'll have to make do with some of mine." He glanced at a trunk shoved in a corner. "Go through my duds and take anything you want. Everything is clean."

Rue stood up and held out her hand. "Thank you, Adams, for everything. I'd be frozen to death by now if you hadn't come along."

Adams gently squeezed her hand. "I'm not a religious man, but I am a believer. I guess God does work in mysterious ways. It's like He set it all up by havin' you and Masters spend the night here, back aways. He knew you'd need a friend later on."

He saw the moistness that sprang in Rue's eyes and cursed himself for being an old fool. He shouldn't have brought up her husband's name. The dog whined and nudged his knee and Adams jumped at the chance to put her mind on something else.

"Me and Dog is gonna go outside for a minute, so dig a pair of woollies out of the trunk." At the door he paused, looking uncomfortable. "My wife's chamber pot is under your bunk," he finally said.

Rue felt a little ill at ease herself, but managed to thank him. As soon as the door closed, she bent down and retrieved the white enameled vessel from where it had sat for many years. She had needed its use half an hour ago.

The long-legged underwear lay on top of the

neatly folded clothes in the leather-bound trunk. Rue hurried out of her clothes and put them on, then crawled into bed. Utterly drained, emotionally and physically, she was almost asleep before she finished pulling the covers around her shoulders.

A pale winter sun fought to penetrate the cabin's single grimy window when Rue awakened the next morning. All was quiet in the small room, and she leaned up on an elbow and looked over at Adams's bed. It was neatly made. She supposed he was running his traps already, and wondered how early he started out.

A fire burned cozily in the fireplace, still Rue hated leaving the warm cocoon of her bed. Once she left it, she'd have to face the cold reality that life didn't hold much in store for her. She was back where she had started, a bleak future stretching ahead of her.

"At any rate," she muttered, "I can't lie in bed all day." She sat up and swung her feet to the floor, then jerked them back with a little cry. Her bare toes had touched something furry. She peeked a look over the edge of the bed, then gave an embarrassed giggle. Adams had placed a pair of fur-lined moccasins next to the bed where she was sure to find them when she got up.

What a caring, considerate man he is, she thought, shoving her feet into the pacs' warmth.

She crossed the bare floor to the fireplace

and smiled. The coffeepot sat on the hearth, steam still issuing from its spout. A tin cup and canned milk sat on the mantle, a scrap of white paper sticking out from beneath the tin. A note from Adams.

"Rue," she read outloud, "me and Dog are runnin' the traps. Shouldn't take too long since all I'll be doin' is baitin' em. Keep the door barred, and don't leave the cabin. There's all kinds of varmints in the woods. Four-legged ones as well as two-legged ones."

It's a good feeling having someone care for you, Rue mused, pouring a cup of coffee then adding milk to the dark brown liquid. Truly cared for, not an act that was put on because something was wanted from her.

Don't think about the past, she sternly reminded herself, and got busy frying several pieces of salt pork over the fire.

After a second cup of coffee had washed down her breakfast, Rue rummaged through Adam's trunk. She found several pair of twill trousers, flannel shirts, and woolen socks. There were also a half-dozen pair of long-legged underwear.

When she rose and walked back to the fire, a change of clothes lay over her arm. She pulled on a pair of twills that fit quite well except for the waist and length. She gave the cuffs a couple turns, then shrugged into the shirt. Its sleeves were too long also, but that was quickly remedied as she rolled them up just below the elbows.

"They'll do," she muttered to herself. "Anyway, who's to see me except Adams and Dog?"

Rue looked around the single room, grimacing as her eyes fell on the kitchen area. She doubted that it, or the table had been scrubbed since she had done it months ago. She could use up half the day cleaning the cabin.

Her first act, however, was to empty the chamber pot, to rinse it out with snow, then shove it back under the bed. When she had smoothed the covers over her bed, she went back outside to scoop up a pail of snow. While it melted and heated, she grabbed the broom, which she doubted had been used in months, and swept into the fireplace a small mountain of dirt and rubble. Like most men, Adams never wiped his feet before entering his home.

The water was steaming by then and Rue dug out a battered dishpan and dropped a bar of yellow lye soap into it. After pouring the hot water over it, she placed the plates, cups, forks, spoons, and knives into it to soak. She would scrub the pots, pans, and skillets last.

While the tins lay in their hot bath, Rue laid another log on the fire, then looked at the single window speculatively. If it was clean, the cabin would be ever so much brighter. This would never occur to Adams since he was never here in the daylight hours, at least in the winter.

She went back to the trunk, and smiled when at the very bottom she found several folded fustain towels. She lifted them out and placed them on a chair. Then, with a pan of vinegar water in one hand and a towel and dishrag in the other, she attacked the built-up grime of years on the windowpane.

When the glass sparkled from her rubbing, Rue gazed through it, a wide smile of pleasure curving her lips. She had an unparalleled view of the valley. She stared at its magnificence. Spruce and pine towered over the thick blanket of snow, and the nearby stream was a clear blue. As she gazed enraptured, she saw through the trees a buck pawing at the covering of snow for some tufts of dry grass. She remembered Hawke saying that cows were too dumb to uncover something to eat. That in the winter when snow covered the ground, hay had to be brought to them or they would starve to death.

Rue gave herself a mental kick, once again ordering herself to stop remembering anything that had to do with the past.

By lunch time she had the old cabin set to rights, years of ground-in dirt scrubbed away. She gave the room a sweeping look and nodded her head in satisfaction. There was no comparison to what it looked like when she first started in on it. It looked like people lived here now.

What to do now? Rue wondered, then spotted her soiled dress and underclothing. She marched purposely to the wooden tub hanging on the wall. She made several trips outside for snow before she had enough water heated to half fill the tub.

Altogether, it took close to two hours before her clothing was washed and placed near the fire to dry. After that, time lay heavy on her hands. Her eyes went often to the clock as the afternoon dragged on. She was used to being busy from daybreak to nightfall and didn't know how to handle idleness. She couldn't remember ever sitting down in the middle of the day.

A heavy sigh escaped Rue's lips. She couldn't even start supper. She had no idea where Adams kept his meat, or even if he had any. However, she remembered, she had seen a big bag of beans on the shelf next to the window. Also there was a large slab of salt pork. She would simmer a pot of beans, she decided.

The sun was just setting through the forest fringe when Rue saw Adams and Dog returning home. *He walks the same as all mountain men,* she thought, remembering her grandfather, toe in, like an Indian.

She hurried to unbar the door, lonesome for the sound of a voice. Dog rushed in, almost knocking her over as he pushed against her, whining a greeting, his heavy tail beating a tattoo against her leg. She rubbed his rough head and smiled a welcome at Adams.

But the old man didn't return it. He only stood and stared, a mistiness forming in his eyes. "The place ain't looked like this since my wife died." His voice was gravelly with emotion.

"I hope you don't mind that I cleaned up a bit," Rue said. "It helped me pass the time," she alibied, not wanting to admit that she couldn't abide dirt.

"Not at all, honey. I guess the place was a bit of a boar's nest." He looked down at the clean floor where the snow from his boots was making a dirty puddle. "There's a big heavy door mat out in the shed. My wife always made me take off my boots on it." He opened the door. "I'll go get it right now."

While Adams was gone, Rue filled a basin with warm water from the kettle on the hearth and laid a towel and bar of yellow soap beside it. She was lighting the lamp when he returned.

"Now, how's that?" he asked a minute or so later after unrolling a large square made from several thicknesses of burlap bags.

Rue nodded her appreciation with shiny eyes. "It's just fine," she said, then added honestly, "I do like clean floors."

"Most women do." Adams understood. "Course there's some who are as careless as men when it comes to cleanliness," he said, hanging up his jacket. "Why I recall . . ."

Rue hid her smile as her old friend talked on about slovenly housekeepers, water splashing all over as he washed his face and hands.

She had the beans on the table by the time Adams finished wiping his hands, and was taking a platter of fried salt pork from the hearth where it had been kept warm.

"I didn't know what else to cook," Rue apologized for the skimpy supper as Adams sat down at the table. "I don't know where you keep your supplies."

"The beans are just fine. I'm right partial to them," Adams said, filling his plate from the pot. "I'd cook them myself, but I'm afraid to leave them all day unattended. They could boil dry and burn."

After eating a couple mouthfuls, he said, "My meat and supplies are out there in the little shed. I hadn't meant for you to do the cookin', but I sure do appreciate it. I'll give you the key to the padlock. You have to keep everything locked up around here, or the Indians will steal everything but your back teeth. Especially in the winter if they get hungry, which is most all the time, poor devils."

Adams grew silent then as he fed his empty stomach. But Rue knew it was only the lull before the storm. Once his hunger was sated, and he sat before the fire, he'd regale her with stories from his past.

However, as she sat with him later, mending

her torn dress while he puffed on his pipe, Adams didn't start a long-winded tale. There was a hesitation about him, as though he were searching for the right words to express himself. *And that is strange*, Rue thought. The old man never seemed at a loss for words.

She shot him a curious look when he said suddenly, almost defensively, "You know a man don't age much, livin' in the woods. Oh, his hair might turn white, a few wrinkles appear on his face, but outside of rheumatiz settlin' in his bones from bein' exposed to the harsh elements of winter, his juices remain much the same."

Was he leading up to something, Rue wondered, or was he rambling in his usual fashion? She took a close look at his face. Was he blushing, or was it the flames in the fire lending that redness to his features? And why was he squirming around?

She was startled, stabbing the needle in her finger, when he blurted out, "I never mentioned it before, but I got me a squaw."

Rue stuck her wounded finger in her mouth, staring at Adam's profile. That was the last thing she had expected him to say. Suddenly the humor of his confession struck her and she was hard put not to laugh out loud. She made sure her face and voice didn't reveal her mirth as she answered calmly, "That's nice. Do you visit her often?"

Adams's face relaxed. "I don't visit her. You

get no privacy in her village. She comes visits me. She stays a week out of every month." He waited a few seconds, then announced, "She'll be showin' up tomorrow night, early."

Rue's eyes widened and she knew a moment of uncertainty. What was she supposed to say to that? she wondered. She rocked the chair. Should she offer to sleep in the little barn with Mule?

Adams was talking again and she ceased rocking, giving him her attention. "Rainy will be company for you while I'm out all day. And we won't be too crowded at night. We'll just set another plate at the table and pull up another chair before the fire." He chuckled. "Me and Rainy use my bunk, so your bed will still be your own."

Rue quickly looked away from the beaming Adams, wondering if she wouldn't rather share Mule's quarters. Only about six feet separated the two bunk beds. And the mattresses, filled with hay, rustled every time you turned over. She could imagine the noise the pair making love would make.

She sensed that Adams watched her, waiting for a response. What could she say? That she'd be too embarrassed, knowing what was going on just a few feet away from her? She remembered the squaw's unusual name and grabbed at the subject.

"Rainy's name is as odd as mine, don't you think?" she asked.

"Oh, that's not her real name. That's what I call her. Her father named her Rain On The Face when she was born. Her mother went into labor during a rainstorm. They were caught in it, and as soon as the baby came into the world, it got rained on. Indians give their newborns names like that." He grinned. "I suppose if she'd been born during a snowstorm, she'd be called Snow On The Face. I'd be callin' her Snowy then, instead of Rainy."

Rue laughed, the unusual name cleared up for her. But later, curled up in bed, she tried to imagine white-haired Adams making love to his squaw in the same fashion Hawke had made . . .

She flipped over on her side, giving the pillow a whack. *Don't ever think of him again, not in anyway*! she chastized herself angrily.

Two days passed before Hawke was cognizant of everything that had taken place. In that time, he had tossed and turned in delirium, calling Rue's name over and over. Dark shadows had appeared beneath Jeb's eyes as he ran back and forth, caring for his two bedridden patients. He was too upset over Hawke to put any importance on Susie's rambling about the witch who had taken Auntie Rue away. He told himself that the child raved in a fever-induced nightmare.

When son and granddaughter finally began to mend, Susie stopped asking for Rue and never mentioned the witch again. And Hawke, after he listlessly reported all that had happened in his search for Rue, lapsed into silence.

There were many silences as the weeks passed, some that would last for hours. At first Jeb tried to talk to Hawke to bring him out of his deep despair. But receiving little, or no response for his effort, he gave up, relying on time to heal the pain that gnawed at his son.

Hawke, snowbound, spent most of the daylight hours, standing at the kitchen window, staring up at the mountain. Up there, somewhere, buried beneath the snow, was Rue. His lovely, fiery Rue. Never again would he hear her throaty laughter or hold her in his arms.

When nearly a month had passed, Hawke decided that he could no longer stand being shut up in the house. There were too many memories of Rue inside its walls.

As he slipped into his heavy jacket, Jeb argued that he should wait at least another two weeks before venturing outside. He only wasted his breath as Hawke argued back that his leg was mended, with only a slight stiffness remaining. A few days of activity and he'd never know he'd been shot. Except for the scar that would always remind him of Rue every time he looked at it, he added to himself.

Twenty minutes later Hawke sat his stallion on a small knoll, looking down on the white silence of the snow-covered valley, hurting to his very soul. He had finally accepted the fact that Rue was gone, and it had turned him into a cold, bitter man, an empty shell of what he had once been. Only his father and the children kept him staying on at the ranch. If not for them, he'd have ridden away as soon as he was able to mount a horse.

How I envy Josh, Hawke thought, his eyes dull. His foreman had ridden away as soon as the fever had left his boss, and all his vital signs were good. He had known that his ramrod was deeply attracted to Rue, but in his jealousy had believed that Josh only wanted to take her to bed. He felt sorry for the man now, for he knew the pain Josh, too, must have suffered at her disappearance.

The wind moaned in the trees and there was a feeling of snow in the air. *Another cold blanket for my poor little Rue*, Hawke thought, his shoulders sagging.

The shadows thickened, but still Hawke remained. He dreaded returning home. The house seemed so empty now. Pa went about, his face still, speaking quietly when he did talk. Even the children didn't romp and play, laugh and argue, like they had when Rue was with them.

Clouds of frosty breath issued from the stallion's nostrils as he stamped his hoofs against the cold, anxious to get back to his warm stable. Hawke patted Captain's shiny black neck, and with a sigh of resignation, he turned the mount homeward.

The wind was driving white pellets of snow in his face when the dark shadow of the house loomed in front of Hawke. Through the lighted window, he could see the children sitting at the table, listlessly watching their grandfather as he worked around the kitchen range preparing supper.

A ranch hand moved out of the darkness and Hawke handed Captain to him with a brief thanks. The cowboy wasn't surprised at the single word. Their boss didn't talk much these days, and smiled less. Of course he didn't have much to smile about, losing his young wife and all.

As the cowboy led Captain away, he wondered if Hawke would turn to Lillie Meyers again. He had seen the woman ride up to the house this afternoon. Her being a widow now, she no longer had to sneak around to see Hawke.

"I was gettin' worried about you, son." Jeb looked up from the stove when Hawke entered the kitchen. "I thought maybe your leg had given out on you."

"No, the leg is fine, Pa," Hawke answered, hanging his jacket on a peg, then stamping the snow off his boots onto a rug Rue had laid there and had insisted everyone use. "I was just checkin' if the men had hauled enough hay to the cattle."

"They should have," Jeb grunted, turning

over a steak in the heavy skillet. "They've been workin' ten hours a day bringin' it out to the dumb critters."

By the time Hawke washed up at the dry sink, Jeb had the steaks on the table, along with boiled potatoes and some hard-looking biscuits.

"So, what did you do this afternoon?" Hawke asked, giving Tommy a poor facsimile of his old smile, then ruffling Susie's hair.

"We didn't do much of anything," Tommy grouched. "It was too cold to go outside."

"Yeah, it's cold out there," Hawke agreed, having a hard time sawing through a tough piece of steak he had helped himself to.

When Tommy and Susie gave up trying to cut through their meat and picked it up with their fingers to gnaw on it, Jeb said apologetically, "I know I'm not much of a cook. Not like . . ." He paused and no one finished the sentence for him. It wasn't necessary. All three knew to whom he was referring.

Supper was over and the children had gone to bed when Jeb looked up from his contemplation of the fire. "That Meyers woman was here this afternoon. Her mount was about dead from fightin' its way through drifts of snow. Somebody ought to make her plunge through drifts up to *her* belly. She might think twice then before makin' a poor dumb animal do it."

"It's doubtful, Pa. Lillie Meyers is not one to

have soft feelins' for an animal—or a human, come to that."

"She said to tell you she'd be back tomorrow. Said it real bossy-like, like I was one of the hired hands."

"Don't let her rile you, Pa. She's not worth a second thought."

"She's a shameless hussy, that's what she is. Chasin' after a man when her husband is barely cold in the grave, and poor little . . ." Again Jeb let a sentence dangle.

It grew quiet between the two men, the snapping of the fire a background to whatever paths their memories took.

A log burned through and fell with a soft thud, jarring Hawke and Jeb back to present. "I expect we ought to get to bed, son," Jeb said, standing up.

Hawke agreed, but the last thing he wanted to do was go to that cold, empty bed and bleed inside because Rue wasn't curled up in his arms.

CHAPTER FOURTEEN

When Rue heard the door latch rattle, her hand froze on the long-handled spoon she'd been stirring the venison stew with. She knew it wasn't Adams. He always made a lot of noise stamping the snow off his boots while Dog whined and scratched at the door.

A gnawing fear building inside her, she moved quietly to the door and stood listening, strained and tensed. The cabin sat at the end of the valley, isolated, vulnerable to attack by white man or Indian.

She glanced at the old flintlock over the mantle and wondered if it still worked, or was it something from the old man's past that he kept out of nostalgia. But even if it still worked, she doubted she could handle the long, awkward thing.

Rue gripped the wooden bar and shook it. It held fast, solid and dependable. A man would have to take an axe to it in order to get inside.

Not so frightened now, Rue told herself that she would just ignore whoever was out there, and sit quietly away from the window.

The window! What if whoever was out there decided to break the glass? She'd better close the shutters real quick and bar them as well.

She was about to hurry away from the door when a feminine voice called tentatively, "Adams . . . are you in there?"

Rue breathed a ragged sigh of relief. It was Adams's squaw. She was early. The old man had said she'd be arriving in the evening.

I can't just leave her standing outside, Rue thought, and lifted the bar from the iron clamp. She swung open the door and gazed at the startled Indian woman, who clutched a snow-covered blanket shielding her head and shoulders.

Adams . . . he is not here?" the woman asked timidly, concern in her voice.

"He's still gathering his furs." Rue smiled at the bulky shape, unable to make out her face concealed by the covering pulled forward. She opened the door wider. "Come on in and get warm. He should be coming along any minute."

The woman stepped inside and removed the wet, ragged blanket.

"Your name is Rainy, isn't it?" Rue took the article from her.

"That is what Adams calls me." There was amusement in the Indian's voice.

"My name is Rue, I'm a friend of Adams," Rue said, hanging the wrap on a peg. "Come sit by the fire and we'll have some coffee while we wait for him."

Rue bustled nervously around, filling two cups with coffee, her ears attuned for Adams's arrival. She wished he'd get home. She didn't know how to entertain the woman, what to talk to her about. Her only encounter with Indians had been a frightening experience.

She handed Rainy a cup, and got her first good look at Adams's lady friend. *She's certainly no beauty*, Rue thought of the fortyish-looking woman. Her features were flat, and her skin badly scarred from smallpox. Her shy smile as she took the cup was beautiful, however, and Rue warmed to her. She had been hungry for a woman's company for a long time.

"Have you walked far, Rainy?" she asked, after taking a sip of coffee. "You must be tired."

"I no walk." Rainy shook her head. "I ride pony. I put in barn."

"Oh." Rue frowned slightly, wondering how it had been possible that she hadn't heard that. She knew that Indians had the ability to move almost noiselessly; were their ponies taught to do this also? She remembered then that Indian mounts weren't shod. With the covering of snow on the ground, it would have been hard for her to have heard hoofbeats.

An awkward silence built between the two women, and Rue searched her mind for some common subject they could converse about. Nothing came to mind. Their worlds were so different from each other.

She repressed a big sigh of relief when she heard the familar sound of Adams stamping his feet, and Dog scratching at the door. She almost ran to lift the heavy bar, then stepped quickly out of the way when Adams rushed in, exclaiming, "Is Rainy here yet?"

Rue grinned. She hadn't known the old man could move so fast. She watched curiously to see the pair greet each other, and was a little disappointed. They did not rush into each other's arms as she had imagined they would, but only gripped each other's hands, smiling happily.

"How have you been, Rainy?" Adams asked softly. "You look thinner than the last time you was here. You got enough food in your village?"

"Almost nothing." Rainy shook her head sadly. "The braves have run out of bullets for rifles, and now depend on bows and arrows." The sad lines on her face deepened. "At least smallpox hasn't come to our village like that of the Arapaho tribe to the east. It is bad with them. A few die every week from hunger or sickness."

Rue's hands gripped the back of a chair. Rainy was talking about the tribe that lived near the ranch, the ones Sly had taken her to. She thought of the boy, Little Star, the one who had cut her bonds, setting her free. Was his little stomach gripped with hunger pains tonight? She wondered if he was even alive. She prayed that he was.

Adams interrupted Rue's worrisome thoughts. "That stew sure smells good, honey. Is it about ready to be dished up?"

"Just as soon as you've washed," Rue answered.

A short time later the three of them sat at the table, eating with hearty appetites, especially Rainy. Rue wondered if the woman would ever stop eating. She couldn't believe the amount of food Rainy consumed was a compliment to Rue's cooking, but rather from near starvation.

When the big pot in the middle of the table was empty, Rainy wiped the back of her hand across her mouth, and giving a loud burp, she smiled, and said, "Good stew, Rue."

"Thank you, Rainy." Rue suppressed her shock at the vulgar sound and smiled back.

When she began to stack the dirty dishes, Rainy rose from the table. "I help you."

"No, no, you go sit before the fire with Adams. You must have a lot to say to each other."

Rainy's brow wrinkled in thought. "Me and Adams, we don't talk much," she said. "Do you talk to Adams?"

Rue smiled wryly. "Some. But mostly I listen while he talks."

Rainy clamped a hand over her mouth, smothering a giggle. "Me too. I listen. Adams, he is long of wind."

Rue laughed out loud. The Indian woman had a good sense of humor, she thought as Rainy sat down beside Adams. One needed that in order to put up with the old windbag. She smilingly shook her head when Adams started in on a long, involved tale.

Rue took her time cleaning the kitchen area, giving the pair some privacy. Maybe Rainy wanted to say something to Adams that she wanted kept secret. But when the old man rambled on and on, giving Rainy no opening to speak if she wanted to, Rue joined them, taking a seat on the raised hearth.

It seemed she had barely settled herself when Adams was standing up and winding the clock, his last act before retiring. Was he going to bed already? For goodness sake's, it was barely past seven o'clock. Usually he didn't run down until ten at least.

"I've had a busy day," he muttered, avoiding Rue's startled look. "I'd like to turn in early."

Rainy giggled, and Rue understood Adams's hurry. The old scamp couldn't wait to get the Indian woman in bed. He had meant it when he said that his juices hadn't dried up. Rue got to her feet, announcing that she was tired also. She said good night and quickly disrobed down to her long-legged underwear.

Rue hoped, as she slipped between the covers, that Adams would give her time to fall asleep before he started stirring his juices. She'd be embarrassed to death if she had to lie there and listen to them.

She lay on her back, staring up at the ceiling, willing sleep to come. The more she concentrated on it, however, the more awake she became. She just wasn't used to going to bed so early.

Oh, hell, she wailed inwardly when Adams's mattress began to rustle, accompanied with his grunts, and the slapping of two bare bodies in rhythmic time.

Rue tried to shut out what was going on only a few feet away, but it was impossible. Her old friend was quite gusty as he sought his satisfaction, not at all a silent lover. She pulled her pillow over her head, thinking that surely the bedframe would collapse, tossing the pair onto the floor.

Finally, after several minutes, the thumping and slapping rapidly escalated, the bed creaking in protest. Adams made a strangling sound, then all was quiet, only the sound of his heavy breathing filling the room.

At last, Rue sighed. *Maybe I can get to sleep now*. She eased on to her side, careful not to alert the couple that she was still awake.

She could dimly make out the shapes of the lovers, Adams still sprawled on top of Rainy. After a moment, however, he rolled off her and laid flat on his back. Rue was about to close her eyes when Rainy sat up and moved to kneel between Adams's spread legs.

Giving an impatient snort, Rue turned her back to them, uncaring whether they knew she was awake or not. She pulled the pillow over her head, shutting out Rainy's ministrations and Adams's raspy, heavy breathing.

She was drifting off to sleep when the bunk bed began squeaking again. *Oh no*, she thought, giving her pillow a whack. *Adams, you old fool, you won't be able to walk tomorrow, let alone run your traps*.

The next morning when Rue awakened, however, Adams had already started his rounds. Rainy sat at the table, sipping coffee, a very contented look on her flat face. Rue watched her a moment, thinking that the woman would be terribly embarrassed when she had to face Rue.

Rue was musing how she could make it easier for both of them when Rainy looked up and smiled at her. There was no embarrassment, no guilt. Had the pair of lovers thought she was asleep after all, or did they take the attitude that coupling was a natural act and that she would look upon it as such?

Rue sat up and swung her feet to the floor. "Did you sleep well last night, Rainy?" she asked, hurrying to the fire and turning her backside to it.

"Oh yes, a little." Rainy giggled. "Never sleep much first night with Adams. It takes most of the night to ease his hunger."

"So I discovered," Rue muttered under her breath. "He was like an old hog with a troughful of slop."

To Rue's surprise, she enjoyed Rainy's visit. They spent the afternoons in front of the fire talking together, sometimes comparing cultures. Rue privately gave thanks for being white, while Rainy thought that in the main white women were a useless, pampered lot.

And thankfully, after that first night Adams didn't hustle Rainy off to bed as soon as supper was over. He was content to stay up, talking away until his usual time for retiring. But every night the bunk bed creaked and groaned at least once.

Rainy's week came to an end, and the sun shone bright the morning she prepared to return to her village. Rue was surprised that she hated to see Rainy leave, that she would miss the genial Indian woman. She had grown very fond of her.

Adams looked up from filling cloth bags

with the supplies he'd brought in from the storage shed. "I wish I could give you more, Rainy," he said, tying off a bag of beans, then meting out some sugar. "but it's still a ways until the passes melt and I can get to town to buy more."

"Do not worry about me, Adams." Rainy laid a hand on his arm. "The two deer you shot yesterday will fill many hungry bellies."

Adams walked over to the mantle where he kept his boxes of ammunition for his rifle. He stood a minute, counting the thin shells, then shook his head. "I wish I could give you some shells for the braves to use, but my supply is gettin' low."

"We will be all right," Rainy again assured the old man. "Winter hunger nothing new to our people. We manage."

"Well, let's get started then," Adams said, lifting the bulging haversack off the table. "I want to get you back to your village before dark."

Rue took Rainy's blanket off its peg and drapped it over her head and shoulders. "I look forward to your next visit, Rainy." She gave the woman a quick hug, not knowing whether she should kiss her cheek.

Rainy's face flushed with pleasure. She had not known the warm embrace of a woman since she lost her mother when she was fifteen years old. She blinked away the tears that shimmered in her eyes.

"I am leaving my pony with you, Rue."

"But, Rainy, I can't take your mount," Rue protested. "How will you get home?"

"She's gonna ride with me on Mule," Adams explained, giving Rue a warning look. "It will please Rainy if you take her pinto."

Rue gave a slight nod of understanding. Rainy would be hurt if she refused her generous gift. She smiled her acceptance. "Thank you very much, Rainy. I will take the best of care of him. I only wish I had something to give you."

"You have given me your friendship," Rainy said softly. "No white woman has ever done this before."

"Then it is their loss," Rue said, her eyes suspiciously wet now.

Adams hustled Rainy outside then, anxious to get started. It would take him an hour to get Rainy home and then he had to run his traps. It would be well after dark by the time he returned to the cabin.

Rue watched the pair ride out of sight, then turned from the window with a sigh. The cabin seemed so empty without Rainy's chatter. It had held back thoughts of Hawke, of the pain and bitterness he had done to her. It would all return to haunt her now.

She smiled mirthlessly. Rainy's presence hadn't helped her at night, when she lay in bed, almost dreading to fall asleep. A night seldom passed that she did not dream of

Hawke. The dreams never varied, only their contents differed. She didn't know which was worse. The one in which she dreamed of Hawke's making love to her, stirring the undiluted passion he always roused in her, leaving her aching when she awoke with unreleased passion thudding through her body, and hatred for herself that she still desired her husband.

Or the other kind of dream, Rue mused, pouring herself a cup of coffee and sitting down at the table. She spooned sugar into the black liquid, remembering last night's dream, which had been more of a nightmare. It started out the same as always. She had been back at the ranch, riding Beauty. Then suddenly Hawke and Lillie rode out of a patch of trees and stopped their mounts to stare at her. She could feel their hatred across the distance. After a moment of trying to return their threatening looks, she turned Beauty around and rode away, not knowing where she was going.

But last night the dream had taken a new twist. The pair had chased her. Hawke, his handsome face twisted with hate and determination, had drawn his Colt and she could feel bullets spewing all around her. She had awakened, drenched in a cold sweat, unable to go back to sleep.

Rue shivered, remembering how vivid the dream had been. But it was a dream, she told herself, and finishing her coffee, she cleaned the cabin. As she made her bed and swept the floor, the Masters family stayed with her. She imagined that Hawke and Lillie were married by now, or at least Lillie had moved in with him. How would Jeb and the children like that? she wondered. Especially Susie who didn't like the woman, and actually feared her a bit. Would Lillie treat the sensitive little girl well?

Of course she wouldn't, Rue answered her own question. It wasn't in the self-absorbed woman to pay any attention to the child's needs. She would only concentrate on Hawke's and her own needs.

Hawke had spent half the morning shoveling snow off the ranch house roof. Last night, as he lay staring at the ceiling, thinking of Rue, he'd heard the beams creaking against the weight bearing down on them and had started in right after breakfast to lighten the load that threatened to break the ridgepole.

He straightened up and fished a handkerchief from a back pocket and wiped his sweaty forehead. As he rested a minute, staring out over the white land, his gaze was caught by a horse struggling through the snow, coming toward the house. His eyes narrowed when he recognized the rider. "Lillie, you bitch," he muttered angrily. "You ought to be shot, treatin' an animal that way."

He walked carefully to where the ladder leaned against the roof and stepped off the last rung just as Lillie rode up.

"Well." She smiled down at him. "It's good to see you up and around at last."

"Thank you, Lillie," Hawke answered politely, making no move toward her.

When she saw that he wasn't going to help her dismount, she swung to the ground, the only sign of her displeasure, a tightening of her lips.

"I won't ask you in, Lillie," Hawke said gruffly, turning toward the barn. "I've got a lot of work to catch up on since I was laid up."

"Oh, that's all right." Lillie took his arm and walked along with him. Pressing a heavy breast against him, she said, "I can't stay long. I only wanted to ask your advice on something."

Like hell, Hawke thought contemptuously. *It's not words you want from me. You've got an itch that needs scratchin'.*

As soon as they stepped inside the warm, hay-scented structure, and Hawke closed the door, Lillie was at him. Her fingers tore at the buttons on his jacket, yanking it open. "Oh, Hawke, it's been so long," she cried softly, sliding a hand inside his denims, and trying to pull his head down so that she could reach his lips.

Hawke kept his neck stiff, resisting the pressure of her hand on his nape. He looked around uneasily. What if Pa or Tommy should walk in?

"Come on, Lil, cut it out," he ordered, taking hold of her wrist, trying to remove her hand, to stop her fondling him.

She shook her head and curled her fingers around his manhood, squeezing and stroking. "Bitch," Hawke growled when against his will he felt it stir.

A sly smile of satisfaction curved Lillie's lips as he grew hard and pulsating in her hand. She knew the rancher well, knew his randy nature, and suspected that he hadn't had relief for a long time. She undid the buttons that confined what she wanted, and gave a little murmur as his throbbing manhood sprang free.

"You do want me," she cried, and kneeling on the hay-covered floor she took him in her mouth.

Hawke stared down at Lillie's head and in his mind's eye the black strands turned into silky blond tresses. All carnal desire left him and he pulled himself free of her. As she looked up at him questioningly, he said, "I told you, Lil, I've got a lot of work to do." He gave her his hand and assisted her to her feet. "But I do thank you for your offer. It was right neighborly of you."

Lillie heard the mockery in his tone and her face became distorted with rage. Hawke thought for a minute she was going to strike him. But as he waited, ready to grab her wrist, she wheeled and ran out of the barn. He heard her mount snort in pain as a whip was laid to its flank, then heard the animal thunder away.

"Bitch!" he grated out, ashamed he'd ever wallowed with the vicious woman. He walked to Beauty's empty stall and stood staring into it. He remembered Rue astride the little mare, riding alongside him mounted on his stallion, sometimes a certain look from one or the other bringing them to rein in, and to find a sheltered spot to make wild love.

Hawke turned his head, listening as a horse's snort and a jangle of reins came from outside. Had Lillie returned to pressure him some more? "Well, by God," he muttered, striding to the door, "this time I'll really set her straight."

He relaxed when he saw one of his cowhands swinging from his mount. "Hawke," the young man said, "I rode past that Indian village awhile ago, and from what I could see, them people are sick and about starvin'." He paused, then added, "I met Miz Meyers on the way in and told her about it. She just laughed and said, 'Good, I hope they all die,' and rode on."

The cowpuncher looked away from Hawke as he ventured, "I don't suppose you'd want to help them after what happened to your wife and all."

"Damn straight!" Hawke snapped immediately. "They'll get no help from me." He started to walk away then a small bronzed face with large brown eyes swam in front of him. He owed the little Indian boy. The child had freed Rue from his people, and though she had perished in the blizzard, the youngster had saved her from a worse death.

"Hold on, Tom." He swung around. "Take a couple men and cut out a dozen head from the herd at the lower end of the valley. That should hold them until spring. As for any sickness they have, I can't help them."

"Right away, boss." The soft-hearted Tom smiled widely. "We'll get them right over there." He climbed back in the saddle and Hawke continued on to the house, calling himself a damn fool. He hoped that the child who had generated his good will was still alive and would benefit from the beef.

The weeks following Rainy's departure, Rue came to know the meaning of solitude. And though the winter days were short, to her, they seemed to last forever. When near dusk she'd hear Adams stamping the snow and mud off his feet, she'd become almost giddy with relief. After supper she welcomed the sound of his voice, although she didn't really listen to what he carried on about.

Then one night while the logs snapped and crackled in the fireplace, sending shadows dancing on the rafters, Adams told a tale that she didn't want to miss a word of. When it was finished, she was shaken to the roots of her heart and soul.

"Around fourteen years ago," he began, "on such a night as this one, a young man knocked at the cabin door. He was near froze, and had a fever and wracking cough. I thought that surely he would die. But my wife tended him as though he was a baby and pulled him through the worse case of pneumony I ever saw.

"When his strength returned, he walked the trapline with me, sometimes talkin', sometimes not openin' his mouth all day. I knew somethin' weighed heavy on his mind, but I didn't ask him no questions. If he wasn't a mind to speak about it, I wouldn't pry. You never ask personal questions in these parts. You never know what a man might be runnin' from, not even his real name in most cases.

"At any rate, after he had been with us a few months, he began to open up a bit. It came out slowly that he was anxious to save up enough money to make a home for his little daughter he'd left behind with a whorin' wife. So I extended my line and he became my partner."

Adams paused and looked at Rue. She sat on the edge of her seat, barely breathing. "Did he ever say his daughter's name?"

Adams nodded. "He called her Rue. Rue DeLawney."

Joy and relief blazed across Rue's face. Her

father had loved her after all! Tears of gladness running down her cheeks she opened her mouth to express her overwhelming happiness, then bit off the words. The solemn expression on Adams's face brought a cold chill to her heart. She wasn't going to like the ending of his story.

Adams saw the abject resignation in her eyes and said as gently as possible, "Two years later your father was killed by a poisoned Indian arrow."

When Rue's storm of weeping died to an occasional shuddering sob, Adams said quietly, "I always meant to look for you, to give you a home myself. But then my wife died and I knew I couldn't care for a youngun' all by myself.

"It's funny how things work out sometimes. The first time I saw you I knew who you was. I can't tell you how it pleases me that I have been able to help you in a time of need. Your father was like a son to me."

The old man and young woman rocked in silence, each with their own thoughts, Rue thinking of the heartbreaking letter she must write to her grandparents, Adams thinking how badly he would miss Rue when she left him. For leave him she must.

He broke the silence. "Rue, honey, you know that you are welcome to live here with me for the rest of your life if you want to, don't you?"

Rue gave him a wan smile and nodded.

"Do you also know that a lonely cabin in the wilderness is no place for you?"

"Why not?" Rue demanded. "I like it here just fine."

"You might like it while your heart is mending, but when you come out of your gloom and despair, you'll find it mighty tedious with just me and Dog for company." When Rue didn't respond, he continued, "You're a young beautiful woman who needs to be someplace where you can meet young men, marry one and start a new life."

Rue gave a short, dry laugh. "Aren't you forgetting that I already have a husband? He may think I'm dead and that he is free to marry again, but I know I'm alive."

"Hell, what difference does that make? You'll never run into Masters again. You could go back and live with your grandparents for a while. Start your new life from there."

"I would dearly love to see them again," Rue said wistfully, envisioning her bustling little grandmother and slightly cantankerous grandfather. "I miss them terribly. But they're poor, Adams. They're old and can hardly make ends meet. They've already taken in my half brother, Jimmy, and I couldn't burden them with another mouth to feed."

"Don't let finances worry you." Adams hitched his chair closer to Rue's. "Your father had a good chunk of money saved when that arrow got him. I been keepin' it all these years in case I ever ran into you."

Rue shot Adams a surprised look, and he nodded. "That's right. You'd be able to help the old folks instead of bein' a hinderance."

Wavering hope and excitement flickered across Rue's face. If she could get back to Grandpa and Grandma DeLawney, and even if Hawke learned she wasn't with the Indians and alive, he wouldn't dare show his face there. Grandpa would ruin him. He'd put a bullet in the elbow of his gun arm, then shoot him in his knees. Strangely, Rue didn't like that idea.

She felt herself possessed by a spirit of elation and eagerness as she stared into the flames, totally self-absorbed. Come spring she would return to the country where she was born, but not to live with the old folks. She and Jimmy would fix up the shack where they had grown up and live there together until Jimmy married someday. As for herself, she'd live there for the rest of her life. She had no intention of ever again becoming involved with a man. It had been proven to her, as she had previously claimed, that for the most part men were no damn good.

The clock struck the bedtime hour and Rue disrobed down to her woollies and climbed into bed. She stretched and yawned, a great peace flowing through her. Before too many weeks past she could stop looking behind her, jumping at every alien sound, afraid her whereabouts might have been discovered by her husband.

Her thoughts trailed off and she slept.

CHAPTER FIFTEEN

As Rue stood gazing out the window, it seemed to her that snow always swirled around the cabin, smarting her face, watering her eyes every time she stepped outside.

She didn't mind it as much as she did two weeks ago, though. She had plans now, a purpose in life. Before, she had lived each day as it came, too sick at heart to think of a future.

She still had moments of deep depression, sometimes lasting for hours. It still baffled her how Hawke could have made such sweet, intense love to her while his heart belonged to Lillie. He had made her feel so loved and cherished when, passion exhausted, he held her in his arms as they both fell asleep.

With a deep sigh Rue started to move away from the window where she had been watching for Adams's return, when a movement at the edge of the forest caught her eye. She cupped her hands to her face and peered through the dusk. Silhouetted against the heavy pine trudged a small figure.

Is that a child? she asked herself in wonder. *What is a youngster doing out at this hour*?

She rushed to the door and flung it open, lamplight spilling out onto the small porch. "Little Star!" she gasped, looking down at the face of the Indian boy who had set her free that terrible day when she was a prisoner of his people.

The boy's face was drawn with utter exhaustion, his black eyes dulled with it. "Come in, child," she urged, taking hold of his arm, feeling its thinness through the ragged blanket covering his head and shoulders.

When Little Star walked past Rue, she noticed the bulky shape between his shoulder blades and mused that he must have come to stay awhile, and that his worldly goods were on his back. Had his grandfather died, she wondered. And what would Adams say to additional person in his home?

"Give me your blanket, then go by the fire and warm up," she invited, feeling that Adams wouldn't be too upset. He would never turn the boy out.

When the worn piece of material was unfastened and removed, Rue stood and gaped. It was not Little Star's possessions strapped to his back, but rather a papoose, around seven or eight months old, she judged.

"My brother, Tiny Fist," she was informed proudly as the double sling was untied and the baby carefully deposited in a rocking chair.

"My goodness, Little Star." Rue finally found her tongue. "What are you thinking of, taking him out in such weather? Does your grandfather know about this?" She bent over and felt a thin little cheek and was surprised to feel it was warm. She had imagined the baby was nearly frozen.

"It is bad in our village," Little Star answered, his black eyes grave. "Our people die all the time from smallpox. We have no medicine man."

His throat worked convulsively. "Last week our father and mother die." He swallowed hard, then said, "Grandfather tell me, take Tiny Fist to you. That you are good woman, will care for him."

Rue wanted to pull the brave little boy into her arms, to console him, to dry the tears that weren't allowed to fall. But, remembering that the Indians weren't demonstrative in that manner, she smiled tenderly at him, and said, "Of course I will." A frown creased her forehead at a question that popped into her mind. "How did you know that I was here, Little Star?"

"Rain In The Face told her cousin of the white woman living with old Adams. Cousin told grandfather, and he come look for himself."

Cold fear gripped Rue's heart. "Will your grandfather tell the rancher, Hawke Masters, that I am here?" Her eyes searched the small face.

"No." The boy shook his head. "Your secret is safe with him."

The boy spoke with such earnestness, Rue believed him and she relaxed. Surely she could stay hidden for another month.

Rue squatted down in front of the baby and tickled him beneath the chin and laughed when he only stared owlishly at her. *Are Indians born disliking the pale face?* she wondered in amusement.

She lifted her head to speak to Little Star and saw that he was eyeing the dutch oven partially buried in the coals. The venison roast did smell good, she thought, and the children were probably half-starved.

"I'm going to fix you fellows something to eat," she said, putting on oven mitts and lifting the iron oven onto the hearth. "Adams will be home soon, but he won't care if we don't wait for him."

"Can Tiny Fist eat meat yet?" Rue asked a little later as she sliced the meat in thin strips and piled them on a platter.

"Yes." Little Star moved to stand beside the

table and watched her, his mouth working. "He has six teeth. His food has to be cut in small pieces, though."

Rue wondered what the children had eaten on their trek across country, and as though the boy read her mind, Little Star said, "Me and Tiny Fist, we chewed on pemmican as we traveled."

"I see." Rue smiled and patted the back of a chair. "Sit down and help yourself to the roast while I dig the potatoes out of the ashes."

Little Star directed a troubled look at his small brother. Rue relieved his anxiety when she added, "Then I'll fix a plate for the little one."

The boy nodded and ate. Rue watched him bolting his food down and wanted to tell him not to eat so fast, that he would choke himself. She shrugged then, hoping for the best, deciding again that she might embarrass him.

The baby, smelling the food, began to cry, to lick his mouth and wave his little arms and legs. Rue hurriedly cut a piece of venison into tiny pieces and mashed one of the potatoes. When she picked him up from the blanket, she discovered his front and little bottom was soaking wet. And by now the small face was a dull, angry red, and his shrieks filled the room.

"Damn," she muttered to herself, "what am I going to do?" Now was not the time to change the little screech owl, nor did she want him sitting on her lap while he ate.

Her ears ringing, she sat the tot on a chair and grabbed the dish towel off the table. She placed it across his stomach then tied the two ends to the back of the chair. That done, she sat down in the chair next to the bellowing baby and popped a spoonful of potatoes into his wide, open mouth.

Tiny Fist quieted immediately, his front teeth working like a rabbit's. "He has loud voice," Little Star bragged. "When he become man, he will lead people."

Rue didn't doubt it for a moment. Anyone with a temper like that and a set of lungs to match would scare anyone into obeying him. In her opinion, the baby should be called Big Mouth.

When the potatoes were gone, and Tiny Fist's hunger eased a bit, Rue gave him the meat. She was thinking that surely his stomach would burst soon when she heard Adams cleaning off his boots. Now she'd find out how he felt about having a baby around.

"We've got company," she blurted as soon as she opened the door.

Adams slid the furs off his shoulder, apprehension jumping into his eyes. "It's all right," Rue assured him. "We're in no danger from this pair."

Adams entered the cabin and goggled at the two little Indians. "What the hell?" he exclaimed. "Where'd these little buggers come from?"

Little Star watched Adams's face closely as Rue explained his and Tiny Fist's presences. When the old man nodded and ruffled his brother's hair, and received a wide smile, Little Star's face relaxed and the tenseness left his body. Rue's friend was a good man. He would not harm the little one.

Adams washed his hands and took his place at the table. "So," he said pleasantly, filling his plate with meat and potatoes, "you're gonna have two fine fellows to keep you company, huh, Rue?"

"Oh, I leave as soon as I finish eating," Little Star said hurriedly. "Only Tiny Fist stay with Rue. When snow melts, and the sickness has left our village, Grandfather will come for young brother."

"But you must stay the night at least, son," Adams spoke gravely. "The wind was kicking up when I came in. We may get another blizzard."

Little Star looked longingly at the fire. "I do not want to be late getting back. Grandfather will worry." Rue and Adams watched him chew his bottom lip thoughtfully. "Maybe he won't worry if I'm just one day late."

He looked at Rue. "He was very sick when I left. I hope I find him recovered when I return to the village."

Rue and Adams exchanged a solemn look, their eyes saying chances were the grandfather would be dead by the time he returned.

All this time, in the back of Rue's mind was the question, what could she use to clothe the baby in? And he had to have a bath. He stank so of urine she was loath to pick the poor little fellow up.

She had an idea if Adams was agreeable to it. She looked hopefully at her old friend, who had found new ears to bend, not knowing nor caring that Little Star barely grasped what he was talking about.

"Adams," she broke into his story, "would you donate one of your sheets for breechcloths for the baby?"

"Sure, honey, take anything you want." Adams took time to answer, then quickly picked up where he had left off.

Rue smiled her thanks, then glanced at Little Star. The boy nodded sleepily, trying his best to be polite, to listen to the old man who had provided him his first good meal all winter. *But another couple minutes and he will lose the battle*, Rue thought and walked to the trunk. Lifting the lid, she took out a blanket and spread it over the bearskin in front of the fire.

"Little Star." She nudged his knee. "Why don't you lie down and rest while you listen to the balance of Adams's story?"

"Yes, I will do that," the boy answered gravely, and in minutes after rolling up in the blanket, the even rise and fall of his slight frame said that he was sound asleep.

Adams watched the sleeping child, his grizzled face soft. "What a strong, proud people they are," he said with a sad shake of his head. "It's a shame that the white man will bring ruin to them before this boy is grown."

Rue agreed that unfortunately that was true as she tore a sheet into squares.

It was well after ten o'clock before Rue and Adams got to bed. Adams had taken their wooden bathing tub off the wall and emptied the pot of water Rue had warmed into it. Rue then peeled away the baby's wet clothing, handing them to the old man, asking him to please toss them outside. As he took them away, holding them at arm's length, she lowered the baby into the tub. The little fellow squealed his delight as the warm water enveloped him, slapping at it, splashing it all over Rue. She laughed and told herself that actually the little imp was very pleasant-natured when he wasn't hungry.

When Tiny Fist was thoroughly clean, including his hair, Rue dried him off and tied one of the squares around his bottom. "Now, Adams, where is he to sleep?" She stood up, the baby wrapped in another square, his eyes drooping in sleep.

"Put him in the trunk for tonight," Adams suggested. "I'll fix him some kind of bed tomorrow."

Rue nodded, and Adams emptied the big leather trunk of everything except for two blankets on the bottom. He motioned Rue to wait, and took his long slicker off the wall. "You don't want to have to wash these beddings every day." He grinned, spreading the waterproof material where it would do the most good.

"You're very good at improvising, friend." Rue grinned.

"You learn to do that when you're livin' alone in the wilderness." Adams grinned back.

The baby didn't stir as Rue lay him on his makeshift bed and covered him with a heavy, woolen shawl.

Rue awakened the next morning at daybreak to see Little Star bent over the trunk, looking at his brother. She glanced at the table and saw that Adams had made breakfast, and was now making up a bundle of food, she imagined for the boy to eat on the trail.

"Maybe you can toss in a handful of our dried apples." Rue rose and walked over to watch Adams wrapping fried salt pork and corn pone, then shoving it into a grub sack. "They're very nourishing."

"I already did," Adams answered, a grin on

his face. "I put them in the bottom of the sack where he won't see them until he's et the meat. If he knew they was in there, he'd have em' in his belly before he was out of sight of the cabin."

Little Star walked up to the table, sending Rue and Adams a curious look, wondering why they were whispering.

"We don't want to wake Tiny Fist," Rue explained, somewhat guiltily.

"Oh." The boy's face cleared. "He won't wake up until he's hungry."

"Well, little brave, are you about ready to leave?" Adams tied a loose knot in the cloth bag.

Little Star nodded and Rue gravely shook the small hand he held out to her. "I give you thanks from Grandfather," he said. "He tell me I should stay with you also. But I say to him he needs me."

"You are a very thoughtful grandson, Little Star." Rue smoothed his black shiny cap of hair, praying that he wouldn't catch the sickness, that he would make it safely back to his village.

Adams opened the door then, and they were gone, Dog running ahead of them. Rue stood at the window and watched them walk through the pink dawn, finally disappearing into the forest. The baby stirred and fussed and she hurried to pour sugar and canned milk over the bowl of cornmeal mush Adams had thoughtfully prepared.

"Don't start crying," she begged. "My ears are still ringing from last night."

Little Star was chilled and miserable as he curled his knees under his chin and stared at the fire in the center of the tepee. His lips trembled, but no tears wet his eyes. He must be brave, he told himself. It was expected of him.

A shuddering sigh shook his thin body. He shouldn't have spent the night with Rue and old Adams. Had he acted like a real brave he would have paid no attention to how tired he was and would have returned to his village. Then he would have been there to see Grandfather one last time. But yesterday his beloved relative had been buried on a nearby hill and his best horse killed. The old brave would be able to ride his favorite mount over the happy-hunting grounds.

A handsome brave, in his mid-thirties sat on the dirt floor near Little Star's pallet of furs, watching his young nephew. He knew that his brother's son was suffering, for he suffered also. Besides losing a brother and father, he had lost his wife and two young sons to the dreaded smallpox. Now there was only himself and his two nephews to carry on.

I will make them my own, the brave planned. *I will take myself another woman and when spring comes I will go after the baby, Tiny Fist.*

They will be brothers to the children I will sire on my new wife.

The thought of siring brought a stirring in the Indian's loins. He had been without a woman for three weeks, a long time for a man as virile as he. He slid a hand into his buckskins and left it there until he grew hard in his palm. He rose then and left the tepee.

He knew which other tepee he was headed for. He'd had his eye on a young cousin for a long time. Even before the sickness struck their village, he had decided that she was ready and that he would take her for his second wife. He would try her out now, and if she pleased him, was of long endurance, he would make her his woman today. Besides relieving his ache each night, she could keep his back warm while he slept.

On his way to his destination, the Indian paused and spoke to a woman who, with other women, was preparing a communal supper over a smokeless fire. When he finished speaking, she nodded. As he walked away, she and her companions covered their mouths to smother their giggles. All had seen the evidence of his arousal pushing against his buckskins. They watched to see which tepee he would enter.

"He has watched her for many moons," the woman he had spoken to said as she filled a bowl with the rich beef stew she had been stirring. She left the others, to tramp through the snow to the tepee where Little Star lay.

"I have brought you some supper, little brave," the woman said, kneeling down beside him.

The savory aroma drifted to Little Star's nostrils and he sat up, almost snatching the bowl from her hands. He dipped in his fingers and brought a chunk of meat to his mouth. He chewed rapidly for a moment, then said in surprise, "This is beef. Where did it come from?"

A frown creased his forehead, and before the woman could answer, he exclaimed, "We will be in much trouble if it is discovered we stole a steer from a rancher."

"We no steal." The woman motioned him to continue eating. "The rancher, Masters, sent us several head. He is good man."

After the woman left, Little Star did some deep thinking as he hungrily devoured the stew. Despite his hard, cold looks, the big rancher must be a good man to have given them beef when they were near starvation. Even though he knew the same Indians had kept his wife captive for a while, he evidently didn't blame the women and children. He wondered if the men of the village were too ashamed to eat the man's beef. He hoped so.

Deep regret that he had lied to Rue's husband gripped Little Star. He could still see the anguish on the rancher's face when he thought that his wife had climbed the mountain.

Determined lines settled on Little Star's small features. As soon as the snow melted and the passes were open, he intended to visit Rue's man and tell him the truth.

CHAPTER SIXTEEN

Hawke wiped a palm across the condensation that clouded the windowpane and looked outside. Winter with its lonely innumerable hours would slowly come to an end now. Last night a wind had come out of the south, bringing with it a heavy rain. It still beat against the house this morning.

His eyes ranged over the yard. The snow had almost melted, leaving only a few inches, and even a few muddy patches were revealed. He closed his eyes against the pain that shot through him. Tomorrow he and some of the hands would climb the mountain, searching for Rue's body.

With a ragged sigh, he turned from the window and sat back down at the kitchen table. His father rose and took the pot off the stove and refilled both their cups.

"I suppose when the rain lets up you'll go lookin' for Rue's . . . Rue," Jeb said, sitting back down and spooning sugar into his coffee.

"I won't wait for the rain to stop, Pa. It could go on for a week." He helped himself to the sugar bowl. "Tomorrow morning I intend to take some of the men and start searchin'."

Jeb didn't say aloud what he was thinking, that by now a mountain lion had probably already found Rue's body. Instead, he said quietly, "You'll have to notify her people. You said that she has grandparents?"

Hawke sighed and nodded. "There's a half brother she was awfully fond of." An image of the brother, Jimmy, came to Hawke's mind, of how bravely the teenager had ordered him to stay away from his sister. How was he going to take such news? He remembered then the love that had shone in old man DeLawney's eyes when he looked at his granddaughter.

God, how he dreaded facing those two, telling them that Rue was dead. It had entered his mind once to send them a letter, explaining what had happened. But he had quickly erased the thought. That was the coward's way. As hard as it would be, he would go to them, try to explain how he and Rue had grown to love each other deeply, that it hadn't been his fault that she had died in a blizzard.

A grim smile twitched his lips. He probably

wouldn't be able to say anything past inform-
ing Mr. DeLawney that his granddaughter was
dead. The crusty old gent would most likely
blow his brains out at that point.

And I don't know that I'd care, Hawke
thought morosely, rising and reaching for his
heavy jacket and black slicker. "I'm gonna
ride up past the foothills, see how much snow
has melted on the mountain."

Jeb nodded, and Hawke walked out into the
pelting rain.

Each morning for the past week, Hawke and
six of his men had set out in the gray dawn,
heading for the mountain. And when they
returned every night, only the bulk of the
house and outbuildings were discernible in
the near darkness.

Hawke had searched the mountain with a
single-minded intensity, scouting out every
crevice, every canyon, every boulder.

This particular day, Hawke's eyes raked the
mountain, pausing at a narrow strip of mag-
nificent pine sweeping up and almost out of
sight. Their wide-spread branches came so
close together at the top that in the winter the
snow never penetrated them and in the summer the sun never quite shone through to the
ground.

He remembered with a long sigh how he
and Rue had often ridden there to make love
on the needle-strewn ground. When he had

begun searching for her, he had hoped to find her in their secret place and he might have had he not been shot.

"Let it go, man," he muttered, "you're beatin' a dead horse over what might have been."

The mountain towered higher to the west, and the sun touched its rim. Once it tipped to the other side, darkness would descend and the horses would have a hard time finding their way down the rock-strewn trails. Hawke cupped his hands around his mouth and loudly yelled to his men that it was time to go home.

As his voice echoed through the many canyons, he turned Captain back down the mountain. Weary and dispirited, for the first time he let himself think that he would never find his young wife's body.

The resigned expression was still on his face when later he pushed open the kitchen door. He blinked a moment against the lamplight from the table, then Susie was running to him, her arms raised to be lifted up.

His haggard face softened as he swept her small body up and gave it a quick squeeze. It was when he put her back on the floor he noticed the Indian boy sitting at the table. He recognized him at once, the boy who had tried to help Rue. He wondered why the youngster looked so uncomfortable, almost afraid.

He shot a questioning look at his father, and when Jeb only shrugged his shoulders, Hawke smiled at the boy, and asked, "How are your people doin', young man? Has the smallpox run its course yet?"

"Yes," he answered gravely. "No more sickness in my village. My grandfather was the last one it took."

"I'm sorry to hear that you lost your grandfather," Hawke said sincerely, wondering why the boy was here, and what he wanted. "Will you stay for supper?" he asked, taking off his jacket and handing it to Tommy to hang up.

"No, I must return to the village before night sets in. The wolves will be roaming about as soon as the moon comes up, and they are hungry after long winter."

"I could ride with you if you want to stay," Hawke offered. "It would please me to help the young man who helped my wife."

Little Star looked nervously away from Hawke. Then moistening his dry lips with his tongue, he blurted out, "I lied to you that night about Rue."

Hawke's smile faded and died. His voice dangerously quiet, he asked, "What do you mean, you lied?"

The boy squirmed uneasily in his seat, shooting Hawke a frightened look. He swallowed, then in a quivering voice he said, "Rue didn't go up the mountain. She went down the valley."

Hawke stared at Little Star, a fury, such as he had never known, engulfing him. His hands shot out, gripping narrow shoulders. "You whelp of Satan!" he yelled, shaking the boy until his hair fell over his face. "Your lie cost me my wife. I could have easily found her in the valley."

"Stop it, Hawke!" Jeb pulled him away from the terrorized child. "You're gonna snap his neck."

"I'd like to." Hawke threw himself into a chair. "Why did you lie to me?" he demanded in the tense atmosphere of the room.

Little Star swallowed a couple times then croaked out, "Rue said not to tell you. I don't know why, but she was afraid of you."

"Afraid of me!" Hawke fairly shouted. "Why should she be afraid of me? I'm her husband."

"I know this." Little Star nodded. "But she didn't want to return to you. I don't know why this is so."

Hawke looked at his father as though for an answer. Jeb's sympathic look said he had no idea why Rue should be afraid of Hawke.

They both turned startled looks on the boy when he said, "She is still afraid of you. I could see it in her eyes the last time I saw her."

Hawke caught his breath. "Rue is still alive?" he asked incredulously.

"She was a month ago," Little Star answered, cringing away from the wild look in

Hawke's eyes.

Jeb laid a calming hand on Hawke's arm and said gently to the uneasy boy, "Where is Rue, son?"

"She stay with the old trapper, Adams."

"How is she?" Jeb asked the question his son seemed unable to ask calmly.

"Her health is good. The old man take good care of her." The little boy paused before adding, "There is great sadness in her eyes, though."

Bewilderment stamped on his face, Hawke was only half aware that Jeb and Little Star continued to talk. Why would Rue be afraid of him? What had he done to put fear in her? That morning she disappeared, they had made their usual slow sweet love before rising and as usual she had stood in the kitchen door, waving to him as he rode away.

Maybe, he decided, she had been hit on the head by one of the Indians and it had caused her brain to become muddled, made her forget everything but how he had treated her in the beginning.

The main thing, he reminded himself, was that Rue was alive. He would go to her, set right whatever was bothering her. The bleakness that had been in his eyes all winter disappeared and his whole body throbbed with almost unbearable happiness. He tried to think, to plan, but his brain wouldn't function properly. That Rue was alive was the only thing that came through clearly.

After calling his name three times, Jeb finally penetrated Hawke's state of bliss. "Do you know a fat man who would want to harm Rue, Hawke? Someone who hated her enough to sell her to the Indians?"

Hawke shook his head, his mind going over his men acquaintances. Again he thought of the storekeeper in Jackson, the most harmless man he'd ever known, and an old trapper, so crippled with rheumatism he could hardly get around. Certainly neither man was capable of harming Rue.

Then suddenly a leering face came to Hawke's mind. He slapped the table with the palm of his hand. *Sly Burford!* That one hated Rue with a vindictiveness that nothing would keep him from following her, and extracting his revenge in the most evil way his sick brain could dream up.

But how could he have tricked Rue into leaving the ranch with him? She feared and hated the man.

A smoldering heat of furious rage ran through Hawke's veins, twisting his features. He was sorry the bastard was dead. It would give him the greatest pleasure to kill the man himself, an inch at a time.

"I can see by your face you have thought of a man who might have done this awful thing to Rue." Jeb broke into Hawke's turbulent thoughts.

"Where's the boy?" Hawke looked around the kitchen.

"He left a minute ago. He's still a little afraid of you. You had a mean look on your face for a while there."

"I was feelin' mean." Hawke laughed mirthlessly. "It came to me who had got his hands on Rue."

"Hawke." Jeb pinned his son with serious eyes. "I think it's time I heard the whole story about Rue, how you came to marry her. It was a strange relationship goin' on between you two when me and the kids first got here. I didn't say anything. I figured it was just a case of newlyweds gettin' used to each other."

For the next ten minutes Hawke talked, relating all the events that had made Rue his wife. He left nothing out, not even his shameful behavior toward her at first.

He ended with a wry laugh. "She sure got her revenge, though. I fell so in love with her, it scared me."

Jeb looked sternly at him. "It would have served you right if she hadn't loved you back."

Hawke stared into his empty coffee cup. "If what the boy said is true, and I have no reason to doubt him, she's back to hatin' me again."

"Maybe she's not herself," Jeb spoke aloud one of Hawke's thoughts.

"Well I intend to find out. I'm leavin' for old Adams's place first thing in the mornin'."

"Then I'd better get supper on the table so

you can get to bed early."

For the first time since Rue's disappearance, the evening was eaten in a happy, relaxed atmosphere. The children chattered excitedly about Auntie Rue coming home, and Hawke was hardly aware of what he was eating. His blood was on fire for morning to come so he could go after his wife and bring her home where she belonged.

Although Hawke retired early as planned, sleep was a long time coming. Again and again, his mind ran over Little Star's words. "She is afraid of you. She did not want to return to you." What if Rue refused to come home with him? He couldn't force her to. For one thing, old Adams wouldn't allow it.

No, somehow, he would have to convince her to trust him, to love him again.

The hour was gray and the air chilly when Hawke left the next morning. Jeb watched him and the stallion until they disappeared in the nightlike shadows, then returned to the warmth of the kitchen. He said a silent prayer that all would end well for his son and the woman he had made his wife.

He glanced around the room and a wry grimace twisted his features. It would take him all day to restore it to the condition Rue had always kept it in. And he wanted everything to be just right if she returned with Hawke. Hawke and the children weren't the only ones who had missed her.

When Tommy and Susie left their beds and came sleepy-eyed into the kitchen, Jeb hurried them through breakfast, saying to Tommy, "I want you to help me get the house straightened up, son. Auntie Rue would have a fit if she found the place in the state it is now. While I clean the kitchen, you can make the beds and dust the furniture."

"Uncle Hawke sure is happy, isn't he?" Tommy remarked, a white ring of milk around his mouth.

Jeb ruffled the boy's unbrushed hair. "I think we all are."

Susie, her rag doll with her as usual, sat her silent companion on the table and said to its painted face, "I hope that Lillie woman don't come here again. She took Auntie Rue away. Maybe she'll take Uncle Hawke too."

Jeb, finishing the last bite of his flapjack, froze, the fork midway to his mouth. When Susie stretched her toes to the floor and slid off the chair, he put the fork down and drew the little girl between his knees. Careful to keep his voice calm, he asked, "When did Lillie take Auntie Rue away, Susie?"

"You know, Grandpa." Susie traced one of his eyebrows with a tiny finger. "The day Uncle Hawke got hurt at the line shack. Auntie Rue went with the bad witch to make him better."

Jeb dimly remembered the child rambling

on about a witch the day Rue disappeared, and even after Hawke was brought home shot in the leg. He had paid no attention to what she was saying, thinking it was the fever talking.

He shook his head, thinking of the *ifs* that could have saved so much heartache. If he had listened to Susie, if Little Star hadn't listened to Rue. He became aware of Susie shaking his knee.

"Why didn't Auntie Rue come home after she made Uncle Hawke better?"

Jeb's mind sought a reason that Susie would understand. The five-year-old didn't know that her uncle hadn't seen Rue, that he, too, had tossed and turned in a high fever just as Susie had.

Finally, he answered, "She had to go see her grandparents, and now Uncle Hawke has gone there to bring her home."

"But, Grandpa," Tommy began, "the Indian boy said—"

Jeb gave the boy a warning shake of his head, looking meaningfully at Susie. Tommy nodded his understanding, then Jeb became very active. He must get to Lillie Meyers before Hawke did. He had no doubt that, woman or not, his son would kill her for what she'd done to Rue. And though the bitch deserved killing, he didn't want his son doing it. Once Hawke's rage cooled, he'd regret killing a woman for the rest of his days.

"Tommy," he said, shrugging into his jacket and slapping his battered Stetson on his head, "I have to go out for a while. Keep an eye on your sister until I get back."

"Sure, Grandpa, but where are you going?"

"I gotta take care of some business that's been a long time comin'."

The rising sun cast a red glow on the white paint of the Meyers's ranch house as Jeb approached it. A dim light shone in the distant bunkhouse, and he could see the men moving around inside.

But all was quiet in and around the widow's domicile. "The heartless bitch probably don't get up until noon," Jeb muttered, dismounting and looping the reins around a hitching post. He stood a moment, then stepped onto the porch, his boot heels stamping with purpose. He lifted his arm and thumped a loud fist on the front door, then stepped back.

It was silent inside for a moment, then there came the scurrying of feet and the sound of a woman's voice, low and urgent. A moment later Jeb heard the snap of a door closing in the rear of the house. He walked to the end of the porch in time to see a man running toward the bunkhouse, his shirttail flying, his boots in his hands.

The contemptuous sneer was still on Jeb's face when the door opened and a tousled-haired Lillie gaped at him in surprise. "Mr.

Masters!" she exclaimed, clutching her robe together with one hand while the other tried to smooth her hair. "Is somethin' wrong with Hawke?" Concern leapt in her pale eyes. "Has he been hurt?"

Jeb shook his head. "Hawke is fine. May I come in? I'd like to talk to you a minute."

"Certainly." Lillie moved away from the door. "I'll go put on a pot of coffee."

"No, don't bother on my account. I'll only be here a short time."

"Then have a seat." Lillie motioned toward a chair.

Jeb gave the room a sweeping glance, taking in the red carpet, the bold-flowered wallpaper, the overstuffed chairs and sofa, the bric-a-brac covering every inch of three table tops. *Just like the waiting room in a bordello*, he thought, then looked back at Lillie.

"I'll just stand. But maybe you ought to sit down."

"My goodness." Lillie gave a nervous titter. "That sounds like you're gonna give me some bad news, Mr. Masters."

"I expect that it does, and it will be." Looking at her grimly with cold eyes, Jeb said, "The game is up for you, Mrs. Meyers. My granddaughter just told me a bit of interestin' news, and yesterday a young Indian boy told Hawke somethin' that was also very interestin'. I put both children's stories together and came up with the answer to what happened to Rue."

"I don't know what you're talkin' about."
Lillie's face went paper-white and she
clutched the back of a chair. "Surely you're
not puttin' any importance on children's
ramblins'."

"I'd believe children faster than I would
most adults. My Susie is too young to have
learned the practice of lyin'."

"Well, she was dreamin' out loud then. I
had nothin' to do with Rue bein' sold to the
Indians."

"Aha!" Jeb pounced on the woman's slip
up. "I didn't say a word about her bein' sold to
Indians. How come you know about it if you
wasn't a part of it?"

Lillie floundered for words for a moment,
then choked out, "Sly Burford came and told
me how he had sold Rue, then he took off."

"You're lyin' through your teeth, woman!
We know everything about your dirty dealins'.
An Indian killed Sly Burford the same day he
took Rue to them. He couldn't have told you
anything."

The look of a trapped animal glittered in
Lillie's eyes. "I had no part in killin' Sam,"
she blurted in panic. "That was all Sly's
doin'."

Jeb caught his breath at that unexpected
disclosure. He hurriedly looked down at the
floor to hide his surprise. The scared, witless
woman had just cleared up the mystery of how

an accomplished rider like Sam could have been thrown from his horse and dragged to death. It hadn't happened that way at all. Sly Burford had murdered Sam Meyers, then made it look like an accident. And damn her lyin' soul, the bitch had been in on her husband's death all the way. He could see it in her guilty face.

He took a shot in the dark. "What about the money you paid him to do away with Sam?"

Lillie's face crumpled in defeat and Jeb pushed his advantage. "I think you'd better clear out of this country, Mrs. Meyers. Sam was liked by his neighbors and there's no tellin' what they'll do to you when I tell them you had him killed. The least they'll do is tar and feather you . . . might even hang you. For sure, they'll drive you out of this valley."

Jeb didn't think her face could grow paler, but now a sickly pallor spread over it. "What about the ranch?" she whined. "It belongs to me now."

"I guess it comes down to you makin' a choice," Jeb said coldly. "Which is more important to you, the ranch or maybe your life?"

Lillie only hesitated a moment before rushing toward her bedroom. "Will you have one of the men saddle my mount?" she asked in her hurried retreat.

"Be glad to." A huge smile of satisfaction spread across Jeb's face. He left the house and almost ran to the corrals.

Less than twenty minutes later Lillie hurried from the house, a stuffed saddlebag over her arm, her boot heels kicking up snow and mud.

Jeb, his elbows hooked over the top rail of the corral, grinned as he watched a cowboy, probably the one his arrival had scared from her bed, help Lillie mount her eye-rolling stallion. When she brought her whip across the animal's rump, and it sprang away, the cowpuncher looked at Jeb.

"Where's she off to so early in the mornin', and in such an all-fired hurry?"

"On her way to hell, no doubt." Jeb continued to grin. "That is if the Devil will take her in."

And while the ranch hand stared at him, Jeb walked back to the house and mounted. The stupid bitch was headed straight through Indian territory. She'd be damn lucky if she made it through there alive. Her hatred of the red man was well-known by the renegade tribe.

CHAPTER SEVENTEEN

Little Star sat hunched against his uncle's tepee, his arms wrapped around his bent knees. He shivered occasionally in the cold wind that still held a wintry chill. He'd been there half an hour, listening to the grunts and thumps inside the structure since the women had started the morning cook fire. If everything proceeded as usual, his uncle would walk outside at the first scent of the roasting meat.

He sniffed the air, anxiously testing it. There was only the smell of smoke and burning wood. As he settled back to continue to wait, he became aware that all was quiet inside the tepee. *At last*, he thought, *my uncle is sated*. He carefully lifted the opening flap and peeked inside.

Sighing, he let the hide drop. From the glimpse he'd had inside the dim interior, his Uncle Wolf was again mounting his new wife of a month. It would be another few minutes, but it would be the last time, the boy consoled himself. For faintly on the air, there came the aroma he had been waiting for. His uncle would smell it also and would leave his bed of furs. He wouldn't ride his woman again until the late afternoon when he returned from the hunt.

Little Star picked up a stick and began drawing pictures in the mud as he waited for the tall, handsome brave to step outside, adjusting the breechcloth over his depleted member. He stood up. He would approach his uncle then about going after his small brother, Tiny Fist. He was anxious to see the little brave, and hoped he could coax their Uncle Wolf into leaving for Adams's cabin today. A worried frown creased his forehead. Rue would be looking for Grandfather to come.

He shook away the sorrowful thoughts of his dead grandfather. His uncle treated him like a son, and the new wife saw to his needs. He was very fortunate. The children who had lost all relations to the sickness were now slaves to the other members of the tribe. They worked from sunup until they wrapped themselves in a blanket under some tree when night fell.

Finally the hoarse cry he had been waiting for sounded. And as he had known would happen, his satisfied uncle emerged from the tepee. He stepped to the side of the tepee, pulled aside his breechcloth, and relieved himself. Then straightening his fringed buckskins, he turned to his nephew, hovering nearby.

"So, little brave, you have been patient. What is so important that you have waited so long?"

"It is about Tiny Fist, Uncle. Do you not think it is time to bring him home?"

The tall brave thought a moment, then nodded his head. "You are right. I have been too occupied with my new wife. After I have eaten my morning meal, I will go to this Rue Masters you are so fond of and bring the baby home."

"Shall I go with you? Rue might be frightened, a stranger coming to her door. She expects Grandfather to come."

"No, you will stay here and watch after your new mother. Do not fear for your white friend. I will not frighten her."

Little Star stared at the ground, his moccasin-shod foot erasing the pictures he'd drawn on the ground. When he sensed his uncle's curious gaze on him, he lifted his head.

"Uncle, I would talk to you about Rue. There is something that you don't know about her."

"And what is that, nephew?" Amusement shone in Wolf's eyes. "Is she ugly? Will she scare me?"

"Oh, no. Rue is beautiful, like a sunset on a clear stream. You have seen her; you wanted her for your woman."

Wolf narrowed his eyes on the boy. "Are you talking about the golden-haired woman the fat man brought to our village? The one who somehow escaped?"

Little Star swallowed and nodded dumbly.

"Why have you kept this secret? You know how badly I wanted her."

Little Star hung his head and said in a low voice, "I know this, Uncle, but Rue is not strong like our own women. I was afraid she could not work as hard as they can, and she might die."

"And you think that your uncle wouldn't take proper care of her, maybe abuse her?"

"I wasn't sure." The answer was barely above a whisper.

"You wrong me, little brave," Wolf said soberly. "I, too, realized the Golden One's worth. I would have treated her kindly."

"Forgive me, Uncle," Little Star said shamefully. "But there is another reason I didn't tell you about Rue. She already has a husband. One who puts much value on her. He would fight you to the death to keep her."

"Why is he not with her now?"

"I think perhaps he is with her by now."

Wolf stood a moment, staring off into the forest, remembering the golden-haired woman he had been on fire to possess. "Who is this man that is her husband?"

"He is the rancher, Hawke Masters, the one who sent us the cattle."

Wolf couldn't remember when he had been so frustrated. Until this moment he'd had every intention of bringing the white woman home with him. His blood had sang at the thought of making her his wife, even to keeping *her* back warm on cold, winter nights.

He sighed deeply. He could forget that now. His honor would not allow him to take away the wife of a man who had undoubtedly saved the lives of his people.

With regret on his face, Wolf laid a hand on his nephew's shoulder. "Rest easy, my son. I will not touch the Golden One."

Half an hour later Little Star watched his uncle ride away, proudly erect on his wild little mustang. He knew a great relief. His uncle would keep his word, no matter how tempted he might be to break it.

Rue awakened to Adams's trying to speak softly to Tiny Fist strapped in his chair, but he still sounded like a growling bear. Her smile was a little sad. The old man had grown very fond of the baby and would miss him when he was gone.

As for herself, she, too, could have given her heart to the little one, but she had carefully not done so. She was tired of loving and losing. She had learned it was too painful to love, to let anyone get close to her.

Her grandparents' faces appeared before her. She still loved them, of course, but they were old and she would lose them before too long. And Jimmy, he would fall in love someday and he would leave her also. And there she'd be, living alone in the shack where she had been born, growing old, waiting for death, never having known love from a man.

What was love anyway? Rue laid an arm across her eyes. She knew that the Bible said that God was love, but what did the word mean to human beings? To her way of thinking, there was only one true love, that deep emotion shared between parents and children. As for a deep abiding love between a man and woman, it was too fragile, too easily broken.

Rue thought back to her mother. She must have claimed to love Papa once, but had then lain with any man who came along. Then there was Hawke. He had claimed to love Lillie, but had acted for all the world as if it was Rue whom he adored.

She went on to remember all the men she had known who had lost a wife. After only a month, sometimes only a week, they had remarried. Had the love these men had professed for the dead women been buried with them, setting them free to love again?

Tiny Fist's chortling chuckle brought Rue out of her gloomy thoughts. When was the little fellow's grandfather coming after him? she wondered. The snow had melted until only a few inches covered the ground. She wished he'd hurry. She was anxious to get on with her life, whatever it might be.

Rue frowned at a disturbing thought. What if the grandfather had died as well as Little Star? Would no one come after the baby then? Would she have to take him with her when she left? The little fellow wouldn't be accepted in her old area. Too many people there had lost loved ones to the red man. She shook her head. It would never enter their minds to remember how many Indians *they* had killed.

"Are you awake, honey?" Adams called from the table where he sat spooning oatmeal into Tiny Fist's hungry mouth. "Daylight is about here and I ought to get goin'."

Rue sat up and swung her feet to the braided rug Adams had brought from the small storage shed. Piece by piece, he had brought out many little treasures that had made the small room cozy. There were the two colorful prints he had hung on the rough log wall, and a pewter lamp, with a shiny reflector, placed between them. He had also brought in two tablecloths, one red, one blue. She knew that once she was gone all the homey pieces would go back into the barrel they had been packed in since the death of his wife.

Rue had to admit, though reluctantly, that this old man had loved his wife and was devoted to her memory. *But he only makes three*, she reminded herself sourly. *Grandpa DeLawney, Jeb Masters and old Adams.* Not very good odds when compared to all the men who only used women.

As Rue washed her hands in a basin of warm water Adams always had waiting for her, Tiny Fist waved his arms and kicked his chubby legs in his delight at seeing her. She dried her face on the rough fustain towel hanging beside the window, then tickled the underside of his chin.

"And how are you this morning, big boy?" She sat down beside him, marveling at the difference three months had made in the child's appearance. He was short, as was his brother Little Star, but the little cheeks and limbs were now plump and dimpled, and he had two more new teeth. Right now all eight were displayed in a wide smile.

Adams stood ready to leave, his buffalo jacket laced up, his fur cap pulled over his ears. Although the temperature had risen, it was still winter and bitterly cold. "Well, I'm off," he said, ruffling Tiny Fist's hair. "You behave for Rue while I'm gone," he ordered the baby.

Dog, jumping around Adams's feet, anxious to get out and run, almost knocked the old man down, rushing past him when he opened the door. Rue grinned as, through the closed door, she heard Adams swearing at the animal, promising him all kinds of punishment once he got his hands on his worthless hide. It was all sham threats, she knew. Adams was very fond of his old pet and would never strike him.

After she finished breakfast, Rue went through her usual ritual—making the beds, sweeping the floor, cleaning the kitchen, then bathing and dressing Tiny Fist.

She was getting dressed herself when she had the urge to don her own clothing for a change. She missed the feel of her soft camisole against her skin, the swish of a petticoat against her legs. She bent down and pulled the wooden box from beneath her bed. She took out the undergarments that had lain in the box all winter, putting back the bloomers. The elastic had broken and she had no way of mending it. She pulled the camisole over her head, stepped into the petticoat, then lifted her dress from its peg on the wall.

"Goodness, I've lost weight," she muttered, feeling how the dress hung on her, the fullness of the material across her breasts, the extra inches around the waist. There was no

427

mirror in the cabin for her to have noticed the weight loss before, nor the thinness of her face. She didn't know how sharply the delicate bones were so clearly defined.

But she did know that her hair was shiny and healthy. It crackled and snapped when she brushed it with Adams's brush. However, she had no idea if the part in it was straight. She did that by touch alone.

Rue smiled thinly. What difference did it make how she looked? Who was to see her except an old man and a baby?

Lunch time arrived, and after Rue fed Tiny Fist, she said to him, "We're going to get bundled up and go outside for a while, to breathe some fresh air."

As though the tot understood her, he began to kick his legs, throwing his chubby arms around her neck. Rue wanted to hug him back, to love him, but wouldn't allow herself to do so. She must continue to guard her heart. It wouldn't mend if it was broken again.

With Tiny Fist bundled up to his nose, Rue carried him outside. They both blinked rapidly until their eyes became accustomed to the sunlight. A damp wind blew across their faces, making the baby catch his breath. Rue laughed softly and patted his back.

"We'll just stay for a minute or so," she consoled him. "The pure air is good for your little lungs."

She pulled the blanket up over his mouth,

then gave a startled jerk, followed by a low cry of surprise when from the corner of the cabin came a deep, masculine voice.

"You are wise . . . for a white woman."

Rue wheeled to face the tall Indian walking toward her, his stolid face showing nothing of what he was thinking. "Who are you?" She clutched the baby and moved backward, repeating, "Who are you?"

But even as she asked the question, Rue recognized the brave and her heart pounded so that it shook her chest. This was the brave who had wanted her, had killed Sly Burford in his determination to have her. Apprehension gripped the pit of her stomach. Had Little Star given away the secret of her hiding place, and this tall Indian had come to take her away?

Her mind raced frantically with the necessity of escape. She threw a fast glance over her shoulder. Could she move fast enough to get to the door, inside, and throw the bolt?

She didn't have to wonder. In the split second she took her attention from the brave, he had moved, and now stood only inches away. While she stared at him with wide eyes, he lifted a lean hand to her cheek.

"Do not be frightened, Golden One." His voice was soft, full of regret. "I would never harm you." His hand left her face with a slow, caressing movement. "I am Wolf, uncle to Tiny Fist. I have come for him."

"But Little Star said that his grandfather

would come for the little one," Rue said warily, moving back again.

A flickering sadness shone in the black eyes. "The sickness took my father. So, I have come."

"Oh, I am sorry to hear that," Rue said softly and sincerely. "Little Star must be grieving."

"Yes."

She waited for the brave to add to the single sentence, and when he didn't, she said, "Come in and I'll get Tiny Fist's clothes together." Strangely, she was no longer afraid of the tall, handsome brave.

Hawke poured the remains of his coffee over the red coals of his campfire, then crawled beneath the low, sweeping branches of a pine and rolled up in his blankets.

Actually, it wasn't necessary for him to make night camp, being only a few miles from Adams's cabin. But when he saw Rue for the first time in months, he wanted them to be alone. He knew Adams wouldn't be at the cabin in the morning so he wouldn't have an audience watching him beg. For beg he would, if it were necessary. Besides, that cantankerous old trapper might not even let him come inside if he were at home.

It was clear the next morning when Hawke mounted Captain, the sun bright for a change. Settling the horse into an easy lope, he rode out of a fringe of spruce at noon and gazed at Adams's cabin, smoke curling from its crooked chimney. His heart hammering, his palms suddenly damp, he reined in. In just a few minutes he would see her.

Hawke was about to lift the reins when the cabin door opened and Rue walked outside. The sun struck her hair, seeming to turn it into pure gold. Staring at the glorious sight, remembering its softness in his hands, its silkiness spread across his chest while she slept in his arms, it took a few seconds before he noticed the baby in her arms.

His face blanched. An Indian baby! What was she doing with a papoose? It couldn't be hers, she hadn't been gone that long.

A sharp intake of breath heaved his chest when a tall Indian came from the side of the cabin and walked up to Rue. They stood a minute, the man stroking her cheek, then they went inside, and closed the cabin door behind them. Pain jabbed his heart like a knife. The brave hadn't used force to get inside. Rue had willingly let him follow her.

Hawke's face darkened with explosive rage. Had she been forced to take this man as a lover, to tend to his child? And what about old Adams? Had he been killed?

His eyes narrowed to slits. Had he been lied to all the way? But for what purpose?

The thought was unbearable that another man's eyes and hands had known Rue's body.

He gave Captain such a jab with his heel, the startled animal lunged away, his hoofs kicking up mud and snow. By God, he swore silently, he would put an end to whatever was going on right now.

Hawke pulled the stallion to a plunging halt a foot away from the porch. In one motion he swung from the saddle and flung open the cabin door.

Startled blue eyes and black ones gaped at the barely controlled savagery on his face. Rue felt a wave of weakness sweep through her and her mouth went dry with fear. Questions drummed in her head. How had Hawke learned that she was alive? How did he know that she was here? Had he come to kill her?

She took a step toward Wolf as though for protection, and thought that she saw pain flare in Hawke's eyes. She blinked and the moment was gone. She had imagined it, of course. Suddenly her days of pain and bitterness boiled inside her. How dare this man persecute her? She had never done anything to him but love him.

She sprang in front of Hawke, her blue eyes stormy. "Go away, Hawke Masters! Let me alone! Let people think I'm dead. Go back to Lillie!"

And Hawke, gazing at her, starvation in his eyes, heard not a word she said. He continued to let his gaze wander over her face. He noted worriedly her thin cheeks, her haunted look, the purple shadows beneath her eyes. It was all he could do not to gather her in his arms, tell her that she would never be hurt again.

But deep in her eyes, past her anger, fear of him still lingered. Why? he asked himself. What lies had Sly Burford told her?

From the corners of his eyes, Hawke saw the Indian pick up the baby and walk to the door. He stopped there and turned to look at Rue, an expression in his eyes that seemed to speak of regret. "Rue Masters," he said soberly, "I will give you protection if you want to come with me."

Rue stood, white-faced, laughing hysterically inside. She had a fine choice. She knew what entailed going with Wolf. Become his wife. Which was worse? Living with a wild savage, or taking a chance that her husband might sell her to another tribe of Indians?

While Rue had stood debating her choices, Hawke's body had become tight and threatening. Did that bastard think for one moment he could walk out of here with the woman he loved? His hand dropped to the butt of his Colt. His jaw clenched and taut, he said in a deadly voice: "She is my wife and I'm takin' her away with *me*."

While Rue watched, gripped with trembling, Wolf stared at Hawke, silently studying him. Finally he spoke. "That is good. A woman should be with her man."

"But, Wolf!" Rue cried out. "You musn't let him take me! You don't know—"

"I know that you and your mate have been victims of deceit. The evil Meyers woman preyed upon your mind, Rue Masters, fed it with lies about your man."

"How do you know this?" Rue stared at the red man.

"Before the fat man died, he tells the braves this, tells long story, going back many moons, hoping to save his life."

At first Hawke was bewildered, then not so mystified. He should have thought of that bitch right off, he told himself, questioned her before anyone else.

"Why don't you tell me the whole story, Rue?" He laid a coaxing hand on her arm. "I've been livin' in hell, thinkin' you were dead, then learnin' that you weren't but that you're afraid of me."

Rue gazed up at Hawke for a long, uncertain moment. Lillie had sounded so truthful when she claimed that Hawke wanted his wife out of the way so that he could marry her. But as Rue continued to study his face thoughtfully, the love and longing in his eyes could not be denied. He *did* love her, she knew it beyond doubt.

With a glad little cry, she went into Hawke's waiting arms.

Between hot, hungry kisses Rue related everything that had happened to her, from the morning Lillie came to the house with her lie, up to the present.

"I'll handle her," Hawke ground out, murder in his eyes.

Rue remembered Wolf then, and turned to apologize for her and Hawke's rudeness. The brave and Tiny Fist were gone. When the pair had left, they had no idea.

"I'll miss the baby," Rue said sadly, then pulled away from Hawke. "Are you hungry?" she asked, her eyes aglow, her cheeks flushed.

"Hungry? God, yes, I'm hungry. But not for food." Hawke pulled her back into his arms. He stroked her back, then moved a hand to cup her breast. "I've hungered for you until I thought I'd lose my mind."

"It's been the same for me." Rue clasped her arms around Hawke's waist. "Even when my mind thought it had reason to fear and hate you, my body didn't care. At night when I slept, it took over in my dreams."

Hawke looked at the clock, then slid his hand up her petticoat. "We've got at least three hours before the old man comes home," he whispered huskily, stroking her smooth thighs. "Plenty of time to show how much we've missed each other."

Rue nodded dreamily, and cupping her face in his hands, Hawke pulled her head down until their lips met. For long minutes they clung to each other in a hunger that had been denied for so long.

And as the kiss went on, tongues thrusting and parrying, Hawke's slim fingers undid the buttons that confined breasts that had grown heavy with passion. He lifted his head, then picking her up, sat down in a chair, settling her on his lap.

Rue felt the strength of his arousal rise and press against her small rear as he pushed the camisole over her shoulders, then cupped her breasts with his hands. When his head dipped down, she lifted one of them and directed the hardened nipple to his waiting lips.

"Oh, Hawke." She sighed softly as his tongue urgently stroked the puckered nub, then gently tugged at it with his teeth until it swelled and rose. A pounding ache of desire flashed through her body as he drew the ready nipple into his mouth and suckled at it like a starving man.

When he replaced her hand with his own, holding the ivory-tinted mound as though it were priceless, she knew what he wanted. They had played this game before, sitting in front of the fire at the ranch house.

Her eager fingers quickly opened his denims, and his powerful manhood seemed to leap into her hand, pulsating with its need. Fierce pleasure turned Hawke's eyes almost black when she curled a palm around him and slowly stroked him. He tore his mouth away from her breast, and standing up, he carried her to the bunk bed and stood her on the floor.

With hands that trembled, he removed her clothing, piece by piece, his hands stroking her back, shaping her waist. "You are so beautiful," he whispered huskily, his hands splaying over her breasts. Rue leaned into his hands, her fingers undoing his shirt and sliding it down over his shoulders. Hawke stepped away from her, and after shrugging out of the flannel, unbuckled his belt, pushed his denims past his slim hips, then sat down on the bed and toed off his boots.

Rue dropped to her knees, and grasping each leg of the denims, tugged them down his muscular thighs and off his feet. Tossing them aside, she whispered, "You are beautiful too," as she gazed at the throbbing length and thickness straining toward her.

While Hawke held his breath, she smoothed her palms up the inner sides of his thighs, moving ever closer to that which had given her so much pleasure in the past. Then, almost at the object of her desire, she paused, fingering a small puckering of his flesh.

"What is this?" She looked up at him. "It looks like a gunshot scar."

"It is," Hawke answered, his breathing heavy. "I'll tell you about it later." His hands covered hers, urging her to go on with her exploring.

Slowly, teasingly, her fingers crept upward while Hawke ceased to breathe. He let his breath out when her palms slid under his heavy sacs and lifted them up. As her head bent down, his big body shuddered in anticipation.

"Do it, honey," he rasped.

When her warm mouth closed over him, Hawke threw himself back on the bed, his hands clutching a handful of quilt on either side of him.

The only sound in the room for several minutes was the ticking of the clock and Hawke's husky murmurs of pleasure.

Close to exploding, Hawke sat up and lifted Rue onto the bed. She stretched out on her back, and straddling her hips, he began his own exploring.

Her breasts were caressed, teased, and suckled until she squirmed. His hands moved downward then until he came to her most sensitive part. His palm rested a moment on the triangle of soft curls, then he lifted her legs to hang over his shoulders.

A shuddering sigh fluttered through Rue's lips as he slid his hands beneath her hips and placed his mouth where his palm had been. Mewling sounds escaped from her as his teeth nibbled and his tongue darted and jabbed.

When Hawke felt the tightening of Rue's body, knew she was ready to spiral away without him, he straightened up and positioned her for his entry. They would reach the heights together.

Grasping her hips, he slowly thrust into her, his largeness filling and stretching her. He felt her contracting around him, and groaning her name, he worked his hips, driving in and out of her in slow rhythm. Shortly he felt her tremble, felt her tighten around him. "Not yet, honey," he murmured softly. "I want it to last. It's been so long."

Rue's fingers clutching at his shoulders, loosened as she made herself relax and just enjoy the smooth slide of the powerful manhood that pressed her into the mattress with each long thrust.

Minutes passed, and still Hawke pleasured Rue, a film of sweat gathering on his forehead. He murmured words of praise as her hips reached to meet his, not wanting to lose one inch of him.

Finally, neither could hold back the passion of desire that beat at them like a raging storm. When Rue began to shudder, she felt the convulsions of Hawke's body and she held him tightly as together they reached a climax that left them helpless to move for long moments.

Rue stroked the sweaty head resting between her breasts, her lips quirking as Hawke's body spasmed weakly. She was still throbbing inside also, and when she felt his lips move in a grin, she knew that he felt the slight contraction. She gave his hair a sharp tug, and he moved his head to nip gently a nipple in retaliation, making her giggle.

She lay, curling his hair around her finger, wondering if and when he was going to withdraw from her. She didn't have to wait long to find out.

When Hawke's breathing returned to normal, he opened his mouth against the breast pressing against his cheek and curled his tongue around its nipple. As he tugged and licked, Rue bucked her hips against his, letting him know that she wanted him again. She felt him respond, felt him growing inside her.

She smiled lazily, anticipating the slide and thrust that would bring her to a mindless state of release.

Hawke smiled. He loved his wife totally, but he also lusted after her to a point that sometimes made him feel like a rutting bull because it took so long to satiate his need of her.

He leaned up on his elbows, and calling her "a hungry little misery," began a hard, rhythmic thrusting of his body. The bed squeaked and shook for several minutes.

The third and last time left the pair utterly spent, and Hawke slowly withdrew from Rue. Concern leapt in his eyes as he saw the exhaustion in her eyes, her swollen nipples, the tiny love bites scattered over her body.

"Rue, honey," he exclaimed, "have I hurt

you?" She looked so delicate next to his large body.

She looped her arms around his neck. "You didn't hurt me at all, my love."

He dropped a light kiss on her forehead and fell over on his back, his legs sprawled apart. His limp member lay across his thigh and mischief sparkled in Rue's eyes. Leaning on her elbow, her head resting in her palm, she lifted what was once so gloriously proud with two fingers, then let it flop back on his leg. "He's not so high and mighty now, huh?" she teased.

Hawke smiled lazily. "He's only restin'. Don't get fiesty. He'll lord it over you tonight."

Rue dropped a light kiss on the object in question, then scooted off the bed. "We'd better get dressed," she said, reaching for her clothes in a pile on the floor. "Adams will be home before long. I've got to get supper." She pulled the dress over her head.

While Rue bustled back and forth between the fire and the table, burying potatoes in the hot ashes, then slicing steaks off a piece of venison, she and Hawke talked of the time they were separated. They spoke of their despair, their yearning for each other.

Hawke then told Rue how he had been shot while searching for her and she related to him the hurtful lies Lillie had told her. Then her eyes shining, she told him about her father, how happy it had made her to learn that he had loved her.

Her hands grew still in the act of setting the table. "Hawke." She looked at him, her eyes large with a frightening thought. "If you would have arrived a day later, I'd have been gone. I was only waiting for someone to come for the baby, then I was leaving for my old shack. With the money my father left me, I was going to fix it up, make a home for me and Jimmy."

"I would have found you." Hawke started toward her, then stopped when the door opened and Adams stepped inside. Dog followed behind him and stood on stiff legs, his lips lifted in a snarl, while the old man glared menacingly at Hawke.

"You got a goddam nerve comin' here, Hawke Masters," he growled. The cocking of the rifle still in his hands was loud in the tense air of the room. "I'll blow your head off if you touch that girl."

"Look, Adams." Hawke stood quietly, nor daring to move. "There's already been enough wrong doin'. Don't you add to it."

"He's right, old friend." Rue hurried to grab Adams's rifle arm. "There's so much I have to tell you."

"Then you've forgive him, have you?"

"There's nothing to forgive. He hasn't done anything wrong."

As Rue explained how she had been lied to,

tricked, Adams shook his head at the cruelty some people were capable of. At the same time, however, he was relieved that his judgment of Hawke hadn't been wrong after all. Hawke Masters was the honorable man he had thought him to be.

He voiced this to Hawke, then looking around the room, he asked the question, to which a flicker of sadness in his eyes said he already knew the answer. "Where's the little one?" he asked over the lump that formed in his throat. "Gone huntin'?"

Rue and Hawke smiled at his attempt at jocularity, pretended not to see how badly he was affected by Tiny Fist's absence. Rue looked away from him and said matter-of-factly, "His uncle came for him today. By now he's halfway home to his people where he belongs."

"You're right, of course," Adams said dully. With an effort, he squared his sagging shoulders and shrugged out of his jacket. "We knew he'd be taken away once winter let up."

"That's right," Rue answered, and finished setting the table. But as she placed the plates and added the flatware, thinking how lonely the old man would be with both her and the baby gone, a flicker of an idea came to her mind. By the time she put supper on the table, it was full grown, but she wouldn't mention it until after supper.

Rue thought that Hawke would never finish

eating. She smiled to herself, thinking that he went after his steak the same way he made love to her, as if someone would take it away from him.

Finally he sat back, rubbing his full stomach. "I sure missed your cookin', Rue. Pa cooks worse than I do."

Adams glanced over at Rue's rumpled bed and said slyly, "I gotta a feelin' her cookin' wasn't the only thing you missed about her."

Rue laughed out loud at the red flush that spread over Hawke's face. He was embarrassed!

Adams blushed also when she turned to him and retorted, "Almost as much as you miss Rainy."

He ducked his head and grinned. "That much, huh."

Hawke raised a questioning eyebrow at Rue and she explained, "Rainy is an Indian woman, who visits him one week out of every month." She slid Adams a teasing look. "He's informed me that his juices haven't dried up, and I believe him. He and Rainy bounce on that bed so hard, and so often during her visits, that I think someday it's going to break and fall in on them."

"Hey, is that so?" Hawke asked, surprised. "Does the hankerin' for a woman last into the later years?"

"You damn betcha it does," Adams answered proudly. "Age ain't slowed me down one bit."

Hawke looked at Rue, a warm gleam in his eyes. "I'm right happy to hear that."

"Oh, you." Rue playfully slapped him on the back of his head. "You'll have worn yourself out by the time you're forty."

All three laughed, then took their coffee to the fire. As they stretched their feet to the fire, Rue brought up her idea. "You know, old friend, that I will be leaving with Hawke tomorrow." Adams nodded and she continued, "I won't be going to my grandparents as I had planned." Again, the white head nodded.

"Would it be too much to ask you to take my money to them after you put your traps away for the season?"

"I reckon not." Adams set his empty cup on the floor. "I've never seen that part of the country before."

Rue hesitated, then taking a long breath said, "There's one last request I'd like to make. If you don't agree to it, please say so. I'll understand."

Adams looked at her and scolded, "Haven't you learned yet, Rue Masters, that I don't do anything I don't want to? What's this request you're talkin' about?"

"It's about my half brother Jimmy. He's sixteen years old and he loves the woods, and hunting and trapping. I'm hoping that if you take a liking to him, you might bring him home with you."

While Adams gaped at her, Rue hurried on, "He's with my grandparents now, but their old and don't have too many years left. I would like to have Jimmy settled in a permanent home."

"Now, hang on there, Rue," Hawke spoke rather sharply. "You know that he'd be welcome at the ranch."

Rue laid her hand on his. "I know that, Hawke, and thank you. But I don't think Jimmy would be happy there. He knows nothing about herding cattle, doing ranch work. He's sort of on the wild side. He's what they call back home a woods runner. He'd be so happy running a trap line in the winter and hunting in the summer."

Rue stopped talking and looked worriedly at Adams. "You haven't said anything, friend."

"I've been thinkin'," Adams answered slowly. "If me and the kid take to each other, it's not a bad idea. I'm not goin' to live forever either. I'd like knowin' my traps and cabin would be left to someone who would appreciate them and take care of them."

"Oh, thank you, Adams," Rue cried, then added confidently, "you'll like him. Everybody does."

"We'll see." Adams stood up, and going to his bunk, bent down and pulled from beneath it a heavy bedroll. "Me and Dog are gonna sleep in the shed tonight. We don't fancy bein' kept awake half the night by all the noise that's bound to come from yonder bed."

This time it was Rue's turn to blush furiously, but before she could fire a retort to Adams, he was closing the cabin door behind him. "You old scamp," she muttered, and cleared the table of the supper dishes.

"Are you gonna be long?" Hawke slid her a wicked look, brazeningly massaging the large bulge pressing against the front of his denims.

"Why?" Rue asked, pretending not to notice his crystal-clear meaning. "Do you want something?"

"My friend does." He grinned and moved his hips suggestively. "He's standing proud and ready, just like I told you he would be."

"He usually is, so that's nothing new." Rue went on gathering the dishes.

"Can't we go to bed now?" Hawke coaxed, his voice raspy. "Can't you leave the cleaning until tomorrow morning?"

"Hawke, you are the limit," Rue tried to chastise him, but a stirring had begun in the pit of her stomach. She remembered such times back at the ranch, how Hawke would tease and coax and tantalize her until he got her to do what he wanted.

She walked toward him, undoing her bodice. She whipped the dress over her head, and the camisole and the petticoat followed. "Well," she said, her hands on her hips, "are you coming to bed or not?"

Hawke rose, his heavy-lidded eyes drinking in her naked beauty as he hurried out of his own clothes.

He carried her to the bed and crawled between her legs. "We'll fool around later," he whispered as he entered her with one, long thrust.